SEASONS

LISA GREGORY

WARNER BOOKS

A Warner Communications Company

WARNER BOOKS EDITION

Cover photo by Karen Filter
Hand lettering by Craig De Camp

Warner Books, Inc.
666 Fifth Avenue
New York, N.Y. 10103

 A Warner Communications Company

Printed in the United States of America

First Printing: September, 1990

10 9 8 7 6 5 4 3 2 1

SHARON THOMPSON. Young and vulnerable, she found love only to lose it. But when fate offered her a second chance, would she risk her heart again?

▼

WES MAITLAND. Charming and irresponsible, he was Sharon's first love—a man consumed by jealousy and hell-bent on self-destruction.

▼

REID MAITLAND. To Sharon he was the consummate politician, all head and no heart. But the respected Congressman was caught in a fatal attraction—for his dead brother's girl.

▼

HOLLIS WENDLEY. She was the last person Sharon ever expected to become her friend, a sensual blond beauty with sophisticated ways—and the means to indulge them.

▼

AMES THOMPSON. Sharon's brother was a man dedicated to helping others. But when the time came to choose, would he surrender to his ideals or the arms of a spectacular woman?

From the winner of the
Affaire de Coeur's
Silver Pen Award

Lisa Gregory
SEASONS

"So sensual that it leaves you breathless, so tender that you are awestruck . . . a book to savor, to cherish and to read 100 times."
—*Romantic Times* **on** *The Rainbow Promise*

ALSO BY LISA GREGORY

Before the Dawn
Solitaire
The Rainbow Season
The Rainbow Promise

Published by
WARNER BOOKS

Seasons

Part I

1

August 27, 1973

No two women could have been more unlike than Sharon Thompson and Hollis Wendley. Only an impersonal university dormitory system would have placed them together as roommates. There wasn't a chance that they would become friends; and, in fact, they did not—until Sharon got pregnant and her whole world came crashing down.

Sharon was petite and brown-haired, with huge, soulful brown eyes. She was pretty in a quiet way, her face dominated by her big melting eyes. She was studious and intelligent, and she came from Little Fork, Texas, a small town set in the crook of the Red River just where it turned down out of the Panhandle. Her background was middle class, and conservative; and though she didn't fit into the mold of her family, she retained the depth of conviction that distinguished them.

Hollis, on the other hand, was a wealthy oilman's only daughter and a sorority girl. Her long hair was blond, artfully streaked with lighter blond strands. Her face was strong and sensual, with high, broad cheekbones, a firm jaw, and a wide,

beckoning mouth. Her eyes were exotic, tilted up a little at
the outer corners and of an unusual green-gold color, with
lashes so thick and dark they shadowed her eyes, giving them
an alluring, mysterious quality. An aura of sexuality clung
to her, and everywhere she went men fell all over themselves
trying to talk to her or do something for her. She had little
interest in school and spent most of her time going out on
dates or preparing to go out on dates. Hollis smoked and
drank and never came back to her room before curfew.

Sharon was glad that Hollis, who was already established
in their joint room since she had come early for Rush Week,
was not there when Sharon's parents and brother helped her
move in. If her father had seen Hollis sitting on her bed
smoking a cigarette, her shapely legs curled up under her, a
tank top revealing the ample curves of her breasts, his qualms
about his daughter's attending SMU would have quadrupled.

Her parents were conservative people, quietly but em-
phatically religious. They were the sort who arranged their
life plans in accordance with God's wishes. Sharon, who had
always been uncertain exactly how they knew what God's
wishes were, had never fit in well with her family. Her brother
Ames understood her parents and got along with them; he
was studying to be a minister. But Sharon wanted to major
in art; she wanted to see the world, to do things. She yearned
to break away from the small-town life. Her family felt Sharon
had inherited her inclinations from her grandmother Alice,
who had also drawn a lot and was considered an eccentric
by most of the Thompson clan.

Sharon had finally won the battle to major in art at college,
compromising with her parents by working toward a degree
in art education, so that she would have a practical use for
her major. Her parents had wanted her to attend a small
religious school like McMurry in Abilene, but when she had
won a scholarship to Southern Methodist University in Dallas,
they couldn't afford to turn it down, especially with her
brother Ames still being in the costly Perkins Theological
School at SMU. So they had agreed to let her go, naively
comforting themselves with the knowledge that it was, after

all, a Methodist school. Besides, she would be on the same campus as her brother, who could keep an eye on her.

Hollis wouldn't have confirmed the Thompsons' rosy view of SMU.

Sharon was not shocked by Hollis. She was well aware that SMU had a reputation as being more of a party school than a religious one, having long since lost most of its Methodist direction and acquired a more Dallas–like atmosphere of wealth and privilege. However, she guessed immediately that she and Hollis were not destined to be close friends. Sharon considered herself a rather ordinary person, not the kind to be associating with glamorous, wealthy, sophisticated people, and Hollis was obviously all those things. Moreover, Sharon despised all forms of bigotry, unfairness, and inequality, and, as a result, she looked upon sororities and sorority types with disfavor. There was, she knew, an unbridgeable gulf between her and Hollis.

She was right. When Hollis came into their room, she greeted her politely, but coolly, and after that, they rarely spoke except about their room or the dorm. Hollis lived in her world, and Sharon lived in hers. She made other friends down the hall in the dorm and spent most of her time with them.

Once Hollis came in drunk and sick from a party, and Sharon helped her to the bathroom to throw up. She wet a washcloth and gave it to Hollis to wipe her face.

Hollis looked up at Sharon, her face washed out, her eyes mirroring the queasy state of her stomach. "Thank you," she said, a note of surprise in her voice. Sharon didn't understand why she was surprised. They had never actively disliked each other; it didn't seem odd to her that she should help Hollis when she was obviously feeling so ill, even if she had brought the illness upon herself. In fact, Sharon imagined she probably would have helped Hollis in this situation even if she disliked her.

The next day Sharon brought Hollis lunch on a tray from the dorm's cafeteria. Hollis rejected most of it, eating only the Jell-O salad, but again she thanked Sharon with surprise.

Sharon put the tray aside to return to the cafeteria later and sat down with her biology book.

After a moment Hollis asked, a little tentatively. "You're dating Wes Maitland, aren't you?"

Sharon glanced up. Now it was her turn to be surprised. She felt color rising in her cheeks and hated herself for the easy way she showed emotion. "Yes. I've gone out with him a few times."

Wes was in her freshman English class, and he had asked her over to the Student Union building for a cup of coffee after the first class. He had thick brown hair that he wore a little long, and gray-blue eyes; and even though he, too, was obviously a rich, fraternity-type, Sharon had been drawn to him. The truth was they had been dating a lot since then, and Sharon had fallen head over heels in love with him; but she was reluctant to reveal that to Hollis.

"I thought I saw you at a party last week."

Sharon nodded. She had seen Hollis, too, but Hollis had been across the room, surrounded, as always, by men, and Sharon had made no effort to speak to her. Frankly, she had been unwilling to bring Wes even to the outer rim of Hollis's orbit.

"I know him. He's from Dallas. We went to Highland Park High School together." Hollis looked as if she were about to reveal something more, but then she looked away, shrugging a little, and said only, "He's a cute guy."

Hollis rolled over, facing away from Sharon. She threw back over her shoulder, her voice bored and disinterested, "If you ever want to borrow some clothes or something, feel free to."

Sharon stared, floored by Hollis's comment. It wasn't just Hollis's generosity, considering the lack of warmth in their relationship, that surprised Sharon. What was more amazing was that Hollis must have guessed that Sharon had found her wardrobe inadequate for the number and quality of the parties and places Wes took her to. Sharon had been embarrassed about that fact but hadn't had the money to buy new clothes. Had Hollis really understood that? Or had she simply offered the first thing that came into her mind in an effort to repay Sharon for being kind to her? Or maybe she considered Sharon's clothes so tacky that she pitied her? The thought made Sharon squirm a little.

Sharon didn't know what to do. She was the same dress size as Hollis, though she might have to put a temporary hem on some things since Hollis was taller than she. And she would love to wear some of those beautiful clothes. However, she didn't feel close enough to be comfortable borrowing them. And if Hollis was pitying her, she couldn't stand that!

Although she thought about the offer the next time she went out on a date with Wes, she wore a dress he'd seen many times before. The following night, as Hollis and Sharon were getting ready, Hollis tossed a blue dress onto Sharon's bed.

"You want to wear it?" Hollis asked in a disinterested tone and turned back to her mirror to finish applying her eye makeup.

Sharon picked up the dress. It was a beautiful, slick, shimmery dress, and she wanted desperately to wear it. "Are you sure you don't mind?" She looked at Hollis.

Hollis shrugged. "I'm not wearing it. Why not you?" She tossed down her mascara and turned, flashing that quick, slightly crooked grin of hers that never failed to win people over. Casually, she knocked a cigarette out of her pack, lit it and inhaled, then went on, "Maybe sometime I'll ask you to write a paper for me."

The telephone rang, and Hollis answered it. She listened for a moment, then said, "Yeah. I'll be right down."

She hung up and turned to Sharon, laughing a little. "He said, 'Hey, Hollis, this is Chuck.' I thought his name was Gary." She picked up her purse and swept out the door.

Sharon watched her go. She wondered how a person ever became as confident and cool as Hollis Wendley. Sharon had never seen Hollis angry or unable to come up with a funny quip. For a moment Sharon felt a strange little pang inside, and she almost wished that she and Hollis had become friends. Hollis might have turned out to be fun.

After that, Sharon often wore one of Hollis's dresses when she was going out on a date with Wes. But, still, she and Hollis didn't become true friends. Neither one of them was ever in the room enough to really talk. Hollis was gone on dates with a variety of men at all times of the day—lunches, study dates, coffee and talk dates, as well as evening dates —and Sharon was spending more and more of her time with Wes.

Wes fascinated her. He was handsome and brooding, a troubled, vulnerable young man like the characters James Dean had played in old movies on television. His family was wealthy but cold, he told her. His father was never home; he was always at work amassing more money. His mother was unaffectionate, and what little love she displayed was for his older brother, Reid. Mrs. Maitland's chief ambition was to have a son in politics. Her family had been political for generations, and she had been disappointed when her husband, after one brief, unsuccessful campaign for the state senate many years ago, had chosen to work only behind the scenes in politics. She had put all her energies into preparing Reid for that life.

"Reid's the perfect son," Wes told Sharon with a twisted smile that made her heart ache. "Four point average, captain of the debate team, sports—you name it; he did it exactly right. Now he's finished law school, and in a couple of years he'll run for something. He's been working for one politician or another for years now, ever since he was in high school, getting the experience, building the contacts, earning brownie points—all the stuff he needs to be successful in politics. Mother doesn't think anything exists except Reid. The sun rises and sets on him. 'Course, Reid's just like her. Cool, remote, all head and no heart. He's always telling me I need to get my act together, to grow up. As if I'd want to grow up like him."

Wes's words pierced Sharon, as they always did when he talked about the things that tormented him. She could see him growing up in that cold house, alone and sensitive, creating a shell of rebellion and wildness around him. He often acted in ways that she disapproved of: He drank too much and partied too often, with even less concern for his studies than Hollis showed. He often smoked grass, and once Sharon had opened a drawer in his apartment, looking for a cooking utensil, and had found a plastic Baggie filled with pills of all colors. She had no idea what they were or how many of them Wes took, but the sight of them scared her. All these things were part of the rebelliousness that he wore like a flag. In time, under the gentle outpouring of her love, they would disappear, she knew. Wes would realize that he no longer needed them. Just as he would realize he no longer needed the parties and wild good times or the childish pranks and jokes he enjoyed with his fraternity brothers.

Sharon loved him, and she was flooded with emotions for him that were maternal yet loverlike. She wanted to take care of him; she wanted to heal his wounds; she wanted to bathe him in the warmth of her love. In the overwhelming thrall of her first real love, Sharon thought she would do anything for him, change herself into whatever he wanted—and in the process change him, too.

He wanted her, and Sharon found that terribly exciting. She had dated a little in high school, but no boy had ever fallen for her the way Wes had. No one had called her and talked on the phone till all hours of the night, as Wes did, or met her every chance he got: at the student cafeteria for coffee, for lunch or even just to sit beneath the trees and look at her. No one else had gone out with her every night he could get her to forget about studying. And nobody had ever kissed and caressed her with such fervor, his skin hot and damp, the way Wes had.

He wanted to sleep with her. He wanted to possess her. He wanted her to be his in every way. Sharon had never even come close to sleeping with a man before, but now she found that she wanted to. She wanted to more than anything. She wanted to love and be loved by him, to belong to him, to give him all the gifts she had to give. She knew that it was the right course, the only possible direction for their love to go. So, in all her innocence, she gave herself to him.

Sex proved to be something of a disappointment. Sharon didn't dislike it, exactly, but it didn't seem the stupendously wonderful thing that everyone had always said it was, the earth-shattering excitement that was portrayed in books and movies. It was embarrassing and awkward at first. Later on, as she got used to it, it became pleasant, but the main enjoyment she got from it was in seeing how much enjoyment it gave Wes. For her, sex didn't compare to the great and crashing feeling of love in her chest for him.

She was too shy at first to go to a doctor for birth control pills. By the time she worked up the courage, it was too late. She began to feel sick when she first woke up in the morning and again in the evening. At first she tried to pass her illness off as a "bug" of some kind that would go away soon. After three days of intermittent nausea, she knew she was kidding herself. The doctor confirmed her worst fears: She was pregnant.

For days she went around in a state of suppressed panic, too upset and scared to tell anyone, even Wes or her best friends. She didn't know what to do. Every alternative seemed even worse than the others. So she tried to quell her panic and just not think about it.

She didn't notice that Hollis had looked at her oddly more than once in the last few days. One evening, when Sharon and Hollis were in their room, studying, Sharon's stomach grew queasy. It began to roil, and Sharon stood up abruptly and rushed out of the room.

She ran to the bathroom and into one of the stalls to vomit. When her stomach had calmed down, she left the bathroom stall, her face ashen, and ran right into Hollis, who was standing against the wall, waiting. Sharon blinked. What was Hollis doing here?

Hollis straightened up and pushed away from the wall. "How long you been tossing your cookies?" she inquired conversationally.

"I don't know," Sharon murmured. "I must have eaten something . . ."

Hollis shook her head. "I don't think so. Let's go back to the room and talk."

Numbly Sharon followed her back to their room. She didn't know what to make of Hollis's sudden interest in her. Hollis looked as if she *knew*. But how could she? And why did she care?

The girls sat down on their respective beds, facing each other. For a long moment, neither of them spoke. Hollis went through the ritual of tapping out a cigarette and lighting it. Finally, as she exhaled the smoke, she said, "You're pregnant, aren't you?"

Tears flooded Sharon's eyes, and she glanced away. She felt humiliated. "Yes," she answered in a low voice. "How did you know?"

Hollis shrugged. "It's not the first time it's happened. Have you told Wes?"

Sharon shook her head.

"Why not? Don't you think you ought to?"

"I don't—" Sharon cast Hollis an agonized look. "I don't want to put pressure on him. I don't want him to think that I'm trying to—to—" Tears clogged her throat, silencing her.

"To trap him?"

"Yeah. I wouldn't, ever. I was just stupid." Sharon slammed her fist down against her leg. "I was so stupid!"

"Aren't we all?" Hollis remarked dryly, flicking an ash from her cigarette. She paused for a moment. "So what are you going to do? Not tell him? Make the decision by yourself?"

"I don't know. I'm so confused." Sharon shoved her hands back into her hair and clenched her fingers, pulling at her hair until it hurt. "I'm scared."

Her voice came out almost in a whisper. She had felt guilty, ashamed, and frightened since she had first suspected she was pregnant. It was a relief to let it out to someone, though Hollis was hardly the person she would have picked to tell.

"Of course you're scared. Who wouldn't be?"

Her remark surprised Sharon. She would have thought

Hollis would regard her with scorn, being too worldly not to have thought of birth control. And if Hollis had somehow had the misfortune to get pregnant, Sharon couldn't imagine her being afraid.

"What should I do?"

Hollis sighed. "I'm not exactly the kind of person you ought to get advice from. Fashion's more my line. But, since you asked . . . well, I . . . I wouldn't get rid of it."

"Oh, no! I wouldn't." Abortions were legal now, but Sharon couldn't imagine doing that.

"Then you either have to get married or have it by yourself. Do you want to marry Wes?"

Sharon had thought about marrying him lots of times, but in a vague, sometime-in-the-future way. She hesitated. "Yeah. I mean, I love him. I just—not this soon. And I don't want to force him. I don't want him to feel trapped."

"He can live with it," Hollis retorted callously. "You're trapped with it, aren't you? Why not him? He had something to do with it, after all."

"Well, yes, but . . ."

"I know, I know, 'Sweet Sharon' isn't the kind of girl to do that." Hollis grimaced. "Look, you can't think only of Wes's feelings. Think about that kid inside you. You have to take care of it. How good a life can you give it? But how good a life will it have as Junior Maitland?"

"You're saying I ought to do it for the money!"

"I'm saying money doesn't hurt, especially when you're raising a kid. You love Wes, don't you? You'd be a good wife to him."

"Yes."

"So you aren't being a gold digger." Hollis paused. "I'll tell you the truth: Wes isn't the man I'd pick for a husband, for you or anybody else. He's got . . . problems."

"I know. He told me about his family."

"It's more than that. He's not a real responsible guy. He's into drugs."

"Just grass."

"That's not what I've heard."

"Sometimes pills," Sharon admitted.

"And a lot of booze." Hollis raised both her hands as though to deflect an attack. "I know, I know, who am I to talk? I run with the same crowd. That's true. But, then, I'm not exactly great wife or mother material either. Wes isn't . . . stable." Hollis shrugged. "But he's a nice guy inside, I think. Who's to say he won't settle down? Lots of people do when they get married and have a kid." She grinned wryly. "Maybe the love of a good woman will change him."

"So you think I should try to get him to marry me?"

"I think you should tell him. Look at it this way: Don't you think he has a right to know? He is the father. Do you have the right to hide it from him?"

Sharon sighed. "No. I guess you're right. Maybe I've avoided telling him because I'm afraid of what he'll think of me. I should tell him." She paused. "I will. I'll tell him."

As it turned out, Sharon never had the chance. She had planned to meet him the following afternoon in the Student Union cafeteria, but he didn't show up. That had happened a time or two before, so she thought nothing of it, except to feel a mild irritation. She walked back to her dorm room, and there she found Hollis, sitting on her bed, smoking. Her face was so pale that her eyes and thick, straight brows were startlingly vivid. Hollis looked at Sharon, and in her eyes was such a strange mingling of emotions that fear leapt up in Sharon's stomach.

"Hollis? What is it? What's the matter?"

Hollis stubbed out her cigarette and came over to Sharon, taking her by the arm and propelling her toward her bed. Sharon sat down, her heart pounding. "Hollis! What is it? You're scaring me."

Hollis sat down beside her. She shoved her hand into her hair and pushed it back off her face. "Sharon, I—Scott Harrington just called me."

Scott was Wes's roommate. Sharon's heart raced even harder.

"He, uh, Wes didn't go to his classes this morning, and finally Scott went in to check on him, and he was—well, he'd taken a bunch of pills, apparently, and he—overdosed." She hesitated. "He died, Sharon. I'm sorry; he's dead."

Sharon stared at her. "What?"

"Wes overdosed on something last night. He's dead. They aren't sure whether it was an accident or . . ." Hollis's voice trailed off, and she had to look away from Sharon's face.

Sharon felt as if she dropped down on a roller coaster and had left her stomach up in the air, only this time it was her soul that had been sucked away from her body, she looked down at her arm; it seemed disconnected to her. She looked at Hollis, at the room. Nothing was real or familiar.

"No. That's crazy. Wes isn't—he couldn't be."

Hollis nodded, laying a tentative hand on Sharon's shoulder. "He is. Honey, I'm sorry. I really am. But he's dead. He was drinking a lot, and he popped some pills. Then he went into his room, and he must have taken a lot more of them. It could have been an accident, with him drinking and all."

Sharon hardly heard Hollis's attempt to reassure her that Wes hadn't committed suicide. She was still too stunned even to take in the fact that he had died.

She sat numbly on her bed for a long time. Hollis, not knowing what to do, retreated to her own bed and sat there, smoking continuously, watching her.

Wes was dead. It couldn't be true. It simply couldn't be. She was carrying his baby, and he couldn't be—oh, God, he'd never know about it, never be able to see it, to hold it, to laugh over its antics. Suddenly the tears that Sharon had been too stunned to cry came pouring out. She put her hands to her face and sobbed. Hollis came over hesitantly, drawn by her sorrow yet uncertain what to do, and sat down beside her, putting a comforting arm around her. Sharon turned her face into Hollis's shoulder and cried.

Wes was buried two days later. Hollis accompanied Sharon to the funeral. Still numb with sorrow, Sharon felt disoriented as if everything were unreal. Three days ago Wes had been there, holding her hand and laughing with her, and now he had just vanished. She had been the girl he loved, the most important person in his life, but in death his family had taken over and shut her out. They didn't even know her or speak to her. She was an outsider at the funeral of the man she loved, just one of the many people there.

She looked at the three people sitting in the front row of the family pews: a balding man whom she took to be Wes's father, an aristocratic white-haired woman with Wes's face in feminine form—his mother—and his brother, with coloring like Wes's and a similar frame, but with features more like those of his father. They were a cold group, all right, sitting like statues while the minister eulogized Wes—no crying, no red eyes or trembling hands. It seemed bitter and sad to Sharon that Wes's mourners should be these three. Tears ran unheeded down her face.

After the funeral Hollis drove Sharon back to the dorm. Sharon didn't know what she would have done without Hollis. She had made her lie down and sleep. She'd forced her to eat. She had chosen a dress for Sharon to wear today and had helped her with her hair and makeup. She had fielded telephone calls and turned away visitors, her cool gaze more than a match for their offended feelings.

Sharon continued to stay in their room for the next few days, not going to classes or even bothering to dress unless Hollis dragged her down to the cafeteria. There she just picked at her food, unable to force anything down.

Finally one evening when they returned from supper, Hollis sat down beside Sharon on her bed and took her hand. She gazed straight into Sharon's eyes. Sharon blinked, a little surprised. Hollis chewed at her lower lip, and her hand squeezed Sharon's. Sharon realized, amazed, that Hollis was nervous.

"I don't know exactly what to say. I'm no good with people," Hollis told her. "So you'll have to help me."

"Help you what?" Sharon couldn't imagine what Hollis was leading up to.

"Get you to stop doing this."

"Doing what?"

"This. Staring at the ceiling, not eating, not talking. Giving up."

Tears sprang into Sharon's eyes. She had thought that Hollis understood. She had been sympathetic, yet hadn't pushed or pried, giving Sharon the space she needed.

"Come on, now, don't do that to me." Hollis handed her a tissue. "You know I'm lousy with tears."

Sharon wiped her eyes. "I—I don't understand. What do you want?"

Hollis tightened her grip on Sharon's hand. "I know how upset you are, how scared and sad and everything. But you can't go all to hell like this. You're carrying a baby. You have to eat. You have to sleep. You've got to decide what to do."

"What to do?" Sharon began to cry again. "Oh, God, I don't know. I don't know! I can't decide. I can't do anything. I can't even think."

"I know. That's why I've been thinking for you. You have to pull yourself together and go see Wes's parents. Tell them you're pregnant with Wes's baby."

"What?" Sharon stared. "I don't even know them. Wes hated them."

"So what? Who gets along with their parents? I love my father, but he's so overbearing it drives me crazy. Look, you're going to need a lot of things. This baby is going to need a lot of things."

"You want me to ask them for help? For money? I couldn't."

"You don't have to ask. Just explain the circumstances. They'll offer you the rest. You need taking care of. There are going to be all kinds of bills. You'll have to find a place to live." Sharon opened her mouth to protest, but Hollis held up a hand. "But that's just one side of it. Think of it from their side. Their son just died. Don't you think they'd want to know that he left behind a child? Their grandchild. It's no kindness to keep the fact from them. You'd be depriving them of that comfort. Do you think that's fair? Wouldn't you want to know?''

Sharon closed her mouth. She hadn't thought of it that way. But Hollis was right. It would be unfair of her not to tell them, no matter how much she dreaded the thought. Certainly she would want to know if she were in their position.

"I don't know. Maybe you're right." Her stomach felt uneasy, reminding her forcibly of the baby and the fact that it depended solely on her. It was Wes's child, all she had left of him. She had to take care of it, no matter how bad she felt; she couldn't let anything happen to it. Hollis was right. She had to pull herself together for the baby's sake. She had to eat and get enough rest. She had to think ahead.

It was just so hard! She pressed the palm of her hand against her forehead, as if she could drive it right through and push out all the sorrow and confusion. Tears trickled down her cheeks. They were always ready to flow these days. "I'm so tired, Hollis, I feel—lost. I don't know what to do."

"Then it's a good thing you have somebody bossy like me around," Hollis retorted with a grin.

That brought a weak smile from Sharon, and once again she wiped her eyes.

"First things first: a good meal," Hollis went on. "None of this dormitory crap. I'm taking you out for a steak. Then you're coming back here for a long nap. Tomorrow you can see the Maitlands if you're up to it."

Sharon followed Hollis's orders, surprised to find that the meal actually tasted good. For the first time in days, she was hungry. She was able to sleep that afternoon, too, as though she had crossed some barrier of grief into an easier world.

The next day Hollis drove Sharon to the Maitland mansion. It was an imposing white colonial set back on a wide green lot just off Turtle Creek. When Sharon saw it, her stomach began to do flips, and her hands turned cold. She couldn't go in there and tell them anything, let alone that she had slept with their son! She cast an agonized glance at Hollis.

"Why don't I come with you?" Hollis suggested. "They don't know me, but I did go to school with Wes. And they might know my dad."

Sharon wanted to say yes. Even more than that, she wanted to turn and drive away. But she knew she couldn't do either one. "No. I ought to do it by myself. I think it would be worse for them with another person there."

She opened the car door and slid out. She walked up the sidewalk. It seemed at least a mile long. Her fingers grew colder every second, and her stomach was churning. She reached the door. A huge funeral wreath hung upon it. She looked at it, swallowing the bile that rose in her throat, and pushed the doorbell. A moment later, a maid answered the door.

"I'd like to see Mrs. Maitland," Sharon said, her voice so low she had to repeat herself.

The black woman frowned. "Mrs. Maitland is indisposed today." She started to close the door.

"Please!" Sharon moved forward, putting up her hand as if to block the door. "It's very important that I see her. It's about her son. Wes."

Sorrow touched the maid's eyes. "Wes Maitland is dead, ma'am."

"I know." Sharon couldn't stop the tears, any more than she had been able to for days. "I'm sorry. I knew him. Please, I need to see Mrs. Maitland."

The maid hesitated. "Just a moment. I'll see if maybe Mr. Maitland will see you."

She let Sharon in the door and left her standing in the marble-floored entryway. Sharon waited, clutching her purse to her like a life preserver, and wondered how she would be able to tell her tale to Wes's father instead of his mother. She was surprised a few minutes later when the young man she had seen in the Maitland pew walked into the entry. She hadn't considered the possibility that "Mr. Maitland" meant Wes's brother, not his father. Reid, the perfect son. Her stomach sank. It would be even more shaming to admit it to him.

"I'm Reid Maitland," he said. "I understand you wished to see my mother?"

"Yes." This close, Sharon could see that his eyes were gray, with no hint of Wes's blue to warm them. And his set face was as cool and forbidding as his wintry eyes. "I did. I—" She fumbled for the right words.

"Perhaps I can help you. Alma said it concerned Wes."

Sharon nodded. "Could we talk—" She made a vague gesture. "—someplace more private?"

His brows drew together, making him appear even more forbidding, and suspicion was clear in his face. "Of course. Why don't we go into the study?"

He led her down a hallway and into a wood-paneled room. It was a dark, heavy, masculine room dominated by a large desk and furnished with leather chairs. Wes motioned her toward one of the chairs facing the desk and he sat down behind the desk. Their positions made Sharon feel rather like a wayward student facing the principal. She was certain that he had chosen this room and their positions in order to intimidate her, and anger surged within her, displacing some of her fear.

Straightening her shoulders, she said bluntly, "My name is Sharon Thompson. I'm a student at SMU. I came here because I thought your mother would want to know that— that I'm carrying Wes's child." Her cheeks flamed with embarrassment. But, there, at least it was out.

Reid Maitland studied her without expression. Sharon found herself tilting her chin a little, defiantly. Finally he said, "You're pregnant?"

"Yes."

"And you claim it's Wes's child."

Sharon stared, surprised, jarred by his use of the word "claim," as if it might not be true. "It *is* Wes's child."

"Do you have anything to support that except your word?" His voice was as cool and impersonal as if he were discussing the weather instead of his dead brother and the unborn child he had left behind.

The blood flooded Sharon's cheeks again, but in anger this

time, not shame. "You think I'm lying? That I would actually come here and pretend that Wes and I—How could you think—Why in the world would I do such a thing?"

His brows lifted, and his face was tinged for an instant with bitter amusement. "Money, perhaps?"

"Money!"

"Yes, a neat little trap. You go to a mother torn with grief, longing to have her son back, and you tell her you're carrying his child. She greets you with cries of joy and takes you into her home. She gives you money and whatever you want. Maybe, if she never comes to her senses, she even sets up a trust fund for the baby—provided, of course, that you really are pregnant. Alternatively, if the mother doesn't fall for that, you bargain for a lump sum to keep quiet about the fact that the son left behind an illegitimate child. They pay you in order not to tarnish the name and reputation of their beloved child. You've got them either way—or so you think."

Sharon stared at him, too astounded by his interpretation of her reason for coming here to even deny it.

"Surprised, Miss Thompson? Unfortunately, you weren't the first to think of such a scheme. There are lots of people who would like to get their hands on a little of the Maitland money. I've already been visited by one enterprising young woman, not quite as young and appealing as you, of course, but more confident and articulate. She even provided me with the dates of her assignations with my brother and the names of witnesses who would testify that he had been seen with her. She also threatened me with a law suit to establish legal claim to the money in Wes's trust funds. I tossed her out yesterday morning, and since you hardly seem as prepared, it's obvious that—"

"Prepared!" Sharon found her tongue at last, and the fury inside her bubbled out. "Of course I'm not prepared. It never entered my head that you wouldn't believe me. That you would think first of *money*, rather than the fact that your brother had left behind a child! A child that you and your family could know and love and have a piece of Wes left with them." Her voice choked with emotion, but she hurried on, too furious to care how she sounded. "I should have known. Wes told me you were heartless and cold, all of you! He told me what it was like to grow up in this sterile, unloving home. I was so stupid and naive. I didn't believe him, not entirely. I thought he was exaggerating, but I can see now that he wasn't."

Reid Maitland's eyes narrowed, and he surged to his feet, bracing his hands on the desk and leaning across it toward her. "I'd suggest you leave right now. You don't know a goddamn thing about Wes or this family, and—"

"Oh yes, I do." Tears were streaming down her face now, but Sharon didn't care, didn't even bother to wipe them away. "I know exactly how Wes was treated here. He told me. All any of you care about is money and the Maitland name. Your getting into politics is the only thing that matters, and an illegitimate niece or nephew might hamper that, mightn't it? So you'll sweep that little inconvenience under the rug. Well, let me tell you something: You won't ever have to worry about keeping news of my child quiet! It'll be born a Thompson and it'll live a Thompson. I wouldn't want it to be connected to the Maitlands in any way." Sharon jumped to her feet and stalked to the door and flung it open. She looked back at him, unaware of how lovely and vulnerable she looked, her cheeks stained with color and her huge doelike eyes swimming with tears. "I was foolish enough to think that you would want to know about the baby. I was trying to be fair to your family." Her voice was laced with scorn. "What a joke. You're much happier with your money than you would be with a flesh-and-blood child."

She stormed out of the room, leaving Reid Maitland standing behind the desk, staring after her.

2

Sharon didn't know what she would have done the next few weeks without Hollis. Still reeling from the shock of Wes's death and ill from her pregnancy, she felt hurt, confused, and helpless. Often she was on the edge of sinking into despair, but Hollis would not let her. Besides making sure she ate, slept, and took her vitamins, Hollis set about arranging Sharon's life.

"How about your parents?" she asked when Sharon worried over what she would do. "Can you go live with them?"

"No." Sharon shook her head vehemently. "My parents are kind, but this is something they couldn't accept. They're very religious. I don't know how I'm going to work up the courage even to tell them. I couldn't live with them. Little Fork is such a small place that everybody would know, and it would humiliate my parents. I can't do that. Besides, they'd pray over me all the time, trying to get me to confess and repent what I'd done, which I will not do. They'd want me to put the baby up for adoption, and I refuse to do that, too."

"I get the picture. Cross them out."

"I need to find a job and save some money. I better quit school and get a little apartment."

"Just hang on. Don't drop out yet. You've got a scholarship, so you have free room and board—as long as you stay in school. Besides, you might go back to school sometime, and then you'll be glad you have an extra semester."

"But I can't stay here in the dorm. I'll start to show."

"The baby's due when, August?"

"Yeah. Middle of August."

"Okay, so that means—" Hollis calculated on her fingers. "You'll be six months at the end of school."

"I'll look like I swallowed a basketball by then."

"Maybe. But you aren't showing yet. You have at least a couple of months before you start to show, and then we can get you some bigger-size clothes to try to hide it. The worst that'll happen is that people will suspect. I think you could finish the year. In the meantime, I'll work on a place for you to live this summer."

Sharon went along with Hollis's plans. She felt too weak and indecisive to do anything else. Her studies suffered, but she managed to pass. Before long, her stomach stopped bothering her and she felt less tired, so she got a job on the weekends at a maternity shop. She spent some of her money on maternity clothes, which she bought at a discount there, and the rest she saved. She didn't know how she would ever get enough to pay for the doctor and the hospital when the baby came or for the time she would lose working, but she did as Hollis advised and put such thoughts out of her mind. It was easy enough for her to do. Wes's death, the baby, the future, were all too overwhelming even to contemplate. The only way she could get through it, it seemed, was simply to plod through life day by day.

One afternoon in March as she returned from classes, Sharon saw Hollis sitting in the dorm lobby with a handsome, black-haired young man. Sharon waved and continued on to their room, eager to get her shoes off. Her feet were beginning to swell nowadays when she walked and stood too much. She wondered who the man was. He looked older than college age, maybe a graduate student. Sharon couldn't remember having seen him with Hollis before. But Hollis certainly had looked happy and sparkling talking to him.

Sharon had just slid out of her shoes and sat down on her bed with her feet up when Hollis waltzed into the room, grinning. "Hi!"

"Well, hello." Sharon couldn't help but smile. "Something wonderful must have happened. Who's the guy?"

Hollis chuckled. "No, he's not what's wonderful. At least, not per se. That's Jack Lacey. His father's Horton Lacey; Horton's a wildcatter, and he and my father have been business associates since way back."

Sharon had learned sometime ago that Hollis's father—and his father before him—had made their not inconsiderable fortune in oil field equipment. But she couldn't see much connection between that business relationship and Hollis's happiness. "And that makes you grin like that?"

"No, silly. I was simply explaining that Jack and I have know each other since, well, since I was born. He's a good, old friend. And that's why he's doing me a favor. He was here talking to me about it—and giving me this." She held up a piece of twine, from which a house key dangled, and her grin grew broader.

"A key?"

"A very special key. A key to the Laceys' summer house in Santa Fe. The house you are going to live in."

"What? What are you talking about?"

"Well . . ." Hollis gave the twine and key a twirl and sat down on the opposite bed, still beaming. "I've been trying to think of some place you could live real cheaply, some place you'd like. I remembered that the Laceys used to have a house in New Mexico. I couldn't remember if it was Taos or Santa Fe. Anyway, it was one of those artsy communities, and I figured you'd like that. Plus, I knew that the Laceys don't go there much now that Horton's dead. He was the one who loved New Mexico. I wasn't sure they still had the house;

but I figured that if they did, Jack'd let me have it for free. When I called him last week, he was out in West Texas checking on some well he's digging. Anyway, he got back into town yesterday, called me this morning, and, voilà!, here is the key."

Sharon stared. "He's just turning the house over to me?"

"Yeah. Neither he nor his mother or sister are going there this year. They don't really want to rent it for fear the renters might damage it. So it's just sitting there. Jack was happy to turn it over to a friend of mine for a few months."

Sharon continued to stare at Hollis, not quite able to take it in. A complete stranger was letting her have the use of his house for several months—without any payment?

Hollis's smile faded. "That is—if you want to. Would you mind moving to Santa Fe? It was the only thing I could think of that would be nice *and* free. Daddy has a little ranch in central Texas, but he's there a lot, and, besides, a foreman and his wife live there all the time. I figured you wouldn't want people around."

"Oh no!" Sharon hastened to reassure her. "Santa Fe is fine. In fact, it's marvelous. I'd love to live there—all the galleries and the artists and the scenery! It's just—I can hardly believe it. I can't imagine anyone being so generous."

"Oh." Hollis waved her hand, dismissing that thought. "Jack's a good guy. A lot of people think he's tough, and I guess he is, at least when it comes to business. But he's been a good friend to me. Besides, he doesn't need the house this summer. It'll really benefit them, having someone there looking after it. Someone they can trust."

"But how does he know he can trust me? I'm a total stranger."

"I recommended you. Besides, I told him I'd probably spend the summer there with you." Hollis paused and glanced at her a little hesitantly.

"What? Are you kidding?"

"No. I didn't really want to spend the summer hanging around home, and I thought it'd be fun to go to Santa Fe.

We can run up to Taos and stuff like that. I figured you might not want to be alone. Of course, if you'd rather I didn't go—''

"No! Oh no, that's great! I'd love for you to come with me. It just never occurred to me that you would consider it. It would be wonderful; I wouldn't be as scared.''

"Yeah, that's what I thought. That's how I would feel.''

Sharon's face lit up. "Maybe I can get a job in a gallery or something else to do with art.''

"Sure. In fact, I asked Jack if he knew of anything. They know a few people in Santa Fe, from having gone there so many times. He said he had an idea, and he'd check on it.''

"I can't believe this. He's going to get me a job, too?''

Hollis laughed. "You don't know Jack. He's a dynamo. He does about ten times as much stuff as ordinary people do. It makes me tired just to be around him. Doing something like that is merely a way for him to fill in the cracks.''

But when school was out early in May and Jack Lacey moved Hollis and Sharon to his house in Santa Fe, Sharon understood why he had been so generous and kind to her. He was in love with Hollis.

Hollis didn't seem to know it. Jack made no romantic gestures toward Hollis; in fact, he treated her as a friend, much as she treated him. But there was an intensity in his eyes when he looked at her, a faint softening of his features that was not there at any other time.

What Sharon found hard to understand was why the two of them remained just friends. They made a striking couple, each with vivid, sensual good looks, yet very different coloring. Jack was of medium height, his body lean, tan, and tight with muscle. It was obvious that he had worked in the oil fields much of his life. His pure black hair was thick and slightly shaggy, the kind of hair that made a woman want to reach out and smooth it off his forehead. His eyes were a compelling, startling blue, alive with personality. There was a cocky air about him that was curiously appealing, part confidence, part daring, part exuberance. He moved through life like a whirlwind.

He was sexy too. There was no denying that. Even Sharon, still grieving for Wes, felt that undeniable pull. Surely sparks must fly between him and Hollis.

But when she mentioned the idea to Hollis, her friend just laughed and said, "Me and Jack? No way. We're just friends. He's too much like my father. Pushy and arrogant, hard, driven. I'll never fall in love with a man like my father. Jack would try to run my life, and I can't stand that. I've had more than enough of it with Daddy."

"I think maybe Jack doesn't feel the same way you do," Sharon suggested.

Hollis paused, looking thoughtful. "Jack? Really? No, you must be mistaken. He's always treated me like a kid sister. I don't think there's any romance there."

Sharon was still not convinced.

After they reached Santa Fe, Jack stayed a few days with them, helping them settle in. Wherever they went, any man around was immediately drawn to Hollis, until finally it got to be a joke. One afternoon, they took a stroll through Santa Fe, window shopping and stopping in the little stores and galleries. Hollis left one of the stores before the others, and Jack and Sharon stepped out of the shop to find Hollis standing on the sidewalk, talking and flirting with three grinning, college-age boys. Jack and Sharon cast a glance at each other and had to laugh.

"Damn. She'd be a hard woman for a jealous man to live with," Jack commented.

Sharon glanced up at him. That look was in his eyes again, warm and intense, as he watched Hollis. Feeling Sharon's gaze, Jack turned his head, and their eyes met. He made a funny noise, part laugh, part sigh. "You caught me."

"You're in love with her, aren't you?"

"I'm going to marry her one of these days." His voice was calm and matter-of-fact.

"Then why—"

"You think I'm going to throw myself in with her horde of admirers?" He shook his head, his eyes returning to Hollis. "No. She's testing her wings, trying out her skills on the boys. I can wait. When she's broken all their hearts, I'll still be here."

Sharon stared. "You're serious. You're—waiting for her to grow up?"

He shrugged. "I guess you could put it that way. I've got no ambition to be one in a crowd. People say I don't have any patience, but I do, when it's something worth waiting for."

"But what if she falls in love with somebody else in the meantime? What if another man steals her right from under your nose?"

"It won't happen. I won't let it. I always get what I want."

Looking at him, Sharon could see the steel that his charm often hid. It wasn't hard to understand why, at just twenty-four, he was able to run his father's business with such success. He probably did manage to get pretty much whatever he went after. Sharon suspected, however, that Hollis might be more than a match for him.

Hollis turned and saw them and smiled. Jack winked and motioned to her to join them. "Come on," he said, his voice as light and unimpassioned as ever. "I'm going to take you two lovely ladies out to dinner."

Over supper, Jack turned to the subject of Sharon's employment. "I've found you a job, if you've got the nerve for it."

Hollis's eyebrows slid up. "Nerve? Jack, what have you done?"

"Don't get in an uproar. It's nothing dangerous. But the woman who needs someone is an eccentric not many people can work for. She's had two secretaries quit on her this year."

"Sounds great."

"You said Sharon liked art." He glanced at Sharon questioningly.

"Oh yes. That was my major."

"Well, this old eccentric I'm talking about is one of the top artists in the country, has been for years and years. She's Jane Laskow!"

"Jane Laskow!" Sharon stared, dumbfounded. "You've found me a job with Jane Laskow!"

"Yeah." Jack looked a little uncertain.

Hollis set down her fork. "The Jane Laskow who has one of her oils hanging in Daddy's office?"

Jack nodded.

"The artist whose painting he paid fifty thousand for when I was kid and that's worth God knows what now?"

"The same."

"Jesus." Even Hollis looked impressed. "I didn't know you knew her."

Jack grinned. "She thinks I'm cute. I met her last year when we were up here. Mother knows her. Anyway, she was bitching about an autobiography she's supposed to be writing for some publisher in New York. She doesn't want to have to go through all her old letters and things herself, but she can't keep a secretary. Apparently she's got a poison tongue."

"Jane Laskow." Sharon repeated. "Oh, Jack, I can't believe it. I would never have dreamed in my life that I'd ever meet her. I've always thought she was the most wonderful —oh, there aren't words for her work. She's as famous as Georgia O'Keeffe or—"

"Yeah, well, she's also almost ninety years old and a real pain in the ass. Very few people can work with her. She has a Mexican gardener who fortunately doesn't speak a word of English, so he doesn't understand what she says, and her housekeeper's been with her since time began. The rest of them come and go—art students, servants, gallery owners. She can be difficult. Still, she's a hell of an interesting old lady. I enjoyed talking to her last year."

"That's 'cause she thought you were cute," Hollis put in, grinning wickedly.

Jack grimaced. "It's up to you. You want to see at least if you can put up with her?"

"Definitely. Absolutely." Sharon's eyes were starry. She was more animated than Hollis had seen her be since Wes died. "Just to be able to listen to her, to hear about her life and her work, her techniques, would be marvelous. And to think of reading those letters!"

"Hope you still think so Thursday. She wants you to come for an interview then."

Jack left the next day, returning to Dallas by way of a gas field in the Panhandle and an oil field near Permian. Hollis occupied herself with fixing up the cabin and getting the last of their things put away. Sharon spent the next two days worrying about meeting Jane Laskow.

She found she needn't have. Jane Laskow was eccentric, but she liked Sharon on the spot and hired her almost without talking to her. Sharon wasn't quite sure why. (The housekeeper, Mrs. Caldwell, told her sometime later that Sharon's coloring and features reminded Jane of her favorite sister, Sophia.)

Sharon loved her job. Jane Laskow was tanned and wizened, with a face like a walnut shell. She had broken one hip two winters earlier, and she walked with a cane. There were times when her memory of recent events was terrible. But most of the time she was sharp as a tack, and her memory of the distant past was excellent. She told Sharon anecdotes, both amusing and sad, about herself and other people, some famous, some not, and she talked about her theories of art and life.

When she found out that Sharon was an artist, she had her bring her work, and offered criticism and instruction. Sharon was sure she received a more constructive and important education in art from Jane than she would have gained if she'd finished all four years of college. At times Jane's tongue was sharp, and she criticized Sharon harshly or let rip a string of curses because she had interrupted or annoyed her. But Sharon was good at letting such things roll off her back; she liked Jane too much to allow her occasional nasty temper to drive her away.

Some of Sharon's job consisted of jotting down and typing the artist's reminiscences, and the rest of it was going through old trunks, boxes, and file cabinets and sifting through the letters and documents she found there. These she read to Jane and arranged in some kind of order. Many of the letters were from Mason Reinburg to her, and there were a few from her to him. These interested Sharon most.

Much of the book would cover Jane's famous love affair with Mason, a married Hollywood director. Their love had lasted for four decades, beginning with their meeting at a Hollywood cocktail party when Jane was forty and he was thirty-two and ending with his death seven years before. Their romance had survived his marriage, the separation of miles, time, and many, many battles. They were both passionate, aggressive people, and their fights had been legendary. Sharon read these letters with a kind of awe and excitement.

Her job didn't really seem like work. It was too much fun. Through Jane she met many other artists in the Santa Fe and Taos areas, and Jane encouraged her to pick their brains, too. Sharon was able to experiment with many different media, for Jane seemed to have all the tools necessary. She had dabbled all her life in other art forms in addition to the oils and charcoal for which she was most famous. Up until now Sharon had stuck to oils, acrylics, and pastels; but she was afraid that the fumes of the paints and fixatives might harm her baby, so she was happy to try other art forms. She took on pottery, weaving, sculpting, print blocking and, finally, stained glass. Stained glass intrigued her the most, and she began to take classes two evenings a week in stained and beveled glass art.

However, as she grew heavier, Sharon grew less and less interested in any art, and by August she decided to postpone the rest of her classes for a few months. More and more she stayed at home with Hollis, looking at television, listening to the radio, or talking. She wouldn't have believed it if someone had told her this nine months ago, but she and Hollis had become the best of friends.

She had found out that Hollis was not the shallow, even callous, girl that she had seemed. That was just an image that Hollis chose to present to the world. She was, in fact, amazingly sensitive, as well as funny and bright, and she proved time and again to Sharon that she was kind and generous. Not only had she found this house for Sharon and even insisted on paying most of their bills, but also she had given unstinting support and friendship—personal sacrifices that were far more generous gifts than money.

Sharon still wondered sometimes what had prompted Hollis to act as she had. After all, at the time Hollis began helping her, they had been little more than strangers who shared a room.

One evening late in July, when Sharon had become so big that she had trouble sleeping through the whole night, she got up in the middle of the night and padded into the kitchen for a snack. As she walked back toward her bedroom, wondering wearily if she would be able to sleep, she glanced outside onto the back porch. There was a dark shape in one of the chairs. Sharon jumped in fright. Then the red end of a cigarette flared as a smoker inhaled, and in its glow Sharon could see Hollis's face.

Hesitantly she opened the door onto the back porch. "Hollis? Are you all right?"

"Sure. I couldn't sleep, so I got up to have a glass of wine and a smoke. I like it out here. I'm not a very good sleeper."

"Neither am I—anymore."

"Come on out and join me."

Sharon did. She was glad for the company. She hadn't looked forward to returning to bed. Sometimes the effort of forcing herself to sleep was tiring in itself. She sat down on the wooden lawn chair beside Hollis. The night was cool, as it always was out here, no matter how hot the days. A breeze rustled through the piñon behind the house.

Sharon shivered a little, and Hollis handed her the blanket from her lap. She had a sweater around her shoulders. Obviously she had come prepared for the night. Hollis sipped from her wineglass, and they sat together in companionable silence.

"I'll never forget this," Sharon said softly. "As long as I live, I'll think back to these months and remember how the night felt and smelled, how the sun looked on the Plaza in the afternoon, how sweet and vivid everything seemed.''

"Me, too." Sharon's eyes were more accustomed to the darkness now, and she could see Hollis smile faintly. "I never had a good friend before. I mean, a good girlfriend."

"Really?" Sharon was surprised. "But I thought you had lots of friends. I mean, all those sorority sisters who used to call you and everything."

Hollis shook her head. "They weren't really good friends. I'm not—an easy person to like."

"I don't know why not. You're terribly kind and generous."

"It's not hard when you've got plenty of money."

"You're generous with yourself, too, with your time and effort."

Hollis shook her head. "Not usually. This is out of the ordinary for me. Jack was amazed."

Sharon studied her. "Then why did you do it for me?"

Hollis glanced at her. "I like you. I just told you, you're the first real girlfriend I've ever had."

"No, that's now. I mean before, back at the beginning. When you figured out I was pregnant."

"You'd been nice to me that time I came home smashed and got sick. It surprised me, and I—I guess I wanted to return the favor."

"You did far more than that."

Hollis lit a new cigarette from the butt of her old one, and Sharon knew that the topic was making her nervous. She didn't understand why.

"I'm just a kind soul. How about that?"

Sharon said nothing. Hollis was the most closed-up person she'd ever met; if she didn't want to say something, there was no getting it out of her.

But, surprisingly, Hollis started talking again, her voice low and flattened to conceal a wellspring of pain. "It was because of something I did a few years ago." She took a deep drag on her cigarette. "I've never told this to anyone before. No one knows except Jack. When I was fifteen, I fell in love with this guy, a real bastard. I was wild and I had the hots for him. He was a senior, and I thought he was so cool." She gave a dry chuckle that ended on a sigh. "Anyway, I ended up pregnant. It was the summer after my sophomore year. I had just turned sixteen. I couldn't let my father know. I mean, I rebelled against him and stuff, but half the things I did were to make him notice me. I really loved him, and I knew he'd be furious with me. And so hurt and humiliated. I couldn't bear the look in his eyes. I couldn't stand to have him think poorly of me. So I got an abortion."

"Oh, Hollis!" Sharon's voice throbbed with sympathy.

"Real brave huh? Real loving and kind. I got the name of this guy from a girl at school, and I went to him—this was before they were legal, you see. It was crazy, with code words and everything. His driver picked me up on a street corner in downtown Dallas and drove me out to a house in the country." She stubbed out the cigarette savagely. "He did it, and then they dropped me off at the same street corner, and I drove home. When I got there, I found I was bleeding. It wouldn't stop. I still couldn't tell Daddy, and in a panic I called Jack. He was the only person I could think of who could help, who would be smart and sophisticated and old enough to know what to do. So he took me to their family doctor. The old guy patched me up and never said a word to the police or Daddy."

Sharon reached out and slid her hand into Hollis's. Hollis clutched it tightly. "I murdered my baby. That's why I wanted to help you; I had to help you. I guess I thought it would make up in some way for what I'd done. Killing my baby just because I was ashamed of what Daddy would think."

"Hollis, you were only a kid. You were young and scared."

"And you aren't?"

"I'm three years older; that makes a big difference when you're talking about fifteen and eighteen."

Hollis shrugged. "Maybe. But there's no getting around the fact that what I did was wrong. Wicked."

Tears filled Sharon's eyes. "Wrong, maybe. But not wicked. I know you, and you're not wicked." She squeezed Hollis's hand tightly, and Hollis hung on.

They sat for a long time, silent, gazing out into the pine-scented darkness, their hands clutched together for comfort.

Sharon had the baby the third week in August, one week late. Hollis had had to go to school a week before to register, but she flew back out as soon as she had gone through registration, missing her first three days of class. Sharon remonstrated with her, telling her that she should stay at SMU, but Hollis looked indignant and replied that she intended to be there when the baby was born. And Sharon was glad. She would have none of her family there.

Sharon had written her parents long ago to tell them that she was pregnant and to explain what she planned to do. Her father had written back an angry, hurt reply. Since then she had received several letters from her family, ranging from heartbroken to sermonizing. They wanted her to give up the baby; they wanted her to repent and "come back to God." They had not come to visit Sharon, nor had she visited them; and Sharon knew that that was best, at least for the moment. Perhaps someday her parents would accept her and the baby, but right now she knew that there would be only arguments and tears if she saw them.

Her brother Ames was the only one in the family who had been sympathetic to her. She had talked to him about her decision, and they had kept in touch after she left Dallas. But he was in his last year at Perkins, and he had already begun school, so he could not be there with her. (And, Hollis, with her wry sense of humor and tough strength, was more comfort than Ames would have been, anyway.)

Sharon's labor lasted all one long afternoon, and finally

the doctor gave her a spinal block. After that the pain went away. They wheeled her into the delivery room, and she was able to see and hear, but not feel the birth. The doctor grinned and said, ''A girl!''

Sharon heard the baby wail and saw the doctor hand the flailing red infant to the nurse. The nurse took her to a small table and worked over her for a few minutes, then laid her in Sharon's arms. The baby was red and screaming, her mouth wide open and her eyes screwed shut. Her black hair was thick and plastered down wetly to her head. Sharon looked at her and fell in love.

Sharon named her Janis. Later, when she felt better and the painful headaches from the spinal block had vanished, she and Hollis would walk down the hall to the glass-windowed nursery, to stand and gaze at Janis sleeping. She seemed the most beautiful thing in the world to Sharon, and Hollis was almost as crazy about her. Hollis bought Janis half the stuffed animals in Santa Fe, it seemed, and she kept talking about what else she could bring her as she grew older.

Hollis had to leave before Sharon got out of the hospital, but Sharon had other friends in Santa Fe now, ones she had met through Jane Laskow. They were mostly artists, and one of them volunteered to drive her and the baby home. Two others, Dora McBride and Randy Donalson, even took turns coming by every day for a few hours to cook her a meal and give her a break from baby care.

Years later, when she looked back at that time, Sharon knew that if she hadn't been so young she would have had the sense to be scared, but at the time she didn't know it. She was happy and bubbling with enthusiasm. For the first time since Wes's death, she was not miserable. She enjoyed every minute of her daughter's life. Jane allowed her to bring the child to work, taking pleasure in the new life that the infant brought into the house. Janis slept a great deal, and when she was awake, she was a quiet baby. Jane liked to watch Sharon play with her, and Sharon caught her more than once bent over Janis's infant seat, dangling a rattle in front of her. The housekeeper loved her, too, and was happy to take care of her when Sharon was too busy to hold her.

Sharon's life was full; and if it was sometimes so busy she could scarcely hold her head up by the end of the day, she was too happy to wish that any of it were different. Now that Hollis was gone, she spent more and more time with the new friends she had made. She became particularly close to Randy. He was a handsome young man, an artist of considerable talent, moody and often temperamental, but also kind and warm. He was gay, and his moody nature caused him to be forever in up-and-down relationships with his male lovers. Sharon became his confidante and friend, the only one with whom he felt he could really be himself, without engaging in any of the sexual gamesmanship he carried on with other gays or encountering the contempt he often sensed in those who were straight.

Randy or one of her other friends was always willing to keep Janis in the evenings, so Sharon took up her stained glass classes again. The more she learned about the medium and worked with it, the more excited she became. Along with her burgeoning maternal feelings and her new excitement in life, she found herself bursting with artistic urgings. She threw herself into learning and working and wished only that she didn't have to work so that she could apply herself entirely to her art.

Hollis kept in touch, writing often and flying out to see her now and then. In one letter, she mentioned that Sharon's brother, Ames, had dropped by to meet her and thank her for all she had done for Sharon and to see how Sharon was doing. As the weeks passed, Sharon was surprised to find that Hollis mentioned Ames often, and it wasn't long before Hollis confessed that she and Ames were dating and that she was head over heels in love with him.

Sharon couldn't imagine her gentle, quiet brother with her wise-cracking, sophisticated friend. But apparently the attraction was mutual, for she received a letter or two from Ames, as well, that were a good deal more restrained but obviously full of love for Hollis. Well, there was no accounting. They said that opposites attracted. Hadn't she and Wes been very different types of people, too? Maybe it would be a wonderful thing for both of them, but Sharon couldn't help worrying a little about what would happen to them eventually. She couldn't imagine Ames giving up his dedication to the ministry, but neither could she see Hollis as a minister's wife!

Sharon was happy except for the small, quiet ache she felt sometimes when she thought of Wes. She was even beginning to see hope that someday the rift between her and her parents would be resolved. Her mother had written two letters since Janis's birth in which there had been no preaching, and she had even asked about the health of the baby.

The peace of her quiet life was rocked, violently and unexpectedly, when she returned home from Jane's one afternoon and found a dark blue Mercedes parked in front of her small house. She was instantly filled with foreboding. Slowly she unfastened Janis from her car seat and gathered her up, wrapping her tightly against the chill December air.

She told herself not to be silly. She did, after all, know some people who were wealthy. Perhaps it was Hollis in her father's car or even Jack Lacey, dropping by to see how the house was or to tell her that she would have to leave. There wasn't a reason in the world to assume that the car was connected to the Maitlands—except her own fear.

Since Janis's birth, Sharon had been afraid that the Maitlands might decide that they wanted Wes's child after all and would try to take her away. She couldn't imagine anyone not wanting Janis, even though they had kicked Sharon out the door; and the family was so powerful and wealthy that she knew she would lose any law suit they might bring against her. She told herself that she was being foolish, that they didn't care about Janis any more now than they had when they found out she was pregnant; all they cared about were money and reputation. Still, sometimes she woke at night, sweating, from a nightmare in which she was endlessly chasing Reid Maitland, who had stolen her baby from her.

Sharon strode quickly down the pebbled path to her cottage, ignoring the luxurious car sitting there. The driver's door opened, and a man stepped out. She didn't look in his direction, but she caught a glimpse of a business suit and black hair. She tried to walk even faster, but the man caught up with her and stopped right in front of her, blocking her path. It was Reid Maitland.

Sharon came to an abrupt halt. Her heart started pounding as though it would come up out of her throat. She stared at him, her eyes wide, and unconsciously clutched Janis closer to her chest.

"I'm sorry if I alarmed you," he said. "I just want to talk to you."

"No. Please. I—I have nothing to say."

"No, wait." He reached out a hand, and Sharon backed away from it. Janis, tired of the blanket over her face against the cold and the way her mother was squeezing her, let out a squawk. Maitland glanced down at the blanket, and for a moment there was a sort of eager curiosity in his normally expressionless eyes. "There's no reason to be afraid of me. Couldn't we go inside and talk?"

"I don't see why."

"All right." His jaw tightened, and he drew a breath. "Let's talk about it here. I know you have no reason to like me, Miss Thompson. But I came to apologize." Sharon looked at him, saying nothing. "I was rude to you and very, very wrong. My only excuse is that when you came to talk to me I was still shaken by my brother's death, as were my mother and father. As I think I told you, another girl had tried to get money from us using a similar story. Had I been less upset, I trust that I would have been perceptive enough to have seen the obvious difference between you and that girl. But at the time, I wasn't thinking clearly. I simply reacted. Unfortunately, in my pain and distress, I lashed out at you. I'm sorry. Please accept my heartfelt apology."

"Are you saying that you believe me? That you admit that Janis is Wes's child?" Sharon's heart sank. Perhaps she would have welcomed the words a year ago when her heart was bruised. But they had come too late. She felt only an upsurge of bitterness about the callous way he had thrown her out of his house, combined with the fear that her worst nightmares were coming true. The Maitlands wanted to acknowledge Janis now; next they would try to take her away from Sharon.

"Yes. For weeks after you left, you kept popping into my mind. Finally, I began to think more clearly. I remembered the way you looked and acted; there had been nothing cheap or phony about you. I began to wonder if I had made a dreadful mistake; I realized how awful the consequences would be if I had. I hired a private detective to check into the last months of Wes's life. He talked to Wes's friends and roommates and traced his movements. What he turned up confirmed what you had told me. Wes had indeed been dating you, and only you. He had given every evidence of being a man very much in love. The detective checked into your background, as well."

"Oh, and did I pass inspection?" Sharon asked with sarcastic sweetness.

"I'm sorry. This must sound cold. But I had to be careful, to be sure."

"I understand. You couldn't make a mistake if money was involved."

"I didn't know you, Miss Thompson. How was I to be certain you were honest and aboveboard unless I checked into it?"

"Some people trust their perceptions and instincts."

"Some people have learned that that isn't always wise."

"Or profitable."

"It isn't losing the money that hurts so much when you've been conned. It's the feeling of betrayal, of having been played for a fool by someone you trusted." He sighed. "I didn't come here to argue with you. I came to apologize. If you wish to continue to dislike me, that's your prerogative. I also wanted to offer you my help."

"Now?"

His mouth tightened. "I tried to months ago, when I received the report from the detective and realized that you had told me the truth. But you were no longer attending SMU. I was unable to find you. It took a while for the detective to track you down. Your relatives and friends were very tight-lipped."

"They wanted to protect me."

"I wasn't trying to hurt you. I wanted to take care of you. To give you money for the doctor and the hospital, for living expenses."

"I don't need money. I don't need your help." Sharon had bitterly vowed long ago that she would never take anything from this man, but there was more to her refusal than anger and shame at his cruel rejection of her. She was afraid to let him help her and Janis in any way, for it might give him some claim over her, some right. She knew she must not give in to him, even slightly. It could be disastrous in the future. Sharon knew her weaknesses: She was too soft-hearted, too trusting. But she had learned through her own painful experience that the things Wes had said about his family were true. They were hard and grasping; they were cold. Even now, apologizing to her, admitting that he'd wronged her, acknowledging that his dead brother had left a child behind, Reid Maitland had shown no emotion. He was as stiff and formal, as rigid and cold as he had been that day in his family's house. Sharon knew she must not let her guard down with him. He had too much power, too much money; he could take Janis from her easily.

"Don't be silly. You can hardly be living in high style. You have a job as a secretary, and you have a baby to raise. That's not the life I want for my brother's child. I can provide well for Janis—clothes, food, a place to live. A fine education when she gets older. You could go back to college and get a degree."

And what would he demand in return? A man like Reid Maitland didn't do things for free. "No. Janis and I are doing fine. And we will continue to do so without any help from you."

He grimaced. "Damn it. You're not being fair to your daughter."

"*My* daughter. You're right about that, at least; she's *my* daughter. You have nothing to do with her, nothing to say about her or how she's raised. She is mine alone. You gave up any rights you had to her a year ago when you kicked me out of your house."

"I understand why you're hurt and bitter toward me, but think of your daughter."

"I am thinking of her. The last thing I want for her is to grow up with the 'advantages' of a Maitland. We all know how much those 'advantages' helped Wes, don't we?"

His face tightened, and for an instant his gray eyes were alive with pain. Sharon realized how cruel her words had been, and apologies sprang to her lips, but she managed to swallow them. There was no reason for her to take care of Reid Maitland. If he felt guilt and pain over Wes's death, there was probably ample reason for him to. She had to protect her daughter any way she could; that was all she could allow herself to think about.

"I will raise my daughter by myself, without any help from you, financial or otherwise. You have no say in it. You didn't want her then; you took yourself out of her life. I'm not about to let you back in now. I don't want you to see her or contact her. And I don't want you to bother me again."

He looked at her for a moment, his eyes silvery, his face set. "That's clear enough," he said finally.

There was something in his voice, controlled as it was, that sent a tug of pain through Sharon's heart, but she ignored it. Tough. She had to be tough. Her baby was at stake.

"As you wish, Miss Thompson." His eyes flickered toward the wrapped-up baby, and he started to speak. Then he looked away, at the trees across the road. "Good-bye."

Sharon didn't turn to watch him leave. She hurried into the house and locked the door behind her. She leaned against it, her breath coming in shallow gasps. Her knees started to shake uncontrollably. She had won. He had left without even seeing the baby. Reid Maitland was out of her life forever.

3

Hollis was amazed that she'd fallen in love with a man like Ames Thompson. After all—a theology student! She didn't even go to church.

But when he dropped by her dorm to ask about his sister and to thank her for helping Sharon, Hollis fell for him like the greenest girl. He was handsome, but it wasn't just his looks. Hollis had known other good-looking guys, but she hadn't gone all soft inside over them. She couldn't explain it; there was just something special about Ames—a warmth in his dark brown eyes, a tenderness in his smile, a *goodness* that shone out of him. He had a kind of charisma, not the powerful energy flow that a man like Jack Lacey created around him, but a sweet, gently enfolding aura that made a person want to be around Ames, as if his sweetness would somehow become part of her, too.

With Ames, Hollis felt changed, different, a new and better person. She loved him through and through, giving herself to him heart and soul. No other man had ever inspired such depth of feeling in her. She was shaken by it, even a little scared, but it thrilled her, too. She knew she had found the one man she would love all her life. (It made her laugh to remember how a few weeks earlier she would have said cynically that there was no such thing as one true, great love.)

It also amazed her that Ames loved her back. Hollis was well aware of her sensual power over men; she'd used it often enough. But Ames was not the kind of man to be ruled by his desire. It wasn't that he was a saint; he wanted her. She could see it in his eyes and in the slackening of his mouth; she could feel it burning across his·skin when he held her. But, unlike most of the boys she had dated in the past, he controlled his passion, instead of letting it control him. He refused to make love to her, despite the many times that Hollis tempted him, because he didn't believe in sex before marriage. So when he told Hollis that he loved her, when his eyes glowed at her with love and affection, she knew it wasn't because he was trying to get her into bed with him. He didn't love her because she was lovely or sexy. Nor did he have any interest in her wealth. He loved her, for some reason, just for herself.

Hollis didn't understand it. She didn't think there was anything in her for a gentle, religious man to love. She was too wild. She had done more than a few wicked things. She suspected that it was that Ames was too good to see the badness that lurked in her. So she did her best to continue to keep it concealed from him. Hollis gave up partying, drinking, smoking, and swearing. She even tried to leash her acerbic tongue, biting back sarcastic comments. She was scared that he would find out about the abortion she had had in high school; she knew he would be unable to overlook or excuse that. If Ames knew about that, he would realize how wicked she was. Hollis could imagine the pain and dismay, the disillusionment that would fill his face, and she couldn't bear the thought. It was bad enough that he would eventually have to find out she wasn't a virgin; she certainly wasn't going to let him find out how many men there had been since she lost her virginity.

It was a sweet, romantic year. Hollis met Ames often, though they rarely went out on the sort of dates she was accustomed to. He didn't drink or dance, and he didn't have the money to spare to go to the movies often. Now and then they visited with his friends or went to one of their parties, but Hollis found his friends dull. She preferred simply to spend the time alone with him. They sat in the lobby of her dorm and talked; they studied together in the library, holding hands across the table; they lay on the grass beneath the spreading trees in the warmth of spring. Hollis was happier than she could remember being in her life. She was filled with love for Ames, and more than anything, she wanted to marry him.

There were times, though, when she hated his religion. It occupied so much of his time and thoughts. He talked about it like a man in love, a man obsessed, when the only thing she wanted Ames to be obsessed with was her. It galled her that she wasn't the most important thing in his life.

When he graduated, Ames would become a minister. It was his lifelong dream. Hollis wanted to marry Ames, but she couldn't imagine being a minister's wife. To have to be circumspect and respectable all the time, to have the disapproving eyes of a whole congregation on her, always waiting for her to slip, to be nice to people she didn't like or even want to know, just because they were important in the congregation, would be a horrible way to live.

Worse yet, what Ames really wanted was to be not just a minister but a missionary. When he began to talk about building an orphanage or a hospital in some third world country, his eyes would glow and his voice would rise with excitement. He wanted to bring the poor people of the world education, religion, and medical help. Hollis was all for that, but her idea of helping them was to donate money. The last thing she wanted was to go live in the hot, humid jungles of South America or Africa with poverty, disease, and no conveniences. Even the thought of it made her shudder. Yet no matter how steadily and subtly she tried to steer Ames away from his ambition, nothing seemed to work.

Hollis tried as much as possible to put the future out of her mind, hoping that somehow everything would work out.

If Ames came to love her enough, he wouldn't need those other things. He would be happy with just her. She would make him happy. In her whole life Hollis had rarely been denied anything, so she couldn't really imagine it happening now. Deep down she felt that somehow she would win what she wanted.

But she didn't win this time. The school year ended and Ames graduated. One evening Hollis came home to the dorm to find a sealed envelope in her mailbox, addressed in Ames's hand. Frowning, she took it out and opened it. She read the short note. Her breath stopped in her throat. Disbelieving, she went back and read it over again. Ames had a chance to start a mission in Guatemala that he couldn't pass up. He had left Dallas this morning to fly there. He loved her, but he knew that she could never be a missionary's wife. He hated to hurt her and was sorry for telling her this way, but he hadn't had the nerve to tell her face-to-face. He was too afraid that his love for her would stop him from following his life's work.

Hollis swallowed. She glanced around her, faintly surprised to see that everything looked unchanged when she felt as if her world had ended. Numbly she walked to her room and sat down on the bed. She read the note again. The normal thing to do would be to cry, she supposed, but the tears didn't come. She never cried.

She thought of running after him, of flying down to Guatemala. She would talk to him, make him see how crazy it was to break it off with her. She would seduce him, and this time he would give in and make love to her. Then he would be tied to her; he wouldn't be able to leave her.

But she knew such plans were foolish. Ames was immovable once he had made up his mind—particularly where his precious religion was concerned. She didn't try to follow him.

Instead she moved back into her parents' house and began a long, dismal summer. She kept to her room most of the time; she didn't want to see anyone, including her parents. Nothing interested her, and she spent much of her time sleeping. It seemed to her as if she would never again enjoy anything.

Jack Lacey was the only one who could pull her out of her depression. They had continued to be friends even though Jack disliked Ames and was not reluctant to tell Hollis what he thought of him. Jack dropped by a few days after Ames left and took Hollis out for pizza. Afterward, they went back to Jack's apartment and listened to records. He was amusing and sharp, and he took her mind off Ames. But then suddenly, much to her dismay, Hollis burst into tears. She couldn't stop crying.

"Baby, don't." Jack pulled her into his arms. It was warm and soothing to be enfolded by his heat and strength. "What's the matter?"

She was unable to tell him. She just shook her head and cried. He continued to hold her, giving comfort, demanding nothing, until finally her tears stopped.

"Ames left," she said at last, her voice small.

"Good riddance. Where'd he go?"

"Guatemala."

Jack let out a brief, humorless laugh. "You're joking."

"No. He's going to be a missionary."

"I'm sure he'll save the world," Jack said dryly.

"I wish I were dead."

He squeezed her to him tightly. "Don't say that. Don't ever say that. Ames Thompson's leaving is the best thing that ever happened to you. Trust me. Someday you'll be glad it happened."

"Will I? I wish I could think so."

"Just hang on, and you'll see."

After that, Jack did his best to keep her spirits up. He came by her parents' house often and took her out to movies or parties or over to his apartment for a drink and a few laughs. He was a lifesaver. Hollis didn't know what she would have done without him that dreadful summer.

She visited Sharon in Santa Fe for a few weeks, and that, too, raised her spirits. Janis was adorable; Hollis felt as if she could get lost in her. Hollis didn't talk much to Sharon about Ames and what had happened between them, but it was soothing just to be with her and talk or prowl around the galleries and shops of Santa Fe and Taos or go out to eat Mexican food.

Hollis returned to SMU in the fall and took a small apartment not far from the campus. She rarely went to sorority functions; somehow in the past year and a half she had lost interest in such things. She rarely dated; no man interested her. For once she concentrated on her studies and found herself making good grades, much to her father's surprise.

Jack was often in West Texas, where his company had several wells, but whenever he was in Dallas he dropped by to see her. He wouldn't let her be blue or down; his raw energy swept her along until she had to laugh and have fun.

She didn't stop loving Ames; Hollis doubted that she would ever do that. But gradually the searing pain lessened and went away. She was able to think of him without wanting to cry. She began to enjoy life again.

One evening in February, Jack took her out to a play, and afterward they came back to his apartment. It was cold outside, and Jack built a fire in the fireplace and fixed them hot buttered rums. They sat on the couch, Jack at one end and Hollis at the other, turned sideways, her feet casually propped up in his lap. Hollis felt cozy and warm, both inside and out. Jack pulled off her boots and began to massage her foot. Hollis wriggled her toes inside her sock with pleasure.

"Um, that feels good."

Jack wiggled his eyebrows. "Just one of my special services, ma'am."

"And what other 'services' do you provide?"

He grinned wickedly. "You want a demonstration?"

"You're so bad." Hollis tossed a throw pillow at him, and he raised an arm, deflecting it. Hollis took another sip of her rum. "Jack . . ."

"Mmhmm." He started on the other foot.

Delightful prickles of sensation ran up her leg. Hollis thought about what a wonderfully handsome man Jack was.

She'd always known it but usually it didn't intrude on her consciousness. "Are you dating anybody?"

He shrugged. "Nobody special."

"You spend so much time with me you couldn't have much time for anyone else." She took another drink. She hadn't had much supper, so the drink was beginning to affect her. She leaned forward. "Have you ever had your heart broken? Have you ever been really, really in love?"

Jack glanced at her, and his hands stilled. He regarded her unblinkingly. "Yeah, I've been in love."

"Did it tear your heart out?"

"Sometimes." He began to massage her foot again, keeping his eyes on his hands.

"Me, too. I can see now, though, that it wouldn't have worked out."

"Yeah?" Again he looked up at her, his vivid blue eyes measuring.

"Yeah. He was too good for me."

"Don't be stupid."

"It's the truth. Ames was a very good man. Religious, kind, sincere. All those things I'm not. Do you know that he never even slept with me?"

His hands stopped abruptly. "What?"

Hollis shrugged, the heat rising in her face. She wished she could take back her words; now she felt embarrassed.

"He never made love to you?" Jack sounded stunned.

Hollis raised her eyebrow and retorted with some asperity, "Not everyone does, you know."

"But he dated you for a whole year."

"He didn't believe in it. Sex before marriage, I mean."

"God, what an asshole."

Hollis jerked her feet out of Jack's lap and swung them to the floor. "He was not. He considered it a sin."

"A sin!" Jack slid across the couch and took her chin in his hand. He stared fiercely into her eyes. "It's a sin not to make love to a woman like you." His voice was low and rough. Heat stirred in Hollis's abdomen.

Suddenly, surprising them both, his lips were on hers, and he was kissing her. His mouth was hot and desperate; his tongue filled her mouth. Hollis clenched her hands in his shirtfront. Heat swept her. It was as if her whole body had suddenly ignited. She had never felt anything like it with any man, never known such fast, wild, fierce passion. She dug her fingers into him. She wanted to claw him, to rip at his clothes, to wrap her legs around him and pull him inside her.

She felt Jack's body jump as her fingers bit into him, but he did not pull away. Instead, with a groan, he pressed her down onto the couch, his body stretching out on top of her. He kissed her deeply, consumingly, as though there were no other time, no other chance. His hands moved down her body, touching her breasts, her stomach, her legs. He cupped her buttocks and pressed her pelvis up against him, rubbing his body over hers. Hollis gasped and shuddered, and her fingers tore at his back. All kinds of wild sensations were exploding within her, and she ached to feel him inside her.

"Jack, Jack," she whispered, her words trailing off in a moan.

Hearing her speak his name like that drove Jack wild. He wanted to give her everything, to fulfill her in every way, to be the world to her, the one man who could satisfy her. He cursed, but his shaken voice sounded as much prayerful as cursing. He rolled to the floor with her, taking the brunt of the fall. It was titillating to feel her lying on top of him, but it wasn't nearly enough. He wanted to turn and pull her under him again, but they were wedged between the couch and the coffee table.

Jack reached blindly for the coffee table, caught the edge and shoved it away, sending it crashing to the floor. But Hollis was wriggling on top of him now, and she brought her legs down beside his, locking herself against him. She began to move, rubbing against him as he had done with her moments earlier. She straightened slowly, still moving her hips against him, and looked down at him. Her face was filled with heat and passion. She was the most beautiful thing he'd ever seen. Slowly, languidly, she rotated her hips over the hot, thick shaft of his desire. And as she moved, she reached down and grasped her sweater. She pulled it up over her head and tossed it aside.

She was wearing nothing underneath. Jack's hands slid up her body and covered her breasts. She smiled a slow, mysterious, sensual smile. He watched her nipples harden and thicken beneath his fingers. Hollis gasped, and her teeth dug into her lips. She lost the rhythm of her movements. Jack's hands went to her shoulders, and he pulled her down to his mouth. His tongue circled her nipple, tracing the outer circle and winding in until it touched the darker bud in the center. One hand slid down between their bodies and in between her legs. Her trousers were damp with the moisture of her desire, and he smiled against her breast. His lips closed around her nipple and he began to suckle, while his hand rubbed sensually against her. She moved with him, her breath sobbing.

He murmured against her flesh, and though his voice was too low to understand the words, she knew the tone. He was pouring out the desire in him, caressing her with language, even as his work-roughened hand caressed her body. His passion, his urgency, were dizzying. Hollis wanted him to go on forever, yet she wanted even more to reach the zenith he was propelling her toward with every movement. She unfastened the button of her trousers and slid down the zipper. She ached to feel his hand inside her clothes. He shoved apart the sides of her trousers, and his fingers delved down, sliding over the slickness of her panties. But, again, it was tantalizingly incomplete.

It was for Jack, too, and he rolled over, taking her under him. He went up on his knees and reached down to take off her socks. Then he grasped her trousers and underpants and pulled them down in one swift movement. He knelt there for a moment, gazing at her naked body. The lights were on, and he could see her clearly. She was beautiful. He thought that he could have looked at her forever—if it weren't for this pounding need inside him, the urgent drive to thrust into her and make her entirely his.

He bent and lightly kissed each nipple, then her navel. Then he stood and jerked off his clothes, throwing them aside. As he undressed, his eyes remained on Hollis's body, eating her up.

Hollis watched him. His body was beautiful in a primitive way, lean and muscular from years of working in the oil fields. He was powerful and thoroughly masculine, and he raised an answering femininity in her. She wanted to take him inside her and conquer him with her softness.

Jack came back to her, sliding in between her legs. He paused for a moment, staring down into her eyes, hovering on the brink of knowing her finally and completely. Hollis gazed back up at him. She was on fire and shivering at the same time, lost in a torrent of emotions and pleasures. Her hands slid up his arms to his shoulders. His eyes closed at the feel of her hands on his skin. His hands went beneath her hips, lifting her to receive him, and, at last, he came inside her.

Hollis drew in her breath sharply, the pleasure so sharp and swift, it was almost unbearable. He filled her completely, tightly, and she shuddered at the satisfaction. Then he began to move within her, slow, deep, hard thrusts, and with each movement he filled her, possessed her again. She circled her hips in counterpoint, lost in the thundering buildup of pleasure.

She was slick and tight around him, stroking him with every thrust. It was all he could do to hold on to one last small thread of control, to build her passion with his slow movements. Then he felt her jerk against him and heard the tiny sigh that escaped her lips, and inside she convulsed around him. The explosion rocked him, separating him for a moment of spinning eternity from reason, leaving him all raw, pure sensation.

He collapsed against her. His sweat dampened her skin. Hollis wrapped her arms around him. For this instant there was nothing in her life but Jack.

* * *

That was the way it was with Jack, passionate and explosive. Hollis didn't love him, not in the sweet, compelling way she loved Ames. But sex had never been as delicious, as enticing, as satisfying with anyone else. She had never expected to have a love affair with Jack, but now she couldn't imagine why they had never made love before.

The affair continued for months. Hollis had expected it to burn out quickly, as intense and fiery as it was, but it did not. When Jack was in Dallas, they saw each other several times a week, sometimes going out, other times staying in. But whatever they did, each evening they spent together wound up in bed. When he was away, Jack called her almost every night; and when he returned, they made love as if they hadn't seen each other in months.

Once, when he had been out in West Texas for a week, seeing to a well that had blown out, he showed up at Hollis's apartment in the middle of the night. He'd driven straight through from Odessa, too anxious to see her to wait until after he'd slept—or even to shower and change. He arrived, grubby and tired, at her front door and when she opened the door, he lifted her up and kissed her, then walked with her straight back to the bedroom. They said not a word, just made love frantically, almost desperately.

The next morning he asked her to marry him.

"What?" Hollis asked in disbelief, turning to face him. She was standing in the tiny kitchen of her apartment, scrambling eggs for their breakfast, dressed only in panties and one of Jack's old T-shirts, her hair tangled around her face. He was standing in the doorway, freshly showered and shaved, with a wide bath towel wrapped around his waist.

"I said, 'Will you marry me?' " Jack repeated a little impatiently.

The situation seemed so ludicrous for a proposal of marriage that Hollis had to laugh. Jack scowled at her reaction, and she covered her mouth with her hand to smother the laughter. "I'm sorry. It's just—well, I've never gotten a proposal in circumstances quite like these." She made a vague gesture with her spatula.

"I'm sure you've had enough of them to be an expert in the field." He picked up the bowl from the counter and held it out to her. "You better dish up the eggs before they burn."

"Oh. Yeah." She picked up the skillet and dumped its contents into the bowl.

Jack looked suspiciously down into the bowl. "You're one hell of a cook, Hol."

"Is that why you want to marry me? To get a live-in cook?"

He snorted rudely. "Only if I wanted to starve. Believe me, I'll hire you a cook. And a housekeeper." He set the bowl aside and leaned against the counter, crossing his arms over his chest. "Well?"

"Well what?"

"I asked you a question."

"I thought maybe you were kidding," Hollis temporized.

"No."

"Jack . . ." She cast him a glance. There was no way out of this. "This is crazy. Why do you want to get married?"

He shrugged.

"Things are fine as they are."

"It's not enough. I want you to be my wife." Jack reached out and took her hand. "I want to give you a ring. I want you to have my name. When I'm gone I want to know that you're home in my bed and I don't have to pound on the door when I get back."

"I'll give you a key to my apartment."

"Don't be obtuse."

She pulled her hand away, frowning. "Why do you have to spoil it?"

"Spoil it? Getting married is spoiling it?"

"I don't want to get married. Most of all I don't want to marry some man like my father, so hard and driven and domineering."

"And I am?"

"You know you are. You're all energy and power; you make everything go the way you want it to. I spent my whole life fighting with him and trying to please him, back and forth, all the time. I don't want to spend the rest of my life doing that with my husband."

"You want to marry somebody who's so weak you can push him around?"

"I didn't say that."

"Sounds like it to me. Hollis, I'm not going to try to tell you what to do. Have I ever done that to you? Have I dominated and suppressed you?"

"No, but we aren't married."

"This isn't really why you're reluctant, is it?" His blue eyes were hard and cold now. "It's Ames Thompson. You aren't over him."

Hollis backed up a step. "I still . . . have feelings for him, yes."

"How in the hell can you say you still have feelings for him after what you and I did last night?"

"That was sex, not love."

"I'm talking about both of them."

"Well, sometimes there's a difference."

"So you're telling me that you have no feelings for me; it's just been sex."

"Of course I have feelings for you! You've been my friend ever since I can remember."

"And we have fun together, right?" Jack asked, and Hollis nodded. "We like the same things. We share a lot of past." He paused, and again Hollis nodded. "When we make love, it's the best thing I've ever known."

"Yeah. It's great. You're right about all those things." Hollis looked at him helplessly; she couldn't explain the difference of those feelings, that passion from the sweet, pure love she had for Ames. "I *enjoy* you; I do. But that's not the same thing as love, is it?"

"I don't know, baby. I don't know what love is. Do you? Love's what you felt for that guy who left you pregnant, isn't

it? It's what you felt for Saint Ames, who hightailed it down
to Guatemala without you. What is it? You only love guys
who leave you?''

"I didn't love that first one; I just thought I did,'' Hollis
retorted, her temper flaring to match his.

"When will the holy roller turn out to be a false alarm,
too? Do you want me to come back then?''

"Don't call him that!''

"Oh no, precious Ames. No doubt I'm too dirty and low
to even speak of him. Maybe I am, but let me tell you
something: We're just alike, you and me. I know you inside
out. And that's better, that's more lasting than this romantic
hero worship you feel for Ames Thompson. I'll be with you
when you're happy or depressed or mad, when you're sweating or you've got a cold. I want you every way you are. I
even want you if you love another man. To hell with love!
I don't want it; I don't need it. Let him be the man you love.
I want to be the man whose bed you sleep in.''

"I can't! I can't!'' Hollis began to cry. She turned away
to hide her tears. Behind her she heard Jack sigh. Then his
hands were on her shoulders, turning her around and pulling
her to his chest.

"Okay, baby. I won't press it now.'' He kissed the top of
her head. "We'll go along as always. But someday you're
going to marry me. It's a promise.''

Hollis knew that Jack always got what he wanted. And he
did once again. Day after day he undermined her defenses.
He disarmed her with sweet gifts; he cut through each of her
arguments with cool logic; he enticed her with his lovemaking, at times exquisitely slow and beautiful, at other times
exploding with passion. Finally Hollis said yes.

They were married in an enormous ceremony right after
Hollis graduated from college. Sharon was Hollis's maid of
honor, and Janis, almost three by then, was a flower girl.

Sharon walked down the aisle to the front of the church
and turned to watch her daughter come down the aisle, scat-
tering petals in a carefree fashion. She glanced around the
church. It seemed as if half of Dallas were there. She even

saw Reid Maitland, sitting beside his mother and a lovely, sophisticated blond woman, in one of the back pews on the groom's side. Sharon's stomach tightened, and she glanced away quickly. She wondered if he recognized her. No, she and her daughter probably hadn't had enough importance for him to remember them.

She watched Hollis moving down the aisle with measured grace. Her wide-spreading dress looked like a concoction of spun sugar. Hollis was beautiful. She stopped beside Jack, and he smiled down at her. Sharon knew that Jack would do everything in his power to make Hollis happy. Sharon wondered if that was possible. Only last night Hollis had asked her what Ames was doing now, and Sharon had seen the trace of love and hurt in her eyes. She had never known exactly what happened between Ames and Hollis, or between Hollis and Jack, but she wondered if Hollis was entering her marriage with a whole heart. Did Hollis love Jack? She wasn't sure if even Hollis knew the answer to that.

They began to make their vows. Tears came into Sharon's eyes. She couldn't help thinking of Wes and the way she had once longed to marry him, the fanciful plans she had dreamed up for an ornate wedding. She wondered what would have happened to them if Wes hadn't died.

She blinked away the tears. There was no use thinking about that now. What had happened, happened, and there was nothing she could do to change it. She was happy, and she had a beautiful daughter whom she loved dearly. That should be enough for any person. She glanced back out at the audience, her eyes going to Reid Maitland. She had thought she would never see him again; funny how he had turned up once more. She hoped she would be able to avoid talking to him. Did he realize that the flower girl was his niece, and if so, did he feel anything at seeing her?

Sharon turned her attention back to the bridal couple. The minister was starting a prayer. Sharon bowed her head. She offered up a silent prayer that Hollis would be happy with Jack. She hoped that for all of them, the bad years were behind them, and only peaceful times lay ahead.

Part II

4

March 14, 1987

Sharon carefully checked the crating of her stained glass pieces, then swung closed the backdoor of her Suburban and walked back to her parents' house. This had been one of the best visits she'd had with her parents in years. It had taken them a long time to come to terms with Sharon's decision to keep and raise her illegitimate child and even longer to accept that Sharon made her living creating stained glass art and would probably continue to do so the rest of her life. But this visit there had been no preaching from them, and she hadn't been defensive, waiting for them to say something that would make her angry.

Sharon opened the front door and went inside. "It's time to go. Janis, hon, are you ready?"

She walked back to the den, where her parents and Janis sat. Janis was leaning back in her chair, eyes closed. Sharon wondered if she was sick or just going through some sort of typical adolescent moodiness. She had complained of having a headache this morning when they got up, and she'd been dead quiet ever since. The whole time they'd been here, Janis had seemed sullen and withdrawn. Last night she had complained to Sharon about how boring it was to stay with her grandparents and said she was happy that they would be leaving the next morning to spend the rest of their spring break with Hollis in Dallas. (Hollis was *never* boring.)

The same could be said for having a thirteen-year-old. Half the time Janis seemed almost adult, funny and intelligent, a good companion. Then suddenly she would be a child again, lying in front of the TV watching Saturday morning cartoons or romping in the backyard with Randy's dog. Or she might fall into a fit of sulks or lash out angrily at her mother.

She really wasn't prepared for dealing with a teenager, Sharon thought. If only they could leapfrog past the next few years . . . From the moment Janis was born, they had had such a good relationship: warm, comfortable, loving. Sharon didn't look forward to the next few years and the hammering that relationship might receive from a teenage daughter.

"Jan, we're ready."

Janis opened her eyes. Sharon noticed that they were puffy. Had Janis been crying? She crossed the room toward her daughter, concerned. "Honey, are you all right?"

Janis nodded. "Yeah, it's just a headache. I get them sometimes." She grinned, a ghost of that flashing, knowing smile she had. "Gran says it's part of 'maturing.' "

Sharon couldn't keep an answering grin off her lips. She could imagine just how her mother had said it, in an embarrassed tone as though puberty were something a nice girl shouldn't indulge in. She had heard the same sort of short, uncomfortable pronouncement from Mama often enough in her life.

"Don't look that way, Sharon," her mother said. "You know it's perfectly true."

Sharon pulled her mouth straight. Mama couldn't help being the way she was any more than Sharon could help not being like her. There was no point in ending the visit in bickering, especially over something so trivial. "Of course,

Mama, you're right. I remember having lots of aches and pains. Did you take an aspirin, Jan?''

"Yeah, Gran gave me a couple. I think I'll feel better in a little while.''

"Okay, then, let's get on the road. You can take a nap in the car. Maybe that'll help you feel better.''

They said their good-byes, hugged her parents, and promised to stop again on the drive back to Santa Fe. Betty and Win Thompson followed them out onto the porch and stood watching and waving as Janis and Sharon got into the car and pulled out of the driveway. Sharon gave them a last wave and started forward. As always, she felt a certain amount of relief at leaving. Her parents could neither understand nor support her life-style, and whenever she was around them, she felt a creeping entrapment, as though their life-style might reach out and wrap its tentacles around her. She and her parents got along better, she thought, when they lived a good distance away from each other.

Janis fell asleep almost as soon as they started off, and by the time she awoke they were in Wichita Falls. The nap had taken care of her headache, and she began to chatter in her usual bright way. Glancing over at her, Sharon wondered why she worried about Janis. She might have a few moods now and then—after all, she was thirteen and therefore entitled to them—but basically she still had a sunny, pleasant personality. Even if they hit some rough spots the next few years, they would manage to work them out and get along. They loved each other too much not to.

In fact, Sharon reminded herself, she couldn't ask much more out of life than she had. Janis was a good daughter, and they enjoyed being together most of the time. They owned a lovely house in Santa Fe, secluded and private, with a large studio for her work. In the morning she could sit on the patio, sipping her coffee, and look out over the arroyo behind the house as the sun tinged the landscape with delicate gold and rose. And Sharon loved her work: the design, the clear jewellike tones of the glass, the meticulous piecing together, the excitement of beginning and the satisfaction of completion. Moreover, she was able to make an adequate living for her daughter and herself from it. She knew very few people who could say that they spent their lives doing what they loved doing and got paid well for it.

The years that she had lived in Santa Fe had slipped by peacefully. Less than a year after Janis was born, Jane Laskow had died, and, to Sharon's surprise, had left her a three-bedroom adobe. It was not a terribly large house, but its lines were beautiful, and in the back was a separate studio, for it had been Jane's first house in Santa Fe many years earlier. Sharon had rented out a room and half the studio to Randy, and with the rent and the money she earned from working on the weekends in an art gallery, she was able to support herself and her daughter while she learned, then honed, her craft.

As the years passed, she began to sell more and more of her works, until she was able to give up the job at the gallery. A couple of years ago, Randy had moved out of the house and gone to live with his latest lover; and though she had missed him, she hadn't needed the money he had paid as rent. Seven years ago, Hollis, who had frequently visited Sharon in Santa Fe and had admired and bought many pieces of artwork and jewelry there, had decided that there was no longer room anywhere in her home for more. So she had opened up a store in Dallas in which she sold items made in New Mexico, thus satisfying her urge to buy them, as well as relieving the boredom of her days by giving her a business to run. She had always carried many of the things Sharon made, and between Hollis's store and a couple of galleries in Santa Fe and Taos, Sharon was able to make a good living selling her stained glass panels.

Sharon was, by and large, content, and had been for years. She had her friends, her work, her daughter, and she hadn't needed anything else. There had been no man in her life special enough to remain there for long. But that fact hadn't made her sad. She reasoned that she was the sort of person who loved deeply, but rarely; perhaps there would never be another love in her life after Wes. She could live with that. It didn't frighten her to be alone. She had learned long ago that she could cope on her own; she was used to it.

Sharon and Janis laughed and talked all the way into Dallas, arriving there late in the afternoon. Sharon swung by Hollis's store first to unload her pieces. She hated carrying them around in the car any longer than was necessary, always envisioning some catastrophic rear-end wreck that would crush her months of work to smithereens.

Hollis's store, "East of Santa Fe," was located in an elegant little cream-colored shopping center in far north Dallas. It was decorated inside in the subtle tones associated with New Mexican art, and there was a cunning arrangement of multiple levels reminiscent of a pueblo, so that one felt that one was stepping into the essence of Santa Fe, without the overkill of Indian rugs and sand paintings all over the place common in so many stores.

Sharon never saw the shop without being amazed all over again at what Hollis had done. She had known that Hollis was clever and gifted and had an eye for the striking and the beautiful, but she had never expected Hollis to put her talents to use. Even she had been fooled, she supposed, by Hollis's wise-cracking, lazily sophisticated attitude. She had assumed that Hollis would lose interest in the shop after a while, sell out, and move on to something else. Instead, Hollis had worked hard and made quite a success of it.

Janis jumped out of the car and ran into the store, eager to see Hollis. Sharon followed more slowly, though excitement was rising in her, too. Over the years, Hollis had become closer by far to Sharon than her own family, even though they saw each other only a few times a year. Hollis's help when Sharon was expecting Janis had formed a bond between them that had deepened with time. She regarded Hollis as her dearest and best friend, and Sharon knew that Hollis felt the same way about her. In fact, Sharon would have guessed that she was the only really close friend Hollis had—except for her husband, Jack. Hollis was not one to form attachments easily, and most women were frankly scared of her. She was too beautiful and sharp-tongued, too prickly; few ever got to see the deeply caring side of her that Sharon knew.

She found Hollis in the middle of the store, hugging Janis. "Oh, you're getting so tall!" she heard Hollis exclaim as she squeezed the girl. "You're almost as tall as I am."

"I know. And Mom, too. Wait'll you see what I've been doing. Cindy's teaching me to weave, and I brought you a runner I did. It's really neat."

Hollis smiled, her eyes glowingly fixed on Janis. "I'd like to see it."

Sharon crossed the room toward them, and Hollis straightened and turned at her approach. "Sharon!" Her face shone with pleasure.

At thirty-two, Hollis was even more beautiful than she had been when Sharon first met her. Her clothes were as expensive and sleek as ever, designer jeans and a cashmere sweater that showed her figure beautifully. Her blond hair swung almost to her shoulders in a smooth bob that she wore caught behind her ears. There was never anything frilly about Hollis. She always wore clothes with simple, straight lines and little embellishment, the perfect complement to her rather exotic, strong-boned face, with its deep, mysterious green-gold eyes.

Hollis came forward, arms outspread to hug Sharon. "I thought you'd be in soon. That's why I hung around the store. Oh, it's so good to see you."

"Same here." Sharon hugged her tightly and stepped back. "I swear, you haven't aged a day."

"Neither have you."

"Don't make me laugh." Sharon knew that she was still an attractive woman, but she didn't take care of herself the way that Hollis did. She got her exercise in sporadic walks around the land close to her house, not in daily aerobics classes. There were no saunas, no facials, no body wraps for her. Her own hair was not carefully trimmed and tamed, but cut in a casual, curling fashion that was easy to manage and needed no styling for months. She wore no makeup today; she rarely did. She had no idea that her natural loveliness shone through in a way that cosmetics could not achieve.

Hollis was aware of her friend's loveliness, but she had long ago resigned herself to Sharon's careless attitude about her looks. "Okay, I can't wait any longer. What did you bring me? I have to see your new pictures." She urged Sharon toward the door. "How many?"

"Ten."

Hollis groaned. "I could sell twice that many. Have you thought of having yourself cloned?"

Sharon smiled. "You know me. I don't move at the same clip you do."

Hollis motioned to one of her workers to help them, and they went outside and unloaded the car, bringing in the crates. Inside the store, Sharon carefully opened the crates and pulled out the padded pieces of glass one by one. As she unwrapped each one, Hollis pounced on it with cries of delight.

Hollis hung them on hooks suspended from the ceiling in front of the plate glass windows, so that the sun brought the jewellike colors to life. Hollis walked up and down looking at them raptly, her hands clasped up high against her chest. "Sharon, they're gorgeous. I think they're the best you've ever done." She cast a twinkling look back over her shoulder at her friend. "I know I've said that before, but this time . . . you've outdone yourself."

"I like the dogwood branches a lot," Sharon admitted, nodding toward an intricate design of brown branches and white flowers against a background of fractured glass. "It took forever to do. I almost decided to keep it."

"I can see why. But I'm glad you didn't. I might just buy it myself. Although I know one of your customers I'd probably have to fight to keep it from." She moved closer to examine the glass artwork. "How did you do this? This white glass for the blooms—the way some of it's thicker than the rest."

"Yeah. I thought it made it look more like real petals. See, I have the thicker parts at the base."

Hollis shook her head. "It's so detailed."

"I know. Cindy says I'm crazy to spend so long on details. But I love that lushness."

"Absolutely. It's worth it. And I think the prices will prove that."

"Hollis . . ."

"Would you stop worrying that I'm going to price you out of the market? I know what I'm doing. And the people who buy your work know what they're doing."

Sharon shrugged. Hollis usually turned out to be right when it came to money.

It took some time for Hollis to tear herself away from her contemplation of the pictures, but finally she sighed and turned away. "I'm sorry. I know you guys must be tired. It's just so hard not to keep looking. But I'll stop now and take you home."

Sharon glanced over at Janis. She had fallen silent while Hollis had been examining the pictures, and she looked pale. Sharon wondered if her headache had come back.

They followed Hollis back to her home, a huge, rambling structure built of white stone and wood. Modern in design, it spread out in multiple levels in the center of two acres. In the back there was a swimming pool and a terraced yard with a lily-bedecked goldfish pond and a low, trickling waterfall over mossy stones. Inside there was another pool, as well as a sauna and whirlpool, and many rooms. In the guest wing, where she and Janis stayed, Sharon often felt as if she were in a completely separate house.

It was always fun to go visit Hollis, to taste for a few days the life of the wealthy, but Sharon preferred a far more simple life, just friends and her work and Janis and enough money to live on.

Hollis took Janis and Sharon immediately to their rooms and left them to freshen up. "I'll be downstairs in the den." She glanced at her watch. "Why don't I mix us some drinks?"

"Sure. I'll be right there."

When Hollis was gone, Sharon turned to her suitcase and began to unpack. Janis appeared in the doorway of their connecting bathroom. "Mama?"

Sharon glanced up at her, and she was swept with the familiar fear of a mother. Janis looked awful, pale and clammy, and her face was strangely puffy. "Honey, what's wrong?"

"My head hurts." Janis sounded suddenly very much as she had when she was little. "And I feel kinda sick at my stomach."

"Oh, dear. Throwing up?"

"Not yet. But I feel real yucky."

"Poor thing." Sharon went to her, feeling her forehead with her palm. No sign of a fever, at least not yet. "You must have caught some kind of bug." She felt relief at identifying it. Janis was so rarely sick that Sharon tended to imagine that something was deathly wrong with her every time she was. But Janis had had viruses like this before, and usually the symptoms were gone within a day. It wasn't anything to worry about. "It's too bad that you had to get it while you're on your spring break. Why don't you lie down and rest? I bet you'll feel better tomorrow."

Janis nodded listlessly. "Yeah. Tell Hollis I'm sorry about missing dinner."

"Don't worry about it." Sharon walked with her back into her room and turned down the covers of Janis's bed. Janis kicked off her shoes and crawled into bed. Sharon pulled the sheet and bedspread up over her shoulders, tucking her in as she had when Janis was little. She smiled down at her daughter, then bent and kissed her forehead. "Get some sleep. I'll check on you later. Do you need anything?"

Janis shook her head, and Sharon smiled reassuringly at her once more. She returned to her room and finished unpacking, then went downstairs to join Hollis. She stopped first in Janis's room. Janis was already asleep. Sharon laid her hand on the girl's forehead again—still no fever—and tiptoed out of the room.

She found Hollis in the den, mixing drinks behind the small marble-topped bar. Hollis smiled at her entrance. "Just finished your gin and tonic. That's your favorite, isn't it?"

"When *you* make them." Sharon took the tall, frosty glass that Hollis held out to her, and they sat down in the cozy arrangement of leather couch and chairs across the room from the bar. This was Sharon's favorite room in Hollis's house, the only one that seemed comfortable and truly homey.

"Where's Jan?"

"Upstairs lying down. She seems to have come down with a virus."

"Poor thing."

"Yeah. She's woozy, didn't feel like coming down to dinner. But I imagine she'll be better tomorrow. Kids are amazingly fast to recover. I remember one time when she was little and got an ear infection; she was up all night, crying and in pain, running a fever. The next afternoon you'd never know she'd been sick."

"Good. I hope so." Hollis smiled. "She's such a good kid."

"Yeah." Sharon sipped her drink and looked at her friend. There was a sad quality in Hollis's eyes, even when she'd smiled. There was something wrong, Sharon thought. She couldn't quite put her finger on it. But there was a difference in Hollis, a quietness, even withdrawal, that Sharon had never seen in her before. Though she laughed and talked much as usual, her sparkle had dimmed. Sharon frowned.

"How's Jack?" Sharon asked.

"Jack?" Hollis glanced up at Sharon, and the smile went back into place, but not before Sharon had caught the sadness on her face. "He's fine. Making money, as usual."

"He's acquiring quite a name for himself." Jack had made his father's oil company enormously successful, and after that he had begun to get bored. He had decided to expand the corporation, to make it a conglomerate instead of just an oil company. With more foresight than most, he had said that the oil boom couldn't last forever, and he wanted to hedge his bets. So he began to buy up other companies, at first small ones that were not doing well, which he would then restructure into profitable ventures. He had gone on to bigger companies, and before long he had become known as a corporate raider, taking over what companies he could and extracting top dollars from those who managed to fend him off.

Finally, he had sold the oil business entirely, so that he could concentrate on his corporate maneuverings. His fortune had grown by leaps and bounds, and when the oil recession had hit a few years ago, he had been unaffected by it.

"Yeah," Hollis agreed. "He loves it. He's playing a dangerous game, but you know Jack. He never could stay away from competition."

"You still happy?"

Hollis looked startled. "What? Jack and me? Yeah, I guess. Why do you ask?"

"I don't know. You look . . . sort of blue."

"Oh." Hollis pressed her lips together and glanced away. "I didn't know it was so obvious."

"Not to most people. But I noticed."

Hollis nodded. "Yeah. Jack sees it, too."

Concerned, Sharon moved closer to her friend. "Hol, what's wrong? Can I do anything?"

To her dismay, Hollis's eyes filled with tears. Hollis blinked them away angrily and jumped to her feet. "I'm sorry. I've become an emotional idiot the past few months." She took a gulp of her drink and began to pace the room.

"Hollis, what's the matter?" Sharon stood up, too. It hurt her to see her friend so obviously distraught. Hollis had always been cool and controlled, ready with a sharp, funny remark even in her saddest times. "Are you and Jack having problems?"

Hollis shook her head. "Not the way you mean. We aren't heading for divorce." She paused. "I don't know. We may be, if I keep this up. I'm sure it's driving Jack crazy 'cause there's nothing he can do about it. I—" She drew a shaky breath, and Sharon saw her set her jaw. "I want a baby, and I can't have one."

"Oh, honey." Sharon went to Hollis and put her arm around her shoulder. Hollis stood stiffly within the circle of her arm but did not move away. "Are you sure?"

"I've been trying to for two years, and no luck."

"Have you been to a doctor?"

Hollis let out a chuckle that held no amusement. "Try five. They all say the same thing. Jack isn't sterile. It's me. That—that time when I—"

"Oh, God. The abortion in high school?"

Hollis nodded, biting down on her lower lip. "There was some scarring. They say it's not impossible for me to bear a child, but very unlikely."

"I'm sorry. I'm so sorry."

"They say the things you do always come back on you. Sure enough."

"No. You must not think that way. It's not a punishment for what you did."

"Really?" Hollis shot her a cool look of disbelief. "Somehow it seems connected."

"I don't think God would punish you for a mistake you made when you were just a kid."

"You know, most of the time I don't even believe in God. But when I think about this . . ."

"There's bound to be something you can do. Couldn't you adopt?"

"We put our names on lists with several places, but it takes a long time. And since there is a possibility that I could have children, it counts against us. We aren't in as bad a shape as some couples, so they get priority. We may not ever get one. So Jack shelled out a bunch of money for a surrogate mother. I was so excited. I was planning for it for months; I decorated one of the rooms as a nursery. At the last minute she backed out."

"Oh no."

"I was heartbroken. For a couple of months I didn't do anything except lie around all day feeling sorry for myself. Jack wanted to pursue it in court, but I couldn't face it. And I—well, I couldn't take a baby away from its mother, could I?"

"Why didn't I know any of this? Why didn't you tell me?"

"I don't know. It was something I wanted to hide. When I thought I could get pregnant and was trying so hard to, I didn't want to tell anyone until I'd actually done it. Then when I found out I couldn't, I was so devastated I didn't want to talk to anyone. After we went to the adoption agencies, I got very superstitious about it. I was afraid if I told anyone, it would put a jinx on it. You know, it was like a wish on a birthday candle—I was afraid if I told, it wouldn't come true. Sounds stupid, I know."

"No, it doesn't sound stupid at all. But I wish I had known. I wish I could have helped you."

"Nobody can help. I realize that. Not even Jack. It drives him crazy. He's so used to making things happen. But I have to accept it. That's what's so hard. I've tried. You know, I've said to myself, 'Face it. You won't be having kids. Lots of women don't, and they manage just fine. Lots of women don't even *want* children. They get along okay, and so can you.' I've tried to do like the alcoholics and take it one day at a time." Hollis attempted to smile.

Sharon took Hollis's hand. It lay stiffly in hers. It was difficult to offer Hollis a gesture of affection. "You'll make it. I know you will. It's tough, but you're a strong, strong person, Hollis. After a while it'll get better. And there's always hope. There's still a chance, isn't there, that you could conceive?"

Hollis grimaced. "A slight chance. No." She slipped her hand from Sharon's and moved away. "I'm not going to feed false hopes. I have to accept reality. I've always been able to in the past. This time it's just . . . harder."

Sharon watched her friend, her own heart aching in sympathy. If only she could do something, say something that would ease Hollis's hurt. But she could think of nothing. How could you comfort a woman who wanted a child and knew she would never have one? "I didn't even know you wanted a baby."

"Strange, isn't it?" Hollis's face looked brittle, as if it might crack and fall apart at any moment. "I'm not the maternal sort. You'd think that's the last thing I'd be crying over. I probably wouldn't know what to do with a baby if I had one. Maybe I'm one of those people who always wants what they can't have."

"No. You have a good heart, however much you try to hide it. You'd be a good mother. I know it."

"Well, we'll never find out." Hollis took a deep breath and straightened her shoulders. "What a thing to be talking about. This is your vacation."

"Don't be silly. You think I expect you to sit around and pretend to be happy just to keep me entertained? You're my friend, Hollis. I care about you. Whether you're sad or happy."

Hollis's smile was more genuine this time. "I know. Thank you. Now. Let's sit down, and you tell me all about Santa Fe and the artsy crowd. Take my mind off it."

After an hour or so, Jack came home. He was as handsome and energetic as ever, his blue eyes vivid and compelling, his movements fast and full of leashed power. Sharon found him fascinating but an exhausting person to be around. She could never have lived with a man like Jack Lacey; he would have flattened her out like a steamroller. He was brash, abrupt, dynamic, and so intense she could almost feel the heat emanating from him. Only someone as strong as Hollis could maintain her identity with him.

Jack loved Hollis desperately. Sharon had always been able to see that. Whenever they were together, his eyes followed her with an intensity and hunger that nine years of marriage apparently had not been enough to satisfy. Sharon suspected that there was nothing that Jack wouldn't have done for Hollis. But he couldn't give her the one thing she wanted. And when his eyes followed her tonight, there was sadness and frustration in them, as well as love.

It hurt her to watch Hollis and Jack, and Sharon was quick to excuse herself after dinner, saying that she was exhausted from the drive today. She went upstairs to check on Janis, who was still asleep. Sharon undressed and put on her gown, then sat for a while by the window, looking out and thinking about Hollis. Finally, sighing, she gave up and went to bed.

It seemed as though she had hardly been asleep any time

when something pulled her back to consciousness. She waited, her eyes open, wondering what had awakened her.

"Mama?" She heard it, faint but clear.

"Janis?" Sharon was out of the bed in an instant, rushing through the connecting bath into her daughter's room, maternal instinct sending her faster than her thoughts could form. "Janis?"

"Mama? I don't feel good."

"What's the matter, hon?" She sat on the edge of the bed and smoothed Janis's hair back from her forehead.

"I'm sick at my stomach."

"Let me help you into the bathroom."

"No. I already threw up. It didn't help. I still feel sick. My head's killing me."

"Would you like for me to lie down with you?"

Embarrassed, Janis nodded. Sharon slipped under the covers beside her, and Janis turned, cuddling up against her.

In the morning, Janis declared that she was fine, and, indeed, she looked much better. They went out shopping with Hollis, but after only an hour, Janis wanted to quit. Her head was hurting again.

Sharon frowned. "This is strange. It doesn't seem like a usual virus. Maybe you should go to a doctor."

"Oh, Mom . . ."

"I could call my doctor, Jan," Hollis put in. "I'm sure he'd see you, even on such short notice."

"No, please. It'll go away."

But after aspirin and rest, the headache was still there, and soon Janis was nauseated again. This time Sharon accepted Hollis's offer of a physician, despite Janis's protests that she didn't need or want to go.

They went to the doctor the following morning. He examined Janis and ordered his nurse to take blood and urine samples. Then he ushered Sharon into his office, leaving Janis with the nurse.

"I'm prescribing Darvon for your daughter's headaches. It should ease the pain. But I'm afraid that's only addressing a symptom. Your daughter's blood pressure is unusually high.''

Sharon stared at him. "What? Her blood pressure? But she's too young . . .''

"Yes, she is young. It's unusual. That's why I ordered blood and urine tests; I want to find out what's causing it.''

This sounded serious. Sharon hadn't expected the doctor to find that there was something really wrong with Janis. Her fears always turned out to be groundless when Janis was sick; usually she had just caught some illness that was going around at the time.

When they left the doctor's office, Sharon tried to put on a good face for Janis, not wanting to scare her. But inside her anxiety built. How could a healthy, active child like Janis have high blood pressure? What did it mean? She went over and over what the doctor had said, searching for clues as to how serious he thought Janis's condition was.

The following afternoon, when the doctor called Sharon, a chill ran through her even before he spoke. "I'm going to refer you to an excellent urologist, Mrs. Thompson.''

"Urologist? But why? What's the matter?''

"I'm not sure. That's why I want her to see a specialist. The results of Janis's tests indicate to me that she may be having a problem with her kidneys.''

"Her kidneys?" It seemed absurd. What did headaches, nausea, and high blood pressure have to do with kidneys?

"Yes. I've spoken to Dr. Terry Youngman. He's one of the best in the city. He can see you this afternoon.''

"This afternoon? But it's so late.''

"I know. He'll fit you in.''

Fear crawled up Sharon's spine. The only reason she could see for an important specialist to fit Janis into his busy schedule was because her condition was too serious to be put off, even until tomorrow. "All right. I'll take her.''

Hollis went with them to the urologist, seeing the fear in Sharon's eyes. Janis went this time without complaint. She looked much worse than she had this morning, her face so puffy that it was almost moon-shaped and her eyes dark with pain.

Dr. Youngman took Sharon into his office when he had finished examining Janis. "I'll be frank with you, Mrs. Thompson. I see definite signs of uremia in your daughter. I'd like to put Janis in Baylor Hospital for further tests and call in a renologist, Dr. Ebersol."

"Uremia?"

"Her kidneys aren't doing the job they should. Janis's tests show evidence of protein and blood cells in her urine, and her blood urea nitrogen level is quite high. She also shows signs of anemia."

"I don't understand."

"Kidneys are basically a filter for the blood. They remove waste products from it and send the waste out of the body. But these waste products are showing up in Janis's blood. Things that should not be filtering through into the urine are. That indicates to me that the filter, the kidney, is not working. The waste substances are building up in her body, hence the puffiness and weight gain. High blood pressure and anemia are also signs of kidney failure."

"Kidney failure," Sharon repeated blankly. "But she's never had anything wrong with her. She's always been so healthy."

"It's sudden, I know. Sometimes it happens like that."

"But how? Why? I mean, wouldn't she have had some sort of disease to cause this? She's never sick," Sharon reiterated, as though that fact would disprove what he had told her.

"I don't know why. That's the reason I want to do more tests and consult with Dr. Ebersol. I want X rays of her kidneys, and we will probably do a biopsy."

Sharon's face went even paler, if that was possible. The only thing she connected biopsies with was cancer.

"It's a simple operation," Dr. Youngman hastened to assure her. "Not even an operation, really. We don't make an incision. We just draw some tissue out with a needle. From the biopsy I'll be able to tell what is causing your daughter's kidneys to malfunction and how we should proceed.''

''All right.'' Sharon glanced around her, as though searching for what she should do. She was so stunned she couldn't think. ''I, uh, I'll take her to the hospital.''

When she rejoined Hollis and Janis in the waiting area, Hollis jumped to her feet. Sharon could see the fear rushing over her features, and she knew that what Hollis had seen in her own face had frightened her. Janis, fortunately, had her eyes closed. As she opened them, Sharon forced her face into more pleasant lines.

''Well,'' Sharon said with false brightness. ''It looks like they're going to stick more needles in you.''

Janis groaned. ''Why?''

''He isn't sure yet what's wrong or what to do for it. He wants—'' Sharon's throat closed up, and for a moment she was afraid she wouldn't be able to get the words out without breaking down. ''He wants you to go into the hospital for tests.''

''The hospital?'' Janis's voice rose. ''I don't need to go to the hospital! I'm not that sick.''

''Just for the tests, sweetheart. He must not be able to do them in his office.''

''Are we going to Baylor now?'' Hollis asked. Her face was as white as Sharon knew her own must be at the moment.

''Yes. I—do you mind taking us there?''

''Don't be silly.'' Hollis looped her arm around Sharon's shoulders and squeezed encouragingly. ''Of course I don't mind.''

Sharon leaned into Hollis for an instant. ''Thank you.'' They both knew she was not thanking her for just a ride.

Hollis took them to the hospital and helped Sharon through the admissions process, then sat in Janis's room with Sharon while Janis underwent the biopsy. Sometime later they brought Janis back to the room. She was wide awake, talking, and quite cheerful. She had had only a local anesthetic, and she related the conversation she had carried on with the doctors while they worked on her. Sharon smiled, although she felt as though it would break her jaw to do so, and listened to her daughter calmly. She had to appear cool and confident; that was the one thing she was sure of in her dazed state—she must not let Janis glimpse her fear, or her panic would infect Janis, too.

But when Dr. Youngman, accompanied by Dr. Ebersol, came into the room and asked to talk to Sharon, it was all she could do to stand up and follow them out of the room. She was almost paralyzed with terror. She was going to lose Janis; dread engulfed her.

The doctors led her to another floor and into a small conference room. Dr. Youngman asked her if he could get her coffee or a soft drink. Dr. Ebersol, a younger but more serious-faced man, sat down at the table and folded his hands, looking at her gravely.

Sharon's terror increased. "Tell me."

"Your daughter has glomerulonephritis," Dr. Ebersol said without preamble.

Sharon blinked. "What?"

"In layman's terms, it's a very serious kidney disease," Dr. Youngman interpreted. "I suspected uremia from your daughter's symptoms—the swelling, nausea, and headaches, the amount of protein and blood cells in her urine, the high BUN level . . . but we had to do the biopsy to determine whether her condition is treatable, whether her kidneys could someday function again."

He paused. Sharon's fingers clenched together in her lap. "And they won't?"

He shook his head. Dr. Ebersol added, "I'm sorry to have to tell you this, but Janis's illness is quite serious. Her kidneys have basically ceased to function."

"But why?"

"We're not sure." Ebersol continued pontifically, "Sometimes it happens gradually over a long period of time, without the patient even knowing that he or she is ill. It's not a painful disease until it becomes so severe that one gets the headaches and nausea. Sometimes it happens quickly. I would say that is the case with your daughter."

Sharon felt as if she couldn't quite catch her breath. "How can she —What— Is she going to die?"

"This is painful to hear, and I hate to have to tell you, but I must impress on both you and Janis the gravity of the situation. Yes, without treatment, your daughter will die."

5

For a long moment Sharon stared at Dr. Ebersol. His words didn't make sense. She could hear the blood rushing through her veins, feel it pounding behind her eyes. One word he had uttered came to her like a lifeline. "Treatment?" she repeated. "Then there's a cure? She doesn't have to—"

"Yes, there's a treatment. I'm sorry for frightening you. But it's necessary that you realize that there is no other way for your daughter. She must realize it, too. There is no cure. Janis's kidneys are virtually without function; they are shriveled and useless, and we can do nothing to rejuvenate them. However, it is possible for Janis to live."

"One of those machines!" Sharon brightened as her brain began to function again. "Dialysis. I've read about it."

"Yes. Dialysis is one solution. Three times a week Janis can be hooked up to a dialysis machine here in the hospital." He began to describe the process of using the dialysis machine—the permanent tube shunt in the veins of her arm, the way Janis's blood would flow into the machine to be filtered and returned to her body, the careful diet she would have to follow.

Horror seeped through Sharon as she listened. "My God, it sounds awful. No wonder you have to make it clear that there's no alternative." Tears filled her eyes. She plunged one hand into her hair, rubbing her scalp as though it would take away the pain and tension there.

"There is another alternative. Dialysis is not the best solution long-term. As you said, it will be the rest of her life, and as young as she is, that's a very long time. Many patients resent the machine and their dependence on it. They come to hate it and their way of life. I've even heard of a patient ripping out the shunt so that he would bleed to death, he had grown to despise it so much."

Sharon turned whiter. "She's so active. She'd be trapped."

"As I said, there's another alternative. I think your daughter is a good candidate for a transplant."

"Transplant. But those—are they successful? I thought they were only last-ditch efforts."

"No doubt you are thinking of other organ transplants, such as heart. Kidney transplants are much more common and more successful. Eighty percent of the patients receiving kidneys from a relative donor live—and lead normal lives."

"Really?"

"Yes. Even those with transplants from a cadaver donor have a fifty percent chance."

"I don't understand. What do you mean, cadaver donor?"

"With kidneys we're luckier than with other organs. Everyone has two of them—or at least, normally everyone does. So we don't have to take our donor organs from people who have died. Not only are there more available, they don't have to be removed and shipped to the donee. We can take the kidney from the donor and put it into the recipient right there in the same operating room at the same time. It's much better. Plus, when the kidney is donated by a close relative, there's less likelihood of rejection. That's the reason for the higher percentage of success using the relative kidneys."

Relief flooded Sharon. She smiled and leaned back in her chair. "Then I can give her a kidney. That's what you're saying, isn't it? She'll have a good chance."

"I'm afraid it's not that easy. First, a social worker will need to talk to both you and your daughter. She needs to make sure that Janis understands and accepts what's going on, and she'll evaluate her as to whether she's a good candidate emotionally. Frankly, having talked to your daughter, I don't think that will be any problem. Then she will talk to you and Janis's father about the possibility of donating a kidney."

"Her father's dead."

"Oh. I'm sorry." He paused. "But before you agree to give up your kidney, I want to make sure that you realize the seriousness of it. You would have only one kidney remaining. Should you develop kidney disease yourself or be in a wreck that damaged your kidney, you wouldn't have a second kidney to fall back on, as most people do. It could mean quite a risk to you."

"But if I don't give it to her, Janis will either die or be on that machine for the rest of her life. Isn't that right?"

"Yes."

"Then I don't see how there's any choice. What is there to think about? Of course I want to give Janis my kidney."

"All right. But you also have to realize, Mrs. Thompson, that you may not be able to donate a kidney to your daughter. We have to make tests to determine compatibility. Siblings are usually the most compatible. Does Janis have a brother or sister?"

Sharon shook her head. "No. Just me. Grandparents, an uncle, a cousin."

"Well, we'll test you first. If you don't match, then you'll have to discuss it with the other relatives."

Sharon nodded, but she paid little attention to what he said. She wouldn't need to approach her parents or Ames. She knew in her heart that she would be a match for Janis. She and her daughter had always been so close; it was inconceivable that she would not have the organ required to save Janis.

Dr. Ebersol explained the tests that would be made of Sharon's blood to determine if Sharon would make a good donor, checking both her blood type and the types of the major antigens in her blood. Sharon had little interest in the technical criteria for a match, and again she nodded. "I see. When can I be tested?"

"Immediately, if you wish. I'll send you down to the lab. However, I have to warn you that even if you do match, you still have to undergo a thorough, lengthy physical examination. If you aren't in excellent health, you can't donate."

"I'm never sick. My health is good."

Sharon was certain that she'd be a match. It wasn't hard for her to put on a cheerful face when she and Dr. Ebersol went down to Janis's room to talk to her. For a few minutes, when the doctor had told her Janis would die without treatment, the world had stopped. She had been overcome by a cold, deep emptiness, a fear and sorrow too awful even to name. But as he'd talked about the kidney machine and the possibility of transplant, she had realized there was hope. It would be a serious operation; it would be a bad time. But nothing insurmountable, nothing impossible. Her kidney would match Janis's. The two of them would get through this together, as they always had.

Her confidence held her up through the blood test the next day and the conference with the social worker. It even kept her going through seeing Janis, a plastic tube sticking out of her arm, hooked up to the dialysis machine, her lifeblood flowing through the clear tubes. It lasted until Dr. Ebersol called her into the same small conference room that afternoon and gave her the results of the blood test.

"I'm afraid it's impossible for you to be a donor, Mrs. Thompson."

"What?" Sharon was stunned. "But—but I thought you had to do more tests."

"Only if your blood type is compatible to Janis's. It's not. Your blood type is AB, your daughter's is B. It's impossible for you to give her your kidney."

Sharon felt as if she might break up into a million pieces and fall down upon the floor. This couldn't happen. This simply couldn't happen. "No."

"I'm sorry. You don't know how sorry. I was really hoping that the two of you would match."

"But I'm her closest relative. I'm her mother."

"Do you think any of her other relatives would consider donating their kidney? Your family? Perhaps someone on her father's side?"

"There is no one on her father's side," Sharon said flatly. "I—I'm sure anyone in my family would be happy to. But if I don't match, how will they?"

"There's a chance, even if they are more removed from your daughter. Not everyone in a family necessarily has the same blood type."

Sharon nodded. "I'll call them."

She was in shock. Hope had sustained her earlier, but now she realized how very perilous Janis's situation was. She could die. Or be chained to that machine, sucking out her blood, six hours a day three times a week for the rest of her life. Sharon wanted to cry, to curl up into a ball on the floor and give way to sobs. She wanted to pull the covers over her head, as she had when she was a girl and had imagined monsters in her closet.

But she could not. She was all Janis had. Even if she could not give Janis the one thing she needed, she still had to be there for her. She had to talk to her parents and Ames; she had to do . . . whatever had to be done.

Shakily Sharon pulled herself out of her chair and left the conference room. Everything seemed strange and disconnected from her, but she made herself walk down the hall to the telephone. Lifting the receiver, she called her parents' home.

Her parents drove to Dallas the next day and took the test. Ames was notified in Guatemala and caught the next plane to Mexico City, where he, too, took the test. Her mother, like her, was disqualified by the blood test, but both Ames and her father had compatible types. They were then tested for antigens.

Sharon was desperately afraid. Janis, with the inability of the young to imagine death really touching them, was sure that one of them would be able to be a donor. But Sharon's optimism had vanished when she had turned out to be ineligible as a donor. The odds were growing worse. At first there had been four possible donors, now there were only two. What if there were soon none? What if both her father and Ames failed? Oh, why weren't there more people in her family?

Her thoughts kept turning to Reid Maitland. He was as close in blood relationship to Janis as Ames was. It would be at least one more possibility.

Every time she thought of him, her mind skittered away. It was impossible. She couldn't ask anything of him. She never had, even a small thing. She couldn't go to him now and ask him to risk his life for Janis. He wouldn't do it, even if she did. He wasn't really an uncle to Janis; he didn't know her. He wouldn't want to help.

Maybe not. But how could she not ask him, if it meant her daughter's life? What did it matter that she must humiliate herself by begging him to help her? Her pride was worth nothing, nor her dislike of him. The past, her feelings, even her certainty that he would refuse to help—none of that meant anything compared with Janis's welfare.

The word came in on her father first. Wendell Thompson's H-a antigen cross-match was acceptable. It made it easier to bear when the word from Mexico City came that Ames's antigen cross-match was poor. It didn't matter that only one person in her family matched; that was all they needed.

Sharon's spirits rose. Janis would get the kidney she needed; she was young and healthy; she would live. Her parents held hands and prayed in her father's room. As always, their voluble praying made her uncomfortable. She left the room and wandered downstairs. She walked outside. The night was cool, and the breeze felt good on her cheeks. She looked up at the sky. The lights of the city obscured the stars, but the night was lovely to her, anyway. She closed her eyes and prayed for the first time in a long while.

Janis was saved.

The next day her father began the rigorous three-day physical exam necessary before he could qualify as a donor. While he was carted around the hospital in a wheelchair from test to test, Sharon sat with her mother and Janis, gaily chatting about what they would do after Janis recovered. Janis looked only slightly better after the dialysis. She was still puffy, her color bad, and she was exhausted. Sharon avoided looking at the bandage that covered the two tubes leading into her veins.

Late in the afternoon, Dr. Youngman came into the room. His expression was so grave that Sharon's stomach dropped. *Something had gone wrong.*

He led Sharon and her mother out into the hall. "What is it?" Sharon asked before he could even speak.

"Your father has been ruled out as a donor."

"What?"

"He was walking the treadmill, and he collapsed. They had to revive him with CPR."

"What!"

"He's all right now," he hastened to assure them, his hand going out to steady Mrs. Thompson's arm. "We transferred him to ICU, just to be safe."

"But he's never had any heart trouble!" This couldn't be true. "He's always been healthy."

"It may not have shown up before. But these things happen. He's obviously not up to the stress of an operation and losing a kidney."

"I have to go to him," Mrs. Thompson said quietly.

"Of course." He gave her directions to the ICU.

Sharon stayed with the doctor. All the blood had drained from her face. She thought she might faint. She leaned against the wall, closing her eyes. Oh, God, her father had almost died trying to help Janis. Now there was no one left who could.

The doctor put his hand on her arm, trying awkwardly to comfort her. "I'm sorry, ma'am. But this isn't the end of it. Janis can stay on dialysis until we find a suitable kidney from a cadaver. It's a delay, not the end."

"I've read about how difficult it is to find a donor, how long the waiting lists are."

"Yes, there's a large demand for them. But there's a sophisticated network now for locating them."

"Dr. Ebersol said her chances were poorer than with a relative."

"But not bad. It's still a viable possibility."

Sharon straightened slowly, opening her eyes. "There's one other chance. She has an uncle, her father's brother. I'll talk to him."

Sharon went straight home from the hospital and looked up Reid Maitland's telephone number. She called his office, her heart beginning to race with trepidation, but the secretary there informed her that Representative Maitland was in Washington, D.C. She helpfully provided the telephone number of his office in D.C., but Sharon did not call him. It would be too easy for him to turn her down over the phone. Instead, she made a reservation on the first flight to Washington the following morning.

She left bright and early the next day on the red-eye flight, not even bothering to pack a bag. For better or worse, she expected to be back in Dallas this evening. During the whole flight, she gripped her hands together in her lap and stared out the window of the plane, ignoring her neighbor and refusing all offers of food and drink from the flight attendants.

It wasn't a fear of flying that held her rigid and white-knuckled. It was nervousness at the thought of facing Reid Maitland again, after all these years and the two short, angry meetings between them before. It was fear for her daughter's life—and a heart-stopping terror that Reid Maitland would refuse her.

She hated the thought of seeing him. He had scored her heart and soul with his dismissal of her as a tramp and a bloodsucker seeking to benefit from his family's sorrow. When he had thrown her out of his house, it was as if he had spat upon her and her love for Wes. She had hated him ever since that day, and even though the intensity of her emotion had dimmed over the years, she still disliked him thoroughly. Even his apology after Janis was born had done little to change her opinion of him. He had been stiff and cold, and she was sure that he had not felt any genuine remorse or even any real interest in his brother's child. Only pride in his family name had made him offer to pay for his niece's upbringing.

A man like Reid Maitland felt no remorse or warmth toward any child, even one of his own blood. What he was capable of feeling, though, was deep resentment over the fact that Sharon had scorned his apology and offer of financial assistance. He wouldn't have forgotten her contempt when she flung back his offer in his face. No, he was too proud for that. He was bound to dislike her.

But even though she was afraid he would refuse her request, she had to ask him. No matter how much she disliked Reid Maitland, no matter how afraid she was that he would not do it, she had to ask. It was the only hope Janis had.

The plane landed at National Airport, and Sharon caught a cab to Maitland's office. As the taxi zipped through the capital city, Sharon hardly saw the harrowing Washington traffic, so lost was she in rehearsing in her mind what she would say. She had thought of several different ways to approach the subject, but none of them satisfied her. There was nothing she could say that would compel Maitland's agreement. She wasn't even sure she could catch his interest. What if he turned her away without listening to her?

She couldn't let that happen. She couldn't. If need be, she simply would have to blackmail him, threaten to reveal to the newspapers that he would not help his dying niece. A scandal in the newspapers was the last thing Sharon wanted, but she was determined to do whatever it took.

The taxi pulled up in front of the legislative office building, and Sharon got out. For a moment, she stood looking up at the building. Her breath came fast and shallow in her throat. This was it.

She made herself walk into the building. A guard stopped her and checked her purse, then directed her toward Representative Maitland's office. She took an elevator to the fourth floor and walked down the hallway, looking for the number the guard had given her. Two men passed her, talking earnestly; one of them looked up and gave her an automatic smile.

Sharon stopped in front of Maitland's door. It stood open. The office inside was small and jammed with several chairs, a bookcase, coffee table, and secretary's desk. Three people sat waiting in the chairs. The woman behind the desk held a phone cradled between her ear and shoulder, and as she listened, her fingers were busily typing. She turned, hanging up the phone and wrote something on a slip of paper, shoving it down atop the spike message holder. She looked up at Sharon and smiled toothily.

"Yes? Can I help you?"

Sharon walked to her desk. "I need to see Representative Maitland."

"Do you have an appointment?"

"No, I'm afraid not."

The woman smiled again, but this time it looked more forced. "I'm sorry, but Representative Maitland's schedule is extremely full today. He can't see you without an appointment. Perhaps I could set one up for you later in the week."

"No. I have to see him today." Sharon's fingers dug more tightly into her purse. "It's an emergency."

"I'm sorry. He can't possibly see anyone. He's at the House right now, voting, and his afternoon is completely scheduled." She turned to a large appointment book and began to thumb through it. "Let's see, the earliest possible time you could see him would be day after tomorrow at three o'clock.''

Sharon set her jaw. She was ready to beard the lion himself in his den; she wasn't about to be turned back by a conscientious secretary. "I'll wait for him."

The secretary raised an irritated eyebrow, then shrugged and turned back to her typing. Sharon sat down in a vacant chair.

The minutes crawled by. Sharon's stomach tightened more with every passing moment. She kept thinking of Janis lying in her hospital bed, her face unnaturally puffy, her cheeks robbed of color, prisoner to the dialysis machine. She was dying. Dying! She remembered Reid Maitland's face the day she had told him she was pregnant with Wes's child. It could have been carved from granite for all the expression it showed; his eyes had been the cold gray of a November day. God, she hated to do this but she had to.

Finally there was the sound of men's voices in the hall, and two men strode in. The one in front was tall, with dark brown, almost black, hair, smoothly cut but ruffled from a breeze or perhaps a hand shoved through it. His face was sharp, all planes and angles, and his eyes were gray. He was dressed impeccably, as he had been every time Sharon had seen him. Reid Maitland. He looked older. His expression was grim, his mouth tight. Sharon had seen him look no other way. She doubted that he was capable of smiling.

Sharon rose slowly, as though pulled from her seat. Her heart was pounding, and her lungs squeezed in her chest. Reid didn't glance at her as he walked across the outer office to the receptionist's desk; his head was bent to listen to the shorter man beside him, who talked continuously in a low, intense voice.

The secretary behind the desk greeted him with a smile of genuine warmth. "Good afternoon, Representative Maitland."

"Good day, Martha. I see I needn't ask how the morning's gone." He nodded significantly toward the fat stack of messages as he drew them off the spike.

"Mr. Ronald Martin is here to see you." Martha gestured toward one of the men seated in the office.

Maitland swiveled toward the man and extended his hand. "Hello, Ronald. Sorry I didn't see you sitting there."

"Quite all right."

"Why don't you come on into my office, and we'll—" His gaze slid casually past the man to the woman who stood a few feet away, and his words died in his throat. He stared.

She was a small woman, shapely although she didn't dress to emphasize it. Her dark brown hair was thick and brushed her shoulders in a careless, curling style. Her eyes were huge, brown, and vulnerable, framed with thick dark lashes. She did not have the sleek sophistication he was accustomed to. She wore little makeup, and she was not dressed in the crisp suit favored by professional women. But the soft textures and bright colors of her full turquoise blouse and multihued skirt suited her, and she wore them with a flair. Her soft, peach-tinged complexion needed nothing to cover it. She made him think of the sun and warmth and the West.

She was older than the last time he'd seen her, lovelier and more self-assured. But he had known her immediately. He doubted that he could ever forget her. "Sharon."

At least he recognized her, Sharon thought, and her muscles eased a little. He hadn't dismissed her out of hand. She wet her lips. "Mr. Maitland. I—need to speak with you." She paused. Her stomach was in knots. She stood stiffly, her face remote, almost haughty. Inside her heart begged him to listen to her. "It's important."

"Of course."

His ready acquiescence startled her. She had no idea that her eyes revealed the need and fear that her face would not. Behind Maitland, she saw even greater astonishment written on his secretary's face.

Reid turned toward the man he had just greeted. "Ronald, I'm sorry. This is an emergency. If you will talk to my assistant, I'm sure Phil can help you. He knows everything I do—and more. Phil?"

The assistant looked as amazed as Martha, but he quickly

covered it with a politician's smile. "Of course. Mr. Martin, I'm Philip Denison. Why don't we go into Mr. Maitland's office?"

"Thanks, Phil. Ronald." Maitland nodded toward the two men. "I'll talk to you again soon."

Phil led Ronald Martin into the inner office. Reid turned back to face Sharon. "Why don't we grab a bite to eat while we talk?"

Sharon nodded. "That's fine."

She didn't like the idea of talking about this in the middle of a restaurant, with people all around them, but at least it would be more private than his office.

Reid took her arm and walked her to the elevator. They rode down in silence. Sharon averted her eyes, as one did in an elevator with strangers. She could feel Reid watching her. All the different ways she had thought of introducing her plea had vanished from her head. She couldn't say anything.

Outside, Maitland caught a taxi and gave the driver the name of a restaurant. It did not take them long to reach the place, for which Sharon was grateful. She couldn't broach the subject of Janis's illness in the back of a cab, but the continued silence grew more and more awkward.

"Did you fly in this morning?" Maitland asked politely, to bridge the gaping silence.

"Yes."

"From New Mexico?"

"No. We're in Dallas now."

"I see." For a moment he looked sad, and then the expression was gone. He turned his head to look out the side window.

Neither of them said anything else until they reached the restaurant. Sharon was relieved to see that there were only a few diners inside the hushed, elegant dining room. Reid helped her off with her coat and handed it to the woman in the cloakroom. The maître d' greeted Reid with low-keyed enthusiasm and ushered them to one of the high-backed semi-circular banquettes against the wall. Sharon slid into the dim shelter of the encircling leather seat, grateful for the privacy.

Reid had understood her need for a quiet, secluded place to talk. She felt almost grateful for a moment, until she recalled that he, even more than she, would want to keep any conversation with her a secret. After all, he was a politician.

Sharon took the elaborate leather-bound menu that the waiter handed her and opened it. She glanced down the page disinterestedly. The thought of food made her slightly ill. "I think I'll just have a salad. I'm not very hungry."

Reid glanced at her. She looked as if she had skipped more than one meal lately, and there were lines of strain around her mouth and eyes. He found himself wanting to lay his hand on hers and tell her not to worry, but he was fully aware of how foolish that idea was. Even though she had sought him out, he knew that Sharon Thompson did not want him to befriend her.

"You should try the veal piccata," he told her. "It's delicious here. Let me order you some."

Sharon shrugged. "If you want." It would simply lie there on the plate, as most of her food did these days. She found it hard to choke down anything, with the specter of Janis's failing body always in her head.

The waiter appeared beside them at some barely perceptible gesture of Maitland's and took their orders. He slid away, and Maitland turned toward her. Sharon knew it was time to begin. She swallowed and clasped her hands together. She couldn't bring herself to look at him.

"I need your help," she began bluntly, her eyes directed to the table between them.

A faint smile touched his mouth. "I presumed as much. I know how you feel about me. It must be something pretty desperate to bring you here."

"It is." She forced herself to look up at him. Her fingers dug into her hands. Her daughter's life might rest on this conversation. "It's for Janis."

"Your daughter."

"Yes." For an instant the old, fierce anger flashed in her eyes. "Wes's daughter, too."

"Yes." He waited. "Is she in some sort of trouble? Do you need money?"

Sharon's mouth tightened. "No. This isn't something that can be bought off." She realized how resentful her voice sounded and cursed herself for it. She needed to placate this man, *persuade* him, not alienate him. "I'm sorry. That came out wrong."

"There's no need to apologize. But if it's not money, why have you come to me? Surely it's not a political matter."

"No. It's purely genetic. Janis needs—Janis is—" She broke off. Tears sprang into her eyes, and she struggled to hold them back. She refused to cry in front of this man. She simply could not let herself.

Reid leaned forward, spreading his hands out flat on the table, not quite touching hers but somehow offering a steady strength. His face was drawn into an earnest frown, and Sharon would have sworn that there was concern in his eyes. "What is it? What's the matter?"

"Janis is dying." She closed her eyes, and tears leaked out from beneath her lids.

"What? But she's only—what is it? What's wrong with her?"

"She has a kidney disease. It's—what they call 'end stage' kidney failure." Sharon wiped the tears from her cheeks with the back of her hand and swallowed hard. "Her kidneys have stopped functioning."

"But they've made all kinds of advances in kidney research the past few years. Dialysis and all that. Can't they do anything for her?"

"She's on dialysis. It's keeping her alive right now. But it's not a good solution, especially for a child her age. It's a very difficult thing to live with. She would be literally tied to the machine, unable to live a normal, healthy, active life." She drew in a shaky breath.

Her large brown eyes were damp and velvety, the lashes ringing them stuck together in moist spikes, giving her eyes a starry look. Reid thought he'd never seen a woman look so heartbreakingly beautiful and sad. "I'm sorry. God, I'm sorry."

This time, unthinkingly, Reid did cover one of her hands with his. When he realized what he had done, he was surprised that she hadn't pulled her hand away.

"The doctors tell me that there's one other option—a kidney transplant." Sharon drew a shaky breath. Now was the hard part; the part she had come for. Reid had been surprisingly kind so far; she realized with some astonishment that he'd even taken her hand comfortingly. But sympathy, she reminded herself, was easy. Giving up a part of oneself, risking one's life went quite a bit beyond that.

"Then that's the answer. She'll get a new kidney from a donor. She's young; it'll work."

"It's difficult to get a donor kidney. The wait can be extremely long. Someone has to die, and their kidneys have to match hers, and even then there are such long waiting lists. It could take months, years even. Besides, there's not nearly as much chance of success as when a close relative donates one of his kidneys. It's possible to live with only one, you see. It would be far better for a relative to give her one, but it has to match, and I'm not a good match. Everyone in my family has been tested, and we've all failed." Her voice rose a little desperately, and she sat back, pulling her hand away from his and crossing her arms in front of her. Her face was twisted with the intensity of her emotions.

Reid stared at her for a moment, then comprehension dawned on his face. "But her father's family might match. Is that it? Is that why you came to me?"

Sharon nodded mutely, and the tears began to roll uncontrollably from her eyes.

"You think that I might be able to donate one of my kidneys."

"Yes. I'm sorry to ask." She looked down at the table, unable to meet his eyes.

Reid sighed and settled back in his seat. "I'm sorry you were so afraid of asking it. Of course I'd give her a kidney. What do I need to do?"

Sharon's head came up, and she stared at him. "Just like that? Not even any questions?" She'd come prepared to argue and plead, even to threaten. She could hardly believe that he had agreed as soon as she'd asked.

He grimaced slightly. "You have a decidedly unflattering opinion of me. Did you really think I wouldn't help her?"

Heat rose in Sharon's cheeks. She felt curiously guilty and ashamed. "It's amazing how many times relatives don't. You hardly know her, after all. And I'm aware that you don't like me."

He gazed at her for a long, silent moment. "I wouldn't say that's true. But even if it were, it doesn't follow that I would refuse to help Janis." His voice stumbled a little on her name. "She's my niece. My brother's child. And she's very ill. How could I possibly not do whatever I can to help her?"

"It could be dangerous for you. Any operation presents some danger. And in the future something might happen to the one kidney you would have left, and you could die because you had only one."

"It's a possibility," he agreed. "But I think the slight risk to me, the possibility of some future harm, hardly outweighs your daughter's danger. Give me the name of the doctor in Dallas, and I'll call him this afternoon."

Sharon began to tremble, and tears started in her eyes. She looked down at her lap to hide the sudden rush of emotion. She had been so afraid, so strung tight with tension, refusing to let herself hope. Now suddenly he was offering her all that she could have asked for; he was handing her the last chance to save her daughter's life. It was too much for Sharon's frayed nerves. She thought she had been prepared for anything, but she hadn't expected kindness from him. She wanted to break down and weep.

"Sharon?" Reid leaned closer, his hand going out to touch her arm. "Are you all right?"

She glanced up, and he saw the tears swimming in her eyes. Her mouth trembled a little. She looked soft and vulnerable, and Reid had to fight off a sudden urge to enfold her in his arms and hold her.

"I'm sorry." There was a little catch in her voice. A tear spilled over her lower lid and onto her cheek. "I was just so afraid—and now—" She swallowed and wiped at her wet cheeks. "I can't believe it's real." She gave him a tremulous smile. "Thank you. You're very kind."

One corner of his mouth lifted in a lopsided smile. "That's one thing I never expected to hear from you. I guess you've seen the worst of me—suspicious, overbearing, cruel." He paused and looked down at the table, smoothing out a crease in the tablecloth. "That isn't my entire nature, however. At least, I hope it's not. I apologized once for that day, but I could see you didn't believe me. I am truly sorry. I have no excuse except grief and love and loyalty to my family. I didn't want my mother to be hurt any more than she had been, and—well, it wasn't the first time that people had tried to weasel money out of my family, particularly where Wes was concerned. Even before he died, I'd had to pay off one or two girls for him. But if I'd been thinking clearly, I would have seen that you weren't the same type of woman." He lifted his head and his gaze met hers. "I'm sorry for the pain I caused you."

There was no pleading in his face; his gray eyes were flat and unreadable in the dim light of the restaurant. But for the first time, Sharon didn't take his controlled expression for arrogance and coldness. She sensed a sincerity in his voice, an emotion that had no outlet in the face he presented to the world. She wondered if she had misjudged him all these years; he had, after all, just shown a kindness and humanity that she wouldn't have dreamed existed in him. The hard knot of resentment and dislike she had carried for him inside her began to soften and melt.

Sharon shook her head. "I—it was a long time ago. Perhaps it's time to let it go."

He smiled a little. "Thank you. Now, why don't you write down the doctor's name and number?"

Sharon did so and handed him the slip of paper. "I should think you'd be able to take the tests here."

"Good. That'll mean less rearrangement of my schedule. I'll have to move things around a bit to come back to Dallas for the surgery."

"You know, it's possible that you won't be able to donate the kidney. You may not match, either. No one in my family has."

"Wouldn't that mean that it's likely my side of the family will be the one to match?"

"I don't know. I don't think that's necessarily true."

"Think positively. I intend to be the donor."

"I hope you're right." There was a catch in her voice. She couldn't let herself hope too much; she didn't dare to dream.

The waiter brought their food. It was delicious, but Sharon did little more than move it around on her plate. She was too full of churning emotions—the shaking aftermath of fear and despair, the rising swell of hope—to feel any hunger.

Reid watched her covertly as he ate. Despite the strain that was evident on her face, she was a lovely woman. Maturity had deepened her prettiness, and she had found her own particular style. There was a warmth and ease, an unfettered femininity in her that appealed to him. He felt a tug of attraction, as he had each time he'd seen her, and it made him feel a little guilty. She was too vulnerable, too upset; it seemed crude and unthinking to even feel that spark of desire for her.

When they finished, Reid drove her back to the office building. When she told him she was flying back to Dallas on the next possible flight, he flagged down a cab for her and put her in it, handing the cabbie the fare. He opened the door for her and leaned in.

"Take care of yourself. You won't do Janis any good if you get sick."

"I know." Sharon paused. She didn't know what to say. Reid had surprised her. She was elated, excited—and scared.

What if this, her final hope, turned into disappointment? What if Reid was not a suitable donor? What if he backed out of it, after all? She still could not quite believe that he was so willing to do it. "Well, thank you."

"There's no need to thank me. She's Wes's child. I want to do it. I'd like to do more."

Sharon stiffened a little. "Thank you, but there's nothing else you can do."

"There's a lot, but I won't press it. Good-bye. I'll see you in Dallas soon."

She smiled. He sounded so positive, so confident and strong, that she could almost believe that he would somehow make things happen as he wanted them to. "Good-bye."

Reid pulled back out of the taxi and closed the door. The car pulled away from the curb. He watched it slip into the traffic, then turned and walked into the building and up to his office.

Martha was in the outer office, on the phone, as always, and two more people awaited him. He gave them a smile, wishing they were anywhere but here, and strode into his office. It was a small room, crammed with filing cabinets, bookshelves, chairs, and a huge desk. Phil Denison, his assistant, sat behind the desk, talking on the other line. Phil raised a hand in greeting and began to maneuver his way out of the conversation.

When he had hung up the phone, he rose, holding out a sheaf of papers. "There are some more messages for you. And Martha brought these letters for your signature. Joel Carmichael's waiting outside for you; I'll brief you on what he wants."

Reid shook his head. "Wait a minute. There's something I have to do first. Stall Carmichael or see if you can take care of him."

Phil frowned. "I don't know. Martin took it okay when you unloaded him on me, but I'm not so sure about Carmichael. He doesn't like to deal with the hired hands."

"You'll handle him, I'm sure. Tell him it's an emergency. I have to make this phone call before I talk to anyone; it'll take only a few minutes. But I may have to go to the hospital this afternoon or tomorrow.''

Phil looked stunned. ''Reid! What's the matter?''

''No, no, there's nothing wrong with me. It's . . . a family matter. I just found out my niece is in desperate need of a kidney donor. I have to be tested to see if I qualify to give her one of mine.''

Phil blinked. ''Your niece? What niece?''

''My brother's daughter. Wes's child.''

His assistant looked at him as if he'd lost his mind. ''What are you talking about? Your brother's been dead for—''

''Thirteen years.''

''But he didn't have a child. He wasn't even married.''

''No. He wasn't married.''

Phil put it together. ''Illegitimate? He left an illegitimate daughter?''

Reid nodded.

''Jesus.'' The other man sagged down onto a chair as if the air had been knocked out of him. ''I didn't know. Nobody knows.''

Reid shrugged. ''It wasn't something I talked about. And Sharon would never have revealed it.''

''Sharon. The woman who was just here? The one you had lunch with?''

''Yeah. She came to tell me about Janis. I hadn't seen her in twelve years.'' He sighed. ''My fault. I screwed it up; she wouldn't let me near Janis.''

''Now she needs a kidney, and you're going to give it to her.''

''If the tests come out right, yeah.''

Phil plunged his hands into his hair. ''Reid, no. Slow down. Think this through before you do anything.''

Reid glanced at him, surprised. ''What do you mean?''

''Think about it. What's it going to mean to your career?''

He shrugged. ''I don't know. I hadn't thought about it.''

''Obviously.'' Phil plopped down into a chair. ''Well, put your mind to it now.'' He shook his head. ''I'm not at all sure it's a smart move to make. Think about how it'll look.''

"It'll look like I'm an uncle giving an organ to my niece. What should it look like?" Phil's dismay irritated him.

"She's not legitimate."

"So?"

"So it'll be a scandal."

"Come on. She's my brother's child, not mine."

"What guarantees that?"

"What do you mean?"

"Look. It wouldn't help you if everybody thought your brother had a bastard kid, but we could probably get through that. The thing is, everyone'll think it might be your baby. I mean, here you are giving your kidney to this girl who's been hidden away from the public view for thirteen years. Your brother's name probably isn't on the birth certificate. It'll look suspicious. They're going to whisper that she's really yours, and you're just laying it off on your dead brother. It will look bad."

Reid gazed at him for a long moment. Anger grew in him into a cold, hard knot. "You're saying I should let my niece die because people might gossip about my relationship to her?"

"Reid . . . don't make me out to be the villain here. I'm only saying you ought to think before you jump into something. Remember, you're starting your campaign for the Senate the end of this year. Maybe you should delay your decision, see if there's some other solution that comes up. Dialysis. Another donor, maybe. People die and donate kidneys all the time."

"There isn't any other choice. She's my brother's daughter, and she's facing a long, difficult life on a dialysis machine if she doesn't get a donor. It would take a long time to get a kidney through ordinary donor channels. And even if she did, she wouldn't have a good a chance of surviving as she does if it comes from a close relative. None of her mother's relatives match. That leaves me." He stared at his aide stonily, then shrugged. "If that makes gossip, I'll leave it up to you and Susan to work the press around. Hell, you'll have me coming out a hero."

Phil grimaced. "All I'm asking is for you to wait."

"I can't. Janis doesn't have the time to waste."

His aide sighed and turned his hands palms up in a gesture of helplessness. "I'll talk to Carmichael. Hold him off for a while. But you'll have to see him."

"I will. Give me fifteen minutes."

Phil nodded and left the inner office.

Reid sat down behind his desk where Phil had been and leaned back, clasping his hands behind his head as he often did when he was thinking. He thought about the niece he had never seen. She was the only child in his family, the only remnant of the brother he had grown up loving, supervising, and often despairing of. He wondered what his mother thought about Janis. He had told her about the girl long ago, when he had learned from the detective that Sharon Thompson's story was in all probability true. His mother had never said anything to him about Janis, never inquired after her or evinced any interest in seeing her. Reid had never been sure whether she had been exercising self-control or was simply uninterested.

Reid had thought of Janis many times. He had thought about her mother, too. Sharon. Such a sweet name, as lovely and delicate as the woman herself. The first time he'd seen her, he had felt a ripple of desire run through him. The fact that he could have wanted her at a time like that, considering what he thought she was and what he thought she was trying to do to his family, had made him even angrier at her. He had never forgotten or forgiven himself for how unfair he had been to her that day, blaming her for his own internal reaction.

He was a meticulously fair and scrupulous man. He had steered clear of all underhanded dealings in a profession where they were commonplace. He attributed that quality to the fact that he had been born with so much money he had never needed to take graft. The truth was, had Reid been born poor, he would have had the same strict sense of honesty and fairness. He had been raised sternly and soberly, duty and responsibility melded into him as a child. He was a

Maitland, and Maitlands acted in certain ways. Because of the gifts of his wealth, intelligence, and power, he felt duty bound to use them for the good of the country and other people. It was why he had gone into politics; it was what he had been trained for all his life.

He had regretted for years his mishandling of Sharon Thompson and Wes's child. He had often thought of her young face with those huge, sad eyes and had disliked himself for the scorn and anger he had heaped on her. He had understood when she refused later to let him help her and her baby. He would have reacted the same way himself. But it hadn't made him feel any better. Now he finally had the opportunity to make it up to Sharon and Janis. That was part of the reason he was doing it. Another part was simply the fact that Janis was Wes's child.

And the other part was Sharon's huge brown eyes.

No doubt Phil was right. It would not be the politically wisest thing to do. His ex-wife would have been appalled. But then, he wasn't Phil, and he and Angela hadn't gotten along.

Reid picked up the phone and began to dial the number Sharon had given him.

Sharon was sitting by the window in Janis's hospital room two days later, staring out blankly, when the door opened and Dr. Youngman stepped in. He glanced at the bed where Janis lay asleep, then over at Sharon. There was a big grin on his usually reserved face. Sharon's heart began to pound. She stood up, excitement rising within her.

"Bingo!" he said in a low voice, so as not to waken the sleeping girl. "We got it this time. Dr. Hassman at Bethesda just called. Congressman Maitland cross-matches on three out of four. It's a good match. He passed the physical exam with flying colors. He's coming in tomorrow, and we'll operate the next day."

"Oh, my God." Sharon wrapped her arms around herself. "Oh, my God."

"I'll come back this evening when Jan's awake and discuss the details." The doctor pointed his index finger at her and brought his thumb down like a kid pretending to shoot, then turned and left the room.

Sharon looked at Janis. She was still asleep. Sharon moved back to her chair shakily and sat down. They were going to operate. Tears filled her eyes. She'd hated Reid Maitland for years. And now he was going to save her daughter's life.

6

"You have a donor."

Sharon smiled down at her daughter. She had told her the good news as soon as Janis awakened. Janis stared back at her. Her face was puffy, almost swallowing up her eyes, and her skin was sallow. She looked exhausted and ill and far older than her years. But her eyes were clear and bright, and they were fixed sharply on Sharon.

"What?" she asked. "What did you say?"

"I said, 'Dr. Ebersol just told me that you have a donor.' You'll be able to have the transplant." Sharon's grin widened. She'd been waiting for an hour for Janis to wake up so that she could tell her the good news.

Janis blinked and struggled to sit up in the bed. "Are you kidding?"

Sharon pushed the button to raise the head of her bed and rearranged Janis's pillows behind her back. "Would I kid you about something like that?"

"No. It's just—" A smile broke across her face, and Janis gave a little giggle, strangely girlish in her weary face. "Oh,

Mama, this is great! This is absolutely the best! No more of that awful dialysis. I'll be well again!''

"Well, not immediately. You'll have to have the operation first. You know there's the possibility your body will reject the kidney, and they'll have to give you steroids and immunity suppressants. It'll be weeks, even months before you're out.''

"I know all that.'' Janis dismissed those facts with a wave of her hand. "That's okay. As long as I know I'm actually getting out. When are they going to do it? Tonight? Tomorrow morning?''

"Day after tomorrow.''

"Day after tomorrow? Why so long? I thought they'd fly it in and do it right away.''

"This is different. It's not someone who's died and donated his kidney. It's . . .'' She paused; for the first time Sharon realized that this was going to be a problem. Why hadn't she thought of it before? "It's a relative. Your uncle.''

"My uncle?'' Janis repeated, puzzled. "But the doctors in Guatemala said Uncle Ames's tissue type didn't match.''

Sharon wet her lips and glanced away from her daughter's eyes. "It's not *my* brother. It's your father's brother.''

"My father? He didn't have a brother. You said—'' She stopped and stared unblinkingly at Sharon. "You said they were all dead. You lied to me, didn't you? My father did have a family.''

"Yes,'' Sharon admitted.

"But why? You always told me you wouldn't lie to me. You said—''

"I know what I said!'' Sharon snapped. "And I did tell you the truth.''

"Except about this.''

"Except about this.'' She paused. "Look, must we pursue this now? Can't we just concentrate on the fact that you're getting a donor, that you have the possibility of a whole life in front of you? Let's get excited about that. Isn't it wonderful?''

"Yeah. It's wonderful.'' Janis looked at her mother oddly.

"I'm happy. Happier than I've been in ages. But, Mama, I can't simply forget about some uncle that I never heard of —especially when he's going to save my life. Why didn't you tell me? Is he a criminal? Is he in jail or something?"

Sharon had to chuckle. She could imagine how the aristocratic Maitland family would react to that statement. "No. More like the opposite. Reid Maitland is your uncle. The congressman."

"The congressman? You mean the good-looking guy? The one the newspapers keep saying is going to run for the Senate?"

Sharon nodded.

"But why didn't you tell me about him?" Suddenly Janis's face closed down. For a moment she looked hauntingly like Wes. "Oh, I get it. He didn't want anyone to know about me, right? He and his family are ashamed of me."

"No. No, it's not that. It's—well, Reid and I had a fight before you were born. He didn't believe me when I told him that—that you were Wes's child."

"Sounds like a nice guy."

"I don't know. Maybe he had reasons for thinking like that. Looking back, I can see that it must have been a shock for him. He and his family were mourning Wes, just as I was. Other people had tried to take advantage of them. If he believed that I was just trying to get some money, it must have been painful to him. He told me the other day that he wanted to shield his mother from any more pain."

Janis raised an eyebrow, an expression she had worked hard to achieve over the past few years. "Un-huh. That's why in twelve years they were never once interested in seeing me?"

"That's not exactly true. Reid did come to Santa Fe once, when you were just a baby. He said he'd hired a private detective, and the detective had established that Wes and I had been dating exclusively those months before he died. He wanted to see you; he said he'd come to believe that you were Wes's child."

"Big of him."

"Janis, don't be too hard on him. He wanted to accept responsibility for you. He wanted to provide for you, to visit you. But I wouldn't let him. I was still angry with him, and I was scared that he and the Maitlands might try to take you away from me. I kicked him out; I would hardly even listen to his apology. I told him that I didn't need him or his money and that I didn't want him coming back around."

"Good for you."

"Janis, what I'm saying is that maybe I misjudged him. I was awfully young then, and I was hurt and furious. I didn't consider his side of it or give him much chance to explain. All these years I've figured him for a monster; but when I talked to him the other day, he didn't seem like one."

Janis crossed her arms across her chest. "Well, how did he even know I needed a kidney?"

"I told him. I flew to Washington and told him."

"Why? I wouldn't have even gone to him."

"How could I not go to him? Your life was at stake. I'd have asked the Devil himself if I thought it would save you."

"I have more pride than that. I don't want any part of him. He didn't want me."

Sharon smiled. "The young can indulge in pride more than I can. Besides, we don't know that he didn't want you. I attributed the worst motives to him that time he came to Santa Fe; I didn't really listen to him. I just assumed the worst and refused to see it any other way. But maybe I made a mistake; I might have kept you from having a relationship with your father's family all these years."

"Oh, Mama." Janis smiled and patted Sharon's hand. "I didn't need a relationship with them or anybody else. I've done fine."

"I don't want you to turn away from him now. You can't refuse to accept his help. I won't let you. It means your life, Jan. No amount of pride or loyalty is worth that. You have to accept his kidney."

Janis sighed. "I don't want to have to be grateful to him."

"Then be as rude and ungrateful as you want," her mother retorted. "Just take the kidney. Think about what's going to happen to you if you don't."

"Okay, okay. I'm not going to turn him down. But that doesn't mean I have to like him."

"That's fine." Sharon paused. "But, hon, if by chance he wants to see you and be—I don't know, be a real uncle to you, I think you ought to give him a chance. See what he's like, if he really means it. You mustn't worry that you'll hurt me or be a traitor to me if you like him. I kind of liked him myself the last time I saw him. He's going out of his way to help you; he doesn't have to do this."

"Maybe he thinks the publicity will help his political career."

Sharon chuckled. "Don't be cynical. You're only thirteen."

Janis made a face. "I'm smart for my age."

Sharon's heart twisted a little. She knew that her daughter was trying to maintain a lighthearted attitude for Sharon's sake. Janis didn't want her mother to worry or be scared, and so she tried to show that she herself wasn't scared. Sharon bent over and kissed Janis on the cheek.

"You're a terrific person. Did you know that?"

"You've mentioned it a time or two . . . hundred."

"All right, Miss Smarts. Just for that, I'll beat you at a game of gin."

"Ha. Ha."

Sharon took a pack of cards out of the drawer of the small bedside table and perched on the edge of Janis's bed to shuffle them. She dealt out the cards onto the rolling adjustable table usually used for food trays, and they began to play. Sharon watched Janis fan out her cards and begin to arrange them, her eyes quick and serious. She knew the girl would beat her; she always did, whatever the game. As always, pride surged in her chest as she watched her. Janis handled everything so well; she didn't whine or bemoan what fate had handed out to her. She accepted things and did the best she

could with them. Just as she'd accepted Reid Maitland's offer
of help. She hadn't wanted to, but her common sense and
fairness had won out in the end. Sharon knew she would give
Reid a chance.

The following morning Reid called Sharon at the hospital.
Sharon answered, expecting it to be her mother or Hollis,
and instead a deep voice on the other end said, "Sharon?"

When she didn't answer, he went on, more tentatively,
"Miss Thompson?"

"Yes."

"This is Reid Maitland."

"Yes, how are you?" She didn't tell him that she had
recognized his voice immediately.

"Fine. How are you?"

"Fine." There was an awkward pause.

"I'm in Dallas. I flew in on the red-eye. I'll be checking
into the hospital sometime this afternoon."

"That's good." She didn't know what to say.

"Hopefully the press won't have gotten wind of it yet, and
we can avoid them until after the operation."

Sharon hadn't considered the possibility of press coverage
until this minute. "Oh. Yes, I can see how that could be a
problem." A senatorial hopeful involved in a transplant to
save his niece was bound to be newsworthy.

"Anyway . . . the reason I called . . ." He paused. "I
was hoping that I might be able to see your daughter." He
hurried on before she could say anything. "I'm not pressuring
you or trying to exchange the transplant for a chance to see
Janis. But I thought she might want to meet me, considering
what's going to happen; she might be curious. I don't know
what you've told her about me."

"Very little. Until yesterday, she wasn't aware that you
were her uncle."

"I see." He cleared his throat. "I guess I'm throwing
myself on your mercy. I would like to see her."

A smile touched Sharon's lips. "I understand. I think it would be nice."

"Good. Thank you." She could hear the surprise and relief in his voice. "Then I could drop by her room this afternoon when I check in?"

"Certainly." Sharon hesitated. "I think Janis would like to meet you." She cast a glance toward her daughter, who lay asleep in her bed. "I was very young when I told you to stay away from her. It—was unfair of me."

There was a slight pause, then Reid said, humor lightening his voice, "It's good to know not only one of us was."

His words brought a surprised chuckle from Sharon. "Yes. I guess you're right."

"Then I'll see you this afternoon."

Reid arrived earlier than she had expected, while Sharon was still in the hospital cafeteria eating lunch. When she walked back into Janis's room that afternoon, she found him already ensconced in the chair beside Janis's bed, chatting comfortably with her. Janis was giggling at something Reid had said. There was a tinge of color in her daughter's face for the first time in weeks, and her eyes sparkled.

Sharon felt a perverse tug of resentment. She had been wearing herself out trying to keep Janis's spirits up. Yet Reid, whom Janis didn't even know, who had denied her so long ago, was able to waltz right into the room and make her laugh and her face shine, just with a few minutes of chat. How could Janis like him so easily, so naturally? But, then, he was a politician; no doubt that was one of his basic skills.

Janis glanced up and saw Sharon and grinned. "Hi! Reid's here." There was none of the resentment toward him that had been in her voice the night before.

"So I see." Sharon couldn't quite keep the chill out of her voice.

Reid turned and rose. "Sharon." His expression was warm and relaxed, and Sharon realized that she had never seen him that way before. Suddenly she felt guilty and petty for resenting the fact that he and Janis liked each other. Reid hadn't won Janis over with a smooth politician's patter;

he was enjoying being with her, just as she was enjoying him. Good heavens, she ought to be grateful to him for making Janis cheerful and at ease on the day before her difficult surgery.

"Hello, Reid. How are you?"

"Good."

"I'm sorry; I didn't realize you were here."

"No problem. Janis and I introduced ourselves." He glanced back at the girl in the bed and smiled. "Didn't we?"

"Yeah. Reid was telling me about his ranch. He said I could go there sometime."

"If it's all right with you, of course," Reid quickly added to Sharon.

Sharon looked from Janis's shining face to Reid. There was a trace of anxiety in his gray eyes. "Well, yes, I guess so—if you want her to."

"Good. You can both come, maybe this summer, when Janis is feeling better."

"I didn't realize you had a ranch."

He nodded. "My uncle left it to me a few years ago. It's a working ranch, but I have a foreman who runs it for me. I just use if for a hideout."

"Hideout?"

"From the press, the job, my employees."

"I see." Sharon felt like an idiot. It was awkward standing here with Reid and her daughter, trying to make ordinary conversation as if there were no past between them.

"I do hope you'll come. I think you'd like it."

"I'll think about it." Sharon couldn't imagine that he would really want her to come with Janis. It was hard enough for her to believe that he wanted her daughter there. Had Reid Maitland changed so much, or had she always been wrong about him?

"Well, I better go now." Reid turned back to Janis. "You need your rest."

"Okay. I'm glad you came by."

"Me, too. Maybe this evening I could drop in again for a while."

Janis's smile was wide and spontaneous. "Please. I'd like that."

"All right. I will."

He started across the room and stopped, turning toward Sharon. "I—perhaps I could take you down to the cafeteria and buy you a cup of coffee while Janis is napping."

Sharon glanced at Janis. She could see the energy of the past few minutes draining out of her; Janis would need to sleep now, though she didn't know how Reid had known it. "Well—yes, thank you."

He took her arm and guided her out the door. There was an almost formal courtesy in his manner that Sharon was unused to. It was somehow pleasing. She found herself wanting to relax and let all her troubles slide off onto him.

He walked her to the elevator and punched the down button. She glanced up at him. He was watching her. "Were you upset when you found me talking to Janis? I had the feeling you were."

Sharon shifted her attention to the elevator door. His cool gray gaze was too penetrating. She shrugged. "Maybe. A little."

"I'm sorry. I should have waited until you were there, I suppose. But I was eager to see her."

Sharon nodded slightly. "I understand. It was nothing; just a little maternal jealousy. I wished I could have been the one to make her laugh."

"Sometimes it takes someone new to brighten things up, especially with kids."

"You're right, of course. It wasn't a feeling I'm particularly proud of."

"Nothing to feel down about, either. I imagine it's only natural, considering."

"Yeah. Considering."

The elevator came, and they rode down to the cafeteria. By now it was beginning to empty out, and they were able to find a table a good distance from the other occupants of the dining room. Reid bought them coffee and brought it over to the table. Sharon added a packet of cream to hers and stirred it, keeping her eyes on the cup. She still felt odd sitting with Reid, uncomfortable and almost guilty.

"Would you rather I not see Janis anymore? That she not come to visit me at the ranch?"

"No, it's not that." She met his eyes squarely. "If you want to, if she wants to, I can't see that there's any harm. If she makes it through this, I couldn't deny her a pleasure as easy and simple as that. I told her yesterday that I didn't want her relationship with you to be colored by our differences in the past."

"You have a great deal of character," he said musingly. Sharon's head snapped up and she regarded him narrowly, unsure whether he meant what he said or was making fun of her. "Don't look at me like that. I mean it. It sounds stuffy and old-fashioned, I know, but you have integrity. Compassion, generosity."

She smiled faintly, her eyebrows rising. "How noble of me."

He shrugged. "I told you it sounded stuffy." He grinned. "I'm often stuffy, I'm told. My press aide is always telling me I should lighten up, joke around more with the press. She says I come across as too sober and moralistic. Maybe I was raised too seriously; I can't seem to shake it. It's not that I'm puritanical, really. But I don't know any other way to act."

"There's nothing wrong with being serious. But this time I think you're mistaken. I'm quite ordinary, not noble at all. You, of all people, should realize that I don't forgive and forget easily. It's been thirteen years since you and I quarreled."

"That's a diplomatic way to put it."

"But don't you think a person who carries a grudge that long is less than compassionate and generous?"

"It depends on how much provocation you had. Or maybe on what your view of the other person was. I hope I wasn't really as wicked as you thought I was, but I can understand your dislike for the man who turned you away when you were penniless and carrying his brother's child."

"But I nursed my anger; I certainly didn't give you a chance

to make up for it. That's not exactly kindness. I feel guilty
about it. I didn't think about Janis or what was best for her.
I didn't think that maybe you were really interested in her.
I assumed you were motivated solely by pride in your family
name; that because she was a Maitland you thought it would
look bad if you didn't provide for her. And I was scared that
you might try to take her away from me." '   . _

"Take her away from you!" He stared. "No! Why would
you think that? I would never have—you were her mother.
I just wanted to help; I just wanted to—" He made a vague
gesture, searching for the right words. "—to see her some,
to be able to treat her like a niece."

"I'm sorry. That didn't occur to me. Because I was still
so angry with you, I attributed the worst motives to you. And
now—well, you've been so nice about this that I've begun
to wonder if I wasn't wrong about you. And if I was, if you
would have been a real uncle to her, then I've robbed my
daughter of something, haven't I? When I saw the two of
you together today, I was even more aware of that. She
enjoyed being with you. She needs a male relative. You would
have given her life a different dimension. I've wronged her
by denying her that, and I can hardly do so again. So you
see, it isn't 'purity of spirit' that makes me let her see you.
It's guilt."

"You haven't convinced me. All you've shown me is that
you're a mature, sensitive, caring mother." Reid looked at
her. She was exhausted, he thought. Janis had mentioned that
she spent most of her time at the hospital. Her face was too
thin, as well, and he remembered how little she had eaten
the day they'd had lunch together. Reid thought she was
overtaxing herself; it would be doubly difficult to be a single
parent of a desperately ill child. How had she managed to
bear up under it on her own?

He found himself wanting to put his arm around her and
reassure her, to insist that she rest and eat and not expend
every last bit of energy on Janis. But, then, he hadn't the
right to do any of that. Sharon would be the first to tell him
that she wasn't any of his concern.

"You won't let me blacken my character at all, then?" Sharon teased, a smile lurking in her tired eyes.

"Not a bit. Janis has told me the truth about you."

"Oh? And what did she tell you?"

"Things like how much time you spend here at the hospital with her, how much you do for her."

"She's my daughter."

"She says you're a terrific mother—high praise from a teenager."

"Janis is the terrific one."

"Maybe you both are. You must have done an excellent job with her; she's a beautiful kid."

Sharon smiled. "Yes, she is, isn't she?"

"When I went in there, I wondered if she would remind me of Wes. She didn't at first. Then I noticed her hands; they're feminine versions of Wes's hands. My hands. I began to see him in the shape of her mouth and nose. The curve of her eyebrows. She even has an expression, kind of turning up one side of her mouth when she's making fun of something, that's just like Wes."

Tears started in Sharon's eyes. "I know. I've always thought that. It's so strange; she never even saw him."

"But after I talked to her awhile, she became her own person, a unique, sweet girl. I stopped thinking of her just as Wes's child. I liked her for herself." He glanced away, embarrassed at revealing even this much of his feelings.

"Thank you." Sharon looked at him, bemused. Reid Maitland was turning out to be entirely different from what she had imagined.

"The thing is," he went on, "I would like to see Janis again. To visit her when I'm in Dallas, take her out, you know, spend some time with her. I meant it about coming to the ranch. But I'm not trying to capitalize on giving her my kidney. I'll understand if you don't want to encourage her being with me. But I'd like to see her. I don't have much family. I'm divorced, no kids. There's only my mother. Janis is pretty much it. It would mean a lot to me to be able to visit her."

Sharon nodded. "I think it would mean a lot to her, too. I wouldn't deny her the opportunity. It's all right with me, whenever you want to visit."

"Thank you." He laid his hand over hers on the table, surprising her. It was a pleasant sensation; his hand was warm, strong, and masculine. Sharon would have liked to turn her hand over and clasp his; she thought his strength might flow out of his hand and into her, supporting her, giving her courage. He was a man to be relied on, she thought, a man who took care of things. She had always been an independent woman, used to doing things for herself. She had had to be. She liked it that way. But right now, the thought of having someone else to rely on seemed awfully nice. For a moment she wished that she knew Reid well enough to lean on him.

But that was impossible, of course. He wanted to help Janis, but that didn't mean that he wanted to help Janis's mother. She was, after all, nothing to him. Sharon straightened, pulling her hand out from under his, and gave him a tight, brief smile. "There's no need to thank me."

She was a very private person, Reid thought. He understood; so was he. He didn't give his friendship or his love easily; he usually distrusted other people's instantaneous friendliness. He suspected that it was the same with Sharon. He pulled his hand back. He wouldn't push her.

"There's going to be a certain amount of publicity about this," he began, shifting the conversation to a less personal track. "I don't know if you've realized that."

Sharon shrugged. "I hadn't really thought about it until today. But I can see that the media would be interested in a political figure donating one of his organs to help a relative."

He frowned a little. "I'm afraid it won't be quite as simple as that."

"What do you mean?"

"I mean that we aren't a typical family situation. I'm afraid they may seize on a niece that nobody's ever heard of. Some reporters might decide to dig into your past."

"Oh." Sharon felt chilled. She hated the thought of anyone prying into her life.

"I'm sorry. Anything connected to a politician is likely to come under scrutiny. I wish that I could shield you from it, but I can't. I thought about checking into the hospital under an assumed name, but they would have found out somehow, and then my secretiveness would have looked suspicious. I decided it was better to be straightforward."

"Yes. Of course." Sharon shrugged. "Well, I won't like it, but there's nothing to be done. I'll just have to take a little embarrassment; it's not much compared to Janis's health."

Reid gazed at his coffee cup, his thumb tracing the rim. "It may be more than a little embarrassment. My aide warned me that because I'm donating the kidney, because you and Wes weren't married—well, there may be some speculation that Janis is my daughter."

"What? But why?"

"You know—a politician hiding his indiscretions."

Sharon stared. "But—how unfair! You're only trying to help, to be kind."

He smiled. "The press is not always fair, I'm afraid. An illegitimate daughter who's been concealed for years makes a juicier story than helping a niece."

"Well, I'll just tell them that she's Wes's child, not yours."

"Thank you. But that doesn't guarantee that they'll believe you."

Sharon frowned. "I'm sorry. This could hurt your career, couldn't it? I mean, if there are lots of rumors, if people believe them."

"I suppose it could."

"Then you're sacrificing even more than I thought. You knew when you agreed to do it that it could hurt your career, didn't you?"

"I didn't think about it until Phil pointed it out to me. But it doesn't make any difference. A little dirt on a political image hardly stacks up against a child's life." He smiled at her; he rather enjoyed the warm concern for him in her eyes. "Don't worry about me. It'll blow over before you know it. These things are always a tempest in a tea pot. In a week something new will come along, and they'll be chasing off after it. Within three months, no one will remember. Besides, my press assistant is very good. Susan'll probably manage to make me come out looking like a hero."

"That's the way you should look," Sharon put in stoutly.

His smile broadened. "I would never have expected to hear those words from you."

Color tinged Sharon's cheeks. "I'm sorry. I was very wrong about you."

"Not as wrong as I was about you the first time we met. I can never make up for my cruelty to you then."

Sharon shook her head. "You don't need to. I can understand why you reacted the way you did. People who have lots of money must have to be on their guard against people trying to con them out of it. You didn't know me; you had no way of knowing that I wasn't conning you. We were both very upset; it wasn't a good time for either of us to have discussed it."

"Then you've forgiven me?"

"I don't know that I'm anyone to forgive anyone else. I've made too many mistakes in my own life. But, no, I don't hold any hard feelings against you anymore." She smiled, realizing with some surprise that she actually didn't feel the old grudge against him any longer.

"Good. I'm glad."

"It's probably a relief to get rid of the bad feelings." Admitting that Reid hadn't been totally in the wrong years ago and that she had unfairly nursed a grudge against him made her feel lighter, freer—almost as if she had been released. She had gone to Maitland because her daughter needed him, but now she realized that in helping Janis, Reid had helped her, too. She was no longer bound to the chains of the past.

She rose. "I better get back to Janis." She held out her hand to him. "Thank you for the coffee . . . and everything."

He shook her hand. It was small inside his, but firm, as honest and straightforward as she was. He watched her walk away across the cafeteria. She was a lovely woman and unlike most women he knew. There was no maneuvering in her, no gamesmanship, no artful pretense. He wondered what it would be like to be loved by a woman like that. A woman who gave of herself and lived her feelings, who cared with all her heart. Reid was afraid he would never know.

The surgery was scheduled for eight o'clock the following morning. That evening Reid stopped in for a brief chat with Janis. Sharon walked down to the soft drink machines and bought a cola to give them a few minutes alone. He didn't stay long after she returned. He understood how easily Janis tired. Janis was keyed up, her pale face eager, yet strained, but a nurse brought in a sedative for her, and soon afterward she fell asleep.

Sharon sat in the chair beside her bed for a few minutes, watching her sleep, keenly aware that there was a possibility she would never again be able to do it. Janis could die on the operating table; she could die of complications anytime after that. Her body could reject the foreign kidney, and she would sink into complete renal failure. Sharon leaned forward, resting her face on her hands. Janis was the jewel of her life, the precious entity around which the rest of it revolved. From the moment Sharon had learned of her existence, she had shaped her world around the child. The thought that she might lose her filled her with a pain and fear almost too great to bear. She had faced many frightening times in her life, but even the darkest of them hadn't begun to compare with this.

She spent the night curled up in the large, padded chair in the corner of the room. She couldn't leave Janis. Sharon slept little in the awkward position, but she knew that she would have slept very little in her own bed at home, too. Periodically throughout the long night, she got out of the chair and walked

over to Janis's bedside to look down at her. She wanted to
cry and beg Janis not to leave her. She walked to the window
and gazed out at the darkness. Leaning her head against the
cool glass she prayed.

Sharon awoke early the next morning, feeling rumpled and
ragged and utterly weary. Janis was awake not long afterward.
She was jumpy and talkative, and Sharon struggled to keep
up a calm and cheerful front, hoping it would soothe Janis.
Soon they shooed Sharon out of the room while they prepped
Janis for surgery, and a short while later, two attendants
transferred Janis onto a gurney and wheeled her from the
room. Sharon walked down the hallway with her, holding
her hand, to the elevators. They stood, waiting. Sharon wasn't
sure she could let go of Janis's hand when the time came.
Janis looked up at her sleepily, the pre-surgery tranquilizer
taking effect.

"Mommy?" Her tongue was thick. Sharon's heart twisted
at her use of the childhood name.

"Yes, sweetie?"

"I love you."

"I love you, too, sweetheart."

"Won't it be nice? Afterward . . ."

"Oh yes." It was a struggle to make her lips curve upward.
*Please, God, don't let her die. Anything, anything, but don't
let her die.* "It will be great."

The elevator doors opened, and the attendants wheeled
Janis inside. Her hand slipped from Sharon's. Sharon stood,
watching, her hands knotting together in front of her. The
thick metal doors came together, shutting Janis off from her
view. Sharon turned numbly and walked back down the hall
to Janis's room. She sat down in the chair and began to wait.

7

The hours of Janis's operation seemed interminable to Sharon. Hollis joined her in Janis's room soon after they wheeled Janis up to surgery. Sharon was grateful for Hollis's presence, but even her conversation couldn't distract her. Soon Hollis herself lapsed into silence. After a few hours they went up to the surgery waiting room, where the doctors would come when it was over. The room was half-filled with people, and the air was thick with cigarette smoke. The room was quiet; the few people who were talking among themselves spoke in low, hushed tones. They were all waiting in fear, like herself, Sharon thought.

She glanced around the room, wondering if any of these people were waiting for Reid. She didn't see his mother; she would have recognized that white-haired aristocratic woman even though she'd seen her only once, years ago, at Wes's funeral. Nor did any of the women look to be the age or type to be romantically involved with Reid Maitland. Once, shortly after Sharon arrived in the waiting room, Reid's press assistant, Susan O'Brien, called to ask if there was any word about his condition yet. Sharon promised to call her back when she heard anything.

It was rather sad, she thought, glancing around the room. Reid was a busy, influential congressman, constantly surrounded by people. Yet there seemed to be no one who cared enough about him to sit here waiting for the results of his surgery. Reid had said he was divorced and had almost no family. But one would think that there would have been someone close enough to him to worry. Yet not even his mother was there. Sharon remembered how Wes had talked about growing up lonely in a cold household. Reid had grown up in the same place, among the same people. He had probably known no more affection and warmth than Wes. Although she would never have believed it possible Sharon found herself actually feeling sorry for Reid Maitland.

It was nearly mid-afternoon when Dr. Ebersol and Dr. Morris, the surgeon who had headed the transplant team, stepped into the waiting room. Sharon jumped up, and Hollis stood up beside her, reaching out to take Sharon's hand. Sharon gripped Hollis's hand so tightly that her ring bit into her finger, but Hollis hardly noticed it. Her attention, like Sharon's, was all on the doctors.

"Mrs. Thompson." The surgeon smiled.

Relief washed through Sharon so strongly her knees almost buckled. He was smiling! "Yes?"

"Perhaps we should step out into the hall."

Sharon followed him out the door, with Hollis behind her. Dr. Morris began to speak. "The operation went well. Your daughter is in ICU now."

"May I see her?"

"For a few minutes. She won't be awake, however. It will be some time before she regains consciousness."

"She's all right?"

"She came through the surgery fine. Of course, there's always the possibility of rejection of the donated kidney. I'm sure Dr. Ebersol has discussed this with you." Sharon nodded. "But right now, all her signs are stable; she went through surgery without a hitch."

"Thank God." Tears welled in Sharon's eyes. She wanted to laugh and burst into tears at the same time. "How is Mr. Maitland?"

"He's in recovery. His surgery was over before we finished Janis's. They should be bringing him back to his room before long, if you'd like to see him."

"Thank you."

"I'll drop in to check on your daughter later, as will Dr. Ebersol and Dr. Youngman. If you have any questions, one of us will be happy to answer them. I realize that right now you're probably feeling a little fuzzy. After awhile you may think of something you want to ask us."

Sharon nodded. He was right. She felt numb and shaken, almost in a state of shock. It was all she could do to remain on her feet and not dissolve into tears.

"Well, then, good day, Mrs. Thompson." He nodded in Hollis's direction.

"Good-bye. Thank you. Thank you."

They watched the doctor walk away from them. Sharon turned to Hollis, who was grinning like a Cheshire cat. "She made it." Hollis laughed and threw out her arms.

Sharon flew into them, laughing, tears streaming down her face, and squeezed Hollis tightly. "She's all right! She's all right!"

Hollis stayed with Sharon the rest of the afternoon, so that by the time she left she was right in the middle of rush hour traffic. It took her an inordinately long time to get home, and when she arrived, she found Jack already there, reading a newspaper and waiting for her in the upstairs sitting room.

"Hi." She trailed into the room, dropping her purse by the door.

He looked up and smiled in his slow, charming way. "Hi, shug, you look exhausted."

"I am tired," Hollis admitted, rolling her head to get out the kinks in her neck. She plopped down on the love seat beside him, and Jack turned to her and began to massage her shoulders and neck. "Mmm, thanks, that's heavenly."

Jack bent his head and kissed her hair. He wished he could take away her weariness, just as he wished he could shield her from every pain and adversity. After nine years of marriage, he still felt that way about her; she was the sexiest, most beautiful woman he knew, and he loved her far more than was wise.

"How is Janis?"

"All right for the moment. She handled the surgery okay, the doctor said. So one hurdle is over with. Now they have to get her body past rejecting the kidney. She's in ICU, still sedated."

"How's Sharon?"

"Pretty rocky. She's relieved and happy that the transplant went all right, but she knows that Jan's still in a lot of danger. She'll feel better, I think, when Jan opens her eyes and talks to her. Sharon really needs some rest. There are dark circles under her eyes, and I know she hasn't slept well since this whole thing began. She's too thin. If she doesn't watch it, she'll be sick."

"You don't look as if you had a particularly pleasant time yourself."

Hollis grimaced and groaned when his probing fingers hit a particularly stiff spot. "It's unbelievably tiring to sit and wait in anxiety. You don't do anything, but it wears you out. I was worried, but there wasn't a thing I could do. It's so frustrating."

Jack leaned back, pulling Hollis into the circle of his arm. She rested her head against his shoulder and closed her eyes.

"You love them a lot, don't you?" Jack asked softly.

"Yeah, I guess so." Hollis sighed. "Sharon's the only good friend I've ever had." Her voice turned wry. "You know me; female friendships are not my forte."

He grinned. "I've noticed you seem to have an affinity for the male of the species."

"Most women get along with me because they're scared not to. Scared that I'll whisk their lousy husband or boyfriend away from them or that they'll appear bitchy and jealous if they aren't my friends."

"Or maybe it's because you keep everyone at arm's length."

Hollis was silent for a moment. "Maybe." She sat up. "Well, I don't want to, but I suppose we better get dressed."

"For what?"

"The Robinsons' party. Did you forget?"

Jack rolled his eyes. "Oh, hell! Let's not go. You're tired. The Robinsons are bores."

"He's also one of your senior executives. Everyone will think he's out of favor if we don't show up. There'll be rumors all over the office tomorrow, and he'll be quaking in his boots, wondering what he's done wrong."

"All right. All right. Let's get it over with, then."

There wasn't time for the long, soaking bath Hollis longed for, so she made do with a quick shower. She sat down to make up her face again. Gazing at herself in the mirror, she brushed eyeshadow over her lids, blending the colors artistically into muted beauty. She began to line her eyelids with a fine pencil, and as she stared into her own eyes, suddenly they filled with water.

Hollis tossed down the pencil and turned away, drawing a breath and forcing back the tears. She would not cry; she would not. Janis was going to be fine; Sharon would be happy again. There was nothing to cry about. It was just the draining weariness that made her want to cry. Just the anxiety that had worn away her usual defenses, slicing into the great well of sadness within her.

When she had swallowed back the tears, she returned to her task. She didn't think of begging off from the party and throwing herself across the bed for a good cry. That wasn't her way. Instead she just went on, as she always did, covering up the hole inside her, pushing back the threatening darkness. There was nothing she could do about her childlessness, she told herself, and, *damn it*, she would not sit around and cry about it; she would go on and live her life.

By the time she joined her husband downstairs, she was

stunning in a simple crinkle gold sheath, gathered at one hip. Only someone close to her would have noticed the tightness in her face or the dark quality in her eyes. Jack saw it, but he said nothing; he knew she wouldn't welcome his comment.

The party was as boring as Jack had predicted, but they weathered it with the easy social charm that both of them possessed. No one would have guessed that with each passing moment Hollis's heart grew heavier inside her, until it was all she could do to keep a smile painted on her face. Jack watched her, concerned. They never should have come tonight, not with the nerve-racking day Hollis had had. He should have insisted that they stay home, made up some reason why he couldn't go. As it was, all he could do was make their appearance as short as was politely possible. Within an hour, he was saying good-bye to their hosts and whisking Hollis out the front door.

She was silent all the way home. Usually she would have been laughing and wittily dissecting the party with him. When they stopped for a light, Jack glanced at her. She was leaning back against the seat, her eyes closed, and he could see the crystal gleam of tears on her cheeks. His heart wrenched inside him. When they reached the house, she slipped out of the car and hurried inside, almost running up the stairs to their room. Jack followed her, catching up to her on the stairs. He took her arm and turned her around to face him. Her face was crumpled up, and she was crying, trying to choke back the sobs.

"Honey, what is it? What's wrong? You said Janis was doing well."

"It's—it's not that." She tried to pull away from him.

Jack sighed. "Damn it, Hollis, don't turn away. Tell me what's wrong. Let me help you."

"You can't!" she shrieked, and she began to cry in horrible, racking sobs.

"Oh, sweetheart." He wrapped his arms around her and held her tightly. Hollis clutched his shirtfront, burying her face in his chest. It was physically painful to him to hear the wretched, rusty sound of her crying. "Baby, it's okay. It's okay. Tell me what it is. I'll take care of it."

She shuddered against him, crying and crying, and he held her. He knew how hard it was for her to cry, how humiliated and powerless it made her feel. At least she had come to trust him enough over the years to sometimes let down and cry in front of him. Hollis had once told him that he was the only person who had seen her cry since she was a teenager.

Finally her tears stopped, and she leaned against him quiescently, exhausted by the emotional bout. Jack slipped an arm beneath her legs and lifted her, carrying her up the last few steps and along the hall into their bedroom. He laid her softly on the bed, then sat down beside her, smoothing her hair back from her face.

"What is it, Hol? You can tell me; it's just ole Jack."

She gave him a watery smile and took one of his hands between both of hers. Her hands were freezing, and her motions were slow and oddly remote; she seemed almost to go into shock whenever she finally broke down and cried this way. "Ole Jack," she repeated, her voice uneven. "Ole Jack. Why'd you marry me? You deserve better."

"Are you kidding? You're exactly what I deserve. More than that, you're what I want. You know that."

"I must look awful."

He smiled. "You look beautiful. You always do."

"You always had a way about you." She wet her lips, then sighed.

"What's the matter?"

"I'm such a mess. Inside, I mean."

"Why?"

"I can't—I can't convince myself to—give up."

"Give up? What are you talking about? Why should you give up?"

"Today—" She let out a long, shuddering breath. "Today I was so worried about Janis. And I realized: She's the closest thing I'll ever have to a daughter."

"Oh, Hollis." His face turned soft and sad, and suddenly he wanted to cry, too.

"I'll never have a baby. I can't even adopt one! Goddamn it!" She slammed one fist down into the bed and pounded it again and again. "They'll never give me a baby."

"That's not true. Look at how much we can give a child; they consider things like that."

"Yeah, but the doctor said it was physically *possible* for me to have a baby. They'll give the babies to someone who doesn't have any chance at all. Those women in the adoption agencies look at me, and they think I won't be a good mother. I know they do. They think, she's only interested in money and clothes and good times. I can tell. And they're probably right; I probably wouldn't be a good mother. I just *want* to be one so bad!"

"You'll be a terrific mother." He squeezed her hand hard. "Don't you dare say anything different. You're the only woman I'd pick to raise my child. We'll get our chance; it'll just take time."

"I want a baby now! I want to hold him and play with him. I'm dying inside. I've been trying to have a baby for two years! I don't want to wait any longer."

"I didn't realize you felt so strongly about it. After that thing with the surrogate mother fell through, I thought you had accepted it, that you were going to wait until one of the agencies—Why didn't you tell me?"

"What could you do?" Hollis looked at him, her eyes pools of sadness. "What can anybody do? Even money and power can't give me a baby." She looked away, and her voice dropped to a whisper. "It's because of what I did. It's punishment."

"Because you had the abortion?" Hollis nodded. "Sweetheart, you were only sixteen years old. You were scared and unhappy. Anybody could have made that mistake."

"Sharon didn't."

"Sharon was two years older than that. She also had a very good friend who helped her through it."

"No. It was because she's a better person. She knew what was the right thing to do. She would have done the same thing even if I hadn't been there. Even if she'd been only sixteen.'' Hollis rolled over onto her side away from him. ''I wouldn't admit it to anyone but you, 'cause you know me like I am—I'm wicked.''

''You're wicked to do this to yourself. And I want you to stop it right now.'' He lay down on the bed behind her and wrapped his arms around her. ''Do you know what you would say if someone else talked about herself the way you just did? I can tell you, exactly. You'd say, 'What a goddamn crock.' Wouldn't you?''

Hollis had to smile a little. ''Maybe.''

''Definitely. It's not punishment. It's a sad, sorry quirk of fate, that's all.''

''It doesn't change anything. I still won't ever have a baby. I know it's crazy to want it so bad when I can't have it. But sometimes I think about holding a baby, and my arms and chest and heart just *ache*, I want it so much. I can almost feel him there. I want to touch his skin and play with his toes and watch him smile and babble. All of that! Damn it, damn it, damn it!'' She struck her fist against the bed. ''It's not fair. I read all the time about people hurting their kids, even killing them. Killing them! And I think, why in the hell do they have children, and I can't have one? Everywhere I go, I see pregnant women, and I hate them all. I think, I could give a child everything. Everything!''

''I know you could.'' He kissed her hair, and rested his head against hers. ''We'll get a surrogate mother again.''

''No. She might back out, like the other one did.''

''I can afford to lose the money. We'll find one who'll follow through eventually.''

''I can't. I can't go through that again—getting my hopes up and then having them crushed. It's—I couldn't take it.''

''Then we'll get one another way. I swear it. I'm not going to let you be miserable like this.''

''Oh, Jack. Even you can't give me a baby.''

''The hell I can't.'' His voice was low, but fierce. ''I'll pull every string I know; I'll spend whatever it takes. Just give me a little time.''

Warmth spread through Hollis's chest. She could almost

believe he would do it for her. When Jack Lacey went after something, nothing stopped him. She didn't know of anything yet that he'd wanted and hadn't gotten. Including her.

She turned in his arms and snuggled into him. He kissed the top of her head. "I promise," he whispered. "I promise."

Sharon sat in the ICU waiting room, staring blankly at the television. A picture flickered across the screen, but the volume was turned too low for her to hear. Sharon and the other four occupants of the room neither noticed nor cared. Sharon had been in the same position ever since Hollis left late this afternoon. She was exhausted, and her mind was blank, but her nerves sizzled like high-voltage wires.

It seemed like years since Janis's surgery was over, but she had not opened her eyes. Sharon had been in to see her for five minutes every hour, as the ICU rules allowed. Janis had looked lifeless and frighteningly frail in her bed, with tubes running in and out of her and machines and stands holding plastic bags of liquid grouped around the head of her bed. Sharon had cried again each time she saw her.

"Ms. Thompson?"

Sharon's head whipped around to the doorway, where the voice had spoken. A nurse stood there. "Yes?" Sharon's voice barely came out. Her stomach froze with fear. She had come to tell her Janis was dying.

"Your daughter just woke up. I thought you might like to see her."

Sharon shivered as relief washed through her. She jumped up, her reflexes a few beats slow. "Yes. Yes, of course. Thank you."

She hurried down the hall to Janis's room. When she reached the room she entered cautiously. Janis slowly turned her head toward her. Her eyes were vague, but they were open. "I'm thirsty," she croaked.

"I'm sorry." Sharon came up to the bed and slipped her hand around the one of Janis's that had no needle taped into it. Tears welled in her eyes. "I don't know if you can have any water. I'll ask the nurse as I leave. They won't let me stay long, you know."

Janis wet her lips clumsily and made a little movement with her head that might have been a nod. Her eyes fluttered closed and opened again. "Am I that bad?"

"What?"

"Crying."

"Oh." Sharon smiled. Her tears flowed even faster. "No. You look wonderful. I'm just happy to see you awake."

"Crazy."

"I know." Sharon swallowed. She wanted to babble and cry and laugh. She could feel her control slipping away in the aftermath of the fear and waiting. "You did great. The doctors told me that the transplant was a success. All you have to do is lie there and get strong again. Oh, Janny." She squeezed Janis's fingers.

"Janny." Janis smiled a little.

"I haven't called you that in years, have I?" Sharon brushed her tears away with her hand. "You look beautiful. I wish I could stay with you, but the nurse is signaling that I have to go. I love you. I'm so happy."

"Love you," Janis murmured, her eyes drifting closed.

Sharon left the room and walked down the hall. She was too shaken and excited to return to the waiting room. For the first time in months hope flooded her, sharp and piercingly sweet. Somehow she hadn't quite believed that the operation had been a success until she saw her daughter conscious again. But now she knew; she was sure. Janis was going to live. She would be healthy again. Sharon wanted to shout, to run, to throw herself down in a paroxysm of tears.

She went down the elevators and walked aimlessly through the halls until she found herself in front of the chapel. She stepped inside. Candles flickered in one corner below a statue of the Madonna. Sharon wished she were Catholic so that she could light a candle; it seemed so symbolic and purposeful. Instead she went to one of the short pews and sat down on the end. She wrapped her arms around herself and cried, rocking, and in her mind, over and over, ran the words "Thank you."

When she left the chapel, Sharon went up to Reid's room. She had to share her elation with someone. Besides, she wanted to see how he was doing after his own surgery.

Reid was asleep when she tapped softly on the door and stepped inside, but he opened his eyes at the sound of her entrance and looked at her. He smiled. "Sharon."

"Hello, Reid." Her voice was hushed. She walked closer to him. He was pale, and an assortment of tubes ran out of him, too. "How are you?"

"All right." He shrugged as if to dismiss any concern over his health. "A little sore. How is Janis?"

"She just came to. She spoke to me." Sharon couldn't keep the tears from starting in her eyes again; she would have thought that by now she was all cried out. "I—I really think she's going to come through it all right. Dr. Morris told me that the surgery went well."

"I'm glad. She'll be okay. I understand there have been a lot of successful kidney transplants."

"Yes. You're right." Sharon paused. She didn't know quite what to say to him. He looked so different lying there in the hospital bed. She glanced around the room. It struck her as odd once again that there was no one there visiting him. "Your office called, a Ms. O'Brien."

"My press assistant."

"Yes. She wanted to know how the operation went. At the time you were still in surgery, but I called her back later to tell her you were okay."

"Thank you."

"Well, I'd better go. I don't want to tire you."

"You aren't tiring me. Please stay for a little bit at least. The pain medication is wearing off, and it helps to have someone to talk to."

"Would you like me to get a nurse?"

"No. They'll bring the stuff in soon. Just sit and talk to me a little."

"All right." Sharon pulled a straight-back chair closer to the bed and sat down. For a moment they just looked at each other.

"It's hard as hell to think of something to say when you're trying to cheer someone up, isn't it?" Reid commented.

Sharon grinned. "Yes. But I'm afraid it's not that. My brain is fuzzy from sitting around waiting all day."

"You ought to go home and rest."

"I can't. Not with Janis still critical."

He shifted his position, grimacing. Sharon stood up.

"Could I help you? Move the bed a little or put pillows behind you?"

"All right. I'd like to sit up some so that I can see you better."

From Janis's long stay in the hospital, Sharon was familiar with the buttons operating the bed, and she brought the head of his bed up partway, then arranged two pillows behind his shoulders and head. He smiled. "You're a very maternal sort, aren't you?"

Sharon shrugged, embarrassed. "Force of habit."

"I didn't mean it as a criticism. It's nice, actually, to have someone fuss over me."

Sharon cast him a doubting look. "Uh-huh, and you're trying to make me believe you don't have a lot of women fussing over you?"

"Not really. Most women I meet spend their time trying to impress me."

Sharon knew she wouldn't have the first idea how to do that. Not, of course, that she would try. She glanced away, suddenly uncomfortable. "I should go now. You'll wear yourself out if you continue to talk."

"Then you do the talking. I'll listen."

She glanced at him. "Talk about what?"

"I don't know. What do you talk to Janis about all the time she's in a hospital bed?"

She chuckled. "Movies, movie stars, rock singers, boys

—the kind of things a teenager's interested in. I wouldn't think you'd want to know about how wonderful Tom Cruise is.''

"Probably not. What about your life? Tell me about you."

"I'm very ordinary."

"You're an artist."

She nodded. "I work with stained glass—and some etched or beveled glass.'' She smiled a little, reminiscently. "I've always loved art. My grandmother was an artist—not professionally, of course. That wouldn't have been acceptable. She was a housewife. But in her spare time she painted and drew. I remember I loved to go to her house to her sewing room —that's what she and Grandy called it, but what she really did in there was paint, mostly. It smelled good to me: paints and linseed oil, turpentine, banana oil, charcoal fixative. Not very pleasant odors, actually, but I loved them. Grandmama taught me how to sketch, how to use oils and watercolors and pastels. When I was little, she'd let me fingerpaint to my heart's content. She'd lay newspapers down on the floor and let me at it. No one else would. Mother was always too concerned about my clothes.''

Sharon paused and glanced at Reid. His eyelids were drifting closed. She smiled. "I can see my conversation is scintillating.''

His lips curved a little. "Not boring. You're just restful.''

Sharon stood up. "I'll let you sleep now. I'll come back tomorrow to see you—that is, if you don't mind.''

"Of course not. I'd like it. Thank you."

She went to the edge of his bed. "No. I'm the one who should thank you. You've given Janis her life. I can never repay you.''

"Don't. I don't need thanks. I—'' He stopped and sighed, too sleepy to collect his thoughts. He shook his head. "I'm glad Janis came through all right.''

Sharon smiled, swallowing against the lump of emotion in her throat. "Me, too. And I'm glad you did, too. Good night, Reid.''

"G' night.'' His lids were closed by the time she reached

the door. Sharon looked back at him and smiled. Then she
started toward the elevators that would take her back up to
her daughter's room.

Around midnight one of the nurses finally persuaded
Sharon to go home and sleep, pointing out that Janis would
probably sleep through the night and that it would be more
reasonable to be at the hospital the next day. Sharon knew
she needed to sleep if she were going to get through the next
few days; nevertheless, she hated to leave. She felt guilty,
almost as if she were abandoning Janis. It didn't matter that
if she stayed at the hospital, she could be with Janis only five
minutes every hour and would not be in Janis's room if she
should get worse and die. Deep inside her was a dark, primitive fear that if she slept, death would creep up on Janis and
seize her.

However, Sharon forced herself to go home soon after
midnight. She was utterly exhausted, and as soon as she
walked into her room at Hollis's house, she flopped down
on her bed, not even bothering to undress. Almost instantly
she was asleep, and for the first time in almost two weeks
she slept deeply, dreamlessly, throughout the night.

She woke up late the next morning, curled up into a ball
on top of the covers. She blinked, her mind adjusting to where
she was. Suddenly she sat bolt upright. The sun was streaming
through the windows! It was late; she had overslept.

Shedding her clothes as she went, she hurried into the
bathroom and took a quick shower. She dressed quickly and
pulled her hair back, securing it with a wide barrette. She
didn't take time for makeup or breakfast, just grabbed her
purse and ran out to her car.

It was almost eleven o'clock when she reached the hospital.
She rushed upstairs to the ICU, heart pounding, supersti-
tiously sure that because she had overslept, Janis's condition
would have gotten worse. Instead, the nurse told her that
Janis had slept the night through and that her vital signs were

stable. She had awakened once that morning and said a few words to one of the nurses, then slipped back into sleep.

Sharon went in to see her; Janis was sleeping, so Sharon stood and gazed at her daughter, trying to decide if it was only her imagination or if Janis's color really was better this morning. After a few minutes she left her daughter's bed and took up her post in the waiting room.

Calmer and more in possession of her senses, she chatted for a few minutes with one of the other occupants of the waiting room, an older woman whose husband had suffered a heart attack and who was being held for observation, then read the newspaper. She noticed a small article on one of the inside pages that stated that Representative Reid Maitland was in Baylor Hospital, having undergone surgery for undisclosed reasons. His condition was listed as good. Sharon read the article through twice. She supposed the information must have come from the press release that Reid's assistant had sent out yesterday. It made no mention of Janis, for which she was glad.

During the afternoon Hollis dropped by and spent a couple of hours with her. Janis was awake two of the times Sharon was allowed in to see her, and they talked a little. Janis looked weary and in pain, but her mind was clear, and her spirits seemed good, if somewhat subdued.

After dinner Sharon went down to Reid's room. There was a young man sitting beside Reid's bed, a pad of paper on his lap. Both men stopped talking and turned toward the door when Sharon walked in. A smile spread across Reid's face. "Sharon. How good to see you."

The young man stood up, nodding at her politely.

"Sharon, this is Curt Vanicek. He works in my office here in Dallas. Curt, this is Sharon Thompson. Janis's mother."

Sharon and Curt exchanged hellos. Sharon walked over to the bed, smiling teasingly. "Working already?" she asked. "Didn't you know that people only one day out of major surgery are supposed to rest?"

The smile hadn't left Reid's face as he looked at her. "Not working, exactly. Curt brought me a few messages."

Curt motioned toward the chair. "Sit down, please. I was about to leave. I'm sure Reid will enjoy your company a lot more than mine."

"Thank you."

The young man slipped the pad and pen into his briefcase and snapped it closed. "Good-bye, Reid. See you tomorrow."

Reid nodded. "Sure. Thanks."

"It was nice to meet you, ma'am," he added, nodding toward Sharon, and left the room.

"I hope I didn't run him off."

Reid shook his head. "He was through with business, and Vanicek isn't one for small talk. Besides, he's right. I'd rather talk to you."

Sharon smiled. "Thank you."

"Although you may not want to talk to me, after what I have to tell you."

"What?" Sharon straightened uneasily.

"Reporters have been calling the hospital, my offices, and my home all day, trying to get information about why I'm in the hospital. The main thing Curt came to tell me was that Susan—my press aide—has decided we ought to issue another, more detailed press release."

"You mean one about Janis and the transplant?"

"Yeah. Curt brought me the release to approve. I told him to go ahead; they'll give it out late this afternoon. Susan thought it would cause less stir if we told them about the transplant instead of trying to hide it. That only arouses their curiosity and makes them think there's more to it than there is."

"You said that Janis is your niece?"

"Yes."

Sharon drew a breath. "That Wes and I weren't married?"

"Of course not. It isn't pertinent."

"They'll find out quickly enough."

"Probably." He sighed. "I'm sorry. I'm afraid that the reporters will start hounding you for a comment. They're damnably persistent and have absolutely no compunction about asking one anything."

"What—what do you think I should say to them? I don't know how to handle it; I've never even talked to a reporter before."

"You could refuse to comment on the whole thing. After all, you are a private citizen; you have no obligation to them. Or you could decide what you want to say and then say nothing else. The worst thing, I think, would be for you to participate in any give-and-take with them, any answering of questions. Don't try to justify or explain, because they can pull you in and get you so turned around and confused that you wind up saying things you never intended. I wish I could protect you from them altogether."

"It's not your fault."

He raised his eyebrows. "No? If I weren't who I am, they wouldn't even ask you a question. You might want to stay somewhere else for a while, so you could avoid them at your house. But there's no way you can avoid them outside the hospital."

Sharon looked at him, startled. "Do you think it will be that bad?"

"I don't know. It's possible. If a big news story breaks, probably not. They'll harass you for a little while, then go on to something else. But if it catches their interest or if the rest of the news is slow . . . well, they could hound you everywhere you go. Perhaps I better give you a driver who could get you through the press, as well."

Sharon stared. She found what Reid said hard to believe. She had seen mobs of reporters surrounding a person, almost attacking him, in movies and television shows, but surely that was exaggerated. It didn't happen in real life—at least not to someone like her. Perhaps reporters pursued Reid Maitland with zest, but she could hardly imagine them doing so with her. She was, after all, an ordinary person, not the kind of woman people were eager to read about. The reporters might ask her a few questions, which she didn't relish. But that was something she could weather, and she was sure they would soon lose interest in her and her story.

"That's very kind of you, but, really, I don't think it's necessary," Sharon told him. Imagine her with a driver/bodyguard!

Reid studied her. "I hope you're right. But, frankly, I'm afraid you're in for a rude awakening."

They went on to talk about something else, and Reid's warnings slipped out of Sharon's mind. But she remembered them the next morning when the telephone rang at 6:30, jarring her awake. On the intercom Hollis's sleepy voice informed Sharon that the call was for her. Sharon picked up the receiver, her heart racing, sure that the hospital was calling with bad news about Janis.

A voice on the other end of the line said, "Ms. Thompson?"

"Yes."

"This is Bryce Anderson, with the *Daily Express*."

"What?" For a moment she was in utter confusion.

"I wanted to talk with you about your daughter's transplant."

"Oh." Her brain cleared. Irritation surged through her. She wanted to bark that he had nearly scared her to death, but she swallowed her hostility. "I'm sorry. I have no time for interviews. I'll be at the hospital with my daughter all day."

"I'd be happy to talk with you there."

"No. I'm sorry. Really, I don't have any time."

"Rumors are already starting to fly. This would be your chance to tell the straight story."

"No, thank you. I have to go now."

"Then let me ask you a few questions now, while I have you on the phone."

"I don't think so. Good-bye, Mr.—uh—"

She couldn't think of his name, and as she faltered, he

asked quickly, "Were you married to Wesley Maitland, Representative Maitland's deceased brother?"

Sharon hung up the phone. She flopped back on the bed, hugging her pillow to her, and gazed up at the ceiling. Her stomach was jumping. Well, it had begun.

8

Sharon got two more calls after that: one from a local newspaper and one from a weekly tabloid offering her $5,000 for her personal story. After that, Hollis put the phone on the answering machine.

When she drove out of the Laceys' electronically controlled gates later that morning, she saw a car parked across the street with a woman leaning against it. Sharon stopped the car to close the gates with the remote control, and the woman hurried over and knocked on her car window. "Miss Thompson? I want to ask you a few questions about your daughter's transplant."

Sharon shook her head. "No. I have nothing to say." She pressed down on the gas pedal, half-afraid the woman would grab her door handle and hang on. Instead, the woman hurried back to her own car. Good heavens, did she intend to follow her? Sharon speeded up, feeling thoroughly unnerved.

She lost sight of the car and breathed a sigh of relief; but when she pulled into the hospital parking lot, she saw the woman standing beside the emergency room exit. Of course.

She wouldn't have to follow her; the press knew what hospital Reid and Janis were in.

Sharon left the parking lot and drove to one farther away on the other side of the hospital. As she passed the front door of the hospital, she noticed a car with a long antenna and the name of one of the local television stations written on its side. Feeling furtive and beleaguered, she parked her car and darted in another side entrance. She was grateful she'd been around the hospital long enough that she knew its layout.

She reached the ICU waiting room without running into another reporter. A man and the woman with whom she had chatted the day before were already there, and Sharon exchanged a few pleasantries with the woman before she went down to Janis's room.

Janis was awake and seemed better. She was rather cranky, but Sharon seized on that with hope. Before this, Janis had been too weak to gripe about anything; she must be getting stronger. Dr. Morris came by while Sharon was there, and after he examined Janis, he walked out into the hall with Sharon.

"I'm encouraged by Janis's condition, Mrs. Thompson. She seems to be responding well; so far the anti-rejection drugs are working."

"Really?" Sharon beamed. "Oh, Doctor, I'm so glad to hear you say that! You're hopeful, then?"

He paused, weighing his words. "Let's say that I'm guardedly optimistic."

Her eyes glowed. "Thank you. I'm so happy." She laughed a little. "I don't know what to do, I'm so happy."

"Well, it's not yet time to celebrate. But I think you can hope."

"I will. Believe me, I will."

After that, even the threat of the news media lurking around didn't bother her. She hurried down to tell Reid the good news. She found him up and shuffling across his room, aided by a nurse.

"They tell me I've been lazy too long." He grinned.

"I should think so—lying on your back for two days in a

row.'' She tsk-tsked, her eyes dancing. Personally, she thought he looked worn out and belonged in bed, but she had become expert at keeping conversations about illness on a light plane—otherwise, she and Janis would have sunk into melancholy days ago.

The nurse helped Reid into the bed, and he leaned back with a sigh. ''All I did was walk over to a chair, sit up a few minutes, and walk back, and I feel like I've run a marathon.''

''You can hardly expect to be physically fit right after surgery.''

''I guess not. But I thought I'd do better than this. I'm never sick.''

''That's your problem. People who are always healthy don't know what to do when they're ill.''

''Maybe you're right.'' He settled into his pillows more comfortably. ''How's Janis?''

Sharon was happy to pass on the doctor's carefully worded optimism regarding Janis. Reid thought that the glow on her face could light up half of Dallas. He liked watching the play of emotions across her face. She was so open and straightforward, unembarrassed to talk about her feelings. He wondered what it was like to love with such intensity and honesty; he wondered what it was like to *be* loved that way.

Finally Sharon came to a halt, smiling shamefacedly. ''I'm sorry. I've been rattling on, haven't I? It must have tired you.''

''No. I enjoyed it. I'm glad to hear about Janis.'' He paused. ''And I'm glad to see you so happy.''

She smiled. ''Thank you.''

Sharon stayed a little longer, asking after Reid's health and discussing the efforts of the press to contact them. ''Give it a few days,'' Reid advised. ''It will get better; they'll find another story to pursue.''

But Sharon wasn't so certain, especially when she started out of the hospital late that evening and saw two reporters lounging in front of the main entrance. Quickly she stepped back inside and left by the side entrance.

   The next morning each Dallas newspaper carried a front
page article about Reid and the transplant. Both articles related the basic information given out by Reid's office, adding
that no record had been found of a marriage by Reid's brother.
On an inside page of one newspaper was a distant picture of
her entering the hospital; she looked distinctly furtive.

   That morning when she walked past the nurses' station on
her way to Janis's room, she saw two of the attendants talking
together in a low voice. They broke off their conversation
abruptly when they spotted her and busied themselves at the
counter. Sharon was certain they had been gossiping about
the stories in the papers.

   Janis was awake and smiled at her. Sharon smiled back.
If this transplant saved Janis's life, it was worth any amount
of embarrassment and public attention. At least it was to her;
she hoped that Reid would not come to regret it, either. While
all this caused her no more than personal discomfort, it could
seriously damage his career in politics. It seemed grossly
unfair that a generous gesture on his part should expose him
to scandal.

   By the end of the week it was worse. Three weekly tabloids
had luridly titled articles about Sharon and Reid, two speculating that they were lovers and Janis their illegitimate child,
the other reportedly giving the true story of the love affair
between her and Wes, cut short by his untimely death. One
of the scandal sheets even had her picture and Reid's on the
front.

   Reporters were often outside the Laceys' house when she
left or returned. She knew they were a terrible nuisance to
Jack and Hollis as well as to her. One morning one enterprising reporter climbed over the closed gates and walked
right up to the door. Sharon regretted all the trouble it was
causing her friends, and she decided to find herself an apartment. Hollis protested, insisting that she was better pro-
tected from the reporters here than she would be in an
apartment.

   However, Sharon felt that she had already imposed on their

hospitality long enough, without putting them through the irritation of fending off reporters. So she spent her time in the waiting room looking through the apartment ads in the newspapers, then looked at two of the places, and made a quick decision. There was little problem involved in moving, since she had brought only two suitcases of clothes, intending to stay a week.

The reporters did not know her new address, so she was blessedly free of them at her home the next few days, but she still had to face them at the hospital. They all knew what she looked like by now, so that it was difficult to elude them. Each day she had to play an irritating game of hide-and-seek when she arrived or walk past the reporters, stoney-faced, refusing to comment. Either way, she felt like a criminal.

The ICU waiting room became a sanctuary to her. But one day even that was violated. A woman who had been sitting in the waiting room with her all morning struck up a conversation with Sharon, and Sharon responded politely, as she had to several other people waiting there for the past few days. It was some minutes before Sharon realized how many questions about Sharon the woman was asking and how often she turned aside any question about herself.

"You're the mother of that little girl who's getting the transplant, aren't you?" the woman asked.

Sharon's skin prickled. "Yes."

"A terrible thing, what happened to her father. It must have been hard for you."

"Yes. It was."

"I guess the congressman's been supporting you all this time."

Sharon looked at the woman. "Who are you?"

"Why, Trish Colson, like I told you."

"I mean, are you a reporter? Whom do you work for?"

The woman smiled as though they shared a clever joke. "*Probe*. We want to be the first to run an interview with the mystery woman in Representative Maitland's life."

An anger so fierce it made her tremble surged through

Sharon. She jumped to her feet. It was all she could do to keep her voice low. "Get out of here."

"Now, Ms. Thompson, I don't think you understand. This is your chance—"

"No!" Sharon's face was white with rage. She wanted to lash out at the woman, to scream at her to leave the room. How could anyone have the audacity, the utter lack of sensitivity to come to a waiting room where everyone was in fear for the life of a loved one and try to sneak a story out of her? "Get out now, before I call the hospital security."

The woman shrugged, obviously unperturbed by Sharon's outrage, and stood up. "By the way, were you married to your daughter's father?"

Sharon glared at the woman silently. She shrugged again and sauntered out the door. Sharon flopped back down into her chair, seething.

Later that afternoon, after Sharon had recovered her temper, she went down to visit Reid, as had become her habit. The door to his room was closed, and there was the sound of loud voices inside. Sharon paused, puzzled, then knocked on the door.

"Come in!" Reid's voice barked, and Sharon opened the door cautiously and stuck her head inside.

"Reid?" She glanced from Reid, sitting up in his bed, his face set, to the woman standing beside the bed. The woman was short, with flaming red hair and freckles splattered all over her face. She wore thick glasses, and her expression was decidedly pugnacious. "Is something wrong?"

Reid looked at her, and unconsciously his face changed, turning softer and warmer. He smiled. "Sharon. Come in. No, there's nothing wrong. Susan and I are having our usual kind of discussion."

The woman chuckled. "Yeah. Full volume." She turned toward Sharon. "Hi, I'm Susan O'Brien, Reid's press manager. I believe we spoke on the phone the other day."

"Yes, of course. It's nice to meet you." Sharon smiled and shook Susan's hand. "I'm sorry to interrupt. I was afraid you were one of those reporters and had managed to worm your way into Reid's room. One of them started in on me in the waiting room today.''

Susan cast Reid a speaking look but said nothing.

"No, you weren't interrupting," Reid said pointedly. "Susan was just about to leave."

"No, I wasn't."

"Susan—"

"Don't try to threaten me, Reid. You know as well as I that if you fired me, there'd be half a dozen other politicians happy to hire me—and they'd probably pay better, too."

Reid grimaced. Sharon looked from one to the other, puzzled. "I don't understand."

"He doesn't want me to tell you what we were talking about," Susan explained, then added, "—because he knows I'm right."

"About what?"

"The press conference. The hospital and our office has been besieged by reporters."

"I know."

"Yeah. Reid told me you had to move out of your house to get away. They're splashing hints and innuendoes all over the papers about you and Reid and about you and Reid's brother. In short, they're harassing everybody. I know reporters, and they won't stop until we give them something. That's why I want Reid to hold a press conference."

"Oh no," Sharon protested quickly. "Reid is much too weak. He's still recuperating."

"I'm not too weak," Reid put in. "The hospital plans to discharge me in a couple of days. They have me up and walking around the halls half the time. I'm strong enough to face a few annoying reporters." He gave Susan a dark look. "Anyway, that's not what we were arguing about. I agreed that we need to hold a press conference."

"Reid, I know you're feeling stronger, but there's always the possibility of a relapse, you know," Sharon put in worriedly.

"Jeez," Susan groaned. "You two ought to get your act straight. Which one of you is weak? To hear you guys talk, you'd think both of you would blow over in a strong wind.''

"What?" Sharon frowned. "I don't understand. Reid is ill; he's just undergone major surgery."

"He says he can handle a press conference; I believe him. He's a healthy guy, and he's getting over his surgery. Besides, it's not a great strain on him. He has to sit in a wheelchair and answer questions; FDR did it for years."

Sharon thought that Susan was awfully flippant about the state of Reid's health. Then she realized, embarrassed, that it was really none of her business. She had nothing to say about what Reid did. "I'm sorry. Of course, if Reid wants to and thinks he can—''

"Great. One down and one to go. What Reid and I were arguing about was who would be with him at the press conference. I want to have a full and complete question-and-answer session, one that will put an end, I hope, to all the speculation. I suggest that one of the team of surgeons also speak.''

Sharon nodded. "I see."

"And you."

"Me?" Sharon stared at her. "Me? Are you serious?"

"As a bad dream."

"But I've never done anything like that. I'm not any good at speaking in public. I wouldn't know what to say."

"That's what I was telling Susan," Reid put in triumphantly. "I told her there was no need for you to do it, and it would be too much of a burden for you."

"Reid . . ."

"No, Susan, I won't hear of it."

"Why do you want me to be there?" Sharon asked the woman. "I don't see why I'd be any help."

"Your presence will add verisimilitude to the story. If you're there, answering questions openly, they'll think, 'She's telling the truth; she's got nothing to hide.' If you aren't there, they'll wonder why not. Why is Reid answering for you? Because he's a politician and more skilled at lying? Are you too likely to blurt out the truth? Or is it because he's protecting you? Well, that's what your lover would do, isn't it?''

"My what?" Sharon glanced sideways at Reid, feeling the color rise in her cheeks.

"Your lover. Haven't you read the newspapers, listened to the stories? That's what people are implying. They're suggesting that you didn't know Wes, that Janis isn't his child, that that's merely a convenient cover-up. They're saying that Janis is actually Reid's daughter, that you're his mistress, and he's kept you hidden all these years.''

Sharon swallowed. "Well, yes, I had read the stories. I mean, I realized what they were saying, but, well, it just didn't seem . . ." Her voice trailed off. She didn't know why Susan's calling Reid her lover should affect her so; she *had* seen the articles and she wasn't stupid enough not to know what they were implying. But reading the suspicions was somehow different from hearing Susan refer to him as her "lover." That was such an intimate word, so sensual and evocative.

Sharon cleared her throat, admonishing herself to be adult about it. "Well, yes, I can see that it might give that impression. But I'm afraid I'd be so awkward and inexperienced that I'd mess it up.''

Susan shook her head eagerly. "No, that will be wonderful! You're obviously not a politician or a polished speaker. It will make you more believable. Seeing you, I'm even more convinced you should speak.''

"Susan, could I remind you that it's not your decision?" Reid broke in crisply.

Susan ignored him, talking straight to Sharon. "You're pretty, but not ravishing or slick. You don't look like a mistress.''

"Thank you. I think.''

"You know what I mean. You look like a real person, a normal woman. Your face has a wholesome quality; you're believable and trustworthy. More important, you look vulnerable. It's one thing to tear apart a politician; everyone knows they're fair game. It's quite another thing to crucify a pretty, sweet-looking woman. You look like a sister, a wife, a daughter. You see?''

''I think so.''

''Then what do you say?''

''Well, of course I'll do it if I would help.''

''I know you will.''

''No,'' Reid put in adamantly. ''Absolutely not. Sharon, there is no reason for you to do this. I can handle the whole thing myself.''

''Oh, Reid, get real.'' Susan grimaced. ''You don't have to be a white knight about this. It's not going to hurt Sharon, and it will help you a great deal. I mean, picture it: this sweet mother whose child is sick, who's worried and maternal. If the reporters tear her up, it'll put the public on your side. Think of her looking out at them with those big brown eyes and telling them that you saved her daughter's life. You'll look like a goddamn prince before the thing's over.''

''Damn it, Susan, that is not my intent!'' Reid barked. ''I won't let you use Sharon to sweeten my image.''

''Come on, Reid, it'll be great. The one problem that people have with you is that you appear too reserved, too cold. This is your chance to warm up that image. 'Loving uncle, unselfishly risking his own life, etc.' ''

''I didn't do it for that!''

''That doesn't mean you can't use it. Look, right now this thing is working against you. Why not turn it around and make it work for you?''

Reid glanced at Sharon. He hated for her to think that he would use her or Janis. She had hated him for years, and now he didn't want her to suspect he'd done it for the publicity. ''Sharon, I don't want you to do this. You don't realize what it's like to sit in front of those barracudas. It takes years to get used to it. They could slice you to ribbons.'' He shot a fierce look at Susan. ''And don't tell me that it would get us a lot of sympathy if they broke Sharon down and made her cry.''

Susan shrugged innocently.

"No, wait, Reid," Sharon put in quietly. "Don't you think that this is my decision to make?"

"Of course. But you don't know what you're getting yourself into."

"I've done a lot of things in my life that I'd never done before, that I didn't know what I was getting into, and I've managed to get through them. I'm a lot tougher than you think."

"I won't ask it of you."

She smiled a little. "Maybe not. But I can volunteer, can't I? Reid, I know you're not doing this to make yourself look good; I know you wouldn't use me. Isn't that what's worrying you?"

Susan's eyebrows rose, and she glanced sharply at Sharon, then at Reid. She sensed that there was something going on here. Something beyond generosity and gratitude and avuncular love.

"Maybe," Reid admitted.

"I was wrong about you years ago. I know that now. I've come to know you. You did this simply because you wanted to save Janis's life, nothing else. And I know that you wouldn't make me your shield at a press conference." She walked over to him, her face earnest. "You've given me so much. Don't tell me I can't give you something in return. The last thing I want is for this to hurt your career. People ought to praise you for it, not make sly innuendoes. If my presence at the press conference will help you, I want to be there. It's not something I'm used to, but I don't think I'll crumple under the pressure. I've been staring my daughter's death in the face. A bunch of reporters will be a piece of cake compared to that."

Reid looked at her for a moment. A slow smile curved his lips. "You're a brave and beautiful woman. I don't know why I ever thought you might not be a match for a few measly reporters." He reached out his hand, and Sharon placed hers in it, curling her fingers around his. They smiled at each other. He raised her hand to his mouth, touching his lips lightly to it. "Thank you."

*   *   *

The press conference was held late that afternoon. A meeting room in the hospital had been set aside, and it was filled with reporters. Sharon and Reid came in together, Reid dressed in elegant silk pajamas and robe, sitting in a wheelchair, and Sharon, looking a little pale and frightened, walking behind him, pushing his chair. Even Susan hadn't expected the thoroughly sympathetic picture they presented. Susan hid a smile behind her hand and hoped that they had good TV coverage. This might work out to give Reid a boost instead of hurt him.

The surgeon opened the meeting with a brief account of Janis's disease, the operation, and Janis's present condition. Then they opened the floor to questions. Few of them were medical. Reid fielded most of them, answering the questions about himself, his career, and his involvement with Sharon in a calm, steady voice.

"Representative Maitland, how have you managed to keep Miss Thompson and her daughter hidden for so long?"

He smiled slightly. "I didn't try to hide them."

"Then why was the public unaware of their existence?"

"They are not public people. There's no reason anyone would have known about them, any more than the public would know about Dr. Morris here or any of you."

"Have you provided them with money all these years?"

"No. Ms. Thompson preferred to support her daughter and herself alone."

"There are rumors that you refused to acknowledge Janis Thompson—as a member of your family. That you refused her entrance to your house, as well as financial support."

Reid raised his eyebrows slightly. He started to answer, but Sharon leaned forward to her microphone, interrupting in her soft voice. "I'd like to answer that, if I may. Mr. Maitland offered to support Janis and me; he was quite generous. I was the one, as he said, who refused to take the money. I was proud and wanted to make it on my own. He has accepted Janis as his niece from her birth, and he has never denied her entrance to his home or to any other place.''

Sharon's voice was shaky with nerves, but her words rang with sincerity. Susan, looking at the crowd, could see even seasoned reporters' faces softening a little as they watched her.

"Ms. Thompson, you were not married to Wesley Maitland?"

"No. He—" Sharon faltered a little. "—he died before he knew about Janis."

"Wasn't Wesley Maitland's death a suicide?" a harsh male voice asked from the back of the room.

Sharon drew in her breath sharply, paling, and Reid leaned forward to speak, his voice clipped with anger. "My brother's death was an accident."

"An overdose of drugs?"

"Yes."

"It was an accident," Sharon reiterated. Even after all this time, the suggestion still had the power to wound her.

"Like many young people of that time, my brother experimented with drugs in college, taking things because they were new and exciting, with little idea of the harm they could cause. He was careless, even foolish. But he didn't commit suicide. He was in love with Sharon, and he had a great deal to live for."

Sharon glanced at him, her eyes warm with gratitude.

"Miss Thompson, there are rumors that your daughter is not Wes Maitland's child. That this story is merely a handy cover-up for the fact that Janis Thompson is in reality Reid Maitland's child. How do you respond to that?"

Sharon sat up straighter, her eyes flashing. "It's absolutely untrue. Janis is Wes's daughter. I hardly knew Reid Maitland until this operation."

"Then you deny any intimate relationship between the congressman and yourself?"

"Yes. I certainly do. Reid Maitland has acted toward my

daughter and me with the utmost kindness and generosity, and I find it appalling that the press has tried to smear his name because of it. It's a terrible thing that a man should risk his life to save a child, and the press, instead of praising him for it, vilifies him, printing unfounded rumors and hints. I want to state this clearly and unequivocally: If there was any wrongdoing, it was on my part—and Wes's. Reid Maitland has done nothing but try to help my daughter. He has done nothing wrong!''

Sharon sat back, folding her arms across her chest. Her eyes flashed. Susan hurried forward to grab one of the microphones. "Sorry, that's it for today. The press conference is over."

There was a murmur of discontent across the room, but the reporters stopped asking questions. Susan slipped the doctor, Sharon, and Reid through a door into a smaller room, locking the door behind her. She smiled at them. "You guys were great. Thank you, Dr. Morris, for agreeing to appear."

"You're more than welcome."

"Quite a defense, Sharon."

Sharon looked embarrassed at Susan's words. "I'm sorry if I was rude. I just got so angry at them—"

"No, it was great. I couldn't have been more pleased."

Reid stood up and took her hand. "Thank you. You did more than I could have asked." He smiled faintly. "I had almost forgotten that you had a temper."

Sharon looked into his eyes. His hand felt warm and strong around hers; she liked it. She wondered why she had ever thought his gray eyes were cold; there was such depth in them. Reid was reserved, perhaps too much so, but inside there was warmth. There were times when Sharon thought that he would like to break through the reserve. Perhaps he didn't know how.

When the room cleared, they left. Susan took Reid to his room, and Sharon rode back up to the Intensive Care Unit. She was pleased with herself. She hadn't been too scared or done too badly. Now, perhaps, the reporters would stop hounding them.

When she stepped inside Janis's room, all thoughts of the media or the press conference fled her mind. Janis lay in bed with her eyes closed. Her cheeks were flushed, and she was too still. Sharon knew, without having to be told, that Janis was suddenly worse.

9

Sharon walked out of Janis's room and across to the nurses' station. "What's wrong with her?"

The nurse looked up. "Oh, Ms. Thompson. I'm sorry. I didn't see you go in. I've sent for Dr. Morris; he should be here in a few minutes. He'll be better able to tell you."

Sharon returned to the waiting room and sat, hands clenched in her lap, fear eating at her. Finally Dr. Morris entered the waiting room and sat down beside her.

"Janis's temperature has risen, and so has her blood pressure. She's showing signs of rejecting the kidney," he said in a low voice.

Sharon looked away, releasing a sigh. It was what she had presumed, but the doctor's words made it real and final. "I see."

"We're giving her corticosteroids. But there's a limit to that. We'll just have to wait and see."

Sharon nodded numbly.

"Don't give up hope."

"I won't." Sharon could barely get out the words for the tears choking her throat. The waiting room blurred before her eyes. A regular occupant of the room gazed at her with sympathy. In another moment, the woman would come over to offer her comfort, and Sharon didn't think she could bear that. She couldn't stand to sit still in this room, feeling her daughter's life flowing away from her.

She jumped up, leaving Dr. Morris still sitting, and hurried out of the room. She walked past the elevators and took the stairs to Reid's floor, the high heels she had worn for the press conference clattering on the cement steps. By the time she reached Reid's room, tears were streaming down her face, and her breath was coming in shallow jerks. She knew she was about to lose control, and all she could think of was reaching Reid's room before she fell apart.

She pushed the door open without knocking and hurried inside. She stopped short. Susan was with Reid, sitting in a chair and talking, a binder filled with papers in her lap. Reid stood by the window, looking out. They both turned at Sharon's precipitous entrance.

"Sharon!" Reid crossed the room to her quickly, his hands going out to clasp her arms. "What is it? You're crying. What's the matter? Is it Janis?"

Sharon started to answer, but instead sobs rose up in her throat. Reid's arms went around her, and he pulled her gently against his chest, cradling her head with his hand. He felt warm and strong and comforting. Sharon wrapped her arms around him and held on. Reid said nothing, just stroked her hair with his hand, bending over her, enfolding her.

"Sh, sh, it's all right," he whispered against her hair. "I'm here. It'll be okay." He murmured a litany of comfort, words of softness and assurance, soothing her. Behind him, he heard Susan rise from her chair and stuff her papers away. She eased around him and out the door, closing it behind her.

Finally Sharon's sobs quieted, and she drew a long, shuddering breath. Reid guided her to the bed and sat down on it with her, one arm around her shoulders. Sharon leaned her head against him, her eyes closed, reluctant to leave the comfort of his strength.

"Oh, Reid," she sighed brokenly.

"What happened? Is she—"

She shook her head. "No. She's alive, but she's worse. A lot worse. The doctor said she's rejecting the transplant. Oh, God, if she does, it'll all be for nothing. She'll die!"

Reid's arm tightened around her. "She won't," he told her firmly. "She won't. What did the doctor say? Is there a chance she won't reject it?"

Sharon sighed again, willing up her own strength. "Yes, there's a chance." She straightened and wiped at the tears covering her face. "Dr. Morris is increasing her dosage of the anti-rejection medicine. He said we'd just have to wait."

She left the bed and walked to the box of tissues on the bedside table. "I'm sorry." She blotted the tears from her face and throat. Her eyes avoided his. "I shouldn't have dumped that on you."

"Who else? I'm her uncle. I'm your friend, I hope."

Sharon nodded. "Yes. You are my friend." She looked up at him. Her eyes were so vulnerable, so large and tear-softened, that his heart twisted within him.

Reid couldn't stop himself from laying his hand alongside her face. Her skin was smooth and hot from her bout of tears. It was hard to imagine that once he had thought her conniving and heartless, even for a brief time. He had never realized the real strength and sweetness of her personality. Their lives had become intertwined fourteen years ago, yet he hadn't really known her until recently.

Slowly his hand fell away. Sharon moved back a step, though she found it difficult. She wanted to return to the comfort and strength of his arms; she wanted to lean against his chest and give up her problems. Let someone stronger take them over.

But that was impossible. It wasn't the way life was. She had discovered that fact a long time ago. She must be her own strength, her own comfort. She had to handle it herself, no matter what the problem was. "Thank you."

Reid frowned, sensing her withdrawal. He didn't like the

sense of loss it brought. "There's no need to thank me. I want to help you."

Sharon nodded. "I know. It's kind of you." She glanced around. "I'm sorry. Did I run Susan off?"

"Doesn't matter. I was tired of talking business, anyway."

"I should get back to the waiting room. I—they might call me anytime."

Reid's frown deepened. They both knew that she would be called only if Janis's condition deteriorated. "Don't think that. She'll get better."

Sharon summoned up a little smile. "Yes. She has to." Her smile trembled, and her eyes were washed with tears again. "She's all I have. She's been everything to me for thirteen years. I can't let anything happen to her."

"Sharon . . ." He took a step toward her, his hands reaching out.

She backed up quickly, shaking her head and swallowing hard against her tears. "No. I have to get hold of myself. I can't break down again. Janis needs me."

"If there's anything I can do . . ." Reid felt helpless, a position he was not used to being in. But this was something that money and influence, even his strength of will, could not change. "Maybe I should go with you. You shouldn't be alone."

"Oh no, you're only a week out of major surgery yourself. I'm sure the hospital wouldn't let you sit outside ICU. It would be too hard, too tiring."

"They're releasing me in a couple of days."

"To go home and rest, not to sit on hard chairs in a waiting room. Please, stay here. I'd only worry about you, too, if you were there. I'll let you know how Janis is."

"All right." It didn't satisfy him. It was infuriating to be weak at a time when Sharon needed support. "But you need someone with you."

"Hollis will be by before long. She comes practically every day. And my mother is flying back here this weekend."

"Good." He took her hand and squeezed it. "Don't wear yourself out. Remember that you need rest, too."

She nodded, paying little attention to his words. There was no way she could rest with Janis near death. Anyway, unless Janis recovered, there was nothing for her to save up her strength for.

Sharon returned to the waiting room and sat down to her vigil.

Sharon had never known hours that lasted so long. By the end of the day she would have said that she'd been there three days, and by the end of the next day, she had completely lost track of time. She didn't go home but caught what sleep she could on the couch in the waiting room. Every hour she went into her daughter's room and held Janis's hand and talked to her, willing her strength into the girl. For five minutes an hour she was calm, confident, and determined. Then she would leave the room and return to the waiting room for the rest of the hour, and the strength would flood out of her, leaving her drained, shaky, and weary. She wanted to cry. She tried to pray. She sat and stared blankly, unable to concentrate on anything.

Hollis stayed the afternoon with Sharon and came back the following day. She cajoled and bullied Sharon into eating and tried to take her mind off Janis somewhat with conversation. But Sharon was unresponsive. Fond as she was of Hollis, she hardly noticed whether she was there. Sharon was locked into the isolation of her worry and fear. She felt hopeless and paralyzed.

Janis's temperature spiked. She moved in and out of consciousness. She showed little response to the steroids. The silent battle went on.

The morning of the third day, after Sharon had spent a second almost-sleepless night in the waiting room, she walked into Janis's room and found her daughter quietly sleeping. The red that had stained her daughter's cheeks was gone. Her hand shaking, Sharon reached out and touched

Janis's forehead. It was far cooler than it had been. Janis opened her eyes. She blinked and ran a tongue across her dry lips.

"Hi, Mom."

"Hello, sweetheart. How do you feel?"

"I don't know," she mumbled, and her eyes closed.

Sharon took Janis's hand and stood there, tears running down her cheeks. She was better! When Sharon left her daughter's room she walked to the nurses' station. "How is she? Is she better? She feels cooler."

The nurse looked up and smiled. "It would be better for you to wait until Dr. Morris has a look at her; he can tell you her condition better than I."

Sharon took the nurse's smile as a statement of hope, despite her careful words. Dr. Morris ten minutes later confirmed Sharon's guess. "She's doing better. This isn't to say that we're completely past danger. But she's come through this crisis."

Sharon hurried to Reid's room. He was scheduled to leave the hospital this morning, and she wanted to give him the news before he left.

Reid was up and dressed when she burst into the room. His head snapped toward her, his face stiff, his eyes questioning. Sharon beamed, allaying his initial fear. "She's better! Her fever's down, and so is her blood pressure. The doctor says she's past the crisis."

"Thank God!" Reid hurried across the room to meet her. His hands clasped her arms, pulling her to him, and he bent his head, kissing her hard and briefly. The pressure of his lips stunned her, and for a moment Sharon stood in blank silence. But Reid seemed not to notice, wrapping his arms around her shoulders and squeezing with a strength surprising for a man who underwent surgery only days ago. He laid his cheek against her hair, and Sharon relaxed against him. She began to cry and laugh, all at the same time. She felt bursting with joy, giddy with happiness. And it seemed perfectly right that it should be Reid with whom she shared this moment.

* * *

"How is Janis doing?" Jack Lacey asked his wife, lifting his head from the report he was reading as she came into the room.

"A lot better. Of course, those doctors would never stick their necks out so far as to say she's doing well. But it's been three days since she stopped rejecting the kidney, and she's looking good." Hollis flopped into a chair across from his desk. "Whew, I'm beat."

"Want me to fix you a drink?"

"Mmm. Please."

"Scotch?" He rose and ambled to the small bar in the corner of his office.

"Yeah." Hollis ran her fingers back through her hair, massaging her scalp.

Jack glanced at her out of the corner of his eye as he poured a healthy jigger into a glass and added a splash of soda. "I guess you won't be keeping your watch at the hospital every day then?" He dropped a few ice cubes into the drink and stirred it with his forefinger.

Hollis yawned, shaking her head. "I wouldn't think so. Sharon will camp out there every minute of every day, I'm sure, but I've used up my martyr instincts for a while."

"Good. I was afraid you might be turning into a saint on me." He grinned in that slow, devilish way that would stir any woman's blood.

Hollis smiled back. "Fat chance."

Jack walked over to her, the drink in his hand, and reached down to pull her out of her chair. He led her to the small couch on the opposite wall of his study, and sat down on it sideways, legs outstretched. He pulled Hollis onto the couch between his legs, and she settled back against his chest with a contented sigh. She took the glass from his hand and sipped it.

"Ah. You always did make the best damn glass of Scotch." She twisted her head to flash a teasing look up at him. "I think it's the stirrer that does it. Adds a touch of salt, I think." She took his hand and lifted it to her mouth, closing her lips around the forefinger he had used to stir the drink and sucking the residue of moisture from his skin.

Jack closed his eyes. His skin was immediately searing, and he was already swelling in response to her tantalizing gesture. He bent and kissed the top of her head, murmuring, "Jesus, you know how to play me."

Her laugh was low and sultry. "You're an instrument I've been practicing for years."

He ran a hand down her bare arm, enjoying the feel of her smooth skin. He thought about taking her upstairs to bed. Or perhaps they would do it here, undressing each other slowly, kissing and caressing, until they were naked on the couch. Or on the floor. He smiled a little, remembering once when he'd been so eager, he'd swept his desk clean, dumping all the contents haphazardly on the floor, and they had made love on top of his desk.

But later. Right now he needed to talk to her. He would enjoy the anticipation, the long, slow pleasure of arousing them both bit by bit. Who said he hadn't acquired discipline over the years?

"If you aren't going to be at the hospital, maybe you could take a trip with me."

"Sure. Where?" Hollis took another sip of the drink and handed it to Jack.

Jack chuckled. "That's a surprise." He drank from the glass and set it down on the floor beside them.

"A surprise? Sounds exciting." Hollis tilted her head back, smiling at him. "Is it?"

"Any trip with you is exciting." He grinned.

Hollis made a little pout. "I don't know whether that's a compliment or not."

He continued to grin and let his hand slide off her arm and onto her torso, exploring in light, gliding caresses. Hollis reached up and kissed the tender underside of his jaw. "Tell me where we're going. Come on, tell me. You know, I haf vays of makink you talk."

"Mm. Show me."

She giggled and trailed her mouth down his neck. "At least give me a hint."

"Well, it's warm. Hot, in fact."

"Mexico."

"Wrong."

She began to unbutton his shirt. "How many guesses do I get?"

He chuckled. "At this rate you could go on all night."

She pressed her mouth against his bare chest. "Maybe I will." Her tongue circled his nipple. He made a little noise, and his hand slipped up under her blouse, caressing the velvet skin of her back, tracing the rigid line of her backbone.

He nuzzled her hair. "I'm all for that."

His low voice melted her, as it always did. In calmer moments, it amazed Hollis that she and Jack had never grown bored with each other, that she still found him so sexy that just looking at him across the room could turn her hot and damp with desire. But right now, thinking didn't enter into it. She slid her mouth down his bare chest, shoving apart the sides of his shirt. Her tongue delved into his shallow navel.

He tightened all over. His hands tangled in her hair. "Baby . . ."

"Hmmm?" Her hands went to the fastening of his slacks, unbuttoning them and pulling down the zipper. Her hands slid inside.

Jack groaned softly. Hollis looked up at him. His eyes were so bright a blue they could burn right through her. His mouth was wide and heavy with passion, his face flushed. She'd seen the look a thousand times before, but still it made her heart accelerate in her chest. She smiled slowly. She knew him. She knew his strength, his scent, his taste, the textures of his flesh. But knowing didn't mean staleness or boredom; rather, it brought its own pleasant anticipation.

He reached down, and his hands dug into her shoulders. "Come here." He pulled her slowly up his body, his gaze intent on her face. The faint sadness that lived in Hollis's eyes had receded, replaced by passion.

He moved his head the last few inches and kissed her.

Hollis thrust her hands into his hair, sliding the strands through her fingers. Her fingers tightened on his hair, pulling it, but Jack hardly noticed the sharp prickles of pain. He was aware of nothing but Hollis's mouth and the feel of her body pressed against his.

She pulled away from him and left the couch. Jack frowned and started to reach for her, but then he saw that she was unfastening each button with careful slowness, and he settled back to watch. Hollis smiled and started a strip routine that was somehow amusing, playful, and wildly erotic, all at the same time. By the time she had worked down to her panties, Jack had had all that he could bear. Making a noise that was something between a laugh and a growl, he stood up and grasped her arms, pulling her to him for a long, deep kiss. She could feel him hard and urgent against her. They melted to the floor in a tangle of legs and arms, and rolled across it, kissing and stroking, trying to taste everything of each other all at once.

He kissed her breasts, reveling in their exquisite softness, and his tongue traced circles around the small raspberry buds of her nipples. He pulled one nipple into his mouth and sucked at it, laving and teasing it with his tongue. Hollis arched up into him, silently asking for more, and he answered her by pulling hard and deep.

Hollis groaned and jerked a little, jolted by a pleasure so intense it was almost painful. Her fingers dug into his back, crumpling up the material of his shirt, blindly seeking his skin beneath it. She wanted to touch him, had to touch him. She made a noise of frustration, and impatiently he shrugged out of his open shirt.

His hands were all over her, touching her, caressing her, so eager that he trembled. His fingers slid over the white satin and lace of her panties, drifting across the brief garment, cool as snow, to the damp center of heat. His finger slipped beneath the material, delighting in the moisture that gave full evidence of her desire for him. Her flesh was slick and supremely soft, fiery hot.

"Hollis. Baby. Hollis." He could say nothing else as he kissed his way down the smooth expanse of her skin, too incoherent with desire to say any of the raging things he felt inside. He was consumed with passion for her, driven by his need, his love. In that moment there was nothing in the world for him but her.

He had to be inside her. Had to feel her heat surround him, her softness taking him in. He fumbled at the fastening of his trousers, cursing at the impediment, and shoved them down, kicking them off. Hollis skinned out of the tiny triangle of her panties, as eager as he to be joined with him. She opened her legs to him, and he thrust into her. They groaned together at the exquisite satisfaction. He buried his face in her neck, clenching his fists as he struggled to hold back the tide of his passion, to let them ride it as long as they could.

He thrust into her again and again, hard, slamming, driving into her very core. Hollis's fingers tore at his back, and she met each driving thrust eagerly, taking him as deep into her as she could. She sank her teeth into his shoulder, holding back the wild whimpers that rose in her throat.

Then at last he climaxed, and Hollis convulsed around him, their world shattering with fierce pleasure, until at last it drifted back together, slowly, peacefully, and they lay together, trembling in its aftermath.

Jack refused to reveal the destination of their weekend trip, continuing to tell Hollis only to pack light, casual clothes. She felt vindicated when they reached the airport on Friday and boarded a plane bound for Mexico City. Jack was taking her to Mexico, just as she had guessed at first. But Jack smiled mysteriously and told her that it was dangerous to make assumptions.

All she saw of Mexico was the airport in Mexico City, where they disembarked and immediately boarded a small private plane. "Jack, where are we going?" she asked, buckling herself in, more and more intrigued.

He smiled again and put on his sunglasses. "You'll find out."

What resort was so far off the beaten track that they couldn't take a commercial flight to it? Perhaps Jack just wanted the privacy and luxury of a private plane, but in that case why wouldn't he have taken one all the way from DFW? Not that this plane was exactly what she would consider in the luxury class. "You're renting your own private island," she guessed.

He chuckled. "Nope."

"You're buying one."

"Give it up, Hol. You'll never guess it."

When they landed some hours later and walked into the airport, Hollis had to admit that Jack was right; she never would have guessed it.

"Guatemala!" She turned to stare at him. "We're in Guatemala City? Jack, are you crazy? What in the world are we doing here? And don't tell me 'you'll see.' "

"All right," he replied mildly. "I won't."

"Jack! We're talking hellhole of the world here. Jungles. Revolutions. Torture and assassinations."

"Home of the Federated Ministries 'Hope Mission.' "

"Hope Mission!" Hollis repeated. She felt as if the ground had moved beneath her feet. "Ames Thompson's mission?"

"One and the same." Jack's voice was light, but his face was carefully blank.

Hollis wet her lips. She could think of nothing to say. She could only stare at him. What in the world was going on? "You despise Ames."

Jack shrugged noncommittally. "Maybe I've gotten religion."

"Jack—" Her voice singsonged with exasperation. "Would you kindly tell me what you think you're doing?"

"Well, right now I'm looking for the man who's supposed to meet us at the airport."

"Who?"

"I don't know his name, but Ames said he'd send someone."

"You talked to Ames?"

"Afraid I'm comparing notes with your old boyfriend?"

Hollis grimaced and turned away. Jack sighed and reached out to touch her shoulder. "I'm sorry. You know, it's not as if I've never spoken to Ames. We're regular contributors to his mission, after all."

"Well, yes, but that's because I write out a check to it every year."

"I've exchanged a few words with him over the years."

"But to come to Guatemala to visit him? There's something weird going on here."

"It won't hurt you. I promise." Jack bent and kissed her lightly on the lips.

"Mr. Lacey?" A voice broke in on them, and they turned to see a young American man hurrying toward them through the airport. Jack nodded. "I'm Chuck Remmert. Sorry to be late. Looks like you've managed to get through the red tape of entering the country."

"Yes. It's probably fortunate you were late."

"Is this your luggage? We better get in the Jeep and go if we want to make the mission before dark."

They followed the young man out of the airport building. He stopped beside a delapidated Jeep and piled their luggage into the open back. They climbed into the beat-up vehicle, and Chuck started it. It roared and chugged and shook. Hollis exchanged a look with Jack, sitting in the backseat, and they had to grin. As they clattered into the street, Hollis leaned back against the seat. Well, one thing at least, with Jack she was always able to laugh.

The ride to the mission was long, winding first through the grimy, overpopulated city, and then into the mountainous countryside. As they gathered speed on the rural roads, Hollis clung to her seat. She thought she might be jounced out at any moment. Even her insides felt bruised, and it seemed a miracle that she hadn't regurgitated her airline breakfast. In

the oppressive humidity the back of her light cotton dress
was quickly soaked, and her hair hung damp and limp, clinging to her sweating face.

It was, she thought, a perfectly miserable country. Everywhere she looked she saw poverty—slums in the city, open-
air ramshackle homes in the country, children in rags, old
women bent under burdens. How could Ames stand it here?
But, then, she guessed that that was exactly why he had
chosen it. Such human misery would be what Ames would
want to heal.

That didn't explain what she and Jack were doing here,
however. She hadn't the faintest idea what her husband was
up to. She couldn't fathom why he would even want to visit
Ames, let alone bring her along.

She was positive that Jack still carried a dark jealousy deep
inside him because she had loved Ames. He had known that
she still loved Ames when she married him, and to a man as
proud and competitive as Jack, that must have been galling.
She remembered that the one time that Ames had been in
Dallas, raising funds for the mission, Jack had suggested that
they fly to Paris for a week. She had gone, of course; there
was no point in stirring up Jack's jealousy, and, besides, the
idea of seeing Ames again had scared her then.

Hell, it scared her now.

What would she do when she met Ames again? What would
she feel? She wondered how he would look. It had been over
ten years since she'd seen him. She remembered him with
the gloss of youth and love. Would he still be handsome?
Inspiring? Would he again awe her with his power and com-
mitment? Or would she find the clay feet this time? He might
be pudgy, balding, and utterly ordinary now, the kind of man
who wouldn't cause her heart to skip a beat.

Or he might stop her heart all over again.

She glanced at Jack. One hand was looped through a strap
on the door, and he was leaning back, his eyes closed, despite
the way the Jeep was tossing them around. He was hard and
powerful. She loved him. Life with him was exciting. He
aroused her as no other man had ever been able to. Jack was

her husband, and they had a good marriage. Didn't they? As good as a woman like her could have, she thought.

But Ames was buried deep in her heart; there was still something raw and aching inside her when she thought of him. She had loved him in a pure, true way. The love she felt for Jack had always been mixed up with the passion and excitement he aroused in her. There wasn't the clarity, the gentle goodness she had known with Ames. There were times when she disliked Jack, and there were times when she manipulated him; she felt sure that there were times when he manipulated her. They played games; they hurt each other; they had loud, screaming arguments that ended in passionate lovemaking. The love she had had with Ames was sweet, untainted, as clear and sparkling as water. She had never lost it. Through all the years with Jack, through the desire and the fun and the fights, Ames had lain in her heart like a sweet ache.

She didn't know what would happen when she saw him again. The love could crumble into nothingness. It could flame up inside her all over again. She didn't want either one to happen. She didn't want to hurt Jack—and she knew she couldn't hide it from him, whatever she felt; she could never hide things from Jack. It would be better if she didn't see Ames at all. Yet she was too curious and eager and excited not to. Besides, there was no way she could avoid it now. Jack was forcing her to see him.

Hollis dug her fingers into the seat and mentally cursed her husband. Why in the hell had Jack decided to put them both in this position?

They arrived at the mission a few hours later, after a spine-jolting ride down a narrow dirt track. Hollis stepped out of the Jeep, amazed at what she saw. She had expected white-washed adobe buildings, like a Mexican church in a movie. Instead she found a large number of small, flimsy thatched-roofed huts with open sides or walls made of branches lashed together. There was one long building with a thatched roof and no walls. It was filled with people, mostly children, eating supper at long wooden tables. There were three other buildings, one a small frame house, two made out of cinder blocks. One must be the church because it had a wooden cross above the door, and the other had a large red cross painted on two sides—the hospital, she assumed.

As she and Jack got out of the Jeep, a man broke away from the others in the pavilion and hurried toward them. "Hollis. Lacey. It's so good to see you." He extended his hand to Hollis.

"Ames." Hollis's heart jumped. He looked so much the same. Older. Tanner. His hair was a little longer, and he wore glasses. But his hair was thick and still the rich dark brown color of Sharon's. His face was just as gravely handsome as before, his eyes the same deep brown under thick black brows. He still looked at her as though he knew her innermost thoughts and secrets but loved her anyway.

His hand was callused against Sharon's skin; that had changed. He clasped her hand briefly, warmly, and for a moment his eyes gazed straight into hers. Hollis squeezed his hand. She didn't know what to say. She didn't even know what she felt. It made her breathless and confused to be this close to him again after so long.

He released her hand and reached out to shake Jack's. "Was your trip all right?"

"Fine."

"We were eating supper. Would you like something?"

They agreed that they were hungry, and Ames led them toward the pavilion. A woman in a khaki skirt and sleeveless blouse was walking toward them, her steps slow and a little hesitant. "Lynn." Ames smiled and motioned toward her. "Come here. I want you to meet Jack and Hollis Lacey."

She stopped beside Ames. Her hair was a light wispy brown, tied back on the nape of her neck. Strands had escaped from it and straggled around her face. Her eyes were a pale, indeterminate color. In fact, everything about her seemed a little pale, despite the fact that she was as tanned by the sun as Ames. She looked as if she had faded, like an old photograph.

Ames took her hand. "Dear, this is Hollis Lacey. And her husband Jack. This is my wife, Lynn."

Hollis felt a jolt of surprise. Of course, she knew he was married; Sharon had mentioned the fact to her several years ago. But Hollis had never pictured him with a wife; she still thought of him as she had known him.

Hollis's smile was stiff. "It's nice to meet you." She extended her hand, and the woman took it; her handshake was limp. Hollis continued to smile.

If Hollis had pictured him with a wife, Lynn wouldn't have been the type she would have imagined. She knew his wife would not be someone like her, of course. That had been a fluke, a once-in-a-lifetime error on Ames's part. She would be stable and responsible, steeped in religion and duty, as Ames was. But Hollis would have thought she would have color, beauty, and personality, unlike this pale, quiet woman before them.

Jack gripped Lynn's hand, flashing her his patented charming grin, and Lynn had to smile back at him. But the smile changed only the lower half of her face; in her eyes there was still a worried, wary look. Hollis suspected she wasn't used to smiling much, at least not with anything more than her lips.

"Chuck and I'll put your bags in the house," Ames offered. "Lynn, why don't you take the Laceys to a table? I'm sure they'd like something to drink, too."

"Yes, I'm dying of thirst." Hollis smiled full-wattage at Lynn, but the woman's return smile was mechanical. She turned away quickly and led them across the dirt courtyard to the open-air dining room. Hollis wondered if Lynn knew that she and Ames had once been in love. Or was she this reticent with everyone?

Jack had more luck getting Lynn to talk, of course, as he did with everyone. By the time she had helped them dish up their food from the serving table and brought them bottled drinks, Jack's lazy, humorous chatter had relaxed her. She began to tell them about the mission, pointing to the various buildings around them and explaining their purposes.

"We're hoping to build a bigger house for an orphanage," she told them. "We hadn't really expected to start an orphanage here. We were thinking in terms of a hospital and church, but so many of these poor children are parentless. We take them into the clinic and heal their wounds. Then where do we send them?" Her mouth curled down and she looked away. "I'm sorry. I'm afraid it still upsets me, even after all the time I've been here. This is such a harsh, cruel life." She sighed, then continued. "We've been taking most of them in. But we have nowhere to put them. At first we boarded them in part of the hospital, but we need that space for the sick and wounded. So we placed them in these houses. However, that's hardly adequate."

Hollis glanced around. "Yes, I can see."

"Ames's next project is to build an orphanage. He prays about it every night."

Hollis glanced away. She didn't know how to respond to a statement of such candid, simple faith. How did praying about it every night get an orphanage built? To her it would have made more sense to spend the time working on a fundraising campaign. Her mind went always to the practicalities. Even before, no matter how much she had loved Ames, she had never been comfortable with his religion. She looked around her at the humble cluster of buildings and tried to imagine herself fitting into this life with Ames. But, of course, she would never have been able to; that was why Ames had left her. A bittersweet sadness pierced her. She had loved Ames so desperately, yet their love had always been impossible.

Ames walked back toward their table through the dimming light of dusk, and Hollis turned her head to watch him. They would never have worked out, yet she could not help but wonder what it would have been like to have married Ames, to have known his lovemaking, to have shared his life.

Ames sat down at their table, smiling. His gaze turned to Hollis. For a moment, they looked at each other. Her heart jittered.

"Lynn's been telling us about the new building you need," Jack said beside her. Hollis was grateful; she couldn't think of anything to say. Driving up, she had wondered if she still loved Ames. She still didn't know.

"The orphanage?"

"Yeah. You'll need to do extra fund-raising for that."

"I know." Ames sighed and ran a hand through his hair. "I'll have to come back to the States, I guess, and stump for funds. I hate to leave here." Beside him, his wife nodded in agreement.

Hollis took a swallow of her drink and said nothing. She couldn't imagine not wanting to run from here as fast as she could.

"You have to be there in person to raise anything substantial," Ames went on. "Begging letters don't do it. I'm working with a man back home about setting up a 'crusade.' Six weeks or so."

"You mean touring around? Preaching in different cities?" He nodded.

"Why don't you come to Dallas?" Hollis asked. "I can throw a fund-raiser for you. That's something I've learned how to do over the years. A big dinner, a dance, maybe an auction of donated items. The proceeds go to your mission."

"She's right," Jack put in. He grinned sideways at Hollis. "You know how to separate a man from his money, don't you?"

Hollis tilted her chin pugnaciously, her eyes laughing. "You better believe it."

Jack slid his arm around her shoulders, and he bent to kiss her forehead. He turned back to Ames, a look of challenge in his eyes. Jack was laying claim to her, Hollis thought, pointing out to Ames that she belonged to him. Hollis didn't know whether to laugh or to cry. Ames was the last person Jack needed to warn off. He had given her up long ago; she had never meant as much to him as his religion. He certainly wouldn't compromise that religion by trying to seduce her now.

Ames held Jack's gaze for a moment, then looked away. "I thought you'd want to get settled in at the house; then I'll take you to the children."

Hollis tightened. She wasn't sure she wanted to see the children. She loved children and enjoyed playing with them, but whenever she did, there was a worm of jealousy inside, eating away at her. Being with kids made her long for what she couldn't have, until sometimes she thought she'd break her heart. "Well, perhaps tomo—"

But as she spoke, Jack cut in, "Why don't we run over there right now?"

"All right," Ames agreed.

He and Jack stood up, and Jack reached down to pull Hollis up. She glanced at him oddly. Jack was acting decidedly strange. Why did he want to look at Ames's kids right now? "What is going on?" she whispered as they walked across the dusty courtyard behind Ames.

"Going on?" Jack repeated and looked at her blankly.

"Yes, going on. You're acting oddly, and the look on your face is so innocent I expect angels to congregate around you any minute."

He chuckled. "Hollis, love . . . you don't trust me?"

Hollis snorted inelegantly.

They reached one of the small houses, and Ames ducked to enter the low door. For a moment Hollis hung back, but Jack took her hand and pulled her in with him.

The house consisted of one room with a dirt floor. Several toddler-size children were playing on the floor. Against one wall were two baby beds and a bassinet. There were also three rectangular woven baskets. Hollis realized that there were babies in all of them. A middle-aged woman was feeding a bottle to one of the babies, and an adolescent girl squatted on the floor, playing with the toddlers. Hollis looked around the room, her heart swelling with sympathy. Several of the children were bandaged. One tyke was missing one leg from the knee down, and he scooted across the floor in a fast, awkward crawl. All the children were thin, and they gazed up at her with unnaturally solemn faces.

Ames crossed the room and lifted a baby from a basket. He handed it to Hollis, and automatically she took it. She looked down at the baby. Thick black hair covered his head. His skin was light brown, and his eyes were huge and dark, surrounded by a brush of black lashes. He was a beautiful child, only a few months old. His fist was in his mouth, and he sucked at it steadily as he stared back up at Hollis.

Hollis's heart contracted. She wanted to cry. He was beautiful. It seemed so unfair he should be here, condemned to a life of poverty and strife, when she would have given anything to have a baby. She brushed her fingertips across his forehead, pushing back his hair. He blinked and reached up with one hand to grasp the large white beads of her necklace. Her throat was so swollen with tears that it hurt, yet she couldn't keep from smiling down at the baby. "What a lovely little thing you are," she whispered to him, putting her index finger against his hand and watching his fingers curl tightly around it.

Her eyes filled with tears, blurring her vision. Damn Ames for putting her in this situation, anyway.

Jack came up behind her. "Cute, isn't he?"

Hollis nodded, not trusting herself to speak. She straightened out the baby's clothing, unable to keep from touching him, aching to run her fingers over his tiny face and body.

"You like him enough to take him home with us?" Jack asked nonchalantly.

Stunned, Hollis whipped around. "What?"

"Would you like to adopt him?"

10

For a moment Hollis couldn't speak. She stared at her husband. She began to tremble, and Jack slid his arm around her. "Hol? You okay?"

"Jack. Oh, Jack, are you serious? You—you aren't making a joke?"

"Jeez, honey, you think I'd joke about that?"

"But we can't—could we?" She swung around to Ames, hope surging through her. "Could we? Can we adopt one of your orphans?"

"Yes. Both Paco's parents are dead; he has no family except a grandmother, and she has given up rights to him. She wants him to go to a good life in the United States."

"She wants him to go—" Hollis repeated dazedly, then stopped and looked at her husband. "You already knew, didn't you? You planned this!"

"I told you I had a surprise for you."

"Jack . . ." She didn't know what to say. She felt breathless. Hollis looked back down at the baby, now cheerfully gnawing on her necklace. She reached out and touched his cheek. Her fingers trembled slightly against his soft flesh. "Sweetheart." Tears ran freely down her cheeks. She bent to kiss the baby's forehead. She cuddled him close to her, rocking a little, and cried.

Jack pulled her against his chest, his arms securely locked around both her and the baby. He kissed her hair, and his hands soothed her back. "Are you all right? Do you want him?"

"Want him!" She began to cry even harder. "More than anything! He's the most beautiful baby I've ever seen." Her words were interspersed with hiccuping sobs, and her face was wet with tears. But she glowed as if lit from within. "Thank you. Thank you."

She reached up to kiss Jack. Then she turned to Ames. "Thank you." She giggled, looking first at the baby then up at Jack. "I don't think I've ever been so happy."

Jack grinned. "I'm glad."

Hollis walked around the room, jiggling the baby, talking to him, reaching down to touch his toes and hand. Jack watched her. Seeing her so happy made his heart swell with joy. He didn't even care that she had looked to Ames in her happiness and thanked him. All that mattered was that the sorrow had left her.

"What's his name? Can we name him? How old is he? Oh, Ames, tell me everything about him."

"His name is Francisco Munez; we call him Paco. But no doubt you'll want to name him yourselves. He's too young to know his name, only six months."

"Six months? He's so small."

"Yes. He suffered from malnutrition; he was close to starvation when we found him."

"Poor baby," Hollis crooned to him, her face as blissfully silly as any new parent. "We'll fatten him up, won't we? Huh? Yessir." She bent her head to rub her nose against his. "Oh, Jack, what shall we name him?"

"Whatever you'd like." He came over and gazed down at the baby.

"Here. You want to hold him?" Jack hesitated, then

grinned. "Sure." He took the baby, supporting its back and head with his hands, and held it up close to his face. The big, grave brown eyes stared back into his. "Hello, fellow. My, you're a solemn one, aren't you?"

Hollis turned to Ames. "Can we take him back to the house? Can he stay with us tonight?"

"Of course. Tomorrow he will be your son legally."

Hollis's eyes widened. "What? You mean we won't have to wait for papers and court hearings and everything?"

"I managed to cut through most of the red tape," Jack told her. "I hired an excellent attorney, and he's already taken care of everything but the final court hearing. That will be tomorrow afternoon, and we have to be there. The court will award him to us, and we can fly back home—with our son."

"I just died and went to heaven." Hollis put her arm around Jack's waist and leaned her head against his arm, looking at Paco. "I could burst, I'm so happy," she murmured. "I'll never be able to thank you enough for this."

"You don't need to." He kissed the top of her head. "I'd do worse things for you."

They took the baby and his small bag of belongings to the house where Ames had put their luggage. The house appeared to be Ames's and his wife's residence. There was only one bedroom, and their bags were in it. When Hollis protested about putting Ames and Lynn out of their house, he assured them that it would be no problem. "We're a lot more used to sleeping in the native houses than you two are, I'm sure," he said with a smile.

"Thank you. Thank you for everything."

Ames gave her a brief nod. "I'm glad you're so happy." He seemed awkward and uncomfortable, as though he wished to say more, but could not think of what to say. After a moment he left.

Hollis hardly noticed his exit. She was once again absorbed in the baby. When he began to cry, she bounced him in her arms, but when Paco's screams grew louder, she turned to Jack, panic-stricken. "What's the matter? What do I do?"

"I don't know. Maybe he's hungry. Or he needs his diapers changed."

"How do I know which it is?"

He chuckled. "Check the diaper. If it's okay, feed him."

Hollis did as he suggested. The diaper was wet, and she laid Paco down on the sofa and removed it, then struggled for a few minutes with an old-fashioned cloth diaper, finally getting it pinned on in a very lopsided manner. She and Jack stood looking down at the baby, waving his arms and legs around vigorously, his diaper bunched and askew. They glanced at each other and began to laugh. Soon they were laughing hysterically, holding their sides and leaning against each other.

In the end, when they had calmed down, they found that feeding was necessary, also, and Hollis gave him a bottle. She had never felt as peaceful as she did then and there, holding the warm little bundle of flesh against her chest and watching him gulp down his food, his tiny hands kneading at the bottle and her hand.

After she burped him, Paco went to sleep on her shoulder. Hollis found it wonderful and amazing that she could feel the change in his little body as it grew utterly limp with sleep.

She laid him down on the bed, and she and Jack lay down on either side, propped up on their elbows, watching him sleep.

"What is it about a baby that makes you feel like saying so many trite things?" Jack wondered.

"I don't know. He makes me feel melted and gooey inside, like a chocolate bar in the sun. I think I'd like to name him Daniel. Or Dean. What do you think?"

"Whatever you want."

"Dean. Dean." Hollis tried it out, looking down at him. He cooed, and she laughed. "I think he likes it." She lifted her gaze to Jack's face. "This is the most wonderful thing that anyone's ever done for me. How did you manage it?"

He shrugged. "I knew I had to do something when I saw how unhappy you were. I couldn't let you go on like that. So I thought of Ames. I figured he must have orphans here, and I knew he'd do it for you. The rest was just hiring a sharp lawyer who knew what to do and greasing a few palms—as well as pulling all the strings I knew how in the State Department.''

"I can't believe you went to Ames for a favor. You've always seemed, well, you know . . .''

"I hated his guts.''

"Yeah.''

"Hollis, don't you know? I'd have gone to the Devil himself for you.''

She smiled and leaned across the baby to kiss him on the cheek. "Thank you. I'll never forget what you did for me. I love you.''

"I love you, too, babe.'' He looked at her, wondering if her words were true. She was grateful to him now, but he had seen the way she had looked at Ames when he walked across the courtyard toward her. Her heart had been in her eyes; her face had glowed. She still loved Ames. He had dreaded her seeing Ames again. But he hadn't had any choice. He'd have done whatever it took to make her look like this, the shadows gone from her eyes. "I love you.''

After Janis passed the rejection crisis, life began to return to some semblance of normality for Sharon. She no longer camped out in the waiting room at night, but resumed visiting Janis only during the day. The press grew less and less persistent, and the story died down.

After he was released from the hospital, Reid called her once or twice a day to check on Janis, and, much to Sharon's surprise, a few days after he had left the hospital, he walked into the ICU waiting room.

Sharon jumped to her feet, setting aside her knitting. "Reid! What are you doing here?''

"I came to see you. And Janis, if they'll let me.''

"But surely you aren't feeling well enough. Here, sit down. Shouldn't you be at home in bed?''

"I'm fine. Getting stronger all the time; I heal quickly. It's been two weeks since the surgery."

"I know, but you mustn't push yourself."

He smiled. "Thank you for being concerned. But I'll probably get more rest here than I would at home. There, my phone's ringing all the time or one of my people is dropping by to bring me some work."

A worried line creased her brow, and Reid found himself wanting to lean over and lay his lips to it. It was both amusing and warming to think that Sharon was overly concerned about his health. Instead he changed the subject. "What are you working on?"

"What? Oh, this. I've been knitting to keep my hands occupied. I'm too distracted to read, and I don't enjoy television. This must be at least my third sweater."

He touched the soft material. "It's beautiful."

"Maybe you'd like one," she joked.

He glanced at her. He thought of her hands making something for him, and he felt a flash of warmth. "Are you serious?"

"Well, yeah—if you are." Her face brightened. "You know, that would be fun. I've never knitted a man's sweater. My father doesn't like them, and Ames hardly has any need for one in Guatemala. It would be nice to have a project; right now I'm knitting aimlessly." She didn't add that she found the prospect a little exciting. It would be nice to do something for Reid, of course, a sort of small repayment, but there was more—an almost sexual feeling to creating an article of clothing for his body.

The thought shocked her, and Sharon turned her face away quickly, busying herself with picking up the knitting and tucking it back into her bag. Surely she didn't feel anything sexual, anything romantic, for Reid Maitland. It was absurd. He was a rising politician, a man who could no doubt pick and choose from some of the most eligible women in Washington and Dallas. He would have no interest in her. She should have no interest in him. The only thing between them was his relationship to Janis. Once Janis was well, he would be out of their lives, except, perhaps, for occasional visits to his niece. Sharon was aware of a curious sense of loss at the thought. She had enjoyed their visits. She had almost come to rely on his presence.

"I guess you'll return to Washington before too long since you're feeling better."

"I suppose."

Sharon wondered if his voice lacked enthusiasm or if that was merely her imagination. "I'll miss you," she said honestly, then chuckled. "I never expected to hear myself saying that."

"You don't think you'll get away that easily, do you? I live in D.C. only part of the time. Believe me, I'll be dropping in to visit—that is, if you don't mind."

"No, not at all. I understand that you want to keep up with Janis."

"I'd like to keep up with you, too."

Sharon glanced at him quickly, then away. Her face was warm, and she felt foolishly happy. To hide whatever she felt—and she wasn't sure what it was—she picked up her purse and rummaged through it for coins.

"What are you doing?"

"I'm going to get a drink." She nodded toward the soft drink machine across the room. "Would you like one?"

"Here. I'll get it for you." He stood up, his movements a little slow and cautious—the only real sign she'd seen that he wasn't entirely well—and walked over to the machine.

Sharon watched him find the coins and feed them into the slot. For the first time, she found herself looking at him as a man—not as an enemy or a friend or the person who had saved her daughter's life, but as a member of the opposite sex. He was long and spare, angular in his movements. His hands were large and long-fingered, the kind of hands that it was easy to imagine on her body.

She crossed her legs, amazed at the turn her thoughts were taking. All the hours of waiting in this room must be driving her around the bend. She was not usually particularly interested in men. She had loved Wes, of course, but since then her relationships with men had been brief and few. Her daughter and her art had filled her life. She had found sex enjoyable, but not wildly exciting, and she certainly wasn't one to sit around watching men and fantasizing.

But, now, looking at Reid, she couldn't help wondering if that rather stiff, aloof way he carried himself would melt in bed, if his face ever gave in to hunger and need, if the cool gray eyes could heat up. His hands were nice. They promised strength and gentleness. His body would be hard. He would be serious and intense, no joking, playful lover.

Her face flamed with embarrassment, and when Reid returned, holding out the can of soft drink to her, she hoped her eyes didn't reveal her thoughts. She took the can, and her fingertips brushed his. Her response was immediate and sensual, a tingling that shot straight to her abdomen. She curled her hand around the can, intensely aware of the coolness of the metal and the moisture dotting it. Thoroughly tongue-tied now, Sharon stared down at the drink, circling the rim with her thumb.

It occurred to Sharon that Reid must think her utterly stupid, sitting there like a block, without even looking at him. She felt like a teenager with a crush.

Sharon grimaced and raised her head. She'd be damned if she would let Reid Maitland affect her this much. "It's time for my visit with Janis. Would you like to go instead?"

Reid's first reaction was a pleased smile, but he said, "I wouldn't want to take your time with her . . ."

"I'm here constantly; I get all the hours in the day. I think I can spare one."

"All right. I'd like that."

He rose and left the room. Sharon was glad he was going to see Janis. Not only would it please Janis, but also it would give her a chance to bring her thoughts under control. When Reid returned five minutes later, Sharon was calm and poised again.

For a few minutes they discussed how Janis looked and the amount of progress she had made. Then Reid said, "Janis told me how late you stay here every night and how early you come every morning. You'll wear yourself out.''

Sharon smiled deprecatingly and shook her head. "Janis exaggerates. She has a teenager's view of time.''

"I think she's a very sharp and accurate girl, myself. And I think that you need to escape from this place for a while. You're too thin, and there are dark circles under your eyes.''

"Well, thank you very much.''

"Not that you aren't lovely, even with dark circles. However''—he reached down and wrapped his hand around her arm, pulling her up—"I intend to do what I can to get rid of them.''

"Reid . . .'' she protested, but not too strongly. She couldn't help but like the concern in his voice and the feel of his hand around her arm. She was afraid her smile showed it, too.

"No arguments. I intend to take you out for a long, leisurely, highly caloric meal, and afterward I'll drive you home, where you will immediately go to bed and sleep for at least ten hours.''

"I really don't need—''

"Do you think it will help Janis if you let yourself become so run down you get sick?''

"I won't get sick.''

"You have a guarantee?'' Sharon made a wry face, and he smiled. "I thought not. Now, admit it, a rest and a meal would be nice.''

"Yes, it would.'' She thought of getting away from the boredom and fear of the hospital. The idea seemed heavenly. "It definitely would.''

"Good. Then, let's go.'' He bent to help her gather up her belongings. "You have to promise me: no thinking about Janis and how you should be here instead of out with me.''

"I promise.'' Right now, looking at him, she thought that was a promise that was sinfully easy to make.

The restaurant was relaxed and informal enough that Sharon didn't feel out of place in her casual clothes, but the food was excellent and the service unobtrusively good. They talked easily and happily about things unrelated to Janis, her illness, or the hospital. Sharon wondered if Reid had missed their conversations in his hospital room as much as she had.

She wasn't sure whether it was the wine they drank with dinner or simply being with Reid, but she felt herself relaxing. The tension in her shoulders and neck melted away, and the lines of worry smoothed from her face. She didn't know it, but she looked years younger and much happier by the time the waiter brought their after-dinner coffee and liqueurs.

Sharon hadn't planned to let Reid drive her home; it wasn't necessary, and besides, her car was still sitting in the hospital parking lot. But when the time came, she didn't make a murmur of protest; she was too pleasantly languid and unfocused to make the effort, too happy even to want to. She gave Reid directions to her new apartment and leaned back against the plush seat of his Mercedes, deliciously enveloped by warmth and comfort.

It was a surprise to open her eyes and find that the car had stopped in front of her apartment building. She realized that she had dozed off. "I'm sorry." She turned to Reid with an apologetic smile. "I must be more tired than I thought."

Reid smiled back. "I didn't mind." He didn't add that he had enjoyed watching her sleep.

He came around the car to open her door. Sharon got out slowly. Her face was soft and slack; Reid thought she must be still half-asleep, even yet. He walked with her up the stairs to her front door. Sharon unlocked the door and turned to him. "This was so nice of you. Thank you. I enjoyed the meal very much." She paused. "Would you like a cup of coffee?"

Reid knew he shouldn't accept her invitation. Sharon was ready to fall asleep on her feet; she needed to rest, not talk to him. But he couldn't resist going into her apartment. "All right. But I'll make the coffee."

"Don't be silly."

"Just point me toward the kitchen. I'm hell with a kettle of hot water and instant coffee."

Sharon smiled, too tired to put up much of a fight, and pointed to the kitchen. "The kettle's on the stove. Coffee and cups are in the cabinet to the right."

"Right." Reid went into the kitchen and quickly fixed the instant coffee. A few minutes later, he carried the two cups of coffee into the living room.

He found Sharon asleep on the sofa, sitting up. He smiled, shaking his head, and set the cups on the end table. He eased Sharon down onto the couch in a reclining position, then took off her shoes and put them on the floor. He unfolded an afghan that lay over one arm of the couch and spread it over her. He had the suspicion that Sharon had spent more than one night on this couch, worrying about Janis, the afghan wrapped around her legs, until finally sleep overcame her.

He sat down on the coffee table in front of her and gazed at her, sipping his coffee. She was a lovely woman. He had missed her since he'd left the hospital. He enjoyed talking to her, looking at her, hearing her laugh. Reid reached out and smoothed his thumb across her forehead. The worry line there had eased out tonight, at least for a little while.

His thumb slid down the line of her nose and touched the indentation of her upper lip. What a warm, generous woman she was. When she loved, she gave herself full measure. She had worn herself to the point of exhaustion, sitting at the hospital, patiently giving her strength and love to her daughter. He admired her. He had known few women like her.

Sharon looked so vulnerable and tired. He wished there was something he could do for her, some way he could decrease her burden. Softly he traced her lips. He would have liked to kiss her. He'd thought about that more than once today. If Wes had lived, Wes would have married her; she would be his sister-in-law today. He found he didn't like the thought. Sharon had hated him for years, but she no longer did; she had even come to like him, Reid decided. He had realized in the past few days that he wanted her to do more than like him. He wondered if there was any chance of that.

He stood up, sighing. It would set off the press again if they even dated. Reid didn't want to subject Sharon to scrutiny of the press again just for a casual, temporary relationship. They would both have to be certain; it had to be serious. He must move slowly.

Reid leaned over and brushed his lips against Sharon's forehead. He turned and walked out of the apartment, locking the door behind him.

Janis continued to improve. The nurses already had her up and walking around, trailing her stand of plastic bottles, and the day after Reid's visit, the doctors decided that it was all right to move her out of ICU.

"Boy, am I glad to get out of there," she told her mother, giving an expressive shudder. "I kept hearing people in the other rooms moaning, and one night some man kept crying out. It was awful. Sometimes I thought, I must be going to die, too, or I wouldn't be here."

Sharon reached over and squeezed her daughter's hand. "Don't think about it. You're out, and you're doing very well. You think you're happy to be away from there—think about me! I could jump up and down at the thought of not having to sit in that waiting room all day long."

"No. Now you just sit here in my room all day long."

Sharon made a face. "Believe me, it's much more comfortable."

"I was getting really bored there, too. I couldn't do anything except read. They don't even have TVs." Having reminded herself of how deprived she had been, Janis picked up the remote control and flipped on the television.

Sharon settled down in the easy chair in the corner of the room and resumed knitting. She had abandoned the afghan she had been working on yesterday. This morning she had looked through her knitting manuals until she found a man's sweater pattern that she liked; then she had gone by a yarn shop to buy a rich chocolate brown yarn that would look good on Reid, as well as tan and white for the patterns. She was already well into casting it on.

She glanced up at Janis, who lay propped up in her bed, her eyes glued to the television. Every day she looked better. Her color was coming back, and the old smile often flashed. The lines of strain around her eyes and mouth and across her forehead were smoothing out. The puffiness was gone. Her youth and natural good health were taking over and speeding her recovery.

It was going to turn out all right, after all. A weight had been gradually lifting from Sharon as Janis improved. She still had doubts and fears, of course, but they no longer consumed her. She was able once again to think that there would be a future, not just the awful, frightening present.

Janis felt her mother's gaze on her and glanced up. She smiled when she saw Sharon's radiant face. "What are you grinning about?" she teased.

"Nothing in particular. Just happy. I feel—I don't know —" Sharon heaved a great breath. "—almost as if I've been reborn. Don't you feel like we have another chance? As if life's starting all over?"

"You mean, like maybe I'll really get out of the hospital someday? I've been in here for years!"

"Yeah, I guess that's what I mean. We can make plans again, look forward to something."

"Mom?" Janis's face turned serious. "Do you think I'll be normal again?"

"Oh yes. Dr. Morris assured me that you would, except for having to take your medicine."

"I know that's what he said. But sometimes I think that I'll be stuck in here forever, that I'll never get to do the things I used to. I feel like a freak."

"That feeling will go away. Once you get home and start doing regular things. Going to movies, talking to your friends, giggling, listening to records . . ."

"I hope so. Are we going back to Santa Fe?"

Her question pulled Sharon up short. "I don't know. I haven't decided." She paused, thinking. "Perhaps we ought to stay here, near the hospital and the doctors, just in case an emergency arises. And the doctors will probably want to check you periodically." Staying here was a practical decision, Sharon told herself. It had nothing to do with the fact that in Santa Fe they would never see Reid.

"Yeah." Janis sighed. "I guess so."

"It's April now. Maybe we could stay here through the summer. When you're feeling better, I'll arrange for private tutoring, so that you'll be able to go on with your class in the fall."

"Okay." Janis's voice was less than enthusiastic.

"I'm sorry, honey. I know you'd like to see your friends. But it will be safer this way. And it won't be so bad. We'll do things. There's lots to do in Dallas. You always enjoy our visits here. Come on, it'll be like a long vacation."

"I guess I sound pretty gripey, huh?" Janis made a face. "I oughta be glad I'll be living anywhere."

"No, you aren't gripey. It's perfectly natural. I think you're quite mature. Just remember, it won't be for long. And I'm sure the doctors would prefer it."

Again Sharon shoved back the thought that they would be around Reid Maitland four months longer.

Reid came to visit Janis frequently after she was moved to a regular room. Sharon noticed that Janis's face brightened whenever he walked into the room. Janis liked him. He seemed to know just the right way to talk to her, light and teasing, not as if she were a child, yet not quite as if she were another adult. But there was more than just friendliness between them. There was the connection of family, a certain knowledge in the bones and blood, a familiarity that came from seeing resemblances to oneself in the shape of another's face or in the turn of a head or a casual gesture. All these years, Janis had had no one but Sharon on whom to build her identity. It was exciting for her to have a whole new part of herself to explore.

Sharon wished that she had as simple and logical a reason why her heart always rose whenever Reid appeared. It would be easier if she could say that it was because he reminded her of Wes, but he didn't. His coloring was the same, but the resemblance was slight, and she never thought of Wes when she looked at him. The truth was that she liked Reid for himself. She more than liked him. It was exciting to see him; there was a rising eagerness in her stomach and an electric tension in her nerves. The way Reid's eyes went toward her as soon as he walked in the door, the way he smiled at her made her feel younger and more alive. The truth of the matter was: Sharon knew that she was falling for him, as giddily as a teenager.

She did her best not to show it. Sharon was positive that Reid would have no interest in her in return, and she didn't want to make him uncomfortable by being obvious about her feelings for him. He might stop coming by, and that was the last thing she wanted, for either Janis or herself.

Reid insisted on driving them home the day that Janis was released from the hospital. He stayed in the room chatting with Janis, who was so eager to leave that she could hardly sit still, while Sharon went downstairs to the offices to check her daughter out. After she had filled out and signed the various papers, she turned to the matter of paying her bill. Her insurance would cover a great deal of it, but she knew the amount of money owed to the hospital was so staggering that her insurance wouldn't take care of all of it. She hoped the hospital would agree to let her pay it off a little at a time. Even though she had reached the point where her art supported her adequately, she was anything but wealthy; and she hadn't even been able to work the past few weeks.

When she mentioned the bill, the clerk frowned and referred to her papers. "But your bill's been paid, ma'am."

"What? That's impossible. I paid some money when Janis was first brought here, but since then . . . surely my insurance hasn't covered it all."

"Well, it says here that it's paid in full." The woman looked at her as if she were slightly crazy for protesting a paid-up bill.

"I don't understand." It must be a clerical error, and

eventually they'd discover it. Then they'd probably dun her
as if she had tried to avoid paying it. "Could you check it
to make sure?"

With a martyred sigh, the woman moved to a computer
terminal, where she typed for a few minutes. Then the machine printed off several sheets of wide, green-barred computer paper, which she ripped off and carried back to Sharon.

"Here are the charges." The tip of her pen trailed down
a column of numbers so large that Sharon's stomach went
cold. "And here's a payment." She stopped on a number
with a minus in front of it, then moved on. "Here's a payment
by your insurance company. Another billing to your insurance
company, and this is the remainder, paid again by an indi-
vidual."

Sharon's eye followed the line from the figure across to
the explanatory words, and Reid Maitland's name jumped
out at her. Reid had taken care of the bill! She sat back,
stunned. "I see. Thank you. Sorry for the trouble."

Sharon folded up the computer sheets and took them upstairs with her. For weeks, underneath her worry for Janis
had been the fear that the hospital bill would be so large that
it would consume all her savings—and still take her years to
finish paying off. She felt as if she had been unexpectedly
released from a prison sentence. However, she couldn't just
let Reid take care of the debt. It was her responsibility.

She was going to tell him exactly that, but when she walked
into Janis's room and saw her shining face, Sharon realized
that she couldn't do it now. Janis was chomping at the bit to
leave, and Sharon couldn't spoil her excitement by getting
into an argument with Reid over money. So she just smiled
and said, "You're free."

Reid drove them home in his Mercedes, Janis leaning back
in the leather seat beside him, enjoying the luxury and the
attention. Sharon, sitting behind Reid, watched Janis's face
and thought of all the years she had lived without a father.
It was obvious that Reid had a good effect on her; she loved
to laugh and banter with him. Janis needed the male
companionship—the guidance, the modeling, or whatever it

was—that Sharon wasn't able to give her. She had been wrong to keep Janis isolated for all these years, and Sharon felt guilty. If only she hadn't been so stubborn and hurt! If only she had given Reid a chance when Janis was a baby. She would have grown up knowing the attention of a loving uncle.

When they reached the apartment, Reid carried Janis's things in for her, then stayed to chat with them. Later he went out and brought back Chinese food, which made Janis close her eyes and pantomime ecstasy at the change from hospital food. When Janis grew tired, and finally, after much urging from Sharon, went to bed early in the evening, Reid lingered.

Sharon took a breath. Now was the time to broach the subject of Janis's hospital bill. "You paid the hospital."

"What?"

"Janis's expenses at the hospital. You paid everything my insurance didn't."

"Yes." He waited, watching her. He had expected a fight on this, and he'd prepared himself for it.

"I can't let you do that."

"It's already done."

"I'll pay you back."

"Sharon, that's silly. Why shouldn't I pay my own niece's hospital bill? I have the money; it's no burden to me. It would be to you. What's wrong with my taking on the expense?"

"It's too much."

"I gave her my kidney, and you think paying a few bills at the hospital is giving too much?"

Put that way, it did sound pretty silly, she had to admit. Sharon clenched her teeth. "I don't like being beholden to you."

"You're not. I'm not asking you for anything in return, not even to let me visit Janis if you don't want me to."

"It's not that. You can visit Janis whenever you want. I realize how good you are for her—"

"Then how does it make you indebted to me? You know, I didn't do it for you." That was at least partially a lie; he wanted very much for Sharon not to be weighed down by the tremendous debt of the hospital bills, but he'd negotiated often enough to know when to fudge the truth a little. "I did it for Janis. She's my niece, my family. I have no children, no nieces or nephews except her. I would have liked to help support her all her life; you know that. Now here's something that I can give her, and I want to do it."

"You're manipulating me," Sharon accused.

"What? How can you say that?" He looked so much the picture of outraged innocence that Sharon had to laugh.

"You're putting it on a little thick, don't you think? You're trying to make me feel guilty for not letting you give us money when Janis was a baby, hoping that I'll back down on the hospital bill."

His grin was sudden and brief, a flash of white in his face that left Sharon feeling slightly breathless and stunned. What was it about that brief, rare grin of his that made her always feel a little weak in the knees?

"You caught me," Reid admitted with good humor. "But it's the truth, all the same. I want to do this for Janis, and there's no reason in the world why I shouldn't. We're family. Come on, Sharon. Let me."

"You make it sound as if *I'm* doing *you* a favor."

"You are."

Sharon turned her hands palms up in a helpless gesture. "All right. You win. I won't say anything else about it." She felt she was giving in too easily, but she couldn't escape the truth of his words: He could afford it; he wanted to do it; and Janis was his niece. She smiled at Reid. "You know something? You're a very nice man."

"I'll use you in my next campaign ad," he teased, smiling. Sharon wondered if it was just her perception or if Reid's face really had grown warmer and more open the past few weeks. Had she imagined the remoteness, or was it that he was distant only around strangers? She wanted to reach out and touch his face, but she kept her fingers firmly laced and resting in her lap. It would be sheer insanity to let herself feel any more for this man than she already did.

Still it was hard to keep her feelings from growing when he dropped by the apartment every few days to see how Janis was. Every time she saw him, she liked him more. She wanted him more. She was falling in love with him. And she knew it was dangerous.

One evening when Reid came to visit, he told them that he was going to his ranch in the Panhandle to stay for a few weeks. Sharon's heart dropped; he wouldn't be by to see them anymore, then, for a while.

But Reid went on. "I thought perhaps you and Janis might like to go with me. It would be a change of scenery and a nice place to relax and rest. Both of you need a little relaxation. I have a workroom. You could bring some of your materials and work there, if you wanted." He made a gesture toward the corner of the living room, where Sharon had been trying to work since Janis got out of the hospital. She had had Randy ship her some of her tools and materials, and she had set up her things on a small table in the living room. It was cramped and messy, and Sharon had found it increasingly trying to work there.

"Oh no," she demurred, although the idea of being able to spread out her tools and materials and really work without worrying about damaging anything strongly appealed to her. "I couldn't bring my work. It would be too much—too bulky and heavy."

"Nonsense. I'll have it shipped up there; it won't be any problem."

Sharon hesitated. It would be fun to spend the time with Reid; it would be heavenly, in fact. She had no doubt but that she would enjoy the trip thoroughly, and so would Janis. But she wondered if it was the best thing. It seemed as if her feelings fed on being with him. Every time he was with them, she wanted him more and more. She hated to think how she would feel about him after spending days almost alone with him.

Seeing her hesitation, Reid went on. "I've talked to the doctors, and they gave their approval. They say Janis is progressing beautifully, and the change would do her good. If she should suffer a relapse or something, there's a hospital equipped to handle it not far away in Amarillo.''

She shouldn't do it, Sharon thought. She ought to protect herself against Reid's charm, not rush headlong toward it. If she were smart, she would stay here.

But she knew she wasn't smart. She was falling in love. She smiled. ''I'd say, it sounds wonderful. We'd love to do it.''

11

Three days later, Sharon and Janis flew to Amarillo with Reid. They traveled first class, as Sharon was sure Reid always did. Sharon had not flown often; usually when she left Santa Fe, she was carrying materials or her finished works, so she went by car. The few times she had been in a plane, she had certainly not gone first class. It made her feel acutely unsophisticated compared with Reid; it emphasized the gap between them.

When they arrived in Amarillo, the foreman of Reid's ranch, Paul Davison, met them at the airport and drove them to the ranch fifty miles north of the city. To Sharon, who loved the spare, rough beauty of New Mexico, the land in the Panhandle was beautiful. It was primitive and harsh, the soil fierce red clay, broken by narrow gullies and dotted with low cacti, white-podded yuccas, and the tangled branches of mesquite bushes. Sharon leaned her head against the window and drank in the colors—the dusty grays and greens of plants, the rust red of the dirt, the bright blue of the sky. Already she could imagine the colors in glass, not a realistic western scene, but an abstract, maybe, with the muted tones of the dry land broken by a slash of vivid color.

She glanced up and found Reid watching her. She gave him a little smile, feeling silly at being caught daydreaming. "Sorry. I was thinking about something I wanted to make."

"Don't apologize." He smiled. "I've never known an artist. I find the creative process intriguing. Very few people look at this country with such enthusiasm."

"I think it's beautiful. Stark and basic. Did you grow up around here?"

"No. My uncle owned the ranch, and some summers I'd come up to visit him. Wes, too, when he got a little older."

"Daddy used to stay here?" Janis, sitting in the front seat beside the foreman, turned to look at him. She was always fascinated with any tidbit of information Reid could give her about her father.

"Every now and then. He wasn't as fond of it as I was. A few years ago my uncle died, and his children wanted to sell the ranch, so I bought it from them. I come up here to get away from everything. To be normal."

"Aren't you normal?" Janis asked, grinning.

"I don't always feel that I am, believe me."

"I imagine it's very relaxing after the pressures of your job," Sharon put in.

Reid nodded. "My workers know never to call me here unless it's something of absolutely vital importance. It's nice to deal with basic, tangible things—cattle, fences, blizzards, drought. I like going out and working with my hands—even if it takes me twice as long to do it as it would for one of the hands."

Sharon smiled. "I know that feeling. It's why I went into stained glass. Drawing was too—I don't know, mental, I guess. I have to build something."

"I guess you would know what I'm talking about." His face lightened in a way that told her that he wasn't used to people who did.

The car turned off the highway onto a small road, and

before many miles had gone by, Paul turned once again. They rattled across a cattle guard and up a graveled road. In the distance was a house. As they drew closer, Sharon could see that it was a two-story frame house, obviously old and in need of a coat of paint. It didn't seem the kind of house a wealthy, elegant would-be senator would live in. But then, Reid had just said that he liked to shed his skin of politician here and be himself.

The house was not alone on the landscape. Not far away were a corral and a loading chute, a barn, some sheds, two small houses, and an old windmill.

Sharon liked the place immediately. There was something homey and old-fashioned about it; it seemed western and real, a working ranch instead of the plaything of a wealthy man. It was too barren, of course, the sign of a house lived in only by men for too long. If she were in charge, she would add trees and shrubs, maybe some rosebushes in front of the foundation. But then, of course, it wasn't up to her; she had to remind herself that she had nothing to do with Reid, his houses, or his future. To even let herself start thinking that way was dangerous.

They got out of the car and walked up the steps to the porch. Sharon came to a dead stop and stared at the front door. It was oak, inset with beveled glass panels, and on either side were matching sidelights. It was newer than the house, but it blended perfectly with the Victorian style. The door was lovely, but it wasn't its beauty that had rooted Sharon to the porch. The door was so familiar that for a moment she felt strangely out of place and confused, as if she were experiencing a moment of déjà vu, but far stronger and more real than those vague feelings usually were.

The door looked just like one she had made on consignment for a customer of Hollis's—no, it *was* the door. She couldn't be mistaken about her own work. Sharon turned and stared at Reid. He looked back, first surprise, then understanding, chasing across his face and settling into a look of sheepishness.

"That's my door, isn't it?" Sharon asked. "The one I did three years ago. That's right, I *did* ship it to a little town in the Panhandle. You bought it? You were Hollis's customer?"

Reid nodded. "I confess. I made Hollis keep quiet about it; I knew you wouldn't like my buying it. I've always liked your work."

Sharon's throat tightened. She felt as if she wanted to cry. "You've bought other things?"

"Yes. There are a couple of them in this house. Some in my place in Dallas, the apartment in D.C., my office."

"I can't believe it. How much of my stuff have you bought?"

He shrugged, looking acutely uncomfortable. "I couldn't say exactly. Several pieces."

"Why? So you could contribute to my support without my knowing?" Sharon wasn't sure whether the thought of that made her angry or gratified.

He shook his head. "I'm honestly not sure. I went to Hollis's store when she opened it because I knew she was a friend of yours; I had seen you and Janis at her wedding. I wanted to find out about you. She had one of your pieces in the store, the one that's in the living room here, and it seemed to reach out and grab me. I wanted it. I wanted to own it, to look at it. When I went closer, I saw your name below it. I remembered then that you were an artist. So I bought it, and I wormed a little information out of Hollis about you and Janis and went home feeling very pleased with myself."

He sighed and paused. "I don't know what to say. Yes, I wanted to help you out financially. And every time I went in there I found out a little something about Janis; sometimes Hollis would show me a snapshot you'd sent her. But I would have bought your work even if I'd never heard of you."

Tears welled in Sharon's eyes. Whatever she had felt, his response had touched all her tangled emotions. "Thank you," she said very softly.

"For what? For buying the pictures? For liking them?"

"I don't know. Probably both. And for explaining it to me. All those years . . . I never dreamed that you wanted to know anything about us. At first I was afraid you had come to Santa Fe and offered money because you wanted to take Janis away from me and raise her as a Maitland. Or that you offered me the money to salve your conscience or to keep me from revealing who Janis was and hurting your reputation. When I refused, I figured you were probably relieved or not that interested in Janis. I presumed that you had wiped us off your slate. I never guessed you were pumping Hollis for information about us all that time.'' It made her heart twist inside her to think of him going to Hollis for crumbs of information about his brother's child. It seemed sad and lonely. There was so much about Reid that was lonely.

Sharon reached out and took his hand and pressed it. He slipped his fingers through hers and squeezed back. Then he opened the door she had made for him, and they walked into the house.

Large but unpretentious, the house was furnished with a jumble of pieces from many different times, some cheap and some expensive, the kind of furniture that had just grown up around the people who had lived there. Comfortable, Sharon thought, the kind of house where she felt at ease.

In the living room before an east-facing window hung one of her pieces from several years back. It was an elegant, stylized woman in a vivid red dress. The light through the window brought the ruby tones of the dress to life. Sharon remembered very well making it; it had been one of her favorites. The red glass had been so pure and rich. Her technique had improved since then, but there was still something compelling about the simple lines and bright color. Upstairs, Reid pointed out another one of her pieces in his bedroom. This one was against a west window, so that the afternoon sun poured through its opaque glass. It pictured three purple irises on long green stalks amid a lush tangle of green grass and vines. It was a recent work, more complex and difficult than the one downstairs, full of delicate detail.

Sharon smiled and glanced at Reid. ''You have good taste. You've picked some of my best things.''

It was strange to think of these stained glass pictures, so

much a part of her life, hanging all this time in Reid's house and her not even knowing it. It was as if he had held some part of her here.

After he had showed them around the house, Sharon insisted that Janis rest for a while. While she napped, Reid took Sharon out back to one of the small buildings behind the house. It was narrow and sturdily built of wood, with windows on three sides. Inside there were two chairs, a small, heavy table and a work counter jutting out from the wall. Above the counter the wall was lined with shelves. About half the shelves and part of the counter contained woodworking tools; the rest were empty and recently cleaned. A window air conditioner hummed at one end of the room, and the air was comfortably cool.

"What do you think?" Reid asked. "Will it do for you to work in?"

"Reid! It's great. I—" Sharon glanced around again, flabbergasted. "I never suspected that you meant anything like this when you said workroom. This is perfect."

"Your tools and things came yesterday. Paul put them out here." He pointed to a large box beside the table. "Is it really all right? If there's something else you need, we could get it in Amarillo."

"No, this is fine." The shed was almost as big as her studio back home and pleasantly disconnected from the house. "I'm sure I'll love working here. Thank you." She gazed up at him, smiling, and he bent, surprising Sharon, and kissed her lightly on the lips.

He straightened. They looked at each other.

Sharon was suddenly very aware of herself—the movement of air in and out of her lungs, the pulse of her blood through her veins, the prickling heat creeping over her skin. She stared at Reid. What was he going to do? She wanted him to kiss her. She wanted that overwhelmingly. He bent toward her again, and, with a faint sigh, she went up on tiptoe. Their lips touched and clung. His lips moved against hers, and she opened to him. Then his tongue was inside her mouth, and he was kissing her hard and deep. His arms went around her tightly, pressing her body into his. Sharon wrapped her arms around his neck, stretching up to meet his passion.

She could feel him hard against her, and it made desire explode inside her abdomen, spinning out crazily all over her. She wanted him. *She wanted him.* She couldn't remember the last time she had felt this kind of quick, imperative passion. Could it have been as long ago as Wes? But, no, she hadn't had this full, deep woman's hunger then, only the moonspun dreams of a girl. She had never clung to Wes, aching because she felt his heat, his hardness; she had never strained upward, moving her hips suggestively. Perhaps she had never felt quite this way before.

Reid's mouth lifted from hers, and he drew back slowly. Sharon's eyes opened, and she looked at him. Her gaze was misty and soft in a way that made his heart turn over. He wanted to pull her back in his arms and kiss her again. "I hadn't planned on that."

"Me either." Sharon supposed that it was wisest that he stop kissing her, but her body wasn't interested in wisdom.

Reid sighed and took another step backward. "Not that I haven't thought about kissing you. I have. But I didn't invite you and Janis up here so I could get you into bed with me. I asked you because I wanted your company. I wanted to spend some long, uninterrupted time with you."

Sharon smiled. She was still flushed with heat, but her mind was able to function once again. "I understand. I absolve you from impure motives."

Reid chuckled. "I think that may be a little broad in scope. A man's bound to have *some* impure motives where you're concerned."

"You keep that kind of talk up, and I'll think you're so smooth you did lure me here for a seduction scene."

"Then I better keep my mouth shut while I'm ahead, huh?"

He opened the door and ushered her out, his hand resting lightly on the small of her back. Sharon could feel its heat, its width, the slight pressure of his fingers. She tried to act more sophisticated and calm than she felt, as if she were used to kisses from handsome congressmen. As if she didn't expect anything more than that.

They strolled back to the house, and Sharon excused herself to go upstairs and check on her daughter. Janis was sleeping soundly. Sharon sat down in a rocker by the bed and watched her. Janis looked more like the child she had been than the almost-woman she seemed most of the time now. The lines of stress and illness that had marked her face for weeks were gone now, and her youthful color had returned. Her daughter was alive because of Reid Maitland. Sharon knew she would always be grateful to him for that.

But gratitude hadn't had anything to do with the way she had felt when he kissed her. She wanted him. She was already halfway in love with him. And she didn't know what in the world to do about it.

He would make love to her if she went to him, if she kissed him and pressed her body against his, letting him know that she wanted to be in his bed. She had felt his passion, his heat. He wanted her, too.

It was what her body wanted, the immediate, explosive satisfaction that she craved. But she wasn't a teenager anymore, to throw herself after what she wanted without any thought of the future. She had learned responsibility the hard way. She had to do what was best, both for her and Janis.

Reid was a politician with a future. She was an artist, the mother of an illegitimate child. His dead brother had once been her lover. The press had already speculated heavily on the possibility that Janis might really be Reid's daughter. There was little possibility that anything long-term or stable could develop between the two of them. He couldn't marry her; the press would have a field day, and his political hopes might very well be dead. He probably couldn't even afford to be seen dating her openly. All that was left for them was an affair, probably brief and most certainly secretive.

Many people, including most of her friends, would argue that something was better than nothing, but Sharon wasn't so sure. Feeling the way she did about him already, she was afraid that if they had an affair, she would fall more deeply in love with him. It would have to end someday, and when it did, she would be left with a heart broken far worse than it would be if she stopped things now.

Even if she decided that the future pain was worth the present happiness and pleasure, even if she opted for love at any price, there was still Janis to be considered. Janis's relationship with Reid was precious to her; she had needed it for a long time. If Sharon and Reid had an affair that ended with hurt and loss for Sharon, perhaps even anger and bitterness, it would make it difficult for Reid and Janis to continue their present fond, casual relationship. Reid would dread going to see Janis, knowing he would run into Sharon. Janis would be angry at him for hurting her mother. Knowing Janis, she might even take him to task about it. He would come less and less, perhaps even stop altogether. Sharon couldn't risk that for Janis.

And yet . . . despite all the arguments against it, there was the strong pull of desire in her. Sharon wanted him, and she wasn't sure how effective any of those arguments were against that fact.

Sharon stayed in the big old rocker in her daughter's room, thinking, until Janis woke up. They came downstairs together. Reid wasn't in the den. Sharon wondered if he was in the house or out on the ranch. They found a pack of cards and played a few hands of gin rummy. Not long afterward Reid came into the den, a pen and a stack of papers in one hand. He smiled when he saw them and readily dumped the papers on the coffee table and sat down to join their game.

They played until they got hungry, then the three of them went into the kitchen and threw together a supper, teasing and laughing about their lack of culinary skill. Throughout the evening Sharon and Reid maintained their usual casual relationship, keeping their banter light and carefully avoiding any touch or a glance that lingered. But the sexual tension between them was clear in their very restraint, so careful and so constant that they were supremely aware of each other and of the fact that they didn't touch.

Neither one could keep his mind from the memory of that explosive kiss this afternoon. Just thinking about it, they wanted more. Nor could either keep from looking at the other in quick, stolen glances, eyes taking in the skin, the hair, the features each wanted to touch, the mouth neither could forget kissing.

They made conversation, enjoying each other's company, oddly natural and comfortable yet tense and tingling. Excitement rose in Sharon, a mingling of fear and hope and sexual reawakening. She tried to push it down; there was no point to feeling this way—nothing good could come of it. But no matter how she tried, the emotion refused to go away.

Pleading tiredness, Sharon went to bed early. The truth was, she was wide awake and could have sat up half the night talking to Reid. But the pull of attraction between them, the rising excitement of being with him, the warring warnings of her mind had all tugged and pushed at her so that she could no longer sit still in the same room with him.

When she retired to her room, there was nothing to do but go to bed, but when she did, she couldn't sleep. Turning from side to side, unable to find a comfortable position, she lay wide awake in the dark. The same old thoughts tumbled around in her head. All the nerves in her body seemed to have come to the surface, tingling even at the touch of the sheet upon her skin. Her gown was satin, slick and cool, and with every movement it shifted across her breasts, arousing her nipples to hardness. It lay across her thighs like a caress.

Sharon wanted to scream with frustration. For years sex had been unimportant to her, something she could take or leave without any problem. Why did it have to be that now she would be swept with control-bending desire? Why did she suddenly have to be so sensitive, so aware?

With an impatient sigh, she threw back the covers and got out of bed. She plopped down in the chair by the window and sat staring out, wide awake, halfway aroused, and thor-

oughly irritated. Hours passed before she was calm enough
to go back to bed and go to sleep.

The next morning she slept late. She awoke with a start,
unsure where she was. Her first thought was immediate guilt
that she had awakened so late. But even as she jumped out
of bed, reaching for her robe and slippers, she remembered
where she was and that Janis was all right now. Janis was
out of the hospital and able to fend for herself for a few hours.
Sharon knew she needed to stop being such a mother hen.
She had to loosen up or she'd start to smother her daughter. So Sharon took a leisurely shower before she dressed and
went downstairs. Janis was in the den on the couch, watching
a game show she had become addicted to while in the hospital.

She looked up and raised a hand in greeting when Sharon
appeared in the doorway. "Hi, sleepyhead."

"Hi. What time is it?"

"Late. I got up two hours ago. Reid's already out doing
something with the foreman. He said he'd be gone most of
the day, and I told him we could take care of ourselves."

"Of course." Sharon repressed the small pang she felt at
the thought of Reid's absence the rest of the day. "Have you
eaten?"

Janis cast her a speaking look. "My God, it's eleven
o'clock. I'm almost ready for lunch."

Sharon smiled. "Of course. How could you have waited
this long?" Janis's teenage appetite had returned with a ven-
geance lately.

"There's cereal in the pantry," Janis offered helpfully,
turning her eyes back to the television.

Sharon found the cereal and poured a bowl and sat by
herself at the kitchen table, eating it, glad to be away from
the noise of the television set. She hadn't realized till this
moment just how annoying living in their small apartment
was; there she could never get out of the range of Janis's TV
or stereo. They were going to have to go back to the house
in Santa Fe soon—or move permanently to Dallas.

She grimaced. Where had that come from? It wasn't even
a possibility. Their home, their friends, Janis's school, her

work, were all in New Mexico. They would return there at the end of the summer. Janis's condition was stable; the doctors said she would be fine as long as she took her medicine. She didn't need to live on the doctors' doorstep. There was no reason to stay in Dallas. Really and truly, they could move back to Santa Fe any day now.

Sharon disliked the fact that she found that thought depressing. It shouldn't be; she loved Santa Fe, always had. It wouldn't be depressing if it wasn't for Reid Maitland. She thought about him too much, liked him too much. She was starting to organize her life around him, for Pete's sake! That was something she had never done. Her daughter and her work had always been the center of her world. That couldn't change; somehow she must get back to her old life, her old balance. Basing her life on Reid would be futile—worse than that, it would be absurd.

Sharon rose and rinsed out the bowl and slid it into the dishwasher. She thought about the workshop out back. The best way to reorient herself in her own world was to return to her work. She had neglected it terribly since Janis's illness. If she were busy, if she were involved in what she loved, surely she would stop thinking about Reid. She would get back her priorities.

So, after telling Janis where she was going, Sharon walked out to the small workshop. She pulled a bar stool to the high counter and, taking up pencil and paper, began to doodle. Before long, her brain was humming, and she was sketching the ideas that came into it. Expanding, refining, changing, she was absorbed in her work, and by the end of the afternoon, she had the rough sketches drawn for a set of three stained glass panels. Not until she tossed down her pencil and stepped back to look at them propped up against the wall did she realize that her stomach was rumbling with hunger and her back was one long ache from hours of sitting bent over the counter.

She stretched, bending forward and back and rolling her head on her shoulders, working out the kinks. Her back protested at each movement. How long had she been sitting in the same position? Sharon glanced out one of the windows and was astonished to see that the sun was low in the sky. She must have worked straight through the afternoon.

A low knock sounded on the door. "Sharon? It's six-thirty. Are you about ready to quit?" It was Reid's voice. "Janis and I made hamburgers for supper."

It was even later than she thought, Sharon realized guiltily. She hadn't gone inside once to check on her daughter. She hurried to the door and opened it.

"I'm sorry. I didn't realize what time it was. How long have you been home? I must seem a terribly unsociable guest."

He smiled. "Don't apologize. I've been home awhile, but it doesn't matter. I taught Janis how to shoot pool, and we had a good time." He looked past her to the counter, where the drawings stood against the wall. "What are these?"

Reid walked past her to look at the drawings closely. "Obviously you've used your time well. A set of three?" He turned his head toward her, eyebrows raised, and she could see a gleam of acquisitiveness in his eyes.

"Yes. Those sketches are about a third the size the finished panels will be. Tomorrow I'll start drawing the patterns to size."

"What colors?"

"Muted rusts, browns, yellows, some orange right here." She reached around him to point out a place on the first panel.

"I want them."

Sharon drew back, chuckling. "Reid . . . for heaven's sake, where would you put them? You already have three of my things in your house."

"My office in Dallas," he answered promptly. "It's a corner office, lots of glass. I'll move the one I have there to my secretary's office. She'll love that. These will fit perfectly. You must have known the color scheme."

"You can't keep on buying my pieces like this," Sharon protested.

"Why not?"

Sharon shrugged. "You'll—it's crazy. You told me you

already have them everywhere you live and work. It's too much. You've done too much for me financially—all those pictures, Janis's bills—I can't let you keep on helping to support me."

He gazed at her levelly for a moment. "It doesn't have anything to do with supporting you. I told you, I loved your work long before I—came to know you well. I like having your pictures around me; I like looking at them. They're soothing; they restore something in me; they give me a kind of peace. I want them."

"Then I'll give them to you. A gift to show my appreciation."

"You don't need to show me appreciation."

"Maybe I have the need to give something to you."

For a moment they looked at each other, Reid's gray eyes steady on her deep brown ones. "All right," he said at last. "I'd like that."

Few presents had ever meant anything to Reid; he had always bought himself anything he really wanted. But the gift of Sharon's talent, her handiwork, filled him with pride and satisfaction. He wanted to kiss her again as he had kissed her here in this workroom last night. He wanted to kiss her so deeply he melted into her and she into him. He wanted to bury himself in her, take her in a primal passion that he was a little surprised to find in himself. Reid hadn't realized until this moment just how much he needed Sharon, how deep his passion for her had become. The darkness and depth of it frightened him a little even as it pulled him.

"I want you," he said quietly.

Sharon took an involuntary step backward, jolted by his unexpected words. Her heart began to hammer wildly; she hadn't been prepared for this. How could he switch so easily from talking about her panels to *this*? She wet her lips and swallowed, unable to utter a sound.

"I want to make love to you," he went on in the same low, even voice.

"Reid, I . . ." She didn't know what she wanted to say.

That she wanted him, too? That she had fallen in love with him? That it was impossible? That her heart would be broken?

He raised his hands in a calming gesture. "It's all right. You don't have to say it. I won't push you. I realize this is hardly the time or the place, in a work shed with Janis inside the house, holding supper for us. But I wanted to say it. I had to tell you how I felt about you." He smiled self-deprecatingly. "I must sound thoroughly unromantic. Too practical and straightforward."

"No," Sharon protested quickly, coming toward him a step. "No, just the opposite. There's nothing unromantic about being told you're desired." She drew a shaky breath. "I'm just a bit scared."

"Me, too." Reid smiled, and the atmosphere was suddenly light again. He took her arm, and they walked back to the house.

After supper, Janis trounced Sharon and Reid in a game of Monopoly. Even Janis was astounded at her easy win. Sharon had never been good at games, but she knew that tonight her concentration had been unusually bad. It wasn't artistic ideas or methods that teased at her mind, as it normally was. Tonight she couldn't get her mind off Reid and what he had said to her this evening. She couldn't stop the tingles of anticipation and excitement zipping through her.

Evidently bored by her easy victory, Janis went up to bed early, leaving Reid and Sharon in the den, looking at each other awkwardly. Sharon tried a smile. "I guess we'd better be glad there isn't a video game here, or she'd really have killed us."

Reid's smile was reflexive. "Yeah. Could I get you something to drink? A brandy, perhaps?"

Sharon agreed. At this point anything that would relax her would be wonderful. She didn't know what to do, torn between logic and emotion. She could guess how she would feel if she let herself get involved with Reid, then lost him. But now she wondered how she would feel if she did not give in to her feelings for him. What would it be like if she turned away from him and spent the rest of her life not knowing his lovemaking? She doubted that it would hurt any less. And she would have missed something important, something wonderful. Sharon thought about Reid's arms around her last night, pressing her into him. She thought about his lips moving over hers, his tongue exploring her mouth.

Her face felt hot, and she wondered if she was blushing. Reid came up to her, holding out the brandy snifter, and she took it and swallowed a quick gulp. The alcohol rolled down her throat like liquid fire. She set the snifter on the table beside her, her fingers curled tightly around the glass.

Reid strolled around the room aimlessly, sipping at his drink. Sharon searched for something to say. His footsteps suddenly stopped behind her. She felt his hand on her hair, and she went rigid. His hand slid down the side of her head, tangling in her hair, and his fingers touched her throat. The tips of his fingers were hot and faintly rough against her skin, now exquisitely sensitive. Her breath turned quick and shallow; she knew he must feel her pulse pounding in her throat. She leaned her head back, and his fingers slid caressingly down the line of her throat. Sharon wanted to shiver; she wanted to press her head back into him, arching her neck to his touch like a cat. Her eyes closed. Her lips parted slightly.

Reid gazed down at her face, relaxing now, melting under his hand. God, she was lovely, her face so expressive. Her thoughts and emotions were always right there on her face. She was honest and real, a woman of immediate, warm response. All his life, he thought, all his life he had been searching for such warmth. Aching for it. There had been other women; he'd even thought himself in love. But he had never felt for them what he felt right now for Sharon. He wondered why it had taken him so long to reach for that warmth.

He set his drink beside hers on the table and bent over Sharon. Both his hands encircled her throat, his thumbs drifting up and down against her neck. He pressed his lips into her hair. His hands moved lower, spreading out across her shoulders and chest, touching the soft, slick material of her blouse and the sharp jut of her collarbone beneath it. He slid over the hard plain of her chest to the swell of her breasts. Murmuring something Sharon could not understand, he trailed his lips down her hair.

Shivers coursed through her. Her hands came up to cover his, then slid up his wrist and arm. "Reid." His name was a sigh on her lips.

He reached down to her arms and pulled her up. Sharon went along eagerly, twisting to face him. She knelt on the seat of the chair, and her arms went around his neck. She lifted her face to his. He kissed her. His mouth was gentle and exploring at first, then hardening with hunger. His lips dug into hers, and his tongue possessed her mouth. He wrapped his arms around her so tightly she could hardly breathe.

Sharon didn't want to breathe, anyway. She didn't want anything except to be lost in the scent and taste and feel of Reid. She pressed up into him, kissing him back fervently, her fingers twining in his hair. She had never felt anything quite like this before, such rushing, dizzying passion, and she was starved for more. They clung together, desperate in their need. They pressed closer, aching for each other, their lower bodies blocked by the chair between them, yet unable to part long enough to leave the chair. Reid pulled her up from her knees and out of the chair. It turned over with a crash, but neither of them paid attention.

His lips left hers, and Sharon made a small noise of loss. His mouth moved down her neck, exploring the tender flesh, and Sharon's head fell back. She was crazily limp and tense all at once, and her skin was searing. Her hands moved restlessly on Reid's arms, sliding up and down, frustrated by the cloth of his shirt. She wanted to touch his skin, to feel the heat and dampness, the swell of muscle. Her fingers dug into him. His breath gusted hotly against her throat.

"Sharon . . . Sharon . . ." His hands moved over her hips

and back up. Her breasts were swollen and aching. She moved against Reid, wanting to feel his hands on her breasts. His hand curved under her breast, and his thumb brushed the nipple. Sharon shivered in response.

She opened her eyes and gazed up at him, her eyes limpid and dazed. "Make love to me," she whispered.

"Oh, God." Reid groaned and bent to kiss her again, sweeping her up into his arms.

12

Had he stopped to think about it, Reid would have felt foolish carrying Sharon up the stairs and to his bed like a lover in a soap opera. But he didn't think. He only wanted.

He carried her into his bedroom, closing the door behind him with his foot. Gently he set her down beside the bed, and as he did so, he kissed her, unable to keep from tasting her again. His tongue swept her mouth, hot and demanding. His hands roamed her back and hips, curving over her buttocks in the tight-fitting jeans and lifting her up into his pelvis, so that she felt the obvious, insistent hardness of his desire. His hips moved against her blatantly, his shaft digging into her soft abdomen.

Sharon smiled against his mouth. The evidence of his passion aroused her as much as his hot kiss. He desired her—desired her so much that his usual calm had vanished. There was no reticence in him now, no formality, no coolness or thought of propriety. There was nothing in his head about rumors or safeguarding his career, no caution because she was unsuitable for him, no fear that the reporters would have a field day if they found out. There wasn't even concern for

her. There was only need. There was only the pounding,
urgent throb of desire.

His fingers dug into her hips, grinding her into him.
"Sharon . . ." His voice trembled slightly, as though he were
at the edge of his control. "Ah, sweet. Love. I want you."

In response her fingers went to the buttons of his shirt,
unfastening them and sliding inside. His flesh jerked under
her touch, and his arms went hard with tension. She leaned
forward to place her mouth against his bare skin, and he made
an inarticulate noise. She slid her lips across his chest. His
skin was searing and tasted faintly of salt; it smelled seduc-
tively of him. The curling chest hairs tickled her lips. Her
heart slammed in excitement. Her lips closed avidly over one
flat masculine nipple.

Reid's hands swept up her back and closed in her hair.
His grip was painful, but she scarcely noticed it. Her entire
consciousness was on the taste of him in her mouth, the
feel of his hardened nipple on her tongue. Her tongue circled
and lashed and soothed as her mouth suckled him. Reid
groaned aloud and bent his head to hers, burying his face
in her hair.

Her mouth trailed across his chest to the other nipple. She
could feel the quiver of his flesh beneath her lips, the rapid
drumming of his heart. As her lips played with him, she
tugged at his shirt, pulling it out of his trousers, and when
his shirt hung open, her hands slid around to his back and
up beneath the shirt. Her fingers pressed into the smooth
muscles of his back, exploring their contours.

His hands in her hair pulled her head back so that he could
kiss her. His mouth ground into hers, hard and almost desperate, so hot she thought he must burn her. Her skin felt
hot and very thin to her, as though anything might pierce the
fragile barrier and release the molten, bubbling heat inside
her.

Reid's hands left her hair, sliding down to her sides and
then up and around between their straining bodies to her
breasts. He cupped her breasts through her blouse, squeezing
softly and running his thumbs across her nipples. He broke

their kiss, gasping for air, and reached for the buttons on her blouse. His fingers were clumsy and hasty on the rounded buttons; it seemed to take him forever to undo them, and he tore at them in frustration until finally they were undone. Sharon knew that the buttonholes were doubtless stretched so far she could never wear the blouse again, but she didn't care. All she cared about was getting rid of her garments so that she could feel Reid's fingers on her bare skin and see his eyes as they looked at her.

He peeled her blouse back and off her arms, letting it drop, and his eyes went to her breasts, barely covered by the delicate lace and satin brassiere. His eyes were dark, the light gray almost swallowed up by the huge black pupils. He reached out and covered the mounds of her breasts with his hands, sliding across the cool, slick satin, feeling the lace catch at his skin. His fingers traced the dark circles of her aureoles visible through the thin material, then moved slowly over the smaller, upthrusting buttons in the centers. He bent and touched his tongue to one nipple, traveling slowly around it, feeling the textures of the lace and satin. He kissed the white, quivering flesh of her breast above the line of her bra, trailing down until his mouth met the cloth of the undergarment.

God, she smelled good. He longed to bury his head in her breasts. He reached behind her and unfastened the brassiere, guiding the straps off her shoulders and down her arms until it fell limply to the floor. He kissed the fragile skin of her chest, savoring the hardness of her ribs beneath it and the contrasting softness of her breasts. He nuzzled into the cleft between her breasts, drinking in the taste and scent of her. He wanted to know every inch of her, consume her bit by bit.

His hands slid down her, pressing into her, one hand in front and one behind. His fingers rubbed along the thick denim seam that ran down into the cleft between her legs. He mumbled something against her skin, his voice thick and urgent, the words unintelligible but the meaning clear. Sharon quickly unsnapped her jeans and pulled the zipper down, meaning to remove the obstruction of her clothing, but Reid was too eager to let her do anymore. His hand pushed hers aside and thrust into the opened cloth, rubbing over the slick cloth of her panties, feeling the soft swell of bone and flesh beneath it, the prickle of hair.

He took her nipple into his mouth, worrying it into elongated hardness with his tongue as he sucked gently. Sharon filled his mouth and hands; he could see and feel and taste only her. Still, it wasn't enough. Nothing would be enough until he was inside her, with her hot and tight around him, thundering to that explosion of pleasure. His breath rasped in his throat, harsh and panting.

Reid shoved her jeans down, cursing low and viciously when they clung, obstructing him. Sharon kicked off her sandals and let her jeans slide to the floor. He lifted her, his arms under her buttocks, and walked the few steps to the bed, his mouth hungry on her skin. They fell back onto the bed, their legs twining together, and his hands and mouth moved over her, touching and tasting everywhere. Almost frantically they rid themselves of the last of their clothes, wriggling out of them and kicking them aside, all the while caressing and exploring the other's body.

When at last they were free of the encumbering material, their naked flesh sliding against each other, slick with sweat, he came into her, thrusting upward in a deliciously long, slow stroke. Sharon gasped and shook; it was so sweet, so heart-stoppingly pleasurable that it was almost unbearable. Her fingertips dug into his back, and she moaned out his name. He moved slowly in, then out, over and over, building their passion to such an aching intensity that both of them were almost sobbing. Then, at last, it broke, sweeping over them in waves, deep and powerful, reaching every fiber of their beings. Reid cried out, burying his face in the crook of her neck, and Sharon wrapped her arms and legs around him tightly, holding on through the storm of pleasure.

Slowly the waves receded, leaving them exhausted and drenched with sweat, clinging to each other. With a groan, Reid rolled to the side, carrying Sharon with him. His arms and legs were around her, enveloping her. She felt drained and utterly at peace, and she knew she never wanted to leave this place, this moment.

"I love you," he whispered, and they slept.

Sharon's sleep was deep and dreamless, and when she awoke the next morning it was like coming up out of a drugged state. For a moment she was disoriented and confused. The curtains were open and the sun shone in on an unfamiliar room; a heavy weight lay across her legs. She turned her head, blinking and struggling to put everything in order in her head. Reid lay beside her, his black hair tousled against the pillow, his cheeks heavily shadowed with stubble. It was his leg that lay across her.

They had made love last night.

She gazed at him, remembering. It had been something she wasn't likely to forget, ever. Sex had never been like that for her; it seemed a little unbelievable even now. She had been right to fear making love with him. She had thought she was falling in love with him yesterday; now she felt that it would kill her to lose him.

As she watched Reid, his eyes opened. There was no confusion for him; she saw instant awareness in his eyes. He smiled. "Good morning."

Sharon felt a blush rising in her cheeks. "Good morning." It was idiotic, she thought, considering what they'd done last night, but she couldn't help the surge of shyness.

Reid edged closer and kissed her forehead. His hand stroked down her hair and neck and onto her arm. "I love you," he said.

Sharon buried her face in his chest, throwing her arm around him and hanging on tightly. "Oh, Reid, I love you, too. I love you so much."

He chuckled quietly. It sounded rich and content. "You make it sound like a confession."

"It is. I think I've loved you for weeks. I was so scared it would show, that you'd find out."

He kissed her hair. "I was scared I would rush you."

"I tried to fight it."

"Why fight it?"

"Because—you know, it's so impossible."

"Not impossible. Never impossible. Maybe there are obstacles."

"Yeah, like the press nipping at our heels. Like your career going down the drain."

"Hush." He nuzzled her ear. "I don't want to talk about politics or the press or any of those things. Right now, all I want is you. I want to hold you and kiss you and say all the silly, mushy, very important things that lovers say. That's all that matters."

Sharon lifted her head and smiled up at him. "All right." She was more than willing to throw reality and practicality to the winds. She was a woman of emotion, not logic, anyway. Right here, right now, was everything she wanted, and she was happy to thrust reality aside for the next two weeks.

He bent and kissed her. His beard was rough against her skin, but she loved it. She tightened her arms around him and gave herself up to his kiss.

They made love languidly, exploring their bodies in the light of morning. The passion built more slowly this time, and when the climax came it was not as explosive, but it was just as intense, just as strong. As they clung to each other afterward, they knew they could never again be the people they had been. They had gone too deeply and had lost part of themselves, in the process gaining something new that was a mingling of them both.

Afterward they lay together in lazy contentment. Sharon felt as though she could happily lie there with him for the rest of the day, murmuring words of love, reaching out to gently stroke each other's body, lost in the wonder of what they had experienced.

Finally, however, Reid looked at the clock and sighed. "I have to get up. I have an appointment in Amarillo at eleven o'clock." He smiled a little. "If I run for Senate, then I'll have to keep in the good graces of the folks up here, too."

He kissed her, meaning to make it brief, but finding he couldn't keep from lingering. When his lips at last left hers, he grinned, changing the angle of his head and leaning toward her again. Sharon giggled and gave him a playful shove. "Good graces, remember? Politics? Amarillo?"

"All right. All right." He rose from the bed, stretching, and walked to the bathroom. Sharon watched him go, admiring the smooth lines of his body. At the bathroom door, he paused and glanced back at her, and he smiled again to catch her watching him.

Sharon felt herself blushing and turned ostentatiously away. He chuckled and went inside the bathroom. Sharon lay back on the bed, gazing up at the ceiling. She would have to get up, too. Janis might begin to wonder where she was.

Janis.

Sharon frowned. She hadn't thought about her daughter until now. The few other times that she had had a relationship with a man, she had been careful not to expose Janis to any knowledge of the fact that she had shared his bed. No matter how free and easy her life-style was in some ways, she had never believed in the casual way many of her artist friends let their lovers into their children's lives. But Janis was older now and more likely to catch on to what it meant if she and Reid demonstrated any affection toward each other. Besides, the three of them were together in the same house.

The only way she could keep Janis from knowing would be to sneak around, trying to hide it from her. The idea didn't appeal to Sharon, but what could she do? It made her blush to even think of telling her daughter straight out that she was having an affair with Reid. Weren't there some things you ought to keep hidden from your child, even if you had a generally open relationship?

How would it affect Janis if she did find out? She liked Reid, but that was a far cry from wanting him to have an affair with her mother. The situation could be a real mess.

Sharon sighed. This was the first time she'd ever had to face this problem. No other man had ever meant enough to her to cause any problems with Janis. It had always been clear to her, as well as to any man she dated, that her daughter came first. But Reid mattered. He mattered so much it was scary.

She got out of bed and dressed, then eased open the door of Reid's bedroom. There was no sign of Janis. Quickly Sharon slipped down the hall and into her bedroom. She hurried to shower, then flipped through her limited wardrobe, searching for the most attractive outfit she'd brought with her. She finally settled on a simple dress in a style and color that flattered her. Normally she wore only the briefest of makeup, but this morning she took the time to put on eye makeup as well as foundation, blusher, and her usual lipstick.

The results were satisfying. She knew it when she looked in the mirror, and the fact was confirmed by the double take Janis did when she walked into the kitchen downstairs. Reid was already there, seated at the table with a cup of coffee and the newspaper, and he looked up when she entered, his eyes lighting up and a smile bursting across his face.

"Sharon." He stood up and started toward her, then stopped, glancing toward Janis. He looked at Sharon, suddenly awkward. His fingers curled around the back of his chair. "Good morning."

Janis stared at her. "Mom! Wow, you look gorgeous. Where are you going?"

"Nowhere." She smiled at her daughter, but her eyes went involuntarily to Reid. He looked so handsome. She wanted to go to him and kiss him.

Janis looked amazed. Her eyes followed Sharon's to Reid. Her gaze went back to Sharon's face. "I—uh, I fixed some breakfast. Bacon and stuff. You want some? I'll do a couple of eggs real quick."

"Toast is fine. Don't bother. I'm not hungry."

"It's good," Reid put in, struggling to carry on a normal conversation when all he wanted to do was kiss Sharon breathless and pull her back upstairs to bed with him. "I had some. Janis is quite a cook."

"Comes from having a mother who doesn't cook, I guess."

"Yeah. I was forced to." Janis watched her mother pour a cup of coffee and walk over to the table where Reid stood.

He pulled out a chair for Sharon, and as he released it, Janis thought she saw his hand lightly skim across Sharon's shoulder and down her arm. She blinked and followed her mother to the table, intrigued.

Sharon found it difficult to look at either Janis or Reid. She felt like an idiot. Janis was sure to suspect something. Why was she trying to hide it? She loved the man. She couldn't conceal something like that from her daughter, even if it lasted only a few weeks.

Reid closed the newspaper and refolded it. "I'm afraid I have to leave." He looked at Sharon, wanting to kiss her good-bye, but knowing he couldn't make any move toward her until she'd told Janis about them. "I, uh, I'll be in late this afternoon. Maybe we could go for a ride then."

"I'd like that."

Sharon glanced at Janis out of the corner of her eye. Normally Janis would be asking to go, too, operation or no operation, but this time she said nothing. Reid stood for another moment, awkwardly. Sharon's hand curled tightly around her cup. Then he nodded and left. Sharon looked down at the table. Silence stretched between her and Janis.

There was the sound of the front door closing. Janis leaned forward as if the noise had released her. "Mom . . ." She dragged the word out with up-and-down inflections. "What is going on?"

"What do you mean?" Sharon raised her head and tried to look blank.

"Come on. What do I mean? Is something going on between you and Reid? Did something happen?"

"Well, uh—"

"It did, didn't it?" Janis pounced, her face alight with curiosity and excitement. "Last night after I went to bed. Something happened between you and Reid. Come on, tell me. Did you—"

"Janis!"

Janis giggled. "You did, didn't you? Mom! You're blushing."

"I love him. Jan, I love him." Sharon looked at her daughter, her stomach squeezing as she waited for her response. Oh, God, if Janis was hurt or angry about it, what would she do?

Janis's eyes widened. "Really? I thought once or twice that maybe he was interested, but I couldn't tell about you. You're in love with him?"

Sharon nodded. "Very much, I'm afraid."

"Oh, Mom, I like him. I like him a lot. This is exciting!" She gave a little squeal that Sharon had often heard her utter in conversations with her friends, and reached across the table to take Sharon's hands. She squeezed them tightly. "Why afraid? Why did you say 'I'm afraid?' What's the matter? I think he's great."

"Do you? I mean, I know you like him, but I didn't know whether you'd like him as, you know . . ."

"Your boyfriend? Your husband?" She sat back, her face thoughtful. "I don't know. I think—I think I'd really like that. He's nice, Mom, and he's, well, he's already my family. It'd be nice if you two got married. Are you going to?"

"No, no, wait. Don't start making plans. I doubt very seriously that we'll get married."

"Why not? Doesn't he like you as much as you like him?"

A small, secret smile touched Sharon's mouth as she thought of the words he had whispered to her this morning as they lay in bed, sated. "I don't know. He told me he loves me. But that doesn't mean we will get married. There are lots of other things to consider. This is awfully early; we've just barely—I mean—"

Janis laughed. "You've just what, Mom?"

Sharon gave her daughter a severe look. "Stop that cackling. What I mean is that our relationship has barely begun," she explained in an overly dignified tone.

"Well, you have my blessing. I won't even horn in on the riding party this afternoon."

"You wouldn't, anyway. I'm not taking any chances with that surgery."

"Ah, Mom, you know they said I could resume a normal life, exercise and everything."

"I don't think that includes bouncing around on a horse, at least not yet."

Janis shrugged. She was too interested in the exciting development between her mother and Reid to go into a sulk about not getting to ride. She sat for a moment in silence, thinking, while her mother spread butter on a piece of toast and ate it. After a moment Janis giggled. "Hey, you know what. If you married Reid, then he'd be my uncle *and* my stepfather. How's that for weird?"

"Pretty strange," Sharon agreed, smiling at her daughter. It was amazing how quickly that obstacle had vanished. If only they could all be done away with that easily . . .

Sharon spent the rest of the day in the workroom. She had been afraid she would be too excited or too full of daydreams to get anything accomplished. But once she sat down to draft the first pattern, she found that she could channel her eagerness and good spirits into her work; she couldn't remember the last time that she'd had this much energy. By the time Reid returned late in the afternoon, she had the first drawing finished and color-coded.

Reid took her out riding across the ranch, as he had promised. At first she had thought that she might feel awkward with him, even alone, after what had happened the night before. But she found that she did not. They were able to talk as easily with each other as they always had, except that now he often reached out to touch her or kiss her and when they dismounted to walk along the cottonwoods by the narrow river, they walked with their arms around each other, stopping now and then to hug each other or to kiss. There was an excitement in her, an anticipation, knowing what the night would hold for them, though she did not wish for night to rush faster upon them. She savored every minute with him, and she did not want any of them to slip away.

He talked about the ranch as they rode, pointing out certain vistas he liked, explaining what it was like in the winter and summer, expounding on the cattle and the business operation. His face was alight with enthusiasm as he talked, and the smile that had once seemed so rare flashed often across his face.

Finally, as they were sitting on their horses, looking down on one of the stock tanks, surrounded by milling cattle, Sharon said, "I don't understand, Reid. You seem to love this place—the cattle, the land, the business, everything. Why aren't you a rancher instead of a politician?"

He glanced at her, surprised, as though no one had ever asked him such a thing before. "I don't know. I guess—the ranch is my hobby. Politics is my work, my life. I always knew I'd go into it. Everybody in my family has. Mother's family's been in politics ever since anyone can remember. One of my ancestors was in the original Texas legislature—when it was a country, not a state. She wanted it for me; Dad wanted it. In some ways, I think he wanted it more than Mother did. He'd made lots of money, but he loved that power of politics. And he didn't have the personality for it. He didn't like people; he was remote. He found it difficult even to talk to people at a cocktail party. Socializing was a real effort for him. He couldn't have stood going out and campaigning. But he always worked behind the scenes. Funding, lobbying, whatever. He was indispensable to my uncle's career in the Texas legislature."

"You went into it because your parents wanted it?"

"I never thought of it that way. But, yes, in a way I guess I did. My father was a difficult man to please. That was the one way that I could really make him proud of me. I knew it from the time I was a kid; I always planned to be a politician. No—I always planned to be a senator."

"Do you enjoy it?"

He shrugged, and again there was that same look of surprise

in his eyes. "It's what I do. It's my life. There are things I don't like about it, certainly—the deals, the press, the image-making, the fund-raising. I hate the parties; I guess I'm not too different from my father in that respect. I hate smiling and talking to people I don't know or don't like in order to get votes or money for my campaign. But you have to take the good with the bad, I guess."

"What's the good?"

He thought for a moment. "I can't deny that I like the power. That I like being popular. And I'm good at it. I can help people. Maybe this sounds pompous and egotistical, but I can help our country. That's not something to be taken lightly. I remember when I was a kid, my mother used to tell me, 'You can influence the course of history.' " He smiled a little. "Pretty heady stuff, huh?"

"Yeah."

He turned his head and looked at her, his eyes very serious. "I have a duty to people, a responsibility. I guess that sounds pretty corny, doesn't it? Wesley always thought I was a stiff, old-fashioned idiot."

"I don't think there's anything wrong with having a sense of responsibility. I loved Wes, but . . . well, I can see now that he would have been a hard man to have built any kind of a life with. He was troubled and selfish and irresponsible, no matter how engaging he could be."

Reid sighed. "Yeah."

"You have integrity and honor, and those are wonderful qualities. You're strong, but you use your strength wisely. I wish there were more people around who believed in duty and responsibility." She paused.

"But? I hear a but in your voice."

"But I can't help but wonder if you're pursuing those things to your own detriment. They're fine qualities, but you shouldn't be trapped by them into doing something you don't like. I think you have to be faithful to yourself, too. You have to see to your own happiness, not just everyone else's welfare."

"I'm happy," he answered quickly. "In fact, right now,

I'm the happiest man alive.'' He smiled at her. ''You make me happy.''

"I'm glad."

He moved his horse closer to hers and leaned over and kissed her briefly on the lips. "I love you," he said, and after that the subject of his career was promptly forgotten.

The next two weeks were the most wonderful ones of Sharon's life. Cocooned in the privacy of the ranch, Sharon and Reid spent long hours together, talking and laughing and simply luxuriating in each other's company. They took long walks. They rode around the ranch in the Jeep or on horseback. In the evenings they sat in the old swing beneath the shade tree and rocked, Reid's arm around Sharon and her head on his shoulder.

They weren't always together. Reid usually had things to see to about the ranch for a few hours every day, and during that time Sharon worked in the shed, which she was now beginning to look upon as hers. She was bursting with energy and creativity, and her work progressed rapidly. Even so, her heart jumped when she heard the backdoor close and Reid's boots on the gravel of the drive, and she was happy to quit her work and fly out to meet him.

Janis spent most of her time in or beside the swimming pool, and the exercise and sun did much to restore her health. Except for the small scar, no one could have told that there had been anything wrong with her. Sharon and Reid often joined her at the pool, lounging under one of the umbrellas and talking softly, now and then slipping into the pool to cool off.

They were like a family, the three of them, sharing meals, sitting in the den together in the evenings, reading or playing games or looking at television, sometimes just talking. Once Reid took down an old picture album from one of the den cabinets, and they spent the evening looking through it. He showed Janis photographs of her father when he was a boy and a teenager, and told them stories about the various pictures. Janis peered at the black-and-white snapshots closely, intrigued.

"It's so strange," she breathed. "I've never quite felt that he was real. Even the picture of him that Mother had didn't make him real. But now, seeing him when he was a kid—" She made a funny face and looked up at her uncle. "Thank you."

"Here." He handed her the album. "You can have it if you want. There are plenty of others at Mother's house. This was my uncle's collection."

Janis's grin was broad. "Thank you. Thank you."

"You're welcome. If you'd like, sometime I'll bring over the boxes of his things stored in the attic of the house in Dallas."

"Would you?" Janis looked excited. "I'd love to see them."

"Sure. I'll do it as soon as we get back."

In her excitement, Janis threw her arms around Reid's neck and hugged him hard, and he held her close for a moment, his eyes closed in an expression that was part pain, part pleasure.

Once the three of them drove into Amarillo for dinner and a movie, and several other evenings they went into Hampton, the small town near the ranch, to get ice cream cones at the Dairy Queen. Reid knew almost everyone who came in, and he nodded and spoke to them all. Sharon enjoyed watching the people. There were groups of men; there were families; there were dating couples, alone or in groups of four or six; and there were tables of teenage girls or boys. The town was so small they all seemed to know one another. The friendly greetings and visiting back and forth made it a homey, cozy atmosphere.

One evening a tableful of teenage boys kept eyeing Janis, and she them, and Sharon thought that if they stayed here long, Janis would soon be one of the crowd. She had a moment's sweet image of them living here on the ranch with Reid, a family, and Janis going to the local school, Sharon working in the shop out back all day. She could see them in a few years, talking and laughing across the tables to their friends, Janis sitting in the corner with a bunch of teenage girls, giggling over boys, or, more likely, sitting in the back with a boy, holding hands.

She sighed a little wistfully and shook the picture from her head. That was something that would never happen. Reid was wedded to politics, and she and Janis didn't fit into his life. These few weeks were all she was likely to have with Reid. She was going to have to learn to live with that fact.

If much of the time during the days the three of them were together, the nights were Reid's and Sharon's alone. Locked in the privacy of Reid's room, they made love. Sometimes it was slow and lazy, at other times fast and heated, frantic. There were nights when they laughed as they loved, teasing and carefree, and there were nights when they were intense and serious. But they were always passionate and always loving. Curiously and inventively they explored each other's bodies and responses even as they discovered the sizzling excitement of their own sensuality. Neither of them had ever had a love like this before, so tender and stunning, so deep, so filled with passion.

After they made love, they lay in the darkness, the curtains open to the starry blackness of the night sky, and talked. Their voices were hushed, and their words were of little consequence, the sort of things always spoken by lovers—love and passion and the exquisite beauty each found in the other, their pasts, their preferences. But what they said seemed very important to them, their similarities amazing, their differences amusing. There was so much they wanted to share. Sometimes Reid talked of things he wanted to do with Sharon when they returned to Dallas, places he wanted to take her in Washington. They talked of visiting her home in Santa Fe and of flying to Cozumel for a few days. Sharon tried not to let herself count too much upon such plans.

Originally they had planned to stay only two weeks, but Reid was able to rearrange his schedule and push back his work so that they could remain a few more days. Finally he could hold off the outside world no longer, and he had to leave. He suggested that Sharon and Janis remain on the ranch longer—for the whole summer if they liked, but Sharon found that the ranch lost much of its appeal if Reid were not there, so she refused.

He smiled when she did so and leaned over to kiss her on the nose. "I'm glad," he confessed. "I was trying to be big about it and say to myself that if this was what you and Janis needed, I'd be happy. But, frankly, I hoped like hell you'd want to go back to Dallas, where I can see you all the time."

"All the time?" Sharon echoed.

"Every minute I get a chance. Unfortunately, I have the kind of life where something always seems to be intervening, but whenever I'm free I'll be on your doorstep."

His words made Sharon a trifle breathless. She wanted badly to believe him. She knew he believed himself at the moment, but she couldn't imagine how he could actually do what he promised. When they were back in Dallas, when he was once again involved in his career, the problems would begin to raise their heads and then he would drift away from her.

They flew back to Dallas, and Reid drove them to their apartment. He helped carry in their bags, then walked reluctantly to the front door. Sharon trailed after him, trying to swallow her tears. Damn it, she would not cry! She would not spoil everything by crying now. She had known what she was getting into, and she'd chosen to take the risk. Even if she never saw him again, it would have been worth it. She had found a kind of love she hadn't known existed.

Reid turned to her at the door. His hand curled around the back of her neck, and he bent to kiss her. It was a light kiss at first, but it deepened. They leaned together. Sharon was filled with yearning; she felt as if her heart was heavy and sodden, weighed down with bittersweet tears. Oh, God, what if she never saw him again? How would she live without him?

Reid embraced her fiercely. "I don't want to go." Sharon made an inarticulate noise of agreement. "I probably won't be able to see you tonight. I'll have a ton of work thrown at me the minute I walk in the door. But tomorrow—would you like to go out? A movie? Dinner? What would you like?''

Sharon shrugged. "Whatever." It really didn't matter. All she wanted was to see him again.

"All right." He wiggled his eyebrows suggestively. "Then maybe I'll just take you back to my place."

Sharon smiled. "I like the way that sounds."

He kissed her again. And still he lingered. "I love you."

"I love you, too."

He straightened and stepped back, recalling himself to duty. "I'll call you."

Sharon nodded, her throat suddenly too clogged to say anything. He walked out, and she stood in the open doorway, peering after him. She watched him walk away and get into his car. She continued to watch until his car was out of sight.

He had said he would call her, and he would. She knew Reid; he wouldn't lie. He could call her, and they would doubtless see each other again. But she wondered if it would really be the next night, or if his work would interfere. She wondered how long it would take before Reid faced up to the reality of the situation, before he saw how impossible a romance with her was. Would it be only days or weeks? Would she be lucky enough that it might last another month or two?

Tears shimmered in her eyes. However much time she might be given, she knew it would not last. She closed the door softly and walked away.

13

When Reid called her that night, Sharon could not suppress a pleased chuckle.

"Why are you laughing?" he asked, smiling just at the sound of her voice.

"I didn't expect you to call tonight."

"I said I'd call, didn't I?"

"Yes. But this is sooner than I thought."

"That's because I'm already lonely. Well, if you want the truth, I was lonely as soon as I left you."

"Come on."

"I was. Are you saying that you didn't miss me?"

"Yes, I missed you."

"I feel like an idiot. I didn't act this way even when I was a teenager."

Sharon grinned. She liked to think that she had the ability to shake Reid out of his usual pattern. "Maybe you're making up for the past."

"I don't care. I'm discovering that I like it."

"I do, too."

"My bed is too empty. The apartment's too quiet. Usually

I enjoy the chance to be alone and have some peace. But not tonight. I wanted to talk to you. I even wished I could hear Janis looking at MTV in the den.''

Sharon chuckled. ''That's getting pretty desperate.''

''I am,'' he admitted. ''I miss you like hell.''

They hung on the phone talking for almost an hour, neither one of them willing to say good-bye. When they finally did tear themselves away, Sharon was lonely and sad. Reid was right. The bed was terribly empty without him in it. She'd slept alone all her life, and now, after only two weeks with Reid, it seemed strange to be in bed by herself.

The following weeks were an emotional roller coaster for Sharon. When she was with Reid she was happy; when she was away from him she was lonely. And always, always, she was waiting, wondering when he would begin to pull away from her. They went out often, and he called her even more often, but it was never enough. They made sweet, passionate love at his apartment, but they could not spend the night together. Sharon had to come home; she couldn't leave Janis at their apartment by herself all night. Making love in her own apartment made Sharon so nervous and jumpy she could hardly enjoy it. It had been different at the ranch house, where Janis's bedroom was separated from Reid's by a long hall. But in this small apartment, with its paper-thin walls and single bathroom and Janis's room right across the hall, Sharon was uncomfortable. Reid said he understood, but they were both dissatisfied. Sharon wanted back the wonderful nights that they had spent together on Reid's ranch.

It was not that Sharon's love for Reid was any less strong, nor that her passion wasn't as tempestuous and overwhelming as it had been. If anything, she felt as though she loved and wanted Reid more each day. It was just that she wanted more. She wanted everything. No matter how much she reminded herself that getting everything was impossible, she couldn't keep from wanting it.

One morning Reid called her, catching her in the midst of cutting colored glass for her three panels. She jumped up to answer it, bumping the table and muttering under her breath when the pieces jiggled. (How long was she going to have to cut on this wiggly table, anyway? It was ridiculous. She ought to go home to Santa Fe and her studio.)

As soon as she heard Reid's voice, a smile spread across her face, and she turned away from the pieces of glass on the table. For a few minutes they exchanged the same ordinary morning things they always said—How are you; how did you sleep; I missed you; the bed is empty; I love you. Then Reid said, "I have a function I have to attend Saturday night."

"Oh." Sharon made a virtuous attempt to hide her disappointment. She had expected them to spend the evening together.

"I know it will be hopelessly boring. A dinner for a retiring judge. But he's powerful in the party, and I have to go."

"I understand."

"Are you understanding enough to endure it with me? Come on, now, wouldn't you sacrifice just one evening for me?" His voice turned cajoling. "You'd make the thing a hell of a lot more interesting. I might even be able to keep the glazed look out of my eyes."

"You want me to go with you?"

He chuckled. "That was the general idea."

"I'm sorry. You surprised me. I mean—a public thing. There'll be media there, won't there?"

He sighed. "Probably. Judge Holcomb's a pretty important man. But we can't hide from the media forever. They're bound to catch us at some party or another." He paused, and his voice had an edge of uncertainty as he continued. "That is, unless you plan on skipping them all. Sharon? Do you hate that kind of thing? Are you going to always want to bow out of them?"

"No! That is, well, I imagine that I won't particularly like it; but I've never been to one, so I don't know for sure. But if you want me, I'll certainly go. It's just that I thought, well, you know, that you'd want to keep it a secret."

"I don't plan to shout out what we do in bed together. But

I don't think it's terribly indiscreet for a bachelor politician to escort a lovely woman to a political function. In fact, it might be worse not to.''

"That's not what I meant," she retorted, her irritation at his teasing too laced with pleasure to sound serious. "I meant it probably wasn't a wise idea to be seen with me, after what everyone was speculating at first."

"Yeah, it'll probably revive it. I've tried to come up with a way to spike their guns, but I'm afraid we'll have to take our lumps. Just face it and hope it'll blow over. I certainly don't intend to go everywhere alone now—or take another woman out to throw the press off the scent."

Sharon smiled. "Then I'll be happy to come with you." She probably would have consented to go with him to the moon if he'd asked. "What does one wear to a judge's retirement banquet?"

"Oh, Lord." He began to stumble through a description of the types of dresses he had seen at such an event.

Sharon cut him off quickly. "Never mind. I'll figure it out. I'll call Hollis."

"I'd better warn you: Mother will be at this, too. We'll sit with her."

Sharon's stomach went ice cold. "Your mother?"

"Yeah. She and Dad were friends of the judge's from way back. Dad backed him financially in the early days."

"Oh, Reid, I don't know." She was willing to face the gossip, the whispers, and the reporters, but this! Thinking of the slim, aristocratic-looking woman who was Reid's mother, she couldn't suppress a shiver. Mrs. Maitland would dislike her. She was bound to. This party would be like running the gauntlet.

Almost as soon as she hung up from talking to Reid, Sharon hopped in her car and zipped over to Hollis's house. Hollis, as usual these days, came bouncing down the stairs to greet her, her baby Dean on her hip.

"You look radiant," Sharon told Hollis honestly. Hollis had always been alluring, tempting, even exotic, but now she was beautiful. She glowed as if lit from within.

"Motherhood, my dear," Hollis said with a brilliant smile, mocking her own exuberance. "Apparently it agrees with me."

"I'd say so. You look better every time I see you."

"Having a maid and a housekeeper and a part-time nanny helps." She hefted Dean higher, and he stretched out his arms toward Sharon, babbling.

Sharon chuckled and reached out to take him and swing him up in the air before giving him a hug. He crowed with laughter. "Oh, God, that sounds so good." She nuzzled the baby's fat, creased neck. "And you feel so good. Yum, yum, yum, I could eat you up."

Dean giggled and bounced. Sharon looked up at Hollis. "He is so gorgeous, Hol. Those big, dark eyes—he's going to be a heartbreaker someday."

"He already is. He has Mama and me under his spell. Even Jack. You should hear him swear Dean's saying 'Daddy.' I keep telling him he's trying to say 'doggie.' "

"Hollis! You mean thing!"

Hollis laughed. "Jack's supposed to be a shark, not a pussycat. I keep telling him he'll ruin his image. Come on, let's go into the playroom. It's the most comfortable place in the house."

They went upstairs to a large room that looked like an annex of the Neiman Marcus children's section. Toys, toy chests, slides, a baby gym, and stuffed animals ranging from holding size to gigantic filled the room. Sharon set Dean on the floor, and he began to crawl toward a clear ball with a whirling butterfly inside. She and Hollis flopped down into beanbag chairs in bright primary colors. Hollis was right. This was far more comfortable than most of the elegant rooms in Hollis's house, and it was sheer joy to watch a baby happily at play again. A funny ache started around Sharon's heart. Suddenly she was remembering the sweetness of a baby—and missing it.

Oh, Lord, was she going to start wanting a baby now? A baby of Reid's? Impossible, impossible. She forced her attention back to what Hollis was saying.

"—would have believed it of me. You know, actually I'm not doing too bad at motherhood. I figured I'd be lousy, even though I did want him so much."

Sharon grimaced. "Don't be silly. Why shouldn't you be a good mother?"

Hollis shrugged. "I don't know. That's just the way I viewed myself. But so much of my bitterness is gone. I hadn't even realized how bitter I was. How much I disliked myself." Her gaze followed her thumbnail as it traced a seam of the chair. "I wouldn't say this to anyone but you, but I think maybe I've made up for the abortion, at least a little. Sometimes I used to wake up at night, and my cheeks would be wet and Jack would be holding me. He'd say I was crying in my sleep. I had been dreaming about babies." Her face was pensive and sad, then it brightened, and she raised her eyes, looking toward Dean. "Not anymore."

"I'm so happy for you, Hollis."

Hollis flashed her a tremulous smile and blinked. She straightened. "Well, so what's been happening in the big, bad world? I've been oblivious to everything but Huggies and smushed carrots and peas—and that fund-raiser for your brother."

"Ames?" Sharon looked surprised. "Is he coming here?"

"Not for several months. But there's a lot of preparation for one of these things."

"Why are you giving a fund-raiser for him?"

"Well, he found Dean for us. I thought the least I could do was help his mission. And if there's one thing I know, it's wheedling money out of rich people. Jack says I'm the best, bar none."

"But what does Jack think about your doing it? I've always gotten the impression that Ames was not his favorite person."

Hollis shrugged. "Me, too. But, on the other hand, Jack's one of Ames's biggest donors. And he was who Jack turned to when he went after a baby. I don't know. Maybe he admires Ames, in his own way. Sometimes I can't figure Jack out. I gave up wasting time trying—you just take him as he is.

Anyway, he knows we owe Ames. He hasn't said a word against it."

Sharon was not as sure as Hollis of Jack Lacey's equanimity concerning the fund-raiser. Sometimes she suspected that Hollis wasn't aware of the extent of Jack's feeling for her. But Sharon had seen the expression on his face when he looked at Hollis, and she didn't think he was unconcerned about Hollis doing anything, even a charity party, for the man she had once loved.

"We'll have a silent auction, as well as a dinner and dance," Hollis went on. "I was wondering if you would donate one of your pieces."

"Of course. You know I will, for Ames's work."

"I tried to call you a couple of weeks ago to ask, but I couldn't get you."

"We were out of town. Reid took us to his ranch."

Hollis's gaze sharpened at her words, and Sharon felt heat rising in her face.

"What is this?" Hollis sounded intrigued. "Something's happened. I can tell by the look on your face; you're utterly transparent."

Sharon grimaced. "I hope everyone can't read me as well." She paused. "You're right."

Hollis grinned, bringing her knees up onto the soft chair and wrapping her arms around them. Sharon knew the posture well; it was Hollis's getting-down-to-the-gossip look. "So tell," Hollis urged.

"Hollis, really—"

"That good, huh? You slept with him."

Sharon nodded.

"And?"

"And what?" Sharon looked at Hollis indignantly. "You expect me to give you the details?"

Hollis laughed. "No. You were always too much of a prude for that. Although I wouldn't mind knowing if he's as staid as he looks . . ."

"Hollis!"

Hollis laughed again, tossing back her head in a familiar gesture. "All right. All I want to know is the condition of your heart. And his. Are there going to be any announcements forthcoming from the good representative's office?"

"No. Don't be silly. We're just—"

"Don't say friends."

"No. But we—it's only been a few weeks, after all."

"It doesn't take a lifetime."

"Reid could never be serious about someone like me; he can't afford to."

"He's got that little heart? Sounds too cold for you, my dear."

"No! Of course he's not cold. He's very warm and kind."

"Mmm," Hollis replied noncommittally. "That's not what I'd say about someone who picks his spouse on the basis of his political career. Of course, I've heard that's what he did the first time around."

"It's not like that!"

"No? How is it?"

Sharon glared at her friend, feeling backed into a corner. "It's just impossible for him. I'd wreck his career."

"How can you be certain of that?"

"You saw what happened when he donated his kidney to Janis—all the insinuations and outright accusations."

"Maybe they'd be happy to see him make an honest woman of you."

"Get serious."

"Okay." Hollis leaned forward earnestly. "Do you love him?" Sharon nodded. "Does he love you?"

"He told me he did."

"But you don't believe him?"

"Of course, I believe him. But I don't know if he's faced up to what it will mean yet."

"Listen. I've told you for a long time that I didn't think he was such a bad guy."

"I know. And you were right."

"I hope so. I don't know Reid well—I see him now and

then at a party or something, and he's come in to buy your pictures. But I sense that he's nice, that deep down he's a good guy. If he is, if he loves you, he won't hide you away. He won't make you his secret mistress. If he did that, he wouldn't be worth it. Trust me.''

"He's not hiding me. That's why I came to see you. Reid invited me to go with him to a retirement party for a judge.''

"This is looking better and better.''

"Don't get your hopes up.''

"Why not? Listen, I used to be the Queen of Cynics. But this kid has proven me wrong.'' She pointed to Dean, sitting in the middle of the room with a soft plastic toy, alternately picking at it with his fingers and sticking it in his mouth. "If I can get a beautiful baby like that, and if I can be a good mother, anything can happen.''

Sharon smiled. "You deserved it.''

"Just my point. So do you. Now. Why did you come here because of a retirement party?''

"To find out what to wear. I've never been to anything like that. My fanciest party has been an opening at a gallery, and artists are supposed to look strange, anyway. Tell me what kind of dress to buy.''

"I'll do better than that. I'll lend you one of mine. Let's go look in my closet.'' Hollis stood, holding out her hands to the baby. "Come on, punkin. We gotta go now.''

With a heart-melting grin, Dean dropped onto all fours and crawled to Hollis. She picked him up and settled him on her hip, then led Sharon down the hall to her bedroom and into the gigantic closet that held her clothes. Handing Dean to Sharon, she went to one section of the closet and began to sift through the heavy clear plastic garment bags.

"I want something conservative,'' Sharon warned, knowing Hollis's usual taste in clothes. "Mrs. Maitland's going to be there.''

Hollis stopped, her hand in midair. She turned to stare at Sharon. "His mother? The Dragon Lady herself? This is getting serious.''

Sharon nodded. "Is she that bad?"

Hollis shrugged. "Not if you don't mind coldness, ambition, and a complete absence of humor."

"Oh, God. She's going to slice me up into little pieces, isn't she?"

"She can be intimidating. I don't know her well, mind you. We don't run in the same circles. She's very much old Country Club, you know, and she probably thinks Jack and I are crude and nouveau riche, coming from only a generation or two of money. She's got that old 'Southern lady' demeanor, like a steel butterfly. Very proper, very genteel, and oh, so gracious, but iron-willed."

"Great. You're really building up my confidence."

"Don't worry. You can handle her. You're a strong lady, too, and you have a distinct advantage—her son's in love with you."

"I don't know if that's enough."

"Just be ladylike and smile politely, whatever she says. Cool and very nicely unbending, that's the tack to take with her. Don't let her fluster you. And I have just the dress." She pulled a garment out and held it up in front of her. "Black, chic, but demure."

Sharon took the hanger from her and looked at the dress, turning it around. "Except for the fact that there's no fastening in the back between the neck and the waist and you can see a strip of three inches of skin all the way down."

"This blousy part in the back covers that most of the time." Hollis grinned. "Besides, that's the part Reid'll like."

Sharon chuckled and looped the garment over her arm. "Okay. You sold me." They went out of the closet, giggling together like the girls they had been in college so many years ago. It was strange, but at the moment, Sharon felt every bit as young and hopeful.

Sharon was surprised and pleased to find that she enjoyed the retirement banquet far more than she had thought she would. As always, she loved being with Reid, no matter where or why, and tonight there was an added fillip of excitement in knowing that he was showing the world that he was interested in her, no matter what they thought. But she had been afraid that she would feel ill at ease all evening, that it would be obvious to everyone that she didn't belong here. However, she realized, after her first glance around the room, that she was as attractive and well dressed as any woman there.

Moreover, as Reid circulated through the crowd, speaking to the many people he knew, he didn't leave her alone, as she had feared he might when his politician's blood was flowing hard and fast. He held her arm or her hand, was always very solicitous of her, and he introduced her to everyone. Sharon was amazed at the amount of names he could remember, as well as the countless tidbits of information about each one. She couldn't remember a quarter of the people to whom he introduced her. Everyone smiled at her as if pleased to meet her and engaged her in small talk, easing her inner awkwardness. Although there was a great deal of political conversation, it was too new to Sharon for her to be bored, and she listened intently, wanting to understand this part of Reid's world.

She was surprised that Reid told everyone about her being an artist—and he said it with great pride. People seemed intrigued by her work, which amazed her even more. She would have thought that a political group would dismiss anything artistic as unimportant.

Sharon was beginning to feel pleased with the way the evening was turning out—until she glanced across the room and saw a small, impeccably dressed, white-haired woman sitting at a table as if holding court. Reid's mother. Sharon's stomach dropped. She hadn't yet faced the real acid test.

Reid skillfully made his way past several knots of people, smiling and greeting them and talking just long enough to be friendly, as he steered Sharon toward his mother's table. Finally they reached the table, and Mrs. Maitland turned and smiled up at her son. Her eyes slid to Sharon with only a hint of curiosity.

"Reid." She held out one hand to him, and he took it for a moment. It wasn't what Sharon would have called a warm and loving greeting. "How are you, dear?"

"Fine. And you?"

She nodded. "I'm doing well."

"I'd like you to meet Sharon Thompson. Sharon, this is my mother, Louise Maitland."

Recognition touched Mrs. Maitland's eyes, followed by a fast, bright flash of anger. Neither lasted but an instant, immediately smoothed away into a look of polite interest. "How do you do?"

Sharon responded with a greeting, forcing a smile onto her face. She was sure that Reid's mother was displeased. There was no glacial look, no snubbing of her, but neither was there any warmth in her face. And she had seen that quickly suppressed look of anger.

"Sharon is an artist. She works in stained glass."

The woman seated on Mrs. Maitland's right looked interested. "Really. Are you the one who did the pictures in Reid's office?"

"Yes," Reid answered for Sharon.

"Speaking of Reid's office," Mrs. Maitland slid in, "have you seen it lately? He's had a decorator redo it, and it's most attractive."

"Really?" The conversation was shunted off into a discussion of color schemes and furniture styles. Sharon wondered if she was being overly sensitive or if Louise Maitland had deliberately turned the conversation away from her.

She was certain it had been deliberate a few minutes later when she and Reid were talking quietly together, his mother interrupted to point out that a certain state senator had arrived and urged Reid to go greet him. Reid stood up and looked down at Sharon. "Are you up to meeting yet another person?"

Sharon started to rise, but Mrs. Maitland made a dismissive

gesture toward her son. "Reid, honestly, give the poor girl a rest. Let her sit here and talk to us."

Reid smiled a little sheepishly at Sharon. "Sorry. I have been dragging you around, haven't I?"

"Oh no, I don't mind," Sharon protested quickly. She wanted to go with him, but his mother had effectively cut that off.

"No. You stay here and visit. I'll be back in a minute."

Sharon mustered up a smile. Reid walked away, and Sharon watched him go. When she turned back, Mrs. Maitland was speaking to the woman on the other side of her. Sharon felt isolated and suddenly cold. There were empty spaces on either side of her, and the rest of the table was involved in conversation. Sharon thought of how neatly and politely Reid's mother had just managed everything. Had she hated her on sight? Or was it that she was determined to keep Sharon in the background to avoid any hint of scandal that could affect her son's career?

The man beside Mrs. Maitland leaned across Reid's empty chair. "Hi. I'm Gerald Mikeska. Reid forgot to introduce us."

Sharon smiled, grateful for someone to talk to. "I'm Sharon Thompson."

"So I heard. You're an artist, huh?"

"Yes. I do stained and beveled glass."

"Is that right? You live here in Dallas?" Just then, Sharon could see in the man's eyes that something had clicked in his mind, and she knew that he realized she was the mother of the child for whom Reid had donated a kidney. He recalled the rumors.

She stiffened, her fingers curling into her palms. "Well, not really . . ."

"I believe Sharon's home is in Santa Fe, isn't that right?" Mrs. Maitland entered their conversation.

"Yes, that's right. I've lived there for fourteen years, although originally I am from Texas." Sharon knew she was babbling, as though if she talked enough about this inane

topic, Mr. Mikeska would forget all about her possible connection to Reid.

"Is that right?" Mrs. Maitland was her ally in that regard.
"Where are you from?"

"A little town near Childress."

"You know, an old classmate of mine was from Childress.
My goodness, I haven't thought of her in years. I wonder
whatever happened to her." Louise Maitland offered a self-
deprecating smile. "Gerald, do you think that's a sign I'm
getting old, sitting around thinking about people I knew long
ago?"

"Nonsense," Mikeska returned gallantly, following her
red herring. "You will never be old."

"How kind of you to say so. But, then, I suppose I must
have been fishing for a compliment. Now, I know that's not
a sign of old age—I've been doing it since I was a girl."

A couple walked over to the table and stopped to greet
Mrs. Maitland. She was quick to introduce them to Gerald
Mikeska. As the four of them talked, Sharon sat back with
a sigh of relief. She wasn't cut out for this kind of life.
She didn't know how she would have handled it if Reid's
mother hadn't stepped in and taken over. What would she
have said if he had asked questions about her and Reid?
She didn't know how she could convince anyone that the
rumors weren't true. If she protested, it was likely to make
a person believe exactly the opposite. She supposed she
should feel grateful for Louise Maitland's help. But, looking
at the woman, she couldn't feel anything but a stirring of
dislike.

The woman had not expressed one word of interest in
Sharon or her daughter. Janis was her granddaughter, and
she had not even inquired after her health. Sharon thought
about the long weeks that Janis had been in the hospital. She
must have known that Janis was Wes's daughter, the only
grandchild she had, the offspring of her dead son. Yet not
once had she come to visit Janis or even called to ask about
her condition. There had been no flowers from her and no
cards. It wasn't natural. Mrs. Maitland was cold and un-

feeling. Why, she hadn't even come to visit her own son in the hospital.

Sharon looked down at her laced fingers in her lap. She had clenched them so tightly together that they were digging into her hands. It was ridiculous to let Reid's mother affect her this way. She was nothing to her and never would be.

Reid slid into the seat beside Sharon. "Hi. Sorry I got pulled away. I promise it won't happen again the rest of the evening. Did you and Mother get to know each other?"

"A little," Sharon answered noncommittally. She wondered how influenced Reid was by his mother. She was certain Mrs. Maitland would do her best to see that Reid stopped seeing Sharon.

Sharon straightened, indignant anger surging through her. Maybe it wasn't in the cards for her and Reid to be together; maybe they would have only a brief, sweet love; but she was determined that that wasn't going to be decided by Reid's mother. Louise Maitland was used to getting what she wanted, but this time Sharon Thompson was going to make it damn difficult.

Sharon smiled dazzlingly and slipped her hand into Reid's. "I'm glad you're back."

The look in his eyes told her he found her beautiful. "So am I, sweetheart. So am I."

It didn't surprise Reid the following morning when his secretary announced over the intercom that his mother was in the outer office, wanting to see him. He wasn't sure if Sharon had sensed his mother's animosity toward her last night; Louise Maitland could be subtle about such things. But Reid knew her well enough to realize that she had been appalled and furious when he brought Sharon to the party with him.

"Send her in," Reid ordered and stood up. Might as well get the battle over with now. Otherwise she'd be sniping at him for weeks.

Mrs. Maitland opened the door and walked in. Even at sixty-one, she was still a slender and attractive woman who moved with grace. Her mind was as sharp as a tack, and there were few in the state who knew the political scene any better than she, but she had always cloaked her brain and her steel ambition in a covering of feminine softness and allure. She knew exactly how to get what she wanted. She walked over to greet her son, placing her hands on his shoulders and stretching up on tiptoe to give him a peck on the cheek.

"Reid. How are you?"

"Mother. About the same as I was last night." He kept his tone light as he took her arm and walked her to the couch. She sat down on the couch, and Reid brought one of the chairs from in front of his desk over to the couch for himself. He knew she had expected him to sit on the couch with her, and he had taken away some of her power by staying apart from her. There had always been games of power and control between the two of them.

"I must admit I wondered if you were quite well last night." Louise's voice was laced with irony.

"Perfectly well." He pretended not to understand the thrust of her remark.

Louise gazed at him, her bright eyes assessing him. "You were always one who appreciated straight talk—one might even say bluntness."

He waited, polite interest on his face.

Louise sighed. "I can see you intend to be difficult." She leaned forward, her expression suddenly unmasked and intent. "Reid, have I ever done anything that wasn't in your best political interest?"

"I doubt it."

"Have I ever guided you wrong or given you poor advice?"

"Not in politics, no."

"Then will you trust me when I tell you that you are on the verge of sabotaging your political future—a future, I might add, that many of us have worked long and hard to help you to attain."

"I'm sure that you believe that," Reid hedged.

"That's not the same, and you know it. But never mind. I'm not here to quibble over semantics. I'm here to stop you from making a serious mistake."

"Sharon Thompson is not what I would classify as a mistake."

"Then you aren't seeing clearly. You're blinded, as most men seem to be, by your hormones. Fortunately, I am able to see better."

"Mother, you're getting into something that is none of your business. It would be better all around if you would simply stay out."

"I can't." She sat back. Her mouth was a straight, harsh line, and there was little in her face of the lovely, genteel lady of a few moments before. "Your life is at stake."

"Surely that's a little melodramatic, Mother. You usually aren't."

"I usually don't have reason to be. Not where you're concerned. In the past you have exhibited a clear, coolheaded logic, a thorough grasp of the situation. But not this time. Sharon Thompson may be a beautiful girl, Reid, but she's all wrong for you. Worse than that, she can ruin you."

"You're overreacting."

"I don't overreact."

"Not usually."

Mrs. Maitland's eyes narrowed. "You think I'm saying this because of Wes, don't you?"

Reid sighed. "Yes. I remember that when I told you about her and the baby all those years ago, you decided that Sharon was the reason Wes killed himself."

"I still think so. Wes came from good stock, even if he was somewhat wild and feckless; he would never have committed suicide. She drove him to it. When she told him she was pregnant, he would have known he couldn't marry a nobody like that. I'm sure she hounded and threatened him, told him that she would create a scandal for the whole family. He knew our family's reputation; he knew you were beginning your political career. He didn't want to ruin them. Yet he couldn't have brought himself to marry a girl like that."

Reid let out a snort of disgust. "Jesus Christ. Wes never gave a damn about this family's reputation; he was usually busy trying to ruin it. As for my political career, he would have loved to see it go down the tubes. He thought I was a stuffed shirt, the kid who had always received everything from this family while he had gotten nothing. I remember Wes much more clearly than you do. He was addicted to amphetamines and God knows what else. I don't know whether he wanted to commit suicide or whether he just accidentally overdosed. But it didn't have anything to do with Sharon. You want to have good memories of Wes, and I understand that. There's nothing wrong with it. But you're making up a fantasy. I loved Wes; we all did. He was charming and loveable. But he had problems. He took drugs. Sharon can't be blamed for that."

"And I'm to blame for it? Is that what you think?"

"I didn't say that."

She stood up and walked away from him. She stood looking out the window at the skyline of Dallas. "Whatever the truth of that situation, it's not what I'm concerned about now. It's not the reason you have to stop seeing that woman. Your career is what's important. You know what the rumors were when you donated your kidney to her child. They'll all come back now, ten times worse, when it gets around that you're dating her."

"I think I can handle it. I can weather some bad publicity. You can't expect me to drop her because some people might gossip."

"*Some people*," she repeated caustically, "are your constituents. You need them."

"Don't you think that my voting record, the things I have done, will count more than who I'm dating?"

She turned, shooting him a withering glance. "Don't be naive, Reid. You've been in politics too long to believe that voters act rationally."

"There have been occasions when they have."

"You don't have to give up seeing her, if she is that important to you. Just don't do it publically."

"I see. It's all right if I keep her as my mistress, if I sneak by every now and then to see her, as long as I don't take her out with me. As long as no one knows." His mother simply looked at him, her face closed and hard. "Well, I'm sorry, Mother, but I can't do that. I don't intend to live my life that way, and I sure as hell don't intend to do that to Sharon and Janis. I love her. I love both of them."

"You're a fool if you throw away everything you've worked so hard for, just for love."

Reid knew that Louise Maitland had never been that kind of fool and never would be. It saddened him. For many years he had fought the knowledge, but as an adult he had come to accept it. Wes hadn't.

"I'm sorry you feel that way," he replied evenly. "But I don't agree with you. I'd be worse than a fool if I turned away from Sharon. You might as well resign yourself, Mother. I not only plan to date Sharon, I intend to marry her."

14

Reid hadn't realized what he wanted to do until the words came out of his mouth. But even as he spoke them, he wasn't surprised. It was natural. It was obvious. He loved Sharon, and he wanted to marry her. The past few weeks had been faintly dissatisfying, despite their love, simply because they could not really be together. He wanted to sleep with her, wake up beside her, eat with her, talk with her. He wanted her in his apartment. He wanted his ring on her finger and his name after hers.

As soon as he could hustle his mother out of his office, Reid also left, telling his secretary to cancel any appointments he had. The way he felt right now, he couldn't keep it to himself. He had to talk to Sharon. He had to ask her to marry him.

As he drove to her apartment, his mind hummed with plans: They would get married this summer, the sooner the better. He would have to leapfrog back and forth between Dallas and D.C. some, but that was all right. As soon as they were married, they'd return to Washington. He needed to see about getting Janis enrolled in school there—Heavens, he didn't even know what grade she should be in. He would adopt Janis; he wanted her to be his daughter legally, and besides, that way she could finally have the name she was entitled to.

They would need to buy a house here in Dallas. He had one in Washington, but he'd kept only an apartment here, spending most of his time in D.C. But an apartment wasn't satisfactory for a family. They needed more room, and Sharon would have to have a studio to do her work in. He'd better call a real estate agent as soon as possible. He'd have to rearrange his schedule to open up time for a honeymoon. He wondered where Sharon would like to go.

Reid parked his car in the lot of Sharon's apartment building and bounded up the stairs to her door. His knock on the door was fast and loud, and he shifted on his feet impatiently, waiting for her to open the door. When Sharon did, she stared at him, amazement, then puzzlement chasing across her face.

"Reid?" She said it questioningly, almost as if she weren't sure it was he. It was rare for Reid to skip work; he was the type who worked weekends and evenings, too. He looked different, too. His gray eyes were light and almost glowing, and there was an air about him of scarcely contained excitement.

All day Sharon had been fearful that his mother would try to persuade Reid not to see her again. She had wondered if Mrs. Maitland had talked to him and, if so, how Reid had reacted. She had been afraid that he would come to her tonight and break it off. But in all her imaginings, she hadn't pictured him like this, rushing over in the midst of work, filled with eagerness.

He grinned. "Hi. Can I come in?"

"Of course." Sharon stepped back. "I'm sorry. I—you startled me. It's the middle of the day."

"I have something important to tell you. Ask you, rather."

"What?" She closed the door behind him, and they walked into the small living room.

He turned to face her. "Suddenly I feel foolish—and scared."

"Why?" Sharon felt at sea. What could he be talking about? Surely he wouldn't introduce it that way if he were about to tell her he wouldn't see her again.

"Because—I don't know, it's a scary situation. Being able to speak in front of huge crowds of people doesn't prepare one for this." He paused. "Sharon, I want to—I want to marry you." She stared at him, her eyes wide, not saying a word. "Will you?" he pursued.

"Marry you?"

"Yes."

"I—this is so—unexpected. You can't be serious."

"Of course I can. I am." Reid was stunned. Sharon was acting as if she'd never thought about marriage, never dreamed of it. He had been confident of her love, sure she would want to marry him as much as he wanted to marry her. Why did she stand there looking at him as if she'd never seen him before?

"Reid, I don't know." Sharon sank down into one of the chairs, not sure if she could remain on her feet.

"You don't know?" he repeated, dumbfounded. "You love me, and you don't know?"

"But I—I never thought that you would ask me, that you would want to. I've been trying to prepare myself all day for you coming over to tell me you didn't want to see me anymore."

"Why in the world would I do that?"

"Your career! After last night, with everybody seeing us together, I figured your phone would be busy all day with people telling you what a mistake you'd made."

"Only my mother, but I set her straight, at least in that regard. I told her that I planned to marry you." He paused. "Was I wrong to be so sure? Do you not want to—"

"No! No!" Sharon jumped to her feet, stretching her hands out to touch his arms. "It's not that I don't want to. I'd love to marry you. I can't think of anything that would make me happier. But after what the newspapers said, the speculation about Janis's real father—"

"I'm a politician. I've lived with rumors and speculation

about my life for the past ten years. After a while, you learn to let it slide off your back.''

"But I thought it would hurt your career. Aren't you planning to run for senator next year? That's what everyone is speculating.''

"I've considered it.''

"Well, wouldn't marrying me damage your chances? I mean, the newspapers will dig up those rumors again. Even if they don't hint that you're really Janis's father, they'll lambast me—and your brother. They'll bring up his death, his drug use, Janis's illegitimacy.''

"Your artistic life-style,'' he added, smiling. "The fact that you and your daughter lived openly for years with a man.''

Sharon's jaw dropped. "How did you know that?''

He grinned. "You think I haven't been warned about you? One of my assistants did a background check on you and was eager to show me the results.''

"You never said anything.''

He shrugged. "It wasn't really any of my business. I didn't think you'd lived the life of a nun before I fell in love with you.''

"Well, I wasn't *living* with him. I mean, not in that way.'' Sharon's eyes sparkled with indignation. "We were roommates. He paid me rent! Randy's gay, for heaven's sake!''

Reid laughed. "That just means they'll harp on your unusual life-style.''

"Reid, they'll crucify you. I don't want to burden you, to ruin your career.''

"Look.'' Reid took her hands in his and stared into her eyes. "I believe that I can keep my career and still marry you. I don't think that in this day and age, the public will turn against me, ignore my record and my platform, just because my wife had a baby by a man she loved, a man who died before they could marry. But let's take the worst-case scenario. Let's say they do. If my choice is to have you as my wife or to become a senator, then there's no choice. I love you, Sharon.''

Tears glittered in her eyes. "I love you, too. Oh, I love you more than anything." Sharon threw her arms around his neck and hugged him close. "I'll marry you. Of course I'll marry you."

Reid squeezed her tightly. "Thank God. You had me worried there for a minute."

She let out a watery little chuckle. "But I'm warning you. I don't think I'll make a very good politician's wife."

"Damn a politician's wife. What I want is you."

They told Janis of their plans that evening. As Sharon had expected, she was thrilled by the news. She flung her arms around each of them and hugged them tightly. "We'll really be a family now!" she exclaimed, her eyes shining. "When is it? Where are we going to live? Is there going to be a big wedding?"

Sharon chuckled. "Hold on. We've hardly had a chance to plan anything."

"We'll live in D.C.," Reid offered the answer to one of her questions, watching her closely. "Will you mind moving there?"

Janis looked a trifle uneasy. "I'd like to live in Santa Fe. That's where all my friends are. But I guess that's pretty impossible, huh?"

"I'm afraid so. We'll have a home here and one in D.C., but we'll spend most of our time in Washington."

"Well, I'll make friends, I guess. It won't be so bad." She summoned up a smile, although Sharon could see a touch of fear in her eyes. Janis turned toward her mother. "Will we keep the house in Santa Fe, though? You aren't going to sell it, are you?"

Sharon blinked. "I hadn't even thought about it. This happened so suddenly. I'm sure it will be awhile before we decide what to do with the house in Santa Fe."

"It might be a good idea to keep it," Reid suggested. He,

too, had seen the faint panic in the teenager's eyes. "We can always use it for a vacation home."

Janis smiled. "That'd be great." She had always had only one home. Now, suddenly, she had three—no, four, counting the ranch in the Panhandle. That thought made her grin broaden. "We'll go back to your ranch sometimes, too, won't we?"

"Sure. I go there every chance I get. Maybe we could have our first Christmas there. How does that sound?"

"Great!" The uneasiness had vanished, and all her former enthusiasm returned. She gave her mother a huge grin. "This is great. I can't wait. Can I be a bridesmaid? Can I have one of those gorgeous long dresses?"

"I don't really think it will be anything that elaborate."

"What's it going to be like, then?"

Sharon cast a questioning look at Reid. "I'm not sure. But I would think it will be small. Just family, maybe some close friends like Hollis and Jack."

"Sounds good to me," Reid agreed. "The only thing I care about is that it happen soon. I'm tired of being a bachelor."

"Sometime this summer?"

"As soon as you're ready. I have to go to Washington for a week. You think about it, and when I get back, we'll make definite plans. We'll have to look for a house here. I have one in Washington. If you don't like it, we can always find a different one, but at least we can do that later. We'll have to enroll Janis in school in D.C."

Sharon nodded. It would be easier if they were married before the school year started, so that Janis wouldn't have to change schools. Besides, Sharon didn't have any more desire to wait than Reid did. She was tired of seeing Reid only some of the time. She wanted to be part of his life.

And she would be. Sharon still had a little trouble believing what had happened. It seemed too easy, too good to be real.

During the next week, while Reid was gone, she began to accept reality. Janis and Hollis chattered about the wedding all the time and busily made plans. Her work went on hold again while Hollis dragged her around town looking at dresses.

"Hollis!" Sharon protested as Hollis went through dress after dress in some of the priciest stores in Dallas. "I can't buy these things! I couldn't possibly afford them. And I still haven't found a dress for the wedding."

"Well, you can't expect to find one in just three days. We're talking about a very special dress. Don't worry; it'll come along. We haven't gone to Lou Lattimore, and we haven't even started on the big stores like Neiman's and Lord and Taylor. Trust me. You are in the hands of an expert shopper."

"Hollis, I'm serious."

"So am I. You can't go to Washington without something to wear. After all, you'll be the wife of a very up-and-coming congressman. You have to dress the part. There'll be cocktail parties, charity balls, and God knows how many political functions. Stop worrying about the cost. Your husband belongs to one of the wealthiest families in this city."

Panic rose in Sharon. "I don't know. I don't think I'm cut out for this. I can't do those things."

"Don't be silly." Hollis saw the real fear in her friend's eyes and steered her over to one of the luxurious couches in the store. "Sit down here and listen to me. You can do anything you want to. You've proved it time and again. A few parties aren't going to get you down."

"I don't know. Sometimes I think Reid's making a terrible mistake."

"Reid's a big boy. He can take care of himself."

"There's going to be a scandal. And when we go to Washington, I might do something really stupid and embarrass him."

"Stop talking that way. Do you hear me? I don't know much about politics or Washington, D.C. But I know you. You've always accomplished whatever you've set out to do."

"Oh, Hollis, that's not true."

Hollis began to tick her points off on her fingers. "Your

family didn't want you to go into art. You did. They didn't want you to go to SMU. You did. You wanted Wes Maitland, and he fell in love with you. When he died, you didn't think you'd make it, but you did. You didn't think you could raise a baby on your own, but you've done a damn fine job of it. You made a home for yourself and Janis. You developed a career; you've established your name in the southwestern art world."

"You make me sound like Superwoman," Sharon said with a wry smile.

"Close enough. You want to know something? I love you, but I've also always envied you. I never had your strength."

"That's not true."

"Yes. It is. You're just too nice to think so. I've been bullheaded and selfish and demanded my own way a lot of times, but that's not the same as being strong." Hollis's face was deadly serious, free of the faint touch of mockery that usually lay there. "I wouldn't admit this to anybody but you—but I've had it easy all my life. First my daddy took care of me and then Jack. There aren't many doors that are closed to Mrs. Jack Lacey. It didn't take much to get a loan from a bank to start a business; the bankers fell all over themselves, hoping to impress Jack. And it didn't take much to make a success of the place. It was a symbol of wealth and being 'in the know' to buy something from me."

"You're underestimating yourself. It would have been easy to fail at your business, even with Jack's wealth and influence."

Hollis shrugged. "The point is, I've never had to try too hard. I never took a course that was hard. I had an abortion when I was a teenager rather than face my father's wrath. When Ames went down to that mission and left me here, I could have followed him. I could have found out why he did it. But I didn't. I already knew the answer. He didn't think I could make it in that kind of life; it was too hard. And I knew it, too. I never even thought about trying to live Ames's life; I just kept wishing he'd give it up for me. Well, he chose the way of life, and I didn't have the guts or enough love or whatever it took to go after him. I loved him, but I married Jack, anyway. I knew I wouldn't ever have Ames. Jack was good looking and rich, a real catch. Women would envy me for marrying him. And even though I loved somebody else, Jack set off all the bells and buzzers in bed. He made me feel good. He wanted me. It was so easy to marry him. That's not strength.''

Sharon simply looked at her, unable to say anything. She had never known exactly what happened between her brother and Hollis or between Hollis and Jack. Hollis was a closed person, proficient at blocking with a quip anyone who got too close. It seemed bizarre to be sitting here on a sofa in a fancy dress shop, listening to Hollis reveal her secrets. But Sharon was not about to say so; she didn't want to do or say anything that might disturb Hollis's unexpected revelation.

"But you—" Hollis wagged her forefinger at Sharon. "You have strength. You do whatever you have to do. You don't choose the easiest course; instead you do what you think is right, what should be done."

"Come on, Hol, you make me sound like a plaster saint."

"All I'm saying is that you have what it takes. You've got guts, talent, and brains. More than that, you have staying power. You'll be a match for whatever Washington throws at you."

Sharon smiled. "Listening to you, I almost believe it."

"Believe it, kid, believe it." Hollis glanced around, and her familiar devilish grin appeared, the dimple in her cheek popping in. "Now, look, are you ready to do some industrial-strength shopping or what?"

Sharon smiled, too, and stood up. "Lead the way."

Reid returned to Dallas three days later. He drove straight from the airport to Sharon's apartment. When she opened the door, he enveloped her in a bone-cracking hug and kissed her hard on the mouth. "The kid here?"

"No, she's gone to the movies with another girl who lives in the apartment complex."

Reid grinned and moved toward the living room, all the while kissing Sharon. Her knees hit the back of the sofa, and they tumbled over it onto the cushions. Laughing and kissing, they rolled on the sofa, reveling in the freedom of being alone in the apartment.

They undressed hastily, touching, kissing, and murmuring their love and passion as they did so. Reid kissed her breasts, suckling the deep rose centers until they were tight and hard. Their breath came fast and unevenly; their skin was damp with sweat. There wasn't enough room on the sofa, but they were too eager even to move to the floor. It seemed as if it had been weeks since they'd kissed, months since they'd made love. When he came into her, he was huge and hard, moving in driving thrusts, the embodiment of desire. Sharon wrapped herself around him, loving the feel of his skin beneath her arms and hands, the muscles shifting with his movements. She hugged him tighter to her as he plunged harder and deeper, each of them trying to meld together, to blend into each other until there was no longer a singular him or her, but only one inseparable oneness. Then Sharon shuddered and the climax took them both, sweeping them into that blissful suspended moment of unity and on into the dark, sweet peace beyond.

They lay silently, their breathing slowing, searing skin cooling, too tired and happy to even speak. Reid shifted onto his side, his arm sliding under her head, and kissed her temple softly. His fingertips slid lazily up and down her arm. Their fingers entwined, and they gazed at their joined hands.

"A ring would look nice on that finger." Reid stroked one finger down her ring finger.

"Yeah? On you, too?"

"Sure." He kissed her forehead, his lips again gentle and lingering. "God, I missed you. I never knew six days could be so long."

Sharon smiled. "Mmhmm." She raised his hand to her lips and kissed it. "Next time you'll have to stay home."

"No. Next time you'll have to come with me."

She chuckled. "Already an argument."

"No argument. We agree: We have to be together." He sighed and stretched. "I haven't slept well since we left the ranch. The bed doesn't feel right without you in it." He nuzzled her hair. "And last week I couldn't stop thinking about you. Calling you every night wasn't enough. I'm surprised I accomplished anything. The only way I could get any work done was to remind myself that I couldn't come home until I finished."

"I missed you, too. Without you here, it didn't seem quite real. I kept thinking, I'm going to find out this is a dream, a fantasy."

"No dream. I'm back." He gave her another kiss and sat up slowly. "I'm starving." He gave her a sideways glance, brimming with amusement. "Now that the important things are taken care of, I can eat."

She grinned and sat up, too, pulling her clothes back into some kind of order. "Sandwich or an omelet?"

"Omelet sounds good. And coffee." He paused in the midst of dressing and glanced at his watch. "We have to meet Phil and Susan in an hour."

"Who?"

"My aide and my publicist. You've met them."

"Oh, yeah. She came to the hospital. I don't remember him, though." She started toward the kitchen, then stopped and turned around. "Did you say 'we'?"

"Yeah. It's about the wedding."

"Oh." They must want the details for a press release or something. "But you and I haven't really discussed it yet."

"We'll do it tonight."

He strolled with her into the kitchen and began to make the coffee while she whipped up the omelet. "I don't understand," Sharon said. "Why are we having this discussion with your aide and publicist present?"

"No point in hashing it over twice. Might as well get used to it, hon. Half the time it seems I live by committee."

"That doesn't sound appealing."

He shrugged. "It's not. But after awhile it gets to be second nature. Strategy sessions. You'll be part of them from now on."

Sharon poured the beaten egg mixture into the pan, keeping her eyes on it. She didn't like the thought of making plans for their wedding with other people present. It seemed to her that it was something that should be private. But she wasn't going to voice any more objections. After all, she had known that she would be living in a fishbowl when she married Reid. It would take some adjusting on her part, but it would be worth it.

She folded the omelet over and slid it onto the plate, adding a piece of toast, golden from the toaster. While Reid ate, Sharon changed clothes and freshened her makeup. Reid assured her that there was no need to dress up for Phil and Susan, but Sharon didn't want to show up looking rumpled and plain, no matter how much like family they were. They were, after all, Reid's "family" and she wanted to make a good impression on them. It seemed important. She'd already failed to do that with his mother.

Sharon left a note for Janis, and they drove downtown to Reid's law office. Everyone else in the office had gone home, but Reid's spacious corner office was brightly lit. Sharon had never been there before, and she gazed around her with interest. Even in the darkened reception area, she recognized one of her stained glass panels hanging against the large plate glass window, and there were two more in Reid's office. She smiled. It still amazed and pleased her to find evidence of Reid's passion for her art.

A man lay on Reid's couch, a submarine sandwich in one hand. His suit coat and tie were off, the neck button of his shirt unbuttoned, sleeves rolled up. His shoes lay on the carpet beside the couch. His hair stuck up in spikes all over his head as though he'd been running his hand through it. He was talking to Susan O'Brien as they came in, gesticulating with the sandwich. She was dressed in jeans, a casual blouse, and running shoes, and she sat in the chair behind Reid's desk, her feet propped up on the desk. She, too, held a sandwich in her hand, and was busily munching on it while she jotted notes on the yellow pad in her lap. She glanced up when Reid and Sharon walked in and raised her sandwich to them in greeting, then returned to her work.

The man paused in his monologue. "Hey, Reid."

"Phil. Susan. You remember Sharon."

"Sure," Phil said. He didn't add that he would never forget her; she was the one who was sending Reid's career zooming toward the abyss.

Susan nodded. "We were just working on the announcement for tomorrow."

Phil sighed and rose, finishing his sandwich in two gulps. He ran both hands back through his hair. "Okay. Now that you're here, let's get started."

Reid and Sharon sat down. Phil perched on the corner of his desk. "Okay. What's first?"

"Date," Susan supplied from the chair behind him.

"Right. Reid's right on this point. It needs to be as soon as possible. That way we'll have more time to recover from whatever bad publicity it generates before we begin the senatorial campaign."

Sharon felt guilty. She was responsible for the bad publicity. Still, it irritated her to have this man okaying their decision to marry quickly. He had no right to approve or disapprove, and if they married soon, it was out of love, not to allow more time for the bad publicity to die down.

"We're all agreed on that point," Reid put in. "The question is the date."

Susan flipped through the pages of her legal pad. "I've jotted down some possible dates." She listed three dates, running through a synopsis of the commitments Reid had the rest of the time. "What sounds good? The one in two weeks may be too soon. There may be parties and stuff Mrs. M. wants to do first. The first week in August might be better. There are a few days after that that we can probably free up for a honeymoon. You planning a honeymoon?"

"Definitely."

"Okay. I'll have Diane make the arrangements. Where do you want to go?"

Reid glanced at Sharon. She had thought of the Caribbean or Mexico, but she felt awkward talking about it in front of the other two. She shrugged.

"What about Mexico? Didn't we talk about going to Mexico?" Reid asked.

"Yeah."

"Okay, then. Cancun? Cozumel? Or do you want the Pacific coast?"

"Cozumel's quieter, less crowded," Phil offered.

"Which would you like, Sharon?" Reid asked.

"I don't know. I've never been to either one."

"Cozumel, then. I'd welcome the peace and quiet."

"Okay, that's settled." Phil picked up a small notebook and glanced at it. "But what about the wedding date?"

"Early in August okay with you, Sharon?" Reid asked.

Sharon nodded. She didn't have anything against the date. But it was so unromantic and impersonal to be carrying on a committee discussion about it.

"Right. August eighth, then." Phil made a notation in his notebook. "Now, the place."

"I'd been thinking of having it at the house in Santa Fe. There's a lovely patio that would be big enough for a small—" She stopped. Phil was shaking his head vigorously.

"Nope. No Santa Fe. You have to get married in Texas, can't go out of state. Even D.C. would be wrong."

Sharon stared at him blankly. "What?" Was this man actually telling her that she couldn't have her wedding where she wanted it? "But I have a lot of good friends in Santa Fe. It's where I've lived for fourteen years."

"No. It makes you seem like a foreigner, you know, like Reid's marrying someone who's not a Texan. We have to downplay anything that would make you appear exotic or different. We'll emphasize the fact that you're a native Texan, that you were born and reared here, and we're going to ignore the fact that you've lived somewhere else since."

Sharon was flabbergasted. She looked at Reid. "Is he serious?"

Reid chuckled at her expression. "Phil is always serious. And he's right. It's a small thing, but it will help your image if the voters perceive you as a Texan."

And she had so much going against her that she needed every little bit she could get, Sharon added to herself. Reid was just too nice to say it.

"Does it mean that much to you to have the wedding in Santa Fe?" Reid went on, a concerned frown starting on his forehead.

Sharon swallowed what she would have liked to say and shook her head. Marrying her was going to cause Reid enough trouble with his constituents. She couldn't insist on something that would be yet another liability to him, no matter how small and trivial it seemed to her. "No, that's fine. I'm sure my friends can come to Dallas."

"Or the ranch. That's closer to Santa Fe, and it'll be a good way to keep it small and private."

"Good idea." Phil nodded his head. "We'll have a lot more control over the press there."

Sharon smiled at Reid. She knew he had suggested it to please her rather than Phil. And the ranch might be even better than Santa Fe. It was filled with memories of their love.

"Now, the next question is what angle we're going to take on Sharon."

"I don't understand," Sharon said.

Phil looked at her. "You know, how we're going to present you to the public. What sort of image we want to create for you."

Susan moved out from behind the desk. "Mrs. Maitland will take care of introducing you to society, I presume."

It was all Sharon could do to keep from snorting in derision. Considering the way Reid's mother felt about her, she was more likely to bury her with the local society rather than introduce her to it.

Reid held up a cautionary hand. "Maybe you'd better talk

to her first. Last time I spoke with Mother, we didn't part on the best of terms."

Susan shrugged, dismissing his statement as of little consequence. "I know Louise Maitland. She may object to your marriage, but your career is still the most important thing to her. She'll do whatever it takes to make you senator."

Phil gave a short laugh. "Senator. Hell, she's got her eye on the White House."

"God forbid."

"That'll work with political people and Dallas society, but Mrs. Maitland's stamp of approval won't help you with the voters. I think we need to make Sharon acceptable to them. First of all, let's make your engagement very public. Go out a lot, be seen. Sharon's a pretty woman, appealing, warm sort of looks. I think that seeing her, people will feel sympathy for her."

"Of course they will." Reid looked at Sharon and smiled. "Who wouldn't? I agree. The more they see you, the more they know you, the better they'll like you. What about it? Do you mind going out a lot the next few weeks?"

Sharon had felt awkward and annoyed, sitting there listening to the publicist talk about her as a liability that had to be overcome. However true she might know it to be, it got under her skin; yet when Reid smiled at her like that, her irritation fled. That wasn't the way Reid felt about her. He cherished her, and that was what she needed to remember. What his aide or his publicist thought about her didn't really matter. After all, she and Reid were the commodities they sold, and it was only a job to them. This was politics, and she'd better get used to it.

"No, I don't mind, especially if it means I'll see you more often."

Reid took her hand and brought it to his lips, kissing it tenderly as he gazed at her. "Perhaps you're the one who should be the politician. You know the right thing to say."

Susan quickly brought them back to the business. "Good. Along that line, we'll play up her ordeal with her daughter. I can probably work up an interview or two about that, and

Sharon can throw it in as often as possible in other interviews. Her worry, etcetera, how you saved her daughter. That makes her sympathetic and reminds them what a white hat you are. There's no way to get around the illegitimacy; everybody knows it. But one way to combat it may be to play up the fact that she's an artist. Let her look a little arty, talk up her achievements—awards, popularity, whatever. Show her work. Establish that she's a real artist, not just a dabbler. What I'm banking on is that people tend to accept a more irregular life-style from an artist. They'll say, 'Yeah, but she's an artist, you know.' A subconscious attitude."

Reid and Phil nodded. Susan continued. "Steer clear of the subject of Janis's birth as much as possible, but when we get forced into it, keep reminding them of Wes's tragic death. They were very much in love, and only his death made the daughter illegitimate."

"I don't know," Phil stuck in. "It seems to me that the less Wes is in here, the better. We don't need the stigma of drugs attached to Reid in any way, even if it's just his long-dead brother. Suicide, drug overdose—neither one'll do us any good. Plus, Wes was his brother and now Reid's marrying Sharon, and that could be a little sticky. Better to ignore it. Why not just stick with what was said at the press conference and refuse to comment now?"

Susan grimaced and began to object. Sharon simply sat, listening to them dissect her life, deciding how she would act, what she would say, where she would go. She was appalled and scared. Was this what her life would be like from now on? A publicist's puppet. An image. She glanced at Reid. He looked tired, and the relaxed happiness that had been on his face after they made love had worn off, leaving behind the same tight lines that had always been there. He was used to this, she thought. He lived with it all the time. Sharon didn't know how he endured it. It occurred to her once again, as it had many times before, how lonely Reid must be, even though he was always surrounded by people.

She reached out and touched his cheek with her fingertips. He turned and smiled. The lines of his face lifted, and his eyes were warm and loving. Reid needed her, she thought, and was surprised. She had always thought of him as so strong, so self-sufficient. But she was the only person who loved him for himself, with no regard for his career, his influence or wealth. Tenderness flooded her. With her he could find refuge from the other things and people that plagued him. She wanted to give him that.

What did all the rest of it matter compared with that? They loved and needed each other; together they could have the deep love and closeness they had always wanted. The publicists, the assistants, the media—those were just bothersome annoyances. She could learn to deal with them. She would handle the problems. It didn't matter as long as she and Reid were together.

She linked her hand with his, and he leaned over and kissed her lightly on the mouth. Sharon scooted closer to him and rested her head against his shoulder. She closed her eyes and tuned out the sound of the other two voices, aware of nothing but Reid.

15

Susan had been right. Despite her personal disapproval, Louise Maitland paved Sharon's path into Dallas society. Until the wedding in August, there was one party after another—cocktail parties, formal dinners, a black-tie fund-raiser for a candidate for governor the next year, afternoon teas, even a bridal shower given by three women Sharon didn't know and attended by still more women Sharon didn't know. Sharon's head buzzed with the names and faces she was introduced to, desperately trying to remember them, as well as match them. It was a relief now and then to see Hollis and Jack at a party and be able to relax and talk. The rest of the time she was tense, very aware that she must perform.

Everywhere she went a member of the media was likely to turn up. Susan arranged several interviews for her, carefully coaching her on how to act and how to answer the questions—and, more important, how to avoid answering other questions without giving offense. It took more subterfuge and acting skills than Sharon had ever known she possessed. Far worse than the interviews, however, were the reporters who called her on the telephone or who showed up on her doorstep or at one of the functions she was to attend. Caught unaware, Sharon was always unsure whether she had said and done the right thing. Mrs. Maitland made sure that Sharon was constantly conscious of the fact that she could destroy Reid's career.

Everyone buzzed with speculation about them. There were a hundred rumors circulating about her, some so farfetched that Sharon had to laugh when she heard them. Two of the national scandal sheets ran articles on her; one even had a picture of her with Wes in college. She couldn't imagine how they had found it. There were leading questions from interviewers and often subtle hints in the stories they wrote. But most of all, people talked. Sharon knew that at every party she attended, someone would be rehashing her past and Reid's, speculating on her, on Wes, on Janis, on Reid's past involvement with her.

Hollis told her to ignore it. "If I paid attention to half the things people say about me, I'd have crawled into a hole long ago. People love to talk. In a few weeks it will have blown over, and they'll be talking about something new. Who knows, they may be talking about me."

"I wouldn't care if I were the only one involved. But it can hurt Reid."

Hollis grimaced. "First of all, Reid is a big boy. He can take care of himself. You aren't his guardian angel. He knew, far better than you, I imagine, exactly what would happen when ya'll got engaged. Second of all, that lackey of his was right when he said that it's better to get it over with now. By the time Reid starts campaigning again, it will have been forgotten."

"I wish I could be so sure. Mrs. Maitland keeps telling me about the mistakes I've made and reminding me how I can sink Reid's chances of being senator."

Hollis waved her hand in dismissal. "Don't pay any attention to her. Louise Maitland is an old turd dressed up like a Southern lady, and everybody knows it."

Sharon giggled. "Hollis, you have a very distinctive way of expressing yourself."

Hollis grinned. "Part of my outrageous charm. But I mean what I said. Promise you won't let that bitch intimidate you."

"I promise."

But it was easier said than done. Mrs. Maitland was outwardly gracious and charming to Sharon, but with great subtlety she let Sharon know that she was unwelcome in her family. No warmth sparked in her eyes when she looked at Sharon, even though her lips might be smiling. No chord of affection rang in her voice, even when she praised Sharon to other people. She did what she had to for the purpose of her son's political career. But in private, she never spoke with Sharon except when absolutely necessary. She described the tone of a certain party and the people who would be there; she emphasized who was important to meet or remember and who was not. She reminded Sharon to do this or not do that, to wear a certain kind of dress, to keep her mouth shut or to be friendly, but never did she ask a friendly question or make a comment that wasn't pertinent to the matter at hand. Not once did she inquire about Janis.

From the dry, impersonal way Mrs. Maitland spoke to her, Sharon might have been an employee. Except that every once in a while, when Sharon glanced at her, she caught a glimmer of malice in the woman's eyes, the bitter line of anger in her mouth. And Sharon knew that Reid's mother hated her.

She couldn't understand the woman. If she hated someone as Reid's mother hated her, she would not be able to smile at her and make gracious comments about her to other people. She simply could not put on an act of liking her. It was too cold, too manipulative. Of course, that was what Wes had said about his mother. She could see now that Wes had been speaking the truth, and she felt sorry for both Wes and Reid. It must have been desperately hard to have grown up with a cold mother, never assured of her love and affection, never touched with warmth. Poor Wes had let it twist him and torture him until he'd turned to drugs for release. Thank God Reid had been stronger than Wes.

The days before the wedding were hectic, and Sharon spent far too many of them with Louise Maitland and too few with

Janis and Reid. She accompanied Reid to many places, but they were always public functions, where both of them had to be political. She rarely had any quiet, private moments alone with him. It would change, she told herself. Soon this hurried introduction to public life would be over. They would be married, and then she and Reid would spend time alone at home. This was only for a few weeks; surely she could hold out that long.

Her work suffered, too. There was no time for it. When she wasn't going to parties or attending to wedding details or shopping for clothes, she was busy looking at houses in Dallas and enrolling Janis in the private school in D.C. that she would attend. It seemed as if she never had a spare moment for herself; and if she should find such a rare and marvelous thing, she spent it with Janis, guilt-ridden because she was with her daughter so rarely these days.

Then, at last, the wedding was finally there. They held it at noon at Reid's family's home, a stately white colonial mansion set in an acre of precise English gardens in Highland Park. Somewhere along the way, it had been decided that the ranch was too far away for the wedding, and Sharon had gone along with it, as she had with everything else.

Though it was a small wedding, Sharon felt as if she were in a sea of strangers. In a house that was not hers, with her mother, father, Hollis, Jack, and Janis the only people that she knew, it could as easily have been some other woman's wedding.

But when Reid took her hand in his and smiled down at her, none of that mattered. So what if his mother had taken care of the flowers and the caterers and half a dozen other things. Sharon hadn't had the time to do everything; as it was, she'd been run ragged. None of those details were of any consequence, really, any more than the guest list was. What mattered was that the people close to her were there and that Reid was standing beside her, joining his life to hers.

She smiled up at him, tears shimmering in her eyes. So choked was she with emotion that her voice came out small and shaky on the words, but Reid's was calm and confident.

When the ceremony was over, he lifted up the fragile demi-veil of her hat and smiled down into her eyes before he bent and kissed her. "I love you," he murmured as he straightened.

Sharon's smile was pure sunshine. She couldn't say anything, sure that she would break into tears, but her eyes poured out her love. It was enough for Reid.

She floated through the reception, smiling, shaking hands, and talking, not caring that she didn't know anyone. But she could feel Reid's impatience beside her in the reception line, and that made her want to giggle. Imagine Reid, the seasoned hand-shaker, shifting from foot to foot, his smiles stiff and mechanical, glancing down the line now and then to see if it would ever end. Once he leaned down and whispered in her ear, his voice agonized, "Jesus, there must be a thousand people here."

Sharon giggled. "Don't be silly. Your mother only invited five hundred to the reception."

"Then every single one showed up and brought at least one guest."

It pleased her immensely to know that he was as eager as she to get away from the people and the pomp and circumstance. He wanted to be alone with her. She linked her fingers through his and squeezed his hand.

Finally the reception line dwindled and stopped. They cut the cake for the photographers, then began the first dance. Once a number of other people had joined them on the dance floor, Reid took Sharon's hand and led her off the floor onto the wide veranda of the country club, where the reception was being held. He didn't glance at the view of the golf greens, but pulled her around the side of the building to the front.

A long, black limousine waited in the drive, a chauffeur lounging beside it. When they appeared, the chauffeur straightened and jumped to open the backdoor. "Mr. Maitland."

Sharon glanced up at Reid, puzzled. "Reid . . . what are you doing?"

"Making our escape. Come on." He whisked her into the limousine and closed the door. The driver jumped in, and seconds later they were pulling away from the club.

Sharon glanced back at the club and then at Reid, astonished. She began to laugh. "Have you lost your mind? What about all those people back there?"

"What about them? It's not their wedding. It's ours, and we are leaving."

She leaned back against the seat, feeling giggly and light and happier than she had ever been in her life. "Oh, Reid. I shouldn't be glad, but I am."

"Glad is exactly what you should be." He put his arm around her and leaned over her, resting his weight on his arm against the seat. With his other hand he reached up and took hold of the demi-veil of her hat and smoothed it between his fingers. "I've been waiting to do this from the moment I saw you. You look so goddamn mysterious and sexy under that thing." He pulled the veil up and back, pushing the little hat from her head, crushing the veil in his hand. He bent and kissed her, not the brief, loving kiss of the wedding ceremony, but a hard, passionate, searching kiss. Sharon responded, her hands going up to cup his face and sliding back into his hair.

He rolled back against the seat, pulling Sharon over into his lap. He was already hardening beneath her. Sharon smiled against his mouth and wiggled her hips. She was rewarded by Reid's low groan. Tearing his lips from hers, he whispered into her ear, in long and explicit detail, what he would do if there were not a chauffeur in the front seat and only a glass partition between them and him. Sharon was sorry there was, and she told him so in a low, throaty murmur that made his arms tighten convulsively around her.

They sat quietly together the rest of the ride to the airport, letting their passion subside to a bearable level. "You didn't give me time to change," Sharon said, to change the subject to something safer. "I feel strange traveling in my wedding dress." She looked down at the elegant dusky rose dress.

"You look beautiful," he assured her, and the light in his eyes told her that perhaps even this wasn't a safe subject.

"Well, at least it's not a big white wedding gown." She giggled a little at the thought of sweeping into the airport in one of those.

"There won't be anybody much around to see you, anyway."

That remark puzzled her until the limousine turned into a private terminal at Love Field, the old, smaller airport in the city proper, instead of driving to the regional airport between Dallas and Fort Worth.

"Why are we here?" Sharon asked, glancing around, as she and Reid walked inside, followed by the chauffeur with their luggage. "Aren't we going on a commercial airplane?"

"Nope. I chartered one. I didn't have any desire to spend the first few hours of my marriage on a plane with a couple of hundred other people."

The plane was a Lear jet, small but luxurious. A bottle of chilled champagne and two glasses awaited them. A single rose of the muted lavender shade known as sterling silver stood in a crystal bud vase on the small table beside the champagne.

"Reid!" Sharon cried in delight, bending down to sniff the rose. "How lovely. It's so romantic!" She turned, smiling, and went into his arms.

They kissed lingeringly. Reid popped the cork and poured the champagne and they drank from the glasses, just gazing at each other in perfect happiness. The pilot climbed up the steps into the plane and greeted them, and a few minutes later, they took off.

Sharon sat on the small, plush couch with Reid, looking out of the window at the buildings of Dallas receding below them. She glanced at Reid and smiled. He lifted her hand in his and kissed it.

"I love you."

"I love you, too."

"Are you ready to be called Mrs. Maitland yet?"

Sharon laughed. "No. That's your mother. People will probably think I'm crazy 'cause I won't answer to it."

He poured another glass of champagne. Sharon felt pleas-

antly light-headed and very, very happy. Suddenly she giggled.

"What?" Reid asked, his lips already quirking up, ready
to be amused.

"If anyone had told me ten years ago that I would at this
moment be Mrs. Reid Maitland, I would have told him he
was crazy."

Reid chuckled, but then his eyes turned serious and warm.
"I just wish it had happened ten years ago. I feel like I've
wasted so much time when I could have been with you."

"Maybe it couldn't have happened ten years ago. Maybe
we wouldn't have even liked each other. Well, we didn't,
actually, but I mean even if we'd really known each other,
maybe we wouldn't have liked each other."

"I think I would have fallen in love with you anytime,
anywhere, if I'd stayed around you longer than five minutes.
I think that was one reason why I was so angry with you the
first time I met you. I felt so guilty for wanting you the minute
I saw you, even thinking what I did about you."

He kissed her softly on the lips. For a long time, they
talked and laughed and kissed, luxuriating in the pleasure of
being alone together. They grew hungry; neither of them had
taken the time to eat anything at the reception. Reid explored
the contents of the airplane's cabinets and small refrigerator.
Both were well stocked, and they sampled much of the contents, ranging from the Beluga caviar to the paper-thin slices
of roast beef on dark rye. Afterward Sharon snuggled close
to Reid and fell asleep on his shoulder. He held her, not
sleeping himself, just watching her.

She slept for over an hour, not awakening until the plane
began gradually to descend. She smiled and kissed him, then
glanced out the window. "Oh, look! Isn't the ocean beautiful?"

He looked out, agreeing.

"The sun's getting low. It must be farther to Cozumel than
I thought."

He smiled a little. "Probably it's because it's a small jet.
Not as fast as the big ones."

"What are you smiling at?" Sharon's voice was suspicious.

"Just happy."

"That's not it. You look very smug, like you have a secret."

He chuckled.

She would have questioned him more, but the plane dropped lower and lower, entering its final descent. The small, discreet seat belt light came on above the pilot's door. They buckled themselves in, but Sharon twisted to press her nose against the glass, looking out.

"The water's gorgeous. Have you ever seen anything that blue?"

He smiled, but his eyes were on her rather than the window.

"I can't see any land, though. It looks like we're going to land in the water. There, I can see a beach. Palm trees."

The plane taxied to a halt, and Sharon excitedly unfastened her seat belt. The pilot emerged from the cockpit, smiling, and let down the steps for them. They stepped out into the late afternoon sunlight. Sharon looked around. There was no airport, not even a small one, only a small paved runway surrounded by trees and vegetation. To one side of the runway sat a Jeep.

Sharon walked over to it slowly while Reid and the pilot took the bags out of the plane. She heard the pilot shake his head and laugh, and she heard the name "St. Kitt." She blinked, trying to place the name. It didn't sound Spanish.

They loaded the bags into the Jeep, and she and Reid drove off. Sharon looked back at the small plane, puzzled. "We're just leaving the pilot here? How's he going to get to town?"

"He's going somewhere else. He'll stay there while we're here."

"St. Kitt?"

He glanced at her, surprised. "Yeah. Did you hear us talking?"

"Just that one word."

They emerged from the brush and palm trees, and the track widened into a better road. Sharon could see the sparkling white beach and the blue ocean off to one side. The road began to climb, and the view grew even more lovely.

"Reid . . ." she said slowly. "St. Kitt is in the Caribbean."

"So's Cozumel."

"But it's not near Cozumel."

"True."

"What is going on? We aren't in Cozumel, are we? There's no airport and no people."

"You're right."

"Why? Where are we? I thought we were going to Cozumel."

"That's what Phil had reservations made for. But our honeymoon wasn't something I intended to let my aide take care of. I changed the arrangements."

"Reid!" Sharon laughed delightedly. It had seemed so flat and cold when Susan and Phil had talked about arranging their honeymoon. Thank God Reid had felt the same way. The fact that he had taken it into his own hands and planned something special warmed her all over.

They had reached the summit of the island, and Sharon could now see around her in all directions. They were on a very small island, and the view was breathtaking. "Oh, Reid, it's beautiful!"

He stopped the Jeep on the road, and they got out. They stood, hand in hand, looking out at the ocean. "It's so lovely," Sharon breathed. "I never imagined . . . Where are we, anyway? This island is so small, and I can't see any sign of habitation anywhere."

She pivoted, surveying the island. Then she saw that ahead of them, on the very crest of the island, the road ended at a cream-colored villa. "Oh, my." Her voice came out small. "Is that—"

He grinned. "Yes, it's ours. For a week, that is."

"A week! I thought you only had four days."

"I stretched it." He took both her hands in his and gazed down at her. "It wasn't enough time with you. I didn't want anyone else around, so I rented a private island with a villa.

There's no one here but us. They offered servants, but I told them no. We can have them if you want; I only have to phone. But I—''

"No." Sharon shook her head quickly. "I want to be alone. I've done fine without servants my whole life. This is the last moment I'd want to start having them around."

"Good. I don't want to see anyone but you for the next week."

"Reid, this is so—so beautiful and romantic." Tears filled her eyes, turning them luminous. "To think that you changed the plans, made your own arrangements to be alone in this gorgeous place. It's a dream."

"No. It's not a dream at all. It's reality. And it's going to be our reality. Always."

He bent to kiss her. His lips were soft and sweet on hers. Sharon trembled at their touch and pressed closer. Never in her life would there be anything as magical as this moment. She loved Reid wholly, overwhelmingly. She melted into his arms.

Their honeymoon was glorious, filled with passion, love, and contentment. They walked along the sugar white beach, now and then picking up seashells. Sometimes they talked, and sometimes they were silent, and neither mood was strained. They swam in the turquoise water of the pool beside the house and in the clear water of the ocean. They sat on the terrace, looking out at the view of white beach, palm trees, and water, marveling at the many different and vivid blues of the ocean, in some places deep, royal blue, in others light blue, in still others almost green. In the afternoons, they took a siesta on the wide bed, the wall of louvered shutters open to the breeze yet slanted to block out the bright sun, the ceiling fan whirling above them, sleep-inducing with its faint click and steady drone. At night they walked or sat, enveloped by the velvet darkness, the stars glittering in the clear dark sky, and they listened to the waves breaking rhythmically on the shore, the line of white foam glowing phosphorescently in the darkness.

And they made love. No matter whether it was night or day, all that counted was their love and need for each other. One look or smile or outstretched hand, and they seized upon the moment without hesitation. For the first time in their lives, there were no restraints, no waiting, no decisions, no duty. There was only now and each other and their love.

It was a magical place, a magical time. But it was only a short time taken out of reality; it had to end. The plane and pilot landed on the airstrip seven days later to take them back. As the plane rose into the air, Sharon looked back down at the island. She wanted to cry. Nothing could ever be that idyllic for them again. How could it? There would be work and children and pressures. There would still be the rumors and innuendoes, the denials.

Reid took her hand, and she turned from the window to him. For a moment she gazed at him, almost as if she'd never seen him before, noting the wide, intelligent forehead, the calm gray eyes, the handsome, chiseled lines of jaw, nose, and mouth. He was her husband. Emotion swelled in her chest, filling her throat. Perhaps the fairy-tale week of their honeymoon was gone. But they would have the rest of their lives together, and whatever came she knew she had Reid's love.

16

Hollis Lacey was happy. More than that, she was content. It was an unusual state for her. She had felt rocketing highs before, moments of great pleasure or towering excitement, but there had also always been the long letdowns, the moments of sorrow and pain, the constant faint dislike of herself and what she did. But to feel at peace with herself and the world was astounding—or would have been, had she thought about it. She was too happy drifting along with the good feeling to stop for analysis.

She had money, good fortune, the security of being Jack Lacey's wife, the passion of their lovemaking, the knowledge that she was beautiful, the freedom to do as she pleased. But she had known most of these things for a long time. What had been added to her life was Dean, and it was he who had given the other things meaning. Dean was a gift from God, utterly fantastic and something she could never have acquired for herself. He couldn't be purchased—with money or with her face and figure. He couldn't be wheedled or intimidated out of anyone. She had paid nothing to have him, yet she had been given him. He loved her wholeheartedly, without reason or restraint, no matter who she was or what she did.

Her once-frantic pace slowed as soon as he came into her life. Shopping, possessions, the awe and envy of those who knew her were no longer important. Dean was. Nothing was allowed to interfere with his naps, meals, or playtime with his mother. She had hired a woman to look after him as soon as they returned from Guatemala, but she soon found that she wanted to do so much with and for Dean that she reduced the job to part time and did most of the caretaking herself.

There were still parties related to Jack's business to be given and attended, but otherwise she cut down drastically on her social and charitable activities. She left most of the supervision of her store to the manager, going in only once every week or two to check on it. She was home most of the day now, playing with Dean and devouring baby books; and when she went out shopping, she was more likely to head for a toy store than a dress shop. There were even days when she forgot to put on makeup, and much of her wardrobe hung neglected.

Jack didn't mind the change. He thought her beautiful whether she was dressed in jeans or mink and diamonds, with makeup or without. The shadows that had once lingered in her eyes were gone, and she was lovelier than ever; she glowed. Jack had always loved the sharp edges to her, the tart that overlay the sweet. But he found he loved the new softness in her, too.

One charity that Hollis had not let slide was the benefit for Ames's new orphanage. She applied her usual energy to it, and it turned out, everyone agreed, just fabulously. At the Lincoln Hotel, across from the Galleria, she arranged cocktails, dinner, and dancing to the music of a subdued, three-piece band. Before and after cocktails there was a silent auction of a stunning collection of artwork and unique gifts that Hollis had managed to gather. She had chosen to leave out all mention of religion in her presentation. Let Ames raise money pounding the pulpit in the little towns of East Texas and the South. Here in Dallas, for a two-hundred-dollar-a-plate dinner and a chance to spend more money at the auction, she preferred to tout the cause as a support for a charitable orphanage and hospital.

Late in the evening, as Hollis stood looking at the couples on the floor dancing and thinking smugly about the success of her party, a man came up behind her and murmured, "You've done more than I ever dreamed possible."

Hollis started, surprised, and her heart jumped. It was Ames. She turned to face him. She was no longer sure how she felt about him. Her heart had mended years ago. If Ames were to suggest right now that she toss aside her life with Jack and run away with him, she would laugh and shrug her refusal. Still, there was a tender ache inside her for him, a special feeling for a love that hadn't had a chance, a man whom she had known from the beginning she couldn't have. She guessed one never lost a feeling like that, which had been cut off unnaturally at its fullest strength.

"Hello, Ames."

"Hollis." He paused, and for a moment they stood awkwardly, looking at each other. "I can't thank you enough for what you've done tonight. I never imagined anything so grand."

She smiled, glad that he'd broken the uncomfortable moment. "Ah, but you have to think big if you want to get anywhere."

"I'm more used to begging for nickels and dimes from a hundred different congregations."

"This saves a lot of time and effort."

"It also takes a lot of things I don't have."

"Just find a sucker like me to organize it for you. You're the one who goes through the crowd and charms them. Do you know that I've gotten checks totaling five thousand dollars from people this evening—I mean, out of the blue, not for the items in the auction or the tickets. You've impressed people."

"Then let's say it was a good joint effort." Again he smiled at her. "You're looking very lovely this evening." He couldn't stop his eyes from flickering down her.

Hollis knew how well she looked in her smooth white strapless evening gown. She felt a twinge of triumph to hear that he was impressed. "Why, thank you. I wouldn't think you'd notice."

He let out a funny half-sigh, half-laugh. "I'd have to be blind not to."

His words were another salve to her long-wounded pride. She wondered if he ever regretted his decision, if at moments like this he thought about what he'd thrown away. She hoped so.

Ames glanced away and started another subject. "How is Paco doing?"

"Who? Oh, Dean!" Hollis's smile was blinding. "He's wonderful. Absolutely beautiful. I'll never be able to repay you for him, Ames. No amount of fund-raisers could do that."

"It was Jack who did most of the work," Ames replied honestly. "I was just lucky enough to have a child who would suit."

"Modest, as always."

Ames's wife, Lynn, joined them a few moments later. Hollis thought that her smile was as stiff as her carriage.

"Hello, Lynn," Hollis greeted her, holding out her hand. "It's nice to see you again."

"Mrs. Lacey."

"Please, call me Hollis. Everyone does." Hollis wondered, as she had when she met Lynn the first time, why Ames had married a woman as unassuming and colorless as she was. You would have thought he would choose someone more his equal, someone pretty and with at least a little personality.

"Hollis," Lynn acquiesced. "This is certainly a lovely party." She looked as though she felt distinctly out of place. Hollis thought that perhaps she was simply shy. Away from a crowd she might develop some personality. She wasn't unattractive, just so pale and poorly taken care of that her looks faded into the background. Ames had certainly married someone as unlike herself as possible.

But then, Hollis had to admit, she had done the same thing. Jack Lacey was as far as you could get from a minister running a mission in Central America.

As if her thoughts had made him materialize, Jack came up behind her and slipped his arms around her from behind. He kissed her lightly on the ear. "The lady's a success, as always."

Hollis smiled and leaned back against him with the habit of long years together. Standing in front of him, she couldn't see that his eyes were locked on Ames's as he spoke or that his face wore a flat, hard expression that was almost a challenge.

"Why, thank you," Hollis told him, patting one of his hands at her waist. She twisted to look up at him. "Is this where I'm supposed to say that I couldn't have done it without you?"

"No." He looked down into her face and smiled, his eyes bright in a way Hollis knew well. It still sent shivers down her spine. "This is where you're supposed to say you'll dance with me."

"That's easy enough." She flashed back a smile at Ames and his wife, excusing herself, and walked away with her husband.

They danced for two songs, and after that Jack insisted that they leave early, despite Hollis's laughing, halfhearted protests. She had felt the heat of his skin while they danced and his hardness against her flesh, and she knew why he was so eager to leave early. It was flattering and exciting, like being a teenager at a prom again—except that it had never really been that exciting until she met Jack.

They slipped out of the ballroom, but, much to Hollis's surprise, Jack whisked her to the bank of elevators instead of to the front door. "What are you doing?" she whispered, and he held his finger to his lips. She giggled, wondering what he was up to this time; at least life with Jack was never dull. They stepped out of the elevator on the top floor. He took her hand and led her to a door, where he pulled a key out of his pocket. Hollis stared as he opened the door and whisked her inside.

She stared at the luxurious suite. "You rented a suite?"

"I couldn't wait."

Hollis looked at him. She began to laugh and walked through the room to the bedroom beyond. She tossed down her purse on a chair and kicked off her shoes as she walked. At the door, she looked back over her shoulder at him and smiled a lazy, seductive smile. "Then what are you standing over there for?"

He chuckled and crossed the room to join her.

Hollis didn't get home until the next afternoon. She showered and lay down for a nap, not having gotten much sleep the night before. She had barely awakened from the nap when the maid knocked at her door and told her that Mrs. Thompson was there to see her. Hollis opened the door. "What? Mrs. Thompson?" What would Sharon's mother be doing here?

"Yes, ma'am. She's waiting downstairs. What shall I tell her?"

"Show her into the den. I'll be there in a minute. I have to get dressed."

She pulled on shorts and a top and ran lightly down the stairs into the den. She stopped abruptly when she saw who was in the room waiting for her. It hadn't occurred to her that "Mrs. Thompson" could be Mrs. *Ames* Thompson.

Hollis recovered quickly. "Lynn! I'm sorry. I thought it was your mother-in-law. I couldn't imagine what—well, how silly of me." She smiled, moving into the room and holding out her hand to Ames's wife. Her mind was really whirring now. It was even more bizarre for Lynn to drop by her house. "Could I get you a drink?"

Lynn shook her head. "No, thank you. I hope you don't mind my coming here. It's rude of me, I know, but—"

"Nonsense. You don't need an invitation." Hollis waved aside her apology. "Why don't we sit down?" She went to the couch, and Lynn followed her. They sat for a moment, saying nothing. Lynn stared down at her hands, which she was twisting together in her lap. She looked scared to death. Hollis couldn't imagine why.

Hollis grew more puzzled. This obviously wasn't a call of social obligation, a thank-you for the party last night. The woman was much too agitated, as though she was driven to come here, yet afraid to, also. Hollis found herself feeling sorry for Lynn.

"Is there something I can do?" Hollis asked, keeping her voice neutral and calm.

Lynn looked up at her in an agonized way. "I'm sorry. I always make such a mess of things. Ames would kill me if he knew I was here."

"Ames?" Hollis smiled faintly. "I didn't know he had such a temper."

"He doesn't. Normally. I mean, of course he wouldn't kill me; that's only an expression. He wouldn't even yell at me. But he'd be . . . very disappointed in me. He would be angry."

"Why? Just because you came to visit me?"

"You see, he's told me about you and him, what you meant to him in the past."

Was Lynn jealous? It made more sense now. "But that was a long time ago. We've hardly spoken in years."

"I saw the way he looked at you last night." Lynn's voice was low and broken, as though she struggled against tears. "He still loves you."

"Ames?" Hollis's brows shot up. "Oh no, you're mistaken. Ames and I—"

Lynn's head shot up and she said fiercely, "I didn't say you were having an affair. I know you aren't. Ames is very honest with me."

"Then what—"

"I'm afraid he could be . . . tempted. I don't deceive myself. I'm a plain woman; Ames didn't marry me for my beauty or personality. I'm no competition for you. I came here to ask you, beg you, please, not to see my husband again.''

She looked back down at her hands, unable to face Hollis's gaze. She seemed in an agony of embarrassment and pain. Hollis felt a stab of pity for her.

"Lynn," she began gently, searching for the words, "I think you're worrying over nothing. Ames and I don't mean anything to each other anymore. We have separate lives; we're married, have children. Ames hasn't loved me in years. He left me.''

"But that was only because he wanted the mission in Guatemala so much. When Mr. Lacey offered him the money to start the hospital, he couldn't refuse. He felt as if it would have been choosing you over God if he did. But it didn't end the feeling he had for you. He explained when he asked me to marry him that—''

"What?" Hollis stared. "What did you say? Jack gave Ames money?''

Lynn looked confused. "Yes, you know, to start the hospital.'' She stopped. "Didn't you know?''

Hollis's face was slack, her eyes huge. For a moment she simply stared. At last her lips moved, forming a brittle, bitter smile. "No. I didn't know that. Some husbands, you see, aren't as honest with their wives as Ames is.''

"I—I'm sorry.'' Lynn swallowed. She realized that she had made a horrible mistake. "I don't know what to say.''

"You can tell me exactly what the deal was. How much did Jack bribe him with?''

"Ames wasn't bribed!'' Lynn sounded indignant.

"Bought off. Is that better? Jack purchased him, same way he purchases everything else. No, wait. I guess he really purchased *me*, not Ames, with that little deal. That's only fitting. I'm another one of Jack's many possessions.''

"Mrs. Lacey, I didn't mean to make any trouble for you and Mr. Lacey. I really didn't. I just wanted to beg you not to see Ames anymore.''

Hollis turned a blank, cold gaze on her. "Don't worry. I

have no plans to see Ames nor to entice him to run off with me. I can't really imagine why I'd want to when he sold me to Jack Lacey.''

"It wasn't like that! Ames would never—''

"No?'' Hollis cocked an eyebrow. "What would you call it, then?''

Lynn blinked. "I—'' She glanced around. "I'm sorry. I've made a real mess of things.''

"No. The only mistake you made was being a truthful woman in the midst of a pack of liars.'' Hollis came to her feet. "But I would like for you to go now, if you don't mind. I have a few things to sort out.''

"Yes. Yes. I'm sorry.'' Lynn looked only too glad to get out of there. She scurried from the room, and in a moment Hollis heard the front door close behind her.

Hollis walked across the room and stood staring blindly out the window. Her chest was tight and choked with rage. Damn him! How could he do this to her? He had tricked her! Bought her!

She turned, and a silver tray of glasses sitting atop the bar caught her eye. With one furious sweep of her arm she knocked it off the bar, tray and all. Jack had betrayed her. She could never trust him again. She picked up the cushions from the couch and flung them on the floor, but the lack of noise was unsatisfying to her stormy soul. She grabbed the small ornamental shovel from the stand of fireplace utensils and crashed it so hard against the brick fireplace that it sent shock waves up her arms. She flung it across the room, then sent the other utensils sailing after it. Damn him, damn him, damn him!

By the time Jack came home an hour later, the den was a wreck, but Hollis had brought her temper under control. It no longer flamed, but burned cold and bright in her. She sat in the den waiting for Jack, her arms folded, her legs crossed, her eyes frosty. He walked through the door, loosening his tie, and stopped abruptly. He glanced around the room, taking in the wreckage, and his eyes finally came to rest on her.

"Hollis—'' His expression was wary. "What happened?''

"I got mad." Her voice was like ice.

"I'd never have guessed." Jack walked toward her, reaching down to pick up a cushion in his path and toss it back onto the couch. He stopped in front of her, his hands in his pockets. "You want to tell me why?"

"First, let me ask you a question."

"Okay." His voice was calm, but guarded.

It gave Hollis a flicker of pleasure to know that he was uneasy, waiting for a blow he wasn't prepared for.

"Exactly what was your bargain with Ames?"

He frowned, puzzled. "My bargain? You mean to get Dean? I just—"

"No," she cut in. "I mean to get *me*. What kind of a price did you put on me? I'm just curious. Was I worth more than your Porsche, say?"

His face closed. "What the hell are you talking about?"

"I think you know. Lynn Thompson dropped by to visit me today. In the course of the conversation she let it slip that you had set Ames up in his mission—in return for me. I'd just like to know the details of the arrangement."

Jack blinked. She'd thrown him a punch he hadn't seen coming. Only long years of business dealings kept his voice even when he felt as if the earth were shifting beneath his feet. "On my side, I gave him the money to buy the land and build the building, as well as operating expenses for the first year," he replied honestly. "At the time, it was about a hundred thousand."

"My, that much, huh?" Hollis's voice was mocking.

"Yeah, that much. I'd have paid ten times that to get you."

"And what was his side of the deal?"

"To leave the country. To tell you good-bye with no hope for the future, to not correspond with you or contact you again."

"Well. You carved my life up neatly, didn't you? Did it ever occur to you that I might like to have something to say about the subject?"

He nodded. "I didn't want to hear what I figured you'd have to say."

"Good old Jack. You were raiding a long time before you ever started on corporations, weren't you?"

"You know me, Hollis. You knew me when I married you. I don't pretend to be nice or unselfish. I go after what I want, and I get it."

"No matter who gets hurt."

He glanced away. "I never wanted to hurt you."

"No? You didn't think breaking my heart would hurt me? You didn't think that finding out that our whole marriage had been a lie would hurt me?"

"I had no intention of your finding out. I never dreamed Thompson would be such a fool as to tell his wife about it."

"There are men who are honest with their wives, Jack. I'm sure it must come as a shock to you. But there are people who believe in open and honest relationships, not manipulating other people."

"I couldn't lose you. That's all I knew. I would have done anything not to lose you."

"No wonder you were there at just the right moment to comfort me. You had insider knowledge, right? All these years, you've been pulling the strings, haven't you?"

"Hollis, it wasn't like that. God knows, you have a right to be mad at me, but—"

"Well, thank you very much!" Hollis shot out of her chair. Her pale eyes were icy. "You broke my heart; you manipulated my life. And you allow as how I have a right to be mad! Let me tell you something, mister, I'm not just mad. I'm leaving."

She stalked past him, but Jack's hand shot out, grabbing her wrist. Anger flamed in his eyes, too. "*I* broke your heart," he repeated ironically. "That's real interesting. Tell me something, why am I the bad guy because I was willing to pay anything to keep you? Why don't you let loose that fine, righteous rage of yours on your precious Ames? After all, darlin', he's the one who threw your love away; he's the one who sold you."

"*You*'re the one who's been running my life for me. You're the backstage manipulator. It didn't matter to you what I

wanted. It didn't matter if I got hurt. All you cared about
was acquiring me, like you acquire everything. All that mattered to you was winning. Having an expensive, elegant dec-
oration, a wife that other men wanted.''

"Goddamn it!'' Jack's fingers bit painfully into her flesh.
"You don't have an idea in hell what you're talking about.
I didn't want you hurt. I didn't do it to break your heart or
ruin your life. But *he* would have broken your heart. Sooner
or later, he would have. He'd have taken you and squeezed
all the life out of you, all the beauty and fire, so that you
would fit in his world. He'd have made you a dry-as-dust
preacher's wife, and if he couldn't have done it, he would
have walked, baby. He would have walked.''

"You don't know that! He might have left the ministry if
you hadn't given him that damn mission he wanted.''

"People like him don't leave. He's too almighty holy to
want a woman so bad he'd choose her over his 'calling.'
Christ, he didn't even make love to you.''

"You'd rather he had slept with me?''

"I'd rather the son of a bitch never even looked at you.
But that's not the point. The point is: He was willing to lose
you forever so he could get his hands on that missionary
hospital. He was willing to turn you over to another man,
and all those years, even knowing that you were in my bed
every night, he was willing to take contributions from me.
He loved you about as much as a pimp loves his hookers.''

Hollis made an inarticulate noise of rage and tried to jerk
away from him, but he held tight to her wrist. His eyes pierced
her. "I wouldn't have let you go for any amount of money
or any reward in heaven, either. If I had had your love, I'd
have done anything to keep it. And I did whatever it took to
get you. I love you, Hollis. I always loved you.''

"Loved me! That's a good one. You told me you didn't
even know what it meant.''

"Oh, I knew what it meant all right. It meant wanting you
so bad it nearly tore my guts out. It meant knowing nothing
in my life would ever be worthwhile if you weren't in it, too.
You think I was going to admit I loved you when you were

still hooked on Ames? When you were saying you couldn't
marry me because it wouldn't be fair to me? I'd a been crazy
if I'd told you: You wouldn't have married me. You probably
wouldn't even have dated me. It would have scared you off.
I don't play fair, Hollis; I never said I did. I'm not a good
guy. But nobody has ever loved you or ever will love you
like I do."

They stared at each other for a long moment. His grip on
her arm eased, and she yanked it away from him. "That
sounds real good, Jack. Except that I can't trust you. I found
that out today. You've lied to me from the first. You hurt
and betrayed me. You say you love me? You didn't give a
damn about me. Everything you did was for you. You! You!
When you love someone, you don't break their heart just to
get what you want!"

She strode out of the room. Jack slammed his fist against
the wall in frustration. "Goddamn him!"

He whirled and ran after Hollis. He started up the stairs,
then stopped. Hollis was at the top. Dean was in her arms,
and a diaper bag slung over her shoulder. She was leaving.

She started down the staircase.

"Hollis . . . you can't." His voice came out hoarsely.

"Why not? We've never really had a marriage, Jack. It
was all based on a lie."

"No. The way I felt about you, the good times we had,
none of that was a lie. The way you respond to me in bed
—that's not a lie."

Hollis gave him a cold glance. "That's sex, Jack, not love.
And that's all we ever had—sex."

"We have a hell of a lot more than that, and you know
it." She walked past him toward the front door. "Where are
you going?"

"I don't know. I hadn't thought. I just want to get out of
this house."

"Hollis . . ." She continued walking. He wanted to beg
her to stay, but the words stuck in his throat. Tears stung his
eyes. He watched as she opened the front door and walked
out. The door closed behind her.

* * *

Sharon liked their house in Washington, D. C., a narrow, faded old brick home in Georgetown. Had life been nothing but her and Reid living together in their house, she would have been happy. Unfortunately, there was a great deal more than that. There were late nights for Reid at his office and conferences on the phone and in the living room. It seemed as if there was always someone else in their house, except when they were in bed—aides, other congressmen, and the aides of the other congressmen; members of this committee and that one; constituents; lobbyists; members of the press. Reid was always tired, always rushed, always under pressure.

Sometimes, late at night, when they were alone in their bedroom, he would put his arms around Sharon and kiss her and say, "Thank God I have you to come home to. You can't imagine how peaceful it is, alone here with you."

"This is the only room in the house where you're ever alone with me."

He chuckled. "I'm sorry. Does it seem as if the house is always full of people?"

"It *is* always full of people."

"You're probably right." He nuzzled her hair. "But we're alone now."

He kissed her, and she forgot all about the irritations. *This* was what was important, she reminded herself. Their love for each other was all that mattered. If she had to put up with a stream of people in and out of the house to have Reid, then she would simply have to get used to it.

But she doubted that she would ever get used to the parties. Sharon had never been much of a party-goer. Most of the ones she had gone to had been openings at art galleries or the small, happy, informal gatherings of good friends. There were openings here, of course, and she and Reid attended several of them, but there were no happy, informal get-togethers. Parties in D. C., she found, were not times to have fun. They were times to circulate, to be seen, to gossip and to catch up on the latest gossip. They were ways to score points, to keep track of the subtle and not-so-subtle shiftings of government. They were usually large and often followed rigid, established rules of etiquette.

At the third party Sharon attended, she met Angela Maitland, Reid's ex-wife. Sharon was standing, sipping a glass of white wine and listening to the wife of a lawyer in the Justice Department gleefully wrecking the reputation of someone Sharon had never met. Suddenly the woman stopped in mid-sentence, sucking in her breath. Sharon glanced up, curious as to what could actually shut this woman up. She followed the direction of Faith Kleburg's eyes and saw a tall, cool, elegant blonde. Sharon saw nothing about the blonde that would cause someone to gasp.

"What is it?"

"There's Angela."

"Who?"

Faith blinked and looked at Sharon as if she'd grown a second head. "Why, Reid's ex, of course."

"Oh." Sharon's stomach tightened. "Of course." She'd heard him mention the name, but little else. She'd never been particularly curious about her.

She found that she was now. Her head swiveled in the woman's direction again. Angela Maitland was lovely and very poised. She belonged here. Sharon could see that easily. She had polish and style, as well as beauty. "She's a newspaper reporter, isn't she?"

Again the small woman beside her looked amazed. "Boy, you don't know much about her, do you?" Mrs. Kleburg's southern accent grew thicker. "Why, when I married Gerry, I couldn't find out enough about his first wife. I pumped everybody for information. Heavens, I knew more about her than I did about Gerry."

Sharon smiled. "I guess I'm not normal. But Reid never talked about her, and I, well, I've just been caught up in Reid. His first wife didn't seem important."

"Must be nice to feel that secure."

Was that what it was? Or was it that she didn't look out

for herself, as Hollis was always telling her, that she wasn't sufficiently suspicious?

"She does work for a newspaper." Faith was happy to fill in the gap in Sharon's information. "She's a columnist."

"I see." Angela was part of the political scene. She would enjoy and understand it; she would know how to maneuver safely through it. It seemed to Sharon that she must have been a perfect wife for Reid. What had happened?

Angela turned at that moment, and her eyes locked with Sharon's. Sharon glanced away quickly. But out of the corner of her eye she saw Angela leave the people to whom she was talking and make her way toward Sharon. Sharon looked at Faith Kleburg and forced a smile. "It's been so nice talking to you, but I really must—"

"Why, Faith." Angela stopped beside them. It was too late. "How are you? It's been ages."

"Yes. Too long. We must get together for lunch sometime."

"Aren't you going to introduce us?" Angela looked straight at Sharon.

Sharon couldn't avoid it. She stared right back at her. The woman was trying to rattle her, to make her do or say something stupid. Well, she wouldn't let her.

Faith cast an apologetic look at Sharon. She understood about confrontations with ex-wives. "Of course. I'm sorry. Sharon, this is Angela Maitland. Angela, Sharon Maitland."

Angela smiled just the right amount for an introduction. "Sharon. I'm pleased to meet you."

Sharon could hardly say the same. She forced a stiff smile. "How do you do?"

"Fine, thank you. And you? I understand your wedding was quite recent."

"Yes. About a month ago."

"I hope you all will excuse me. I better go find my husband," Faith declared, although until that moment she had expressed no interest in the whereabouts of her spouse. Much as she loved gossip, she wasn't about to get caught in the middle of what could turn out to be a cat fight. She moved away from the other two. Sharon and Angela hardly noticed her absence. They were too busy sizing each other up.

Up close, Angela was still near-perfect. Her skin was flawless, her hair cut and shaped beautifully, with artful streaks of pale blond running through it. Her makeup was expertly applied to reduce what few things were wrong with her face. She looked lovely and untouchable, a cool woman in command of every situation. Next to her, Sharon felt clumsy, provincial, and unattractive. She stiffened her spine, trying not to let it show.

Angela smiled coolly, a hint of amusement in her eyes. "I must admit I'm surprised. You're not . . . quite what I expected."

"Oh, really?" Sharon felt like an idiot. But what was one supposed to reply to a statement like that?

"It didn't surprise me that Reid would choose someone unlike me. He was rather bitter about our divorce." She shrugged. "I suppose that's to be expected. But I presumed you would be different primarily in physical appearance. I never thought that he wouldn't marry politically."

Hot anger spiked inside Sharon. Her smile was a model of cold dislike. "No. This time Reid married for love."

Angela's eyes widened, which gave Sharon some satisfaction. Apparently Angela had thought that the country bumpkin had no claws. "But one wonders if Reid will be quite so enamored when he loses the senatorial race."

"That's assuming he'll lose."

"Creating a storm of gossip is not the way to win, believe me. A long-term mistress, an illegitimate child—that's hardly going to win Reid votes, particularly in a state like Texas."

Sharon's eyes flashed, and she clenched her fists at her side. "Those things aren't true."

"They don't have to be. The rumor is enough to damage his career. Besides, it most definitely is true that you're an artist, with a background that is, well, dubious, to put it kindly."

"I think the voters of Texas are more astute than you give

them credit for. Reid's record and his stance on the issues are more important than whom he married.''

Angela's smile was at once amused and pitying. ''Naïveté is not in fashion, you know. It won't help Reid any. A politician needs a wife who's savvy, who's politically alert. Do you honestly think you'll be able to navigate the waters of D. C. society? That you can deal with the back-stabbing and the gossip and the maneuvering? Reid doesn't have time for you to grow up and get smart. He'll be smack in the middle of his campaign in a couple of months. And what'll you be doing, sitting at home painting pictures?''

Sharon's fingers itched to slap Angela. How could she manage to look so pretty and detached while her mouth spewed out venom? Sharon knew that her own cheeks were flaming with rage. ''I'll do,'' she said, biting off each word, ''whatever my husband wants me to.''

''My, how noble. How wifely.'' Her eyes were glacial, though there was still an artificial pleasantness to her features. ''Easy words to say when you've already wrecked Reid's career in order to get what you wanted. Well, you have him now. You have his money, and you have his fame. He can hang even more of your little glass pictures around the house. But don't try to move him up. You don't have what it takes. Tell him to stay a representative. Maybe both of you can last there.''

Sharon raised her eyebrows, startled. Understanding struck her. Angela started to turn away, but Sharon reached out and took hold of her arm. ''Wait a minute.''

Angela looked back at her in cool inquiry. Her eyes dropped significantly to her arm, where Sharon's hand gripped her, but Sharon didn't release it.

''That's what's eating you, isn't it? The fact that while Reid was married to you, he was collecting my artwork. Wasn't he? It gripes you. You think he was in love with me all along.''

''Don't be absurd. I was the perfect wife for Reid, and he knew it.''

"Then why did he divorce you?"

Angela's nostrils flared. "What makes you think he did? I divorced him."

Sharon shook her head. "Maybe on paper. But it was Reid who walked out on you. I'd lay odds on it. An ex who wanted to be one doesn't waste her time trying to stab his new wife. It's a long time, Angela, to carry a grudge. After three years, you couldn't have really thought he would come back to you."

Angela bared her teeth in an expression that could hardly be called a smile. "Reid always did think with his hormones instead of his head. This time it's ruined him."

She turned and stalked away. Sharon was glad to see that at least she had managed to shake Angela's composure almost as badly as Angela had shaken hers.

Sharon glanced around her and saw Reid quickly making his way toward her through the crowd. A worried frown creased his forehead, and she knew he had seen Angela talking to her. She smiled, glad to think that he was concerned about her.

"Are you all right?" was his first question. She nodded. "What did she want?"

Sharon struggled to keep her face and voice calm. "Just to compare notes, I guess."

Reid grimaced. "The bitch. Did she bother you? Did she say something to upset you?"

"I can handle her," Sharon lied, knowing she was shaken by the incident, but hoping she could manage to avoid the woman in the future. There was certainly no point in burdening Reid with an account of what Angela had said. "But I think I would like to leave now. Is it okay?"

"Of course it is. Come on, let's go. This place is too boring, anyway."

They left the party after prolonged good-byes and thank-yous to their hosts. Sharon settled back against the car seat with a sigh as Reid drove away from the house. She closed her eyes. She was beginning to realize how very much she disliked living in D.C.

* * *

For weeks after her confrontation with Angela, the woman's words still bothered Sharon. No matter how much she told herself that Angela had only wanted to hurt her, that she was jealous because Sharon had Reid's love and she no longer did, she could not shake the suspicion that Angela had spoken the truth. After all, she herself had worried about the same thing from the moment that Reid wanted to make their love public. She was desperately afraid that she had severely harmed—if not ruined—Reid's career.

She worried about it alone, for that was the one thing she knew she could not talk over with Reid. He would just deny it; he was too kind and loving to admit it. He would not tell her that the grooves that were beginning to wear permanently into the skin around his mouth and eyes or the late nights at the office or the numerous war talks in their library until the small hours of the morning were because his marriage had wreaked havoc with his campaign. And Sharon wasn't about to waste what little time they had together in going over a useless, painful topic.

As the time passed, she found more and more things that she was reluctant to talk to Reid about. It seemed as if the painful topics were piling up, and mention of any of them were bound to make Reid feel hurt and guilty. She missed him terribly; it seemed as if he were gone nearly all the time; and when they were together, there was often another person with them or they were at some obligatory social function or another. Janis didn't like her new school. She was finding it hard to make friends and to adjust to the very different lifestyle. She spent far too much time at home alone in her room, listening to records and writing to friends back home in Santa Fe. She never bugged Reid for his attention or asked why he was gone so often, but Sharon could see the hurt in her eyes because he was so rarely with her anymore. Sharon tried to explain the practicalities of the situation, pointing out to Janis that Reid was having to take care of all his normal duties as well as prepare for a senatorial campaign. Janis nodded and said she understood, but then she would go upstairs and closet herself in her room.

Sharon's work suffered. The creative outpouring of this summer appeared to have dried up. She had little time anymore to work on her stained glass pieces, for there was always some other duty as Reid's wife interfering, but when she did sit down to work, nothing came.

She hated the socializing they were forced to do. She didn't know anyone, and the running chitchat of a Washington party was not the kind of thing that allowed her to get to know anyone. Nor did most of the people she met appeal to her as potential friends. She didn't like the crowds of people, and she didn't like the conversations—often she didn't even understand what they were talking about.

Yet she couldn't tell Reid these things any more than she could talk about her fear that she had damaged his career. He would feel guilty that he had taken her away from the environment she knew and dragged her here where she was unhappy. He would be sorry that he had uprooted Janis and plunged her into a foreign situation. As he did in everything, he would assume all responsibility and then struggle as hard as he could to change things so that they would be happy. Sharon couldn't add that burden to his already heavy load.

Yet that reluctance caused them to have less and less to talk about whenever they were together. Sharon felt as if she were being stifled, cut off from Reid. There were times when she thought wistfully about returning to Santa Fe. Perhaps they could just live there for the school year. Reid would be so busy with the campaign he wouldn't miss them too much, and he could fly out to see them as easily as he flew now to Dallas and Houston all the time to consult and raise funds for his campaign. But, no, again that would be burdening him. And Sharon refused to do that. She was determined that their love would never be a burden to Reid.

17

After her confrontation with Jack, Hollis drove straight through the night. Hurt and confused, her first thought had been to flee to her parents' house, but that was the first place Jack would look for her. Besides, it was too close to him. She wanted to get far away. She wanted to be alone to lick her wounds. So she drove, tears streaming down her face, through the darkness, until finally she was too tired to drive anymore. She checked into a hotel in San Antonio, but sleep wouldn't come to her. The next day, bleary-eyed and exhausted, she drove on to Padre Island and took a room on the beach.

She called her parents to tell them where she was and learned that Jack had already come to their house and had called back twice to see if she had shown up there yet. She extracted a promise from them not to tell Jack where she was. Her mother besieged her with questions, but Hollis couldn't tell her what had happened between her and Jack. Tears kept getting in the way.

She spent two weeks on the Island, taking care of Dean and going for long walks on the beach. She called Sharon once or twice, but it didn't seem fair to burden Sharon with her problems when she'd just been married.

Hollis felt shocked, ripped apart. She tried to think things through, but it seemed as though all she could do was cry. Her whole life was suddenly a shambles.

One afternoon she came in from the beach with Dean, who was happily caked with sand, and set him down in the tub to clean him off. She switched on the radio, then stripped off his clothes and set to work rinsing off the sand. Dean giggled and shrieked, slapping happily at the water and watching it splash. In the background, a song played on the radio, and Hollis hummed along with it. The song ended, and the news came on. Suddenly a word penetrated her consciousness and she sat up straight, turning toward the radio and listening.

". . . unknown how many hostages are actually in the hospital. Early reports indicate that at least four American citizens were in the hospital at the time of the takeover by the terrorists. No names have been released yet, and there has been no comment by the Texas-based Federated Ministries, which operates the Hope Mission Charity Hospital.''

Hollis gripped the side of the tub. Her breath stopped in her throat. Hospital! Federated Ministries Hope Mission was the name of Ames's organization. Could it be the same one?

Pulling Dean out of the tub despite his protests, she wrapped a towel around him, then ran into the bedroom and put him down on the floor. She grabbed the telephone and dialed Sharon's number in Washington. A woman answered the phone and put her on hold after Hollis had identified herself. A few moments later Sharon's tearful voice came over the wire. "Hollis?"

"Sharon! Oh, my God." The sound of her friend's voice confirmed her worst fears. "Is it true? I heard—"

"Yes! It's true; it's true." Sharon began to sob. "Terrorists took over Ames's hospital. They're holding him hostage! Oh, God, Hollis, what if they kill him?"

Hollis went icy. "No. That won't happen. They'll do something. They'll get him out. They'll negotiate, and—"

"No. Reid just heard. Their government has already refused the terrorists' demands. They won't free the prisoners the terrorists want."

"Oh, Sharon, no. This can't happen. This can't happen."

But it had.

Hollis packed and drove to Dallas that afternoon. She left Dean with her parents and caught a plane to Washington. She was still in shock over the news, but she had one clear thought—she had to be with Sharon through this thing. Sharon would be going through an agony of fear and pain. Her friend needed her. They needed each other.

Hollis arrived at Sharon's home late in the evening. Sharon put her arms around Hollis without saying a word and cried. They spent the following days together, sometimes talking, often sitting in silence. Reid did what he could, pulling every string he knew in the State Department to get them to put pressure on the Guatemalan government to negotiate.

The negotiations for the hostages dragged on. It had been days now, and still both sides refused to compromise. One evening Reid came home late; Sharon and Hollis could see from his face that the news wasn't good.

He loosened his tie, sighing, and sank down wearily into a chair. "Nothing." His voice was grim. "All negotiations are at a standstill."

"Oh, Reid, no."

He nodded, and his eyes went reluctantly to his wife. "It doesn't look good, honey. The government won't give them the prisoners, and the terrorists won't settle for anything else. They've been offered asylum, a plane to take them out of there—Jack and Hollis's dad and I tried to negotiate a money ransom, but no go."

Hollis's eyes widened. "Jack? You mean my Jack?"

Reid nodded. "Yeah. We offered them literally millions, but they wouldn't consider it. All they care about is making their statement."

Hollis stared, dumbfounded. She would never have dreamed that Jack would pay a penny for Ames Thompson's life, let alone "millions." She wasn't quite sure what to make of it.

She continued to puzzle over it as the days passed. The terrorists stood firm on their demands. So did the government. The captors threatened to begin shooting their hostages. There was a picture of Ames, bearded and weary, in front of a dated newspaper. There were frantic negotiations, and no killings began.

Hollis was awakened one night by the ringing of the phone. Her heart began to pound. She picked it up; her fingers were trembling.

A familiar voice was on the other end of the line. "Hello, baby."

"Jack!"

"Listen, don't hang up. I've got something to tell you." Dread settled coldly over her. She sat up. "All right."

"You can't let this out. Promise me. But I couldn't let you continue to worry and wait—"

"What are you talking about?"

"I wanted you to know that Ames will be all right. I've made arrangements to free him."

"Arrangements!"

"With a guy who used to be in Special Forces."

"A commando?"

"He specializes in things like this. We'll get him out okay."

We? "Jack! You aren't going, too!"

"Yeah. I'm going to make sure it works."

"No! Jack, that's dangerous. You don't know how to—"

"You forget. I used to go hunting with Horton from the time I was six. I'm a good shot. And I won't do anything that'll mess it up. It won't put Ames in danger, I swear it."

"But that's—"

"I have to go. I just wanted you to know. In a couple of days it'll be over. He'll be safe. You don't have to worry anymore."

"Don't have to—Jack, wait!"

"Bye, baby. I love you."

"Jack!" There was a click. He was gone.

Hollis stared blankly at the receiver in her hand. Slowly she put it back on the telephone. Jack was going to rescue Ames. She wanted to rip the phone out of the wall and hurl it across the room. Damn him! Why did he always have to be in on everything! He was going to get himself killed. And why in the hell was he doing it?

She lay awake all night, unable to sleep. The next morning she told Sharon and Reid about Jack's telephone call. Sharon's face brightened. "Like what Ross Perot did?" she asked. "Can they really do it?"

Hollis shrugged. "Jack wouldn't hire anyone but the best."

"It's a better chance than what they have now," Reid said bluntly. "I know who he's hiring. We talked about it when the ransom was turned down. The guy's good. He's rescued others."

"Really?" Sharon looked even more optimistic.

"But why did Jack have to go himself?" Hollis burst out. "What if he gets killed?"

Reid shook his head. "I tried to persuade him not to. But he was determined. He said he wasn't good at delegating."

"That sounds just like the idiot."

Hollis was furious at Jack. She clung to her anger all day. It kept her from thinking about what was going on right now, about where Jack was and what he was doing. But during the night the rage deserted her. In the darkness, nothing could hold back the fear that boiled up from within her.

Jack was going to get killed. And it would be her fault. He was doing this for her. She knew it. He was bringing Ames back to her, as he always got her everything she wanted.

Hollis buried her face in the pillow and clung to it. She couldn't remember ever praying before, but she prayed now.

Hollis and Sharon sat together in silence the next day, waiting. Hollis was pale, and deep circles of sleeplessness had formed under her eyes. She looked so tight-strung that Sharon thought she might snap at any moment.

The phone rang and a moment later, the intercom came on. "It's Mr. Maitland for you, ma'am."

Sharon answered the phone. She listened, and her eyes widened, her skin suddenly paling. Hollis jumped to her feet. Her pulse pounded so hard there was a roaring in her ears.

"Sharon! Sharon, what is it?"

Sharon turned to her, letting the phone slide from her hand. Tears sparkled in her eyes. "He's alive! Ames is okay. That was Reid. He said he just got word that they're out. They're en route to D.C."

"What about Jack? Is Jack okay?"

She nodded, a grin breaking across her face while tears poured out of her eyes. "Yes! Yes! They're all safe. Three kids and all four Americans. The men who went in after them. Only one man got shot, but he's all right. And it wasn't Jack."

Reid sent a limousine to take them to the airport. A government type hustled them into the airport and through the halls to a windowless room. They sat down and waited. Reid joined them. Sometime later another man entered the room and called Reid outside. Hollis waited in an agony of nerves, certain that he was telling Reid that a mistake had been made, that Jack had not survived, after all.

But when Reid returned to the room, he smiled and said, "The plane's landed. They want to talk to them first, but you'll be able to see them soon."

After some time, the man returned and escorted the three of them down the corridor and past a crowd of journalists into a cordoned-off waiting area. It was empty. Hollis sat down. She felt as if she were about to explode from the constant waiting. It was all she could do to keep herself still.

A door opened at the other end of the large room, and several people came out. Hollis jumped to her feet, watching. There was Ames and beside him, Lynn, then two men she didn't know. Sharon hurried forward to hug Ames, but Hollis stood, waiting, her eyes glued to the door. It opened again, and three men emerged, talking and smiling. One of them was Jack.

He glanced across the room and saw her. He stopped. They looked at each other. Hollis's knees began to tremble. She couldn't move; she could hardly breathe. Jack glanced over at Ames and the knot of people with him, then back to Hollis. He started toward her. Hollis moved forward, pulled toward him. They stopped a foot apart.

"Hollis."

"Jack." She wanted to cry. Her throat was almost too tight to speak.

He looked thinner than when she'd seen him last, and there was two days' growth of stubble on his jaw. But he'd never looked more wonderful to her.

"I don't know whether to slap you or kiss you." Tears spilled out of her eyes. "How could you scare me like that!"

Jack looked startled, then he grinned, the familiar deviltry back in his face. "I'll vote for the kiss."

He held out his arms, and she flung herself into them. They clung together, and she kissed him all over his face, punctuating her kisses with sharp, breathless words, some endearments, some curses. All Jack cared about were the three she said over and over again: "I love you. I love you."

Jack squeezed her to him tightly. "God, Hollis, I thought I'd lost you forever."

"You're never going to get rid of me," she assured him, stopping her kisses to lean against his chest, her arms wrapped around him.

"When you left me, when you wouldn't even take my phone calls—"

"I'm sorry. I was so mad at you. But it wasn't until you told me you were going to get Ames out that I realized why I was so mad." She leaned back and looked up at him.

"Why?" He was smiling down at her.

"Because I love you, not Ames. I never loved Ames like I do you. Maybe I thought I loved him just because he was the one guy I couldn't have. But it's always been you. You were my friend, the man I desired. It was just so good and right between us that I didn't recognize it."

"Hollis, you're crazy." He chuckled and squeezed her again.

"When you told me you were going, I was scared to

death—for you, not for Ames. And I realized that it was you I loved. You were the one I was worried about. Frankly, I didn't care if Ames lived or died, as long as you came back safely.''

Jack nuzzled her hair. ''I've waited a long time to hear you say that. It feels even better than I thought it would.''

''I wasn't mad because you'd kept me from marrying Ames. I realized finally that what made me so furious was the fact that you had lied to me. I felt betrayed. It was the idea that maybe you didn't really love me, but just acquired me like your car or your house—''

''No. Hollis, no, you've never been a possession to me. I love you.''

''I know.'' She snuggled into him. ''That's why you took off to Guatemala—to get me what you thought I wanted. It's what you always do, only this time, you were willing to give me what I wanted even though it might have meant losing me to Ames. You did it because you loved me, with no thought of yourself.''

She stretched up and kissed him softly, lingeringly. ''I love you.''

''I love you, too.'' His arms enfolded her.

Hollis felt warm and secure and breathlessly in love. She'd been looking for something all her life. Funny, how it had been right here all this time. Thank God she'd realized it before it was too late.

''Come on,'' he said. ''Let's leave this place. I want to get you alone.''

He wrapped his arm around her shoulders, and they started walking down the hall.

For a time, when Sharon was racked with fear over Ames's survival, the smaller problems of her life receded. The rock of Reid's love sustained her through the ordeal. But Sharon found that after Ames was rescued and their life returned to normal, the same annoyances, problems, and fears remained. They had just been hidden for a while, not gone. There was still the awful specter of having ruined Reid's career looming over her. If anything, after Reid's gentle concern and support during that time, it seemed even worse that she should be responsible for his losing the Senate seat he had always wanted to hold.

One evening, when Phil was closeted with Reid in the library, Sharon happened to pass by the library door as she left the den. She stopped dead in her tracks when she heard an unintelligible murmur, then Phil's voice clearly said "—make up what you've lost."

"It won't be that hard," her husband replied, his voice weary. Sharon could picture the gesture Reid would make as he said that, rubbing his hand across his forehead, and it made her heart ache a little. "We've slipped only a few points in the polls."

Phil said something indistinct, and Reid chuckled dryly. But there was little humor in his voice. Sharon moved quietly away.

She had hurt Reid's career. Was the damage irreparable? Would he regret marrying her for the rest of his life because of it? She went back to the den and waited for Phil to leave. Sometime later the library door opened and closed, and Sharon hurried into the hall. Phil was alone and walking toward the front door. Sharon hurried after him. "Phil?"

Phil turned and saw her. Surprise flitted across his face. "Hello, Sharon." He glanced at his watch. "Little late, isn't it?"

She was usually upstairs in the bedroom by the time Phil left in the evenings. "Yes, I guess it is. I wasn't sleepy tonight. Where's Reid?"

"I left him going over some papers. I'm afraid it's quite a stack. He'll be at it for some time." He held up his briefcase. "I decided I'd take my work home, too."

"Could I—would you mind staying for a bit? I—there's something I wanted to ask you."

There was a puzzlement in his eyes, but Phil was too well trained to show any emotion in his face. "Of course. What can I help you with?"

"I—uh—" Sharon paused awkwardly. She didn't know how to approach this, and Phil always made her feel uncomfortable. She was certain that he had wanted Reid to marry her as little as Mrs. Maitland had. "I want to ask you a question, and I want you to answer it honestly," she said on a quick breath.

This time he couldn't keep the surprise from marking his face. "I'll try."

"Did Reid hurt his career by marrying me? Am I a liability to my husband?"

Phil's face shut down. He spoke slowly, choosing his words carefully. "Reid loves you very much. He would be unhappy if he were not married to you."

"That doesn't answer my question. I'm not looking for reassurance. I want the truth. I want you to be blunt."

For once his face sparked with humor. "That's a big request to make of a man in my position."

"I want what's best for my husband. I would never do anything to harm him. You can be honest with me."

"Reid'd probably have my head if he knew I told you this . . ."

"But?"

"But, yes, of course, your marriage damaged his career. It couldn't help it."

"I thought so. Reid tried to tell me that it was minor."

"I think it's recoverable. Reid has a good record and an excellent rapport with his constituents. People tend to trust him, even though they are put off by his remote air."

Sharon sighed. Tears pricked at the backs of her eyeballs. "How badly did it affect his campaign?"

"He definitely slid in the polls."

Sharon turned away. Well, now she knew it for certain. What good did it do her? She almost wished she could be more blind, more selfish. "I never wanted to hurt him in any way."

"I'm sure you didn't, Mrs. Maitland. As I said, Reid would have been unhappy if you hadn't married him. That could have affected the campaign as badly."

"Do you really believe that?"

Phil hesitated for a moment, then shook his head. "Frankly, as a person, I like you. You're easy to like. But the only thing that I am concerned with, ultimately, is Reid's career. This campaign. He'd have been better off if he'd never fallen in love with you."

Tears sparkled in her eyes. Phil had seen a lot of women cry, but this time it touched him. "It's no use feeling bad about it. It's done. Over."

"That's not exactly comforting." Sharon blinked back her tears, making her voice purposely dry.

"I'm sorry."

"Is there anything I can do?"

"What do you mean?"

"Is there any way that I can make it up? That I can repair the damage? Can I help Reid to negate the harm I've done?"

He looked at her quizzically. "Yeah, if you're willing to do it."

"You don't think I would be willing."

He shrugged. "I didn't say that. But, from what I've seen of you, you don't seem to have the personality for it. You have no interest in politics."

"I have an interest in Reid's happiness. What exactly would I have to do?"

"Help him campaign. Go out there and show everybody what a sweet and wonderful woman you are, so they understand why he married you. So they think: 'Hell, those rumors can't be true.' Let reporters interview you. Appear on television. Go on the campaign trail in Texas and shake hands next to Reid. Stand on the platform with him when he makes speeches. Talk to women's groups. Attend the little teas and coffees in podunk towns. Have luncheons with the wives of wealthy backers. Talk Reid up all the time. And smile."

Panic bubbled up in Sharon. "But how—I don't know how to do those things. I'd make a mess of them."

"Not if you were coached. Not if you were willing to keep working."

"What do you mean, 'coached'?"

"I'd tell you what to say—the issues, the standard answers, what to steer clear of. We'd hire a consultant for the rest—hair, makeup, poise in front of cameras or people, public-speaking skills, that sort of thing."

"Can you really learn to be confident and likable?"

"You can learn to appear to be."

"Oh."

Sharon looked at Phil. No wonder he had doubted her willingness to do it. She couldn't think of many things she would like to do less than the ones he had named. She thought of Reid and how much he had been willing to give up to marry her. Was she so selfish that she could not make these sacrifices for him?

Phil obviously was waiting for her to tell him that she couldn't do it. Her chin came up. She wouldn't let Reid sacrifice his career for her.

"All right." Her voice was calm.

Phil looked thunderstruck. "What?"

"I'll do it. Get hold of that consultant and set up an appointment for me."

The consultant's name was Amanda Peznick. She came to the house two days later, the first time that she could fit Sharon into her schedule. She was short and wide, but her face, hair, and clothes were impeccable. Brusque and efficient, she made no effort at small talk, but got right down to the problem at hand—Sharon.

She walked around Sharon, her quick eyes assessing her face, form, hair, and clothes. Sharon stood before her, feeling like an idiot, as the woman inspected her. "Good," Amanda said at last. "Good basics. We won't have to do much cover-up. Your hairstyle will have to be changed, of course. Different clothes. Can't have a candidate's wife in jeans and sweatshirt.''

Sharon's hand went to her hair. What was wrong with it? ''I don't wear these clothes except at home.''

''You won't be home often. Okay, let's take a look at your closet.''

Sharon led her up to her closet. Amanda flipped through Sharon's clothes quickly, pulling out a garment now and then. When she was through, she had three dresses and a pair of slacks in her hands. ''These will do.''

Sharon's eyes widened, and she looked back at the clothes hanging on the rod. They included practically everything she wore, as well as several of the dresses Hollis had helped her pick out.

''Now, wait. That's all? What about these?'' She pulled out two cocktail dresses that Hollis had selected. They'd been horribly expensive. And no matter how unsophisticated her own taste might be, she *knew* that Hollis knew what she was doing.

''Very attractive. And, of course, there are occasions when you can wear them here. Maybe a few things in Dallas or Houston, but not for the campaign. They're too sophisticated. The neckline's too low on this one. You want to look smart and well put together, but not intimidating and definitely not sexy. You don't want to look as if you stepped out of *Vogue*, you see. We want clothes that are practical, plain, and elegant. Suits that can do double duty when you take off the jacket and put on another blouse and different accessories. None of these patterned things; they look bad on TV You have too many bright colors. We need to tone it down a little; use pastels. We're trying to combat your wild artist image. We need to make you look softer, paler, more conservative, as well as a little more sophisticated.''

Sharon stared. She had never thought of herself as being flamboyant. She wanted to protest the sweeping dismissal of her wardrobe, but she held her tongue. After all, she had agreed to do this.

Amanda pulled two cards from her purse. "Here. This is Leslie Johnson's number. I'll tell her to call you and arrange a time for the two of you to go shopping. She'll help you select the right clothes; I'll talk to her this afternoon about it. And this is Alan Webster, a very good hairstylist. I'll get in touch with him, too, tell him what I have in mind for your hair. Call him tomorrow and set up an appointment."

She opened her pocket-size appointment book and flipped through a few pages. "Let's see. We can start work next week. I have two times available, two-hour sessions each. I'm sure we'll need both of them." She took out another card, this time one of her own, and jotted down the two times. "Here you are. I'll look forward to seeing what Alan's done with your hair. I have to run now. Another appointment. See you next Wednesday."

"All right." Sharon trailed her out of the bedroom and down the stairs. She felt as if she'd been taken over. It was an uncomfortable feeling, and she wanted to tell Amanda that she could manage her own life, thank you. But she did not. She would see this thing through.

Her resolution was put to the test two days later when she went to her appointment with the hairstylist. He set to work on her hair without a question to her about what she wanted. Sharon gripped the arms of the chair and kept her mouth shut as he began to snip away. She liked her hair long and had worn it down to her shoulders for years, but Alan cut a good two inches off it and curved it under into a smooth, sleek style. When he was through, she had to admit that she looked more sophisticated, even prettier. But she didn't look quite like herself. She knew she would have to take more time with her hair each day, no longer just twine it into a quick braid for coolness and comfort as she worked.

Next she was hustled off for a manicure and pedicure, and her treatment was topped off by a facial mask and a demonstration of how she should use cosmetics. Made up in the new way, she looked even less like herself.

But she did look lovely. That was confirmed that evening

when Reid saw her and let out a long, low whistle. "What have you been up to?"

"Oh, nothing," Sharon replied airily. "Just a day at the salon."

He bent to kiss her. "I'm almost afraid to touch you, you look so perfect."

Sharon threw her arms around his neck. "Oh no. I'm not that perfect, believe me."

He chuckled, and his kiss deepened. They missed the party they were scheduled for that evening.

After the transformation in her looks, Sharon noticed that people paid more attention to her. She was aware she had crossed some kind of barrier, although she wasn't sure exactly what it was. Now she appeared to be a woman to be reckoned with.

She worked hard every day to make that appearance a reality. Phil managed to squeeze an hour out of his busy schedule two or three times a week to give her instructions on politics in general and Reid's work in particular. On the days when Phil could not make it, his assistant took his place to drill the knowledge into Sharon's head. Two days a week she worked with Amanda Peznick, and she spent several other hours with various of Amanda's minions. They taught her how to walk, how to sit correctly, how to stand (at her husband's side, by herself, behind a podium). They gave her lessons in speech making and in giving interviews, taking videotapes each time to play back and reveal her mistakes.

She learned tip after tedious tip about appearing on television. "Don't cross your legs at the knee, only at the ankle." "Don't cross your arms. It looks defensive. Keep your hands folded neatly in your lap." "Don't wear white." "Don't wear patterns, checks, or plaids." "Don't wear big earrings. They're distracting." "Don't wear a big bow or pin at your neckline. It pulls the eye down from your face." "Remember to keep smiling."

Amanda taught her how to avoid questions she didn't want to answer without appearing to be avoiding them and how to turn a negative question to her advantage. She took home Amanda's videotapes of people demonstrating the various techniques Amanda recommended and watched them until she thought she would die of boredom.

Sharon had little time for her own work nowadays, and she neglected it. There were so many other things that occupied her time, not only the preparations she was making for the campaign, but also spending time with Janis, who was still unhappy at her school, and being with Reid whenever he was miraculously freed from work. Fortunately, she no longer needed the money she received from her artwork. But that didn't keep her from missing it. She had ideas that she hadn't the time to sketch, and there were many frustrating afternoons when she worked with Amanda, all the while aching to be in her studio, cutting and fitting pieces of glass. There was such beauty and order to creating in stained glass, and the lack of it left a vacuum in her life.

At least she had the gratification of seeing Phil's surprise and increasing respect as she molded herself into a good senator's wife. There was also the satisfaction of knowing that she could now usually hold her own at parties. Sharon could feel her poise increasing almost daily. The only problem was she no longer looked or felt like herself.

In the meantime, Phil had signed Sharon up for volunteer work with a couple of Dallas charities, another statewide charitable organization based in Houston, and yet another charity in Washington itself. Sharon didn't understand how she could do any work for these charities when they were so scattered. Phil looked pained and explained that her only task was to provide them with publicity, to be a highly visible spokesperson. She would attend their large society fund-raisers and do a few interviews with the media regarding the charities.

"But how?" Sharon blurted out. "I don't know anything about them or what they do."

"Don't worry," Phil assured her. "I'll provide you with

the information you'll need before you're interviewed. It'll be easy. Amanda wants to try you out on a small interview with one of the local dailies for the D.C. charity.''

"A newspaper interview?''

"Yeah. Next Tuesday.'' Phil pulled a manila folder out of his briefcase and handed it to her. "Here's the info. Just review it so you can throw in a few statistics about abused wives and children.''

"Okay.'' Sharon opened the folder. There were only a few pages inside. ''Are you sure this will be enough for me to answer the questions?''

"Sure. You don't have to be an expert. They'll also talk to one of the shrinks at the center. You're there to get a picture in the paper, which they wouldn't do for the shrink. Amanda will walk you through an interview with the questions they'll probably ask you. It'll go fine.''

Sharon practically memorized the sheets of information Phil gave her, and she got through Amanda's mock interview without flubbing any of her answers. Afterward, Amanda went back and pointed out what she had done wrong, then ran her through it again. By the time Amanda finished with her, Sharon was confident that she could handle it.

By the time the reporter came to talk to her two days later, Sharon had lost much of her confidence. Her palms sweated profusely, and most of the facts Phil had given her had flown from her head. However, once they started talking, Sharon's tension diminished, and she was able to answer the questions. When the reporter finished and left, Sharon was flooded with relief. It hadn't been so bad, she realized, and let out a little giggle. She had handled it; the reporter hadn't thrown her any curves; and she'd made it through it. She supposed she should have realized that an interview about a charity wouldn't involve probing, awkward, or embarrassing questions. The reporter wasn't out to get her; she wanted only to whip out a short, informative, public service article.

Sharon did one television appearance and three newspaper and magazine interviews in the following weeks. Only one took place in D.C.; she had to fly to Dallas for the others.

But she didn't stay away long, and none of the interviews
were bad. All but the magazine article were about the charities
she was involved with, and Phil gave her information on each
one, so that she sounded as if she knew what she was doing.
The reporters were friendly, and everything went smoothly,
even the magazine article about her life. Still, she was racked
with nerves for hours before each one and overwhelmed with
relief when they were over. She hoped fervently that it would
get easier with time, as Amanda had assured her it would.

They kicked off Reid's campaign in Dallas at a rally and
fund-raiser. They spent several days in Dallas, shaking hands,
going to functions, and talking. Sharon talked until she
thought her throat would dry up and she would never be able
to speak again, and she listened to other people talk even
more. She sat on the podium with Reid when he gave a speech
and listened to him with a sweet, loving smile on her face.
After the third time she heard the speech, it began to grow
difficult to look loving and interested. Worse was listening
to the other politicos who spoke, either introducing Reid with
fulsome praise or pounding on one or another of the issues
that were dear to the heart of his audience. Even more tor-
turous was standing in a reception line or walking through a
crowd, shaking hands and smiling, smiling, until Sharon
thought her jaw would break.

They left Dallas and toured northeast Texas, stopping at
various small towns for rallies, meetings, teas, coffees, dinners, breakfasts, and luncheons, each with its own long,
tedious reception line. Sharon became familiar with the pattern of campaigning. They arose early in the morning and
jumped immediately into some kind of meeting with the public, usually combined with a tasteless breakfast. Then they
worked throughout the day, meeting and greeting people,
giving short speeches, or listening gravely to the complaints
of farmers, union members, or whoever happened to be there.
Sharon and Reid often split up during the day so as to reach
more people. Sharon talked to women's groups—the wives
of this or that organization or a businesswomen's group or a
women's political organization—or she went to small parties

held by the wife of a backer or some local party bigwig.
Often she lunched with the wives of men important to Reid's
campaign, and she usually dropped by Reid's local head-
quarters to meet the workers and encourage them. The public
day ended with a dinner function and/or evening rally, but
afterward there would be long discussions with Phil and Susan
before they finally went to bed.

Sharon decided that campaigning was as much a test of
physical endurance as anything else. If one were weak or
lacked the necessary spirit, he was bound to fall by the way-
side. She was afraid that she might prove to be one of those
unfortunates.

Phil sent Sharon on a week-long swing of the Panhandle,
one of Reid's weakest areas, while Reid visited Houston.
Sharon was filled with panic. Even though Susan accompanied her to keep her on schedule and help her through any
rough spots, Sharon felt lonely and scared. She had never
considered the possibility that she might have to campaign
without Reid's comforting presence and sturdy support. *She
wasn't cut out for this*, she thought. *She couldn't do it.*

Susan paid no attention to her doubts. She just told Sharon
where she was going, whom she would see, and what she
should say. Then she thrust her out into the day's activities.
It was either sink or swim, Sharon decided, and she swam,
albeit somewhat feebly at times.

Susan seemed pleased with their trip. Sharon, on the other
hand, hated every minute of it. Even when she was with
Reid, she disliked campaigning. She was constantly tired,
yet so wired up with nerves that she slept poorly despite her
exhaustion. She missed Janis, and she missed Reid, whom
she seemed to see only in passing or in the presence of other
people. They rarely had any time alone to talk or even relax
in each other's presence.

Sharon kept telling herself that it would get better as she
grew used to the rigorous schedule. When she had done these
things enough times, they would become easier. Spots would
open up in their schedules when she and Reid could be together.

None of these things happened.

It just got tighter, more harried, and lonelier. Sharon called Janis two or three times a week, but the calls made her want to cry, she missed her daughter so. Once there was a break in her schedule for several days, and she seized the opportunity to return to D.C. and Janis. The visit made her feel worse. Janis's visible unhappiness with the situation flooded her with guilt and sympathetic pain, and the few days of rest and peace with her daughter made her want to stay put, instead of thrusting herself back into the battle.

She was miserable during the whole flight back to Texas. Leaning her head against the window and looking down on the billowing white clouds, she searched for anticipation within herself and found none, only a cold, lonely reluctance. She didn't know how she could continue to do this. She wanted to go home. She longed for the stark beauty of New Mexico and the peace of her small adobe house. Perhaps she should admit that their marriage had been a mistake, that she didn't fit into Reid's life. She had hurt his career, but the effort of making it up to him was tearing her apart.

Sharon wanted to be with her daughter again. She wanted to spend her days working on the things she loved. She wanted to be happy. Tears sprang into her eyes. She thought of leaving Reid. She thought of divorce.

It wasn't what she wanted; everything within her cried out against the thought. How could she be happy away from Reid? Yet, insidiously, the little thought wiggled through her mind like a worm: Wasn't she already "away" from him?

By the time she landed in Dallas, she was exhausted and torn by her thoughts. She stepped into the terminal and glanced around for Phil or Susan or one of the others of her husband's entourage. Instead, amazingly, she saw Reid himself standing there, waiting for her. He was chatting easily with a small knot of people, but when he looked up and saw her, he left them. He swept her up in his arms, hugging her tightly and kissing her hard on the mouth.

"God, I missed you. It seems like a month since you left."

The worry and doubts drained out of Sharon, and she was suddenly refreshed. She smiled.

"How are you? How's Janis?"

"Fine," she lied, still smiling, and leaned her head against his chest.

They made their way through the airport without too many people recognizing them and wanting to chat and shake Reid's hand. A limousine waited by the curb, and it whisked them back to their house. They hadn't really lived in the house yet; Sharon didn't think of it as their home. But at least it was a place she had chosen herself, and it had the style, space, and uniqueness of a house, not the cramped sterility of a motel room. Best of all, there were no aides sleeping down the hall and likely to knock on the door at any moment.

When they stepped inside, Reid flipped the lock behind them and put on the chain for good measure. He took the receiver off the hook and stuffed it between the cushions of the couch. Sharon giggled, feeling lighthearted and years younger. Reid turned and winked. "My schedule is cleared until tomorrow, and I plan to keep it that way."

There were no servants in the house, and they made their own dinner in the kitchen, talking and laughing as they worked. There was not a word said about politics or the campaign. They avoided Susan's and Phil's names, as though even mentioning them might conjure them up on the doorstep.

After supper and a leisurely snifter of brandy before the fireplace, they went upstairs to their bedroom. They undressed each other slowly, pausing to kiss, caress, and murmur soft words of love. Reid laid her back on the bed and kissed her deeply, his tongue exploring her mouth with all the wonder and passion of the first time. His hands drifted over her body, cupping her breasts and teasing her nipples into hardness, sliding down the plain of her stomach and into the crease between her legs. Gently his fingers explored her, separating the satiny folds of her flesh and sliding into her. Sharon moaned and moved her legs restlessly, thrusting her pelvis up in urgent demand.

But Reid did not part her legs and come into her, despite the hunger in him. He wanted this loving to be long and slow; he wanted to savor every minute of it as much as he had missed her earlier. His lips slid from her mouth to her ear, and he nibbled at the lobe. His tongue followed the whorls of her ear and delved inside. He moved down her neck and chest, stopping to feast on the soft globes of her breasts. He nibbled, kissed, and suckled, making love to her breasts as though nothing else existed. All the while his fingers stroked and teased at the hot center of her desire.

Sharon groaned, pressing her fingers into the flesh of his arms, his back, his buttocks. She dug her heels into the bed and pushed upward, her hips circled, in a primal rhythm. She said his name, her voice pleading for release, yet she reveled in the delightful sensations shooting through her, never wanting them to stop. Her hands caressed him everywhere she could reach. Her mouth nipped at his shoulder, and he jerked, moaning at the dart of pleasure-pain.

He slid down her body, replacing his hand with his mouth. His hands dug into her buttocks, holding her tightly against him while his tongue had its way with her, now slow, now fast, retreating, thrusting, forcing her to the rhythm he set until she was almost sobbing for release. Then he gave her the pleasure she sought, shooting white-hot through her.

Gasping, damp with sweat, she lay back, feeling sated, boneless, mindless. But then Reid was inside her, huge and hard, and he was moving slowly, his eyes closed as if he was in the darkest pain or the deepest ecstasy or something that was a combination of the two. Sharon wrapped her legs around him, rocking softly with his motions. They felt suspended in time and place, as if nothing else in the world existed except them and their love. Deep inside Sharon, passion began to build again, welling up from her satiety until she was all blazing heat and unfulfilled yearning once more, aching for release. At last he plunged deep inside her, his seed bursting forth, and they clung together, rocked in an endless explosion of pleasure.

Afterward, Sharon lay in Reid's arms, too dreamy and content to speak or move. She knew, lying there, that she could never leave this man. She would be here for him, no matter what it took.

18

Sharon started feeling sick during their swing through West Texas. At first she was only a little more tired than normal, but with every day she grew more and more weary. It was a strange illness. She felt generally bad, but she had no specific symptoms other than an occasional queasy stomach and the awful, dragging loss of energy. For a while she wondered if she could be pregnant, and a fuzzy warmth filled her at the thought of having Reid's baby. But she was forced to reject that idea. It simply wasn't possible; she'd been using birth control since before their marriage, knowing that this would be a terrible time to get pregnant. Besides, she didn't feel the way she had with Janis. Once she had felt this bone-weary with the flu, but then she had also had headaches and a fever, as well as aching bones and an upset stomach.

Reid was scheduled to cover the Valley while Sharon and Susan took up a tour of the central Texas cities and towns. He was reluctant to leave her feeling unwell, but Sharon smiled and assured him that she'd be fine by the time he saw her next. "It's just a mild case of flu. There's nothing you can do for me anyway."

So, leaving instructions with Susan to call him if Sharon got sicker, Reid left for Brownsville. Susan and Sharon headed for Hillsboro. Sharon hated campaigning without Reid, but she comforted herself with the thought that in a few days she and Reid would be together again in Austin. In the meantime, she concentrated on getting through each day without disgracing herself and Reid by fainting or falling asleep in the middle of a speech. In Waco, Susan brought a doctor to her motel room. He diagnosed her as having the flu, explaining that not everyone had all the symptoms. He prescribed rest and fluids.

Sharon smiled and told him she would do her best. It was out of the question to rest, of course, but perhaps she could manage to get down juice and water. As soon as the doctor left, she dressed and went down to meet a gathering of campaign workers and their friends.

It took every bit of courage and willpower Sharon possessed to get through the days that followed. They hit several small towns and wound up two days later in Austin. Sharon couldn't have said the names of any of the places she had visited. When they reached the hotel in Austin, Sharon stumbled into her bedroom of the suite and barely managed to undress and remove her makeup before she flung herself across the bed and slept.

The next morning the persistent ringing of the telephone pulled Sharon from sleep, though she struggled against it all the way to consciousness. She lay for a moment, aware of what had awakened her but unwilling to make the effort to answer the telephone. She opened her eyes, then closed them again. Lord, she felt as if she hadn't slept a wink, as if she could sleep forever. Finally, the irritation of the ringing grew too great, and she crawled across the wide bed to lift the receiver. A recorded message cheerily told her the time and the state of the weather. Sharon let out a short, succinct curse.

She sat up and swung her legs out of bed. She stayed there for a few minutes, resting her elbows on her thighs, her head in her hands. How long was this flu going to last, anyway? She'd had it for almost a week now, and every day it got worse instead of better. The doctor had told her two days ago that she was through the worst of it and should start to feel better soon. That moment certainly hadn't arrived yet. She thought Susan suspected that her illness was psychosomatic. Even Sharon was beginning to wonder. Maybe this awful tiredness was a result of the stress of campaigning. Maybe she was trying to make herself ill so she would have a good excuse to drop out and go home to Janis in Washington.

There was a knock on the door. "Sharon? You up? You have an appointment in forty-five minutes."

"Yeah. I'm getting ready." Sharon dragged herself to the closet and stared at her dresses. What had she worn yesterday? Did it make any difference? She'd been in a different town. Where? She wasn't sure; her mind was numb. Today was Austin; she was sure of that because Reid was going to join her here, and they would campaign together in Austin and San Antonio.

She slid the four dresses back and forth. The business suit with the jacket would be the most practical; it was the one she had worn most during the campaign. But the pink dress was prettier, and she wanted to look her best since she would be seeing Reid today. She glanced at her image in the mirror above the dresser. She was certainly going to need all the help she could get in that department. The weeks of campaigning had left her several pounds lighter, but it wasn't the indentations in her cheeks that bothered her. It was the dark smudges beneath her eyes and the new lines that had formed there; it was the dullness of her skin.

She tossed the pink dress onto the bed and went into the bathroom to put on her makeup and do what she could with her hair. She'd been too tired to wash and style her hair last night, but she could do it up in a twist that would hide the fact that it was limp and dirty. The makeup was more difficult. She couldn't put on enough to make her look healthy and pretty, and she got so tired in the middle of doing it that she had to sit down on the counter to finish.

She dressed and went into the sitting room of the suite without any time to spare. Susan was waiting for her, briefcase in hand. She handed Sharon her purse and led her out of the room, talking as she went. "First you're going to breakfast with Brenda McDonnell, the wife of R.J. McDonnell, the House Speaker—state Speaker, that is, and Heather Cummins, Bill Cummins's wife. She's very pretty and not too bright; if you talk about clothes and stuff she'll be satisfied. Bill's one of the big contributors to Reid's campaign. A good guy except for his taste in wives. Brenda's sharp, very savvy, but you won't have to be on your toes with her because one, she's very much in our corner, anyway, and two, she knows what Heather's like."

"Then I won't have to struggle to appear intelligent and informed? That's good." Sharon's voice was sharper than she'd intended. Usually she was better at keeping her sarcasm to herself, but the illness must have lowered her customary defenses.

Susan glanced at her, eyebrows raised, but said nothing.

"I'm sorry," Sharon apologized immediately. "I'll keep a better rein on my tongue with them, I promise."

"It's okay. Afterward, you'll hit the campus crowd. There's a reception at Dr. Weingarten's house, lots of intellectuals and arty types. No problem again, they're predisposed to like Reid, and they should like you even more."

Sharon nodded. It was better that she hadn't worn the business suit, then. Susan paused as they crossed the lobby, then continued with the list of activities when they were settled in the back of the limousine. Sharon leaned her head against the window and tuned her out. Susan would remind her of each event as they reached it, and she didn't have it in her to remember them all, anyway. It was going to take all her reserves simply to get through the functions without looking too dumb. She felt even worse than she had when she got up. The glass was cool against her forehead. The day was awfully warm for winter.

They reached the elegant red brick mansion in Davenport Ranch that was the Cumminses' home. Susan jumped out of the car. Sharon opened the door and paused for a moment, marshaling her energy to walk up the steps to the house. For a moment it seemed more than she could do. Susan came around the car and stopped beside her, saying cheerily, "Well, you must be feeling better this morning. You have some color back in your cheeks."

"Really?" Sharon was surprised. She had thought she looked like death warmed over when she'd looked in the mirror of the hotel room.

But when they got inside, she glanced at the mirrored entryway wall and saw that Susan was right—her cheeks were pink and her eyes brighter. But she didn't feel better. In fact, what she felt was hot.

Susan introduced her to Heather and Brenda, then left her. Sharon smiled and followed them into the dining room. The sight of food made her feel queasy, so she drank a glass of orange juice and picked at a croissant. She pushed herself to concentrate on what they said, to laugh and smile at the right times and make appropriate remarks. She couldn't leave them thinking that Reid's wife was a socially graceless idiot. The effort sapped her strength, and by the time Susan came back and hustled her off to her next meeting, she felt wrung out.

She leaned back against the plush seat of the limousine and promptly fell asleep while Susan rattled on about the next meeting. When they stopped in front of the professor's house, Susan had to shake Sharon's arm to awaken her.

"Sharon? Are you okay?" Susan's voice was tinged with concern.

"What?" Sharon blinked and glanced around. "Oh. I'm sorry. I didn't mean to be rude." She looked out the window at the house. How in the world was she going to force herself to go into that house and socialize? She didn't think she could get out of the seat.

But somehow she managed to step out when the chauffeur opened the door. She walked up the sidewalk behind Susan, unable to keep up with the other woman's pace. Her legs were like spaghetti. She was burning up, and she wondered vaguely if she had at last acquired that elusive fever she should have with the flu. Susan glanced back, frowning, and started back toward Sharon just as the front door opened. Susan turned and greeted the woman at the door. Sharon pushed herself the last few steps to the porch. Her mind was like cotton. How was she going to converse? She wasn't even sure that she could smile and nod.

Susan introduced her to the woman at the door. Her name went right through Sharon's head. Sharon followed them down the entryway and into a room stuffed with people. Sharon's stomach was strangely hot, and her legs were still rubbery. The woman began to introduce her to people. Sharon couldn't hear anything that was said, for there was suddenly a roaring in her ears. Her stomach flip-flopped. She knew she had to sit down. She couldn't stand up another moment. She opened her mouth to ask for a chair, but nothing came out. She crumpled onto the floor.

When Sharon came to, she was lying on a couch, with Susan kneeling on the floor beside her. There was a cool, damp rag on her forehead; it felt good against her searing skin. Susan let out a gusty sigh when Sharon opened her eyes. "Thank God. Lie still. We've sent for an ambulance."

Sharon shook her head. She struggled to collect her thoughts enough to explain why that was impossible. "So much—I can't."

"Yes, you can. Reid'll have my head if we don't take you to the hospital immediately. I should have taken you there already. Why didn't you tell me you had a fever?"

"Do I?" Sharon licked her lips. She was having trouble concentrating on Susan's words. In fact, she was having trouble remembering who Susan was.

"You're burning up!"

"Where's Reid?" Sharon glanced around. There seemed to be a great number of people that she didn't know here. She felt very strange and disoriented. She brushed a strand of hair back from her forehead. Suddenly she wanted to cry. "I want Reid."

"I've put in a call to him, but I haven't been able to locate him yet. I reached Phil, and as soon as he sees Reid he'll tell him what happened.''

Sharon felt horribly alone. She reached for Susan's hand. At least she was vaguely familiar. ''I'm scared.'' Her voice was no more than a whisper.

She saw her own fear reflected in Susan's eyes before Susan put on a reassuring mask. ''It'll be all right. I promise. I'll stick right with you until Reid arrives.''

''Where's Janis? Somebody's got to take care of her.''

''Janis is fine.'' Susan squeezed her hand, but again Sharon saw the flash of panic in her eyes, quickly suppressed. ''She's home in D.C., going to school. Mrs. Bell is staying with her.''

Sharon closed her eyes, somewhat comforted. She was so fuzzy she hadn't been able to put together most of what Susan said, but she understood that Janis was safe. ''She's so little.''

Susan turned to the woman beside her, and Sharon heard her whisper, ''How can she be so much worse so quickly? Something's wrong. Something's wrong.''

Sharon drifted in and out of consciousness. The next thing she knew she was being lifted and carried out of the house. She wanted to protest, but she couldn't put the words together. It was too much of an effort. There was a terrible pain in her abdomen, but that, too, seemed too much of an effort to mention. They put her into a vehicle and a man climbed in beside her. He did things around her, touching her, putting things on her. It annoyed her; she wished he would leave her alone.

It seemed that Ames was beside her, and she spoke to him. He answered back, but his words were gibberish. She closed her eyes again, and the next time she opened them, she was rolling down a corridor, flat on her back, watching the ceiling go by. There were people beside her whom she didn't know. One of them was a woman who was busy asking questions and writing things down. The next time she opened her eyes, there were different people around, and a man was asking her questions. She looked at him and thought of answering, but she was too hazy. No words seemed to gel.

"I'm sorry," she whispered, and tears rolled down her cheeks. "Hot."

"Yes, I know you are, and we're working to bring down your fever," the man assured her. He prodded at her stomach, then abdomen, and she flinched. "Is that painful?"

But once again her eyes closed, and she didn't answer.

Each time she awakened, there were people around her. Once there was a large machine over her. Another time, there were tubes running out of her arms. But that wasn't right; Janis was the one with the tubes. She couldn't make sense of this. She heard voices; she heard a man saying her name again and again.

And then—how very odd—she was above herself looking down. She could see herself lying on the bed. There were a man and two women standing beside her bed, and the man said, "Jesus, we're losing her."

He began to push on her chest, and one of the women hurried out. Sharon wanted to tell him not to push so hard; it would hurt her. But even though she felt much clearer, she was way up here and she couldn't speak. It was odd to watch herself. She looked old and bad.

Suddenly there were more people in the room and a machine and excited voices. The man took a paddle in each hand. He put the paddles to her chest, and she jerked. Sharon slid away. There was somewhere she was supposed to go.

Now she was in the hall outside the room. Susan was there, pacing, and so were Phil and another man. Reid was there, too, sitting on a chair outside the door. His elbows were on his knees, and he rested his head on his hands. He seemed weary, no, worse than that—he looked defeated and sad. He looked up at the door to the room, and she saw the shimmer of tears in his eyes. Her heart went out to him. How unhappy he looked. She couldn't go off and leave him. Poor Reid. She loved him so.

Suddenly the pain slammed through her, filling her chest and body, and she wanted to scream, it hurt so much. She heard a jumble of voices. One said, "Heartbeat's back."

Sharon wanted to look, but she couldn't open her eyes. Once again she drifted into the blankness.

After that there was little except nothingness or vague, swirling dreams of color, light, and sound. At last she came up out of the mist and darkness. She was aware of herself and of the world. But it took a supreme effort just to open her eyes.

She was in a hospital bed. Plastic bags of liquid hung on portable racks on either side of the bed, and tubes ran from them into her. Janis was curled up, asleep, in a chair against the opposite wall. Reid sat right next to her bed on a straight chair. He was holding her hand, and he was leaning over, his head resting on the bed beside her.

"Reid." The word came out barely a whisper, but his head snapped up.

He stared at her as if he couldn't believe what he saw, then a grin broke across his face. "Sharon! Sharon, thank God!" Tears filled his eyes, and he bent and pressed his lips against her hand. The warm drops of his tears hit her skin. He looked back up at her. "I'm sorry." He wiped away the tears from his cheeks. "I'm just so glad—to see you again."

"I—what happened?" Her voice was a little stronger this time.

"You've been sick. Very sick. You had some kind of intestinal infection that everybody wrote off as the flu. But the doctors here figured out what it was, and they have you on antibiotics. It's working. You're awake. You're going to be all right."

"I fainted."

"Yeah. That's when Susan realized that it was serious." His face hardened. "Jesus, she must have been oblivious not to have seen how sick you were. If I'd just stayed with you—"

Sharon moved her head in a negative gesture. "No. Not your fault."

"I'd have seen it. I wouldn't have let you push yourself like that. You have too much heart."

"How long have I been—" She made a weak gesture

around her. She was exhausted simply from talking the little bit she had.

"Two and a half days."

"So long?" Looking at Reid, she could see that it must have been a long time. He was rumpled, red-eyed, and unshaven. She smiled faintly at him, then sighed. "I'm so tired."

She slid back into sleep.

For the rest of the day, Sharon continued to awaken and fall asleep. Often there was a nurse by her side, taking her pulse or temperature or fiddling with the plastic containers hanging beside her bed. Once or twice, there was a doctor who asked her a few questions. Always, Reid was there, either by her side or sitting in the chair against the wall. Sometimes Janis was there, too. They would take her hand, talk to her, smile at her. Sharon was beginning to realize that they had thought she was going to die.

Sharon thought she almost had. She remembered that strange sensation of floating above the doctors and nurses, of looking down at Reid sorrowing. Had it been a dream? It had seemed so real. She thought perhaps she had floated that near to death. It was a disquieting thought.

She came to the next morning feeling sharper and less disoriented. Neither Reid nor Janis was there, but Phil came in a moment later and explained that he had sent them both back to the hotel for some rest, now that they knew she would recover. Sharon went back to sleep.

Early that afternoon, Reid returned. He looked tired, but at least he was clean-shaven and a trifle more rested. He smiled when he saw her. "You're looking better." He came to her bed and bent to kiss her forehead.

"I feel better." She managed a smile in return. "I can almost think again. I've been in a haze."

"Your fever's down. You were delirious for a while." He sat down beside the bed, pulling the straight-backed chair up close to her. "God, you don't know how great it is to see you looking alive again. I was scared silly."

"You couldn't lose me if you tried."

"No? I'm glad. I knew that if you died, my ambition would have killed you."

"No! Darling, don't say things like that." Sharon reached out a hand to him.

He took her hand and squeezed it. "It's the truth. I didn't take good care of you. I was too busy chasing after the nomination. I should have been with you. You shouldn't have been campaigning so hard. You should have rested, gone to the doctor."

"Don't be silly. I did go to a doctor. Susan got one for me, and he thought I had the flu, too, just like Susan and I did. You wouldn't have known any different. It wouldn't have been any different if I hadn't been campaigning. If I had been home, I still would have thought it was the flu."

"Maybe. More likely, you wouldn't have caught it. I think it was stress. You've been working too hard."

Sharon thought back to the days when she had dragged through her obligations. In a way, being ill had made it easier. When it took every bit of effort and concentration just to pull herself through each and every duty, there was no room in her mind to think of how much she disliked the campaign or of what a relief it would be not to have to do it anymore. She remembered, too, how she had had to push and push herself, forcing herself always to do the things a politician's wife had to do. Perhaps Reid was right. Perhaps it was the stress that had made her sick.

She sighed, and tears filled her eyes, despite her best efforts to hold them back. Reid saw them, and he reached out to brush away a tear that slid from the corner of her eye. "Ah, sweetheart, I'm sorry. What'd I say? I wasn't blaming you for being sick. You must know that. I feel guilty that you got sick working so hard for me."

Sharon turned her head aside. "It's nothing. I'm just tired. It makes me cry for no reason." She paused, looking for something to change the subject. "Shouldn't you be out talking to people instead of here? You're wasting a lot of campaign time."

He made a face. "To hell with that. You think I'd be out glad-handing people when my wife is in the hospital? You think I'd give a damn about my campaign when you're sick?

"Well, there's no possibility of my dying now. So—you can't let it slip away from you after you've worked so hard. You could go out now."

Reid chuckled and shook his head. "You're too stubbornly loyal. I can live without campaigning for a few days. I can't live away from you." He leaned over and kissed her forehead. His gentle concern made her feel treacherous for having the thoughts she'd had—thoughts of leaving him because she hated the life of a politician's wife, of the awful impossibilities of being torn between this man whom she loved more than anything in the world and Janis and her own wishes.

She couldn't hold back the tears. She put her hands up to her face. "I'm sorry. I'm so sorry. It's not anything."

"I'm disturbing you." Reid sounded guilty.

"No! No, I love having you around. It's just— I failed you! I wanted so much to be a good wife, and I failed."

Sharon's words stunned him. "Failed me! What in the world are you talking about? Sweetheart, what's wrong?" His hand went to her forehead. "Are you delirious again?"

"No." She shook her head, having to smile at his words, even though she couldn't stop the tears from flowing. "I'm sorry. I'm like this when I'm sick. I can't seem to control myself."

"Then don't. Tell me what's the matter."

"I can't do it!"

"You can't tell me?"

"I can't be a politician's wife. Oh, God." She wiped futilely at the tears. "Please, ignore me. Forget what I'm saying. Maybe I am delirious."

Reid frowned. "I don't think so. I think you're so weak you can't hide your feelings the way you usually do. Are you saying—" Reid felt as if he'd had the wind kicked out of him, but he had to say it, anyway. "—Do you want a divorce?"

"No." Sharon began to cry harder, and Reid cursed himself for upsetting her. "No. I love you. I love you."

"Honey, shh. Calm down. Tell me what you meant."

"I can't do it. I've tried. I've really tried. But it's so hard. I didn't want to ruin your career. I never intended to, but I hurt it so badly when I married you. I thought if I could be a good politician's wife, it would make up for it. I wouldn't be responsible for ruining your career. I want to help you; I really, really do."

"Of course you do. I know that. But you didn't ruin my career. Far from it."

"I have. They all say so."

"Who?"

"Everyone. Your mother, Angela—"

"Angela!" Anger pulsed in his voice for the first time. "What the hell does she have to do with this?"

"She told me how I'd wrecked your chances of going anywhere in politics, how you'd be stuck forever as a small-time politician, if you could even manage to get elected as representative again."

"And you believed her? She's a bitch. A jealous gold-plated bitch, that's all."

"Susan said it, too, and Phil. Everyone, when I really pressed them."

His face was thunderous. "Goddamnit, they're off my staff tomorrow if that's the kind of—"

"No, no! They love you, Reid; they practically worship you. They want what's best for you. So do I."

"You're what's best for me."

"I've tried. I've really tried."

"Tried to what?"

Sharon brushed her palms across her cheeks. The tears at least had stopped leaking from her eyes. Her whole life was teetering on the edge now, and it was all because of her stupid tongue. Yet she couldn't stop it; she was too exhausted, too sick. The words kept slipping out. "I've tried not to let you down. To be what you wanted, what you needed. But I hate it; I hate it. I hate having those people around me and never having any time for myself—or for Janis or my work or us. I hate the reporters and the gossip and the sly insinuations. I hate meeting people day after day and smiling 'til my face hurts and shaking hands until I think my arms are going to fall off and never having the slightest idea who any of them are or what they're like. Do you know how long it's been since I saw my daughter? Sometimes I think about running away, giving up you and our marriage and everything, because I'm so weak that I can't take it.''

Reid let out a long, slow sigh. ''Sweetheart. Why didn't you tell me this?''

''I want to be with you. I want to make our marriage work. Sometimes I thought about taking Janis and going back to Santa Fe, but the idea tore my heart out. The other day, when I almost died—it was really strange; I felt as if I were floating up on the ceiling and looking down at everything. I began to float away from the doctors and my body. I felt as if I were going somewhere. Then I saw you. I knew I couldn't leave you. I could never leave you.'' She covered her face with shaking hands. ''I'm so sorry. I shouldn't be saying all this.''

''Why not?'' His voice was quiet and grim. ''I think it's about time you did.''

''It's too much of a burden for you; you don't need anything else to carry right now.''

Reid leaned over and softly kissed her forehead where it flowed into her hairline. ''Don't you know that you're never a burden to me? You're everything I want or need, all day long, every day. I didn't marry you to get a perfect political wife; I married you because I love you, because you're you.'' He sighed. ''I wish I'd known. I wish you'd told me.''

He moved away, going to stand and gaze out the window. ''But, then, I should have known without your telling me, shouldn't I? I've been too wrapped up in myself and in this race to see what was happening to you. I actually thought you were doing the campaigning because you enjoyed it. I didn't realize how unhappy you were.''

Reid came back to her bedside. ''I'm sorry.''

Sharon felt drained now and so exhausted she could hardly stay awake. Her lashes fluttered closed, and she forced them back open. Reid bent and kissed her. She thought she saw tears glinting in his eyes. "You need to sleep. This is too wearing for you. I'll be back later." He kissed her again. "I love you."

The next day Sharon felt much stronger. She bitterly regretted what she had revealed to Reid. He was already pushed and pulled upon by so many people, all acting out of their own interests. The last thing she wanted to do was to add to his burden, to make him feel torn between her and his career.

Janis had come to visit Sharon the evening before, without Reid, and she came alone again this morning. But shortly after one in the afternoon, Reid arrived to take her place, and Janis left. Sharon looked at him, her heart aching to see the lines of weariness and worry etched into his face, the dark shadows smudged beneath his eyes. Once again she cursed herself for not having kept her mouth shut.

Reid took her hand, and she squeezed it, her mind racing, trying to figure out how she could take back what she'd said yesterday.

But Reid spoke before she could. "I've been thinking a lot since they put you in the hospital. When I almost lost you the other day it scared me right down to my toes. I don't think I've ever been so frightened in my life. There's nothing for me if I don't have you. You're the most important thing in the world to me."

"Oh, Reid." Tears gathered in her eyes.

"No. Don't say anything. Just listen to me. I've decided to withdraw from the Senate race."

Sharon stared, slack-jawed. Her amazement went beyond speech.

"When my term is up next year, I don't plan to run again, either."

She found her tongue at last. "Reid! No. You can't!"

He gazed at her calmly, saying nothing.

"You've always been in politics," she protested. "You can't give it up. Please, please, don't give up the life you love for me. You'll wind up hating and resenting me for it."

"That's just the point. I don't love it. I never have. Yesterday when you were talking about how you'd failed at being a politician's wife, I kept thinking: But I don't want you to be a politician's wife. I love you the way you are. I don't give a crap whether you know how to wiggle your way through Washington society or how to use this lobbyist or convince that guy to contribute to my campaign. None of that's important to me. What's important to me is your smile. The way you look at me. Your warmth and gentleness. Your talent. I was putting together an argument to use today to convince you to stay with me and be you, without trying to bend yourself to fit some political wife mold. Then it occurred to me to wonder why I didn't want that from you. Hell, I'm a politician; that's what I need, isn't it? It finally dawned on me that I don't want to be a politician any more than I want you to be a politician's wife."

Sharon's heart raced. She wanted so badly for what he was saying to be true. Yet she couldn't let herself hope. He was only trying to please her; if she let him do it, he would regret it. "But, Reid, you've been a politician so long. How could it be something you don't love?"

"I thought I loved it. But until I met you, I didn't have the first idea what love was. Now I know, and what I felt for politics wasn't it. Remember when we talked about my career a long time ago back at the ranch? You wondered why I hadn't gone into ranching."

Sharon nodded.

"I talked about why I'd gotten into politics. I think you saw then that I didn't have a passion for my career. I'd done it because of duty, responsibility, and love for my parents. I'd gone into it to please my mother and father; I guess I was always trying to win their love by being the perfect son. Same reason Wes did the things he did—we wanted our parents' attention. I was raised to go into politics and fulfill their dreams. I never thought about the fact that it wasn't my dream. I just did it. I was good at it. Mother and Father approved. I married the right kind of woman, and she approved of what I did. All the time I kept thinking I was successful, and I couldn't understand why I felt empty inside. I thought it was my fault that I wasn't happy; here I was achieving everything I wanted, and I couldn't enjoy it. But now I can see it: I wasn't achieving what I wanted. It was what they wanted for me.''

"Reid." Sharon took one of his hands in hers and brought it up to her lips. She kissed his palm gently and laid his hand against her cheek. "I won't deny that I'd be happy to say good-bye to politics. I don't like this life; I haven't from the first moment. But if you walk away from it because of me, I'm afraid you'll regret it. I couldn't bear it if I was the cause of your unhappiness.''

"You could never be that," he assured her. "I don't have to quit politics because of you. I could tell you to go ahead and live as you want, to forget all the political mess. But I realized: I don't want it either.'' He curled his hand up and brushed his knuckles against her cheek. "I don't want to spend the time away from you and Janis. I don't want to live a life my parents mapped out for me. I'm getting close to forty years old. Don't you think it's time I started living for myself?'' He bent and kissed her forehead. "I want us to live at the ranch. I want to forget about the press and all the repercussions of our every action, the nuances of every phrase. I just want to live with you and be happy.''

Sharon's throat clogged with tears. "Oh, Reid, that's what I want, too.''

"Good. Then it's settled.''

"If it's really what you want.''

"It's what I want. It's what I've always wanted—and more than I ever dreamed was possible.'' He bent to slide his arms around her, carefully avoiding the tubes feeding into her arms. Tenderly he kissed her cheeks and mouth. "I love you.''

"And I love you.'' She knew that his decision was right. Their love was what mattered. She turned her head and pressed her lips against his skin. "I love you.''